WHEN THE LAMPS GO OUT

WHEN THE LAMPS GO OUT

a novel by

Megan Spurgin

WestBow
PRESS
A DIVISION OF THOMAS NELSON

Scripture quotations are from The Holy Bible, English Standard Version® (ESV®), copyright © 2001 by Crossway, a publishing ministry of Good News Publishers. Used by permission. All rights reserved.

Scripture taken from the New King James Version. Copyright 1979, 1980, 1982 by Thomas Nelson, inc. Used by permission. All rights reserved.

WestBow Press books may be ordered through booksellers or by contacting:

WestBow Press
A Division of Thomas Nelson
1663 Liberty Drive
Bloomington, IN 47403
www.westbowpress.com
1-(866) 928-1240

ISBN: 978-1-4497-6606-1 (e)
ISBN: 978-1-4497-6607-8 (sc)
ISBN: 978-1-4497-6608-5 (hc)

Library of Congress Control Number: 2012916207

Printed in the United States of America

WestBow Press rev. date: 09/19/2012

For my sister Katelyn,

You are my best critic, my best fan, and my best friend.

Characters

GERMANY:

Hilda van Ostrand - a young woman caught in the middle of World War II and divided in her loyalties

Paul van Ostrand - Hilda's older brother, who tries to cope with the many changes coming with the war, including hostility toward the woman he loves

Dederick van Ostrand - Hilda's younger brother, a loyal Nazi who puts country first

Frederick van Ostrand - Hilda's father, who discovers a shocking secret and pays a terrible price

Benedikta van Ostrand - Hilda's mother, who cannot find her place in the war and struggles with the changes around her

Elsa van Thof - Benedikta's best friend, she helps those who are suffering through the war

Hannah Strauss - A young Jewish woman living in the midst of the Holocaust

Maria van Ostrand - a young girl growing up without her parents in the middle of the war

AMERICA:

Jesse Riker - a young pilot serving his country while struggling through his relationship with a young German woman

Danny Riker - Jesse's father, a pilot who fought in World War I

Mari Riker - Jesse's mother, a nurse who served during World War I

Christina Riker - Jesse's younger sister

Josh Sauders - Jesse's friend in the Eagle Squadron

Luke Pendair - a good friend of the Rikers who served in World War I

Allison Pendair - Luke's wife, who also served in World War I with Mari Riker

ENGLAND:

Jeffrey Rolf - a friend of Hilda's who works in the British Secret Intelligence Service, SIS

Grace Holden - A reporter who has close ties with the Rikers through her parents

John Holden - Grace's father, a doctor who served with Mari Riker and Allison Pendair in World War I

Mary Holden - Grace's mother, and friend to the Rikers

FRANCE:

Marie Badeau - a friend of Hilda's who works against the Nazi regime

Dominique Badeau - Marie's older brother, who is also involved in the Resistance

Julian Rousseau - Elsa's cousin who lives outside of Versailles

SOVIET UNION:

Tanya Berezovsky - a young woman of Russian and German descent who must choose between two difficult paths

Nicholas Berezovsky - Tanya's father, a high official in the secret police of the Soviet Union known as the NKVD

Preface

This is a work of fiction and the characters within are entirely from my imagination. Any involvement in the circumstances of World War II by these characters is purely for the enjoyment of the reader. While Hilda van Ostrand, Jesse Riker, and their family and friends are fictional people, the historical events and battles they find themselves in were very real. A detailed chronology of World War II can be found at the back of the book.

The decision to tell this story from the perspective of a German family will bring readers, I sincerely hope, to a deeper understanding of this time in our history and the changes it evoked on all sides. World War II remains one of the darkest moments in history, but Christ promised those who follow Him that they "shall not walk in darkness, but have the light of life." (John 8:12) It is my hope that these characters and their journeys will inspire you as much as they have me.

"The lamps are going out all over Europe;
we shall not see them lit again in our lifetime."

Sir Edward Gray
British Foreign Secretary
August 3, 1914

Prologue

Mari Riker gulped down the sob that threatened to escape her throat, but nothing prevented the silent torrent of tears that streamed down her face as Dr. Holden slowly pulled the white sheet over Allison Pendair's pale face. As a nurse on the front lines, Mari had seen her fair share of gruesome images, but the wrenching pain of watching her best friend's life fade away left a hole so black and empty that she spun away from the horrific sight.

"Please—Dr. Holden, are you sure?" She choked on the words.

Mari felt the good doctor's hand squeeze her shoulder and send a current that jarred her aching muscles, a reminder of the struggle they had endured over the past several hours.

"I checked three times, Mari. There was nothing we could have done for her. She lost too much blood."

Mari forced herself to nod, to maintain the sense of professionalism that she prided herself on. But the gesture came out awkward and jerky, and when Dr. Holden came around to face her, a fresh flood of tears began.

"I know it is hard, Mari," he said quietly. "She was a friend to all of us. But there is much still to be done. She needs your help now."

They both looked down at the sleeping infant nestled in Mari's arms. From the cute little nose to the slightly open deep red lips, the child

1

looked just like Allison—except for her eyes. Mari remembered when they opened for the first time, and the color took her breath away. She had Luke's eyes.

Mari gently touched a single finger to the baby's velvety cheek. "What will happen to her? And what on earth are we to do if—"

The tent flap opened, and the distant sound of gunfire reminded Mari that they still sat in the middle of a battle. Looking up, she saw a tall man removing his leather cap and goggles, his face smeared with blood, and her heart tightened.

"Danny!"

Her husband looked past her, and his face fell at the sight of the covered body. "No … Allie …" He stumbled forward and reached out a shaky hand to touch the sheet. "When?"

"Only moments ago," Dr. Holden replied. "She fought so hard, right up to the end." The British doctor ran a hand through his hair. Though only in his thirties, he appeared to have aged ten years over the past four. Gray streaked through his hair like tiny rivers, and heavy lines surrounded his weary eyes as he pushed his glasses up his nose. He nodded to the bundle in Mari's arms. "He has a daughter."

Danny turned to his wife, and his cinnamon brown eyes grew wide in wonder as he rubbed his thumb across the baby's smooth forehead. "Would you look at that," he murmured as a small smile broke onto his serious face. "She's the spitting image of Allie."

Mari turned worried eyes to Danny. "How is he?"

"He was sleeping when I left him. The bullet went clean through, but they're still worried about blood poisoning. The rest of the squadron is relatively unharmed." He sighed and shook his head. "There were so many of them, Mari. He didn't see that plane coming until it was too late. But he's a fighter. He always has been."

"He has to make it. God would not let them both die. Not after all they've been through. The child needs him!"

"Calm yourself, Mari," Danny said, gripping her arms. "You've always been the strongest of us all, and you must be strong now."

Mari shut her eyes tightly and gulped in a breath. They were so close, so close. The war was almost over. Her eyes opened and fell on the still form beneath the sheet. How was this tragedy the Lord's plan? Allison had arrived in Europe so eager to fight for the cause, even when her wealthy parents shunned her for it. And when Luke Pendair and Allison Winter fell in love at first sight, the gloom of the war disappeared in their faces.

Mari felt a bright future lay ahead for them. And a daughter … a beautiful baby girl. With a son of her own, she knew well the overflowing blessings of motherhood. So how was this tragedy the Lord's plan?

The little one started to fuss, and Mari rocked her slowly. "She's hungry."

"I sent someone for a wet nurse," Dr. Holden said.

A shell exploded, and the tent shook. Danny put a protective arm around Mari, who gently hushed the baby.

"They'd better hurry," Danny said quickly. "Evacuations are supposed to begin soon."

"Is she dead?"

All three froze at the voice. Turning, Mari felt her heart break anew. Luke's arm was wrapped tightly and hung in a sling, his face as pale as his bandages. His dark green eyes gave away the storm of anguish that raged within him as he took in their faces and the table where he knew his wife lay.

Danny stepped forward and put a hand on his arm. "Luke, you shouldn't be up. You need rest."

Luke's eyes shone with unshed tears. "Why?" he murmured quietly. "There's never been any rest here. I can rest when I'm dead."

"Luke, don't say such things!" Mari said angrily, and her sharp tone brought a cry from her arms.

Luke suddenly noticed the blanketed form clutched to her breast. He walked over to her and let his eyes take in the miracle before him. At the same time, the baby stopped her crying and opened her eyes, as though knowing her father gazed upon her. Every other sound seemed to fade as the powerful silence emanated between father and daughter. Slowly, carefully, Luke reached out, and Mari gently placed the child in his good arm.

"Incredible," he whispered. "I'm a father."

The word seemed to startle him, for he glanced up quickly and caught Dr. Holden's gaze. "Let me see her."

Mari and Danny shared a look. Dr. Holden began to raise his hands in protest, but Luke was firm.

"Please, Doc. Let me see my wife."

Dr. Holden shook his head slowly, but turned to the table and pulled the sheet back from Allison's face. Her golden hair spilled around the pillow, and had she not been so pale, she could have been asleep. Luke's tears fell silently now, and he slowly lowered himself to the edge of the table.

"Oh, Allie, my love. You are still as beautiful as the day I laid eyes on you."

His voice was so low that Mari could not make out his words, but her eyes lowered, and she turned away to give Luke privacy to say good-bye to the woman who had been taken from him too soon.

"You know, little one, we carved our initials in an old tree outside of London the day before we were married. You'll have to see them sometime." Luke laughed softly, and only then could Mari hear the tears in his voice. "She tried so hard to deny her feelings for me, you know. But I wouldn't give up. I knew she'd been watching me from under that tree while I trained. In the end, our love could not be denied, could it, Allie? One for the books, we liked to say. She wrote it all down, you know … in her journal. You can read it when you are older."

At the mention of the journal, Mari lifted her head. Allison's journal was back in the room they shared. She gently touched Danny's arm, and he turned from watching the heart wrenching scene.

"Allie's journal," she murmured. "I know where it is."

"I'll come with you," he insisted.

"You should stay with Luke."

"I'm not leaving you, Mari. Not now."

A nurse who looked to be no older than eighteen stepped into the tent. Her uniform was torn and dirty, and her plaited hair had lost some of its luster beneath her cap.

"Evacuations have begun. Where is the child?" she asked.

Luke seemed to be lost in thought as he gazed into Allison's face. His daughter, perfectly content, had fallen asleep in his arm. Dr. Holden placed a gentle hand on his shoulder and murmured a few words that Mari could not hear. After a moment, Luke nodded and allowed the child to be taken from him. Dr. Holden handed her to the nurse.

"See her to safety. I will find you at the next field station. And see that an ambulance is brought around. This man is in critical condition and must have a medical transport."

"Yes, Doctor." As quickly as she came, the nurse brushed the flap aside once more and vanished. Mari watched her disappear among the hundreds of injured who were being led to the trucks. Her white cap stood out like a rose among the grimy brown haze the soldiers created.

"Mari."

She turned as Luke called her name. His hand now clasped Allison's limp fingers, but his eyes held hers for a long moment. When he finally

4

returned his gaze to Allison's face, Mari could feel the strength and determination of his words even before he spoke.

"Don't let her forget us."

Mari swallowed her pain, marched over, and took his face between her hands so that he was forced to meet her eyes. She kissed his pale forehead and felt the fever rage inside his wounded body. Somehow, she knew. She did not want to believe it, but she knew.

"Never."

Luke's face broke into a relieved smile, and even as he began to tremble with weakness, she let him go. Another shell shook the tent, and Danny pulled her up. Dr. Holden hustled around and called for medics to gather supplies for the journey. As Danny pulled her into the throng of soldiers that moved down the narrow path between the beds, Mari turned once more and looked into the far room that grew smaller with every step she took. Luke now lay on the bed next to Allison with his good arm wrapped around her dead form. The pressure on his shoulder would be too much for him to bear. That was the dim thought in the back of her mind as she caught a final glimpse of the tender scene.

When they finally made it out of the tent, Mari could now see the explosions as shells rained down on the nearby forest and the town beyond. They could not survive such an onslaught for much longer.

"A pencil."

"What?" Danny shouted over the noise of the battle.

"A pencil. I need a pencil!"

"Whatever for?"

"Hurry, Danny!"

He struggled to pull a worn stub from his jacket as Mari ripped a piece of paper from the notepad in her apron. She paused for only a second and scribbled hastily.

"What are you doing?" he yelled.

"Quickly! Where is that nurse?"

"Mari, come on! We've got to get on those trucks. There are dozens of nurses around. We won't find her here. Our best bet is to get to the next field station."

Danny pulled her along, but Mari continued to look around frantically. Moans rose up from the wounded, a whine that grew until it nearly drowned out the shells. It came all the same, as though the sound meant to find her. A baby's cry. She stopped abruptly and strained to see over the soldiers. There it was. Her cap shone like a lamp amid the dirt and blood.

"Mari, the trucks are this way."

A colonel strode past her. Mari stopped him with a swift hand to his shoulder.

"Please, sir, see that this letter reaches that nurse. It's for the child," she pleaded as she pushed the paper into his hand.

He looked at it skeptically for a moment, but the imploring look in Mari's eyes softened his resolve, and he nodded abruptly. "Yes. Lieutenant!"

Mari watched him blend into the mass of soldiers scurrying like ants in every direction. Her eyes narrowed even as her husband pulled her toward a truck filling quickly with soldiers. "Danny, he's going the wrong way!"

"Mari, come ..."

The explosion knocked them off their feet.

"It would be a wonderful thing for all of
humanity if both peoples would renounce
force against each other forever. The German
people are ready to make such a pledge."

Adolf Hitler
October 14, 1933

1

Heidelberg, Germany
August 1935

G ermany had changed. As steam rose up between the cars of the train, Paul van Ostrand stepped onto the platform and breathed deeply. While Paul had been in America for the past few years, Adolf Hitler had succeeded in becoming Chancellor of Germany, quit the League of Nations, and following President Hindenburg's death, appointed himself as Führer, the sole authority over the country. Yes, Germany had changed.

But as he took in the sights and smells of the station, he smiled in spite of it all. Paul was home. As much as he had enjoyed his time in the United States, his heart had constantly yearned for Germany. This land was his home.

Paul turned as his friend Jesse Riker stepped off the train. His cool, intent dark brown eyes swept the crowd and took in the large number of soldiers milling about. Paul wondered at his first impression of the Fatherland.

Jesse smiled, and his white teeth shone against his deeply tanned face.

"Quite a welcoming committee."

Paul shrugged. "It has changed much in two years." His English bore a thick accent.

"Maybe we got on the wrong train," Jesse said wryly.

9

"I barely recognize it from when I left." Paul looked around and searched the faces passing through the gate of the platform. "Mother said she'd be here at five sharp."

Benedikta van Ostrand was never late. It was not in her character. Paul and Jesse walked with the flow of the crowd toward the exit. It was a busy time at the station, and they had to speak quite loudly to be heard above the noise of rush hour.

"So tell me again who's coming to meet us?" Jesse asked.

"Well, I hope my brother will come along, but Mother says he's hardly around anymore. But I know my sister will come."

"Hilda," Jesse said slowly. "That's her name right? And your brother is Dederick."

"Yes. The three of us were almost inseparable as kids. We used to drive Mother crazy, and Father always had to … well anyway, I hope they both come."

Paul grew silent as he thought of his father. Suddenly being home brought his death into starker clarity than it had reading a letter. His heart squeezed tightly, and he cleared his throat to relieve the painful pressure. Jesse poked him, and he looked up. An older woman with wispy blonde hair under a stylish blue hat waved vigorously at him. Paul's face burst into a smile, and he ran toward her. The German flowed off his tongue as sweet as honey after two years at the back of his mind.

"Mother!"

"Paul!"

Benedikta opened her arms to her son, and he embraced her tightly. Her eyes shone when they finally pulled apart, and she smiled.

"Well, look at you! All grown up and handsome. I sent you away as a boy and you come back a strapping young man!"

"I've missed you, Mother."

"And I you, dear. Two years is far too long. We need you now more than ever."

Paul nodded slowly and wrapped his arm around her. "I'm here now. I'm not going anywhere."

She gave him a wobbly smile as tears formed in her eyes. Paul wished he could somehow take away her pain, or give her back the man who had made nearly twenty-five years of her life such a wonderful adventure. Benedikta wiped her eyes and lifted her head high once more.

"Oh, we're being so rude, Paul!" she exclaimed as she turned to Jesse, her English slightly broken. "Pardon, it's just been so long."

"Not at all, ma'am," Jesse said with a smile.

"Mother, this is Jesse Riker. I stayed with his family in Los Angeles. Jesse, my mother, Benny van Ostrand."

Jesse offered his hand, which Benedikta took with a smile. "It's a pleasure to finally meet you, Mrs. van Ostrand."

"The pleasure is mine, Jesse. I've heard so much about you from Paul's letters. It's wonderful to finally meet his best friend in the flesh."

"I've heard plenty about you as well," Jesse said.

Paul, who had been looking around the station, broke in. "Mother, is anyone with you?" His face was full of disappointment at not recognizing anyone else. Benedikta smiled and touched his arm.

"Yes, dear. Hilda saw a friend of hers and stopped to chat. Oh, here she comes."

The men turned to where she was pointing and stopped dead. Tall and slim, a vision in emerald green walked toward them. Her long hair was waved stylishly away from her face, and a charming beret perched atop her head. As she walked through the station, several heads turned to follow her. Her face split into a beautiful smile as she caught sight of her brother. Now it was Paul who poked Jesse.

"Close your mouth," he muttered, then called excitedly, "Hilda!"

"Paul!"

They ran toward each other and Hilda threw herself into Paul's arms. He hugged her tightly. How he had missed his beloved sister.

"It's so good to have you back!"

"It's good to be back," he murmured. "Come and meet Jesse."

Paul took her hand and led her back to where his friend stood with his mother. Hilda smiled, and with a small wink at him, turned her sparkling green eyes to Jesse.

Jesse coolly looked back at the woman who turned to him with an intent gaze. Against his will, he felt his guard going down. He could not deny that women were drawn to him. His mother had said many times that Jesse inherited his father's handsome genes, and the uniform did nothing to deter young women, especially with a war on the horizon.

But this girl was different. He already felt a strong attraction to her, and that bothered him. He did not think the German language beautiful until it came from her lips. Jesse put a cordial smile on his face as Paul turned to him. He could see that an introduction was coming, and he wanted to be well prepared.

"Jesse Riker, my sister Hilda."

Jesse shook her hand quickly and leaned forward. "It's a pleasure to meet you. Paul has told me so much about you," he said loudly.

Hilda's curious gaze grew amused and slightly irritated, and she freed her hand as she leaned away. "Clearly he forgot to mention that I speak and understand English quite well."

Jesse was shocked at how fluently she spoke. Right down to the accent and vernacular, she could have passed for an American any day. He would not have been able to tell the difference if he had first met her in the states. He saw the amused look on her face at his surprise, and it annoyed him to no end. He casually put his hands in his pockets and leaned back as though studying her.

"So you're the little sister," he mused, emphasizing *little*.

Hilda's eyes narrowed. She turned to her mother quickly, and her long brown locks swung ferociously. When she spoke, her German mesmerized him, and he shifted awkwardly to hide the effect her words had on him. It was fascinating gibberish to him, but he thought he heard her mention her younger brother Dederick.

Whatever she said, Paul choked back a laugh and glanced at Jesse, who straightened his jacket and looked uneasily between the three. Apparently the joke was on him. Benedikta looked shocked at her daughter's words and hastily tried to cover the obvious insult with a warm smile.

"You must stay with us while you are here, Jesse. I daresay that we have ample room. I am not one to send a visitor to a hotel, Hilda. Besides, goodness knows we could use another man around the house, with Dederick never at home anymore and your father gone ..." She halted as her voice broke. She wiped her eyes and waved away her children's concerned arms.

Jesse had heard Paul talk of his father often. Since he had not been able to come home for the funeral, his father's death was probably very fresh in his mind. He remembered when his parents had taken him to France when he was a child. He had seen the pain in their eyes as they remembered the friends they had lost in the Great War. Jesse had admired them so much for their sacrifice. The sorrow that he had seen in his parents' eyes was now reflected in the faces of the small family, and he felt their loss. His eyes shifted and settled on Hilda. She and Paul were staring at each other, but she turned and caught Jesse's gaze. He noticed something, something familiar, as though from a story or a photo. Hilda awkwardly looked away, and the moment passed.

"You will stay with us, won't you, Jesse? You are most welcome." Benedikta was addressing him, and he abruptly brought his thoughts back to the train station.

"I would be delighted."

"Splendid! Peter is waiting with the car just outside," Benedikta said.

Paul took his mother's arm and started to escort her through the station toward the car where Peter, their help, waited for them. Jesse turned to Hilda, who was beginning to follow them, and stopped her with a hand to her arm. He smiled wryly.

"I missed something back there, didn't I?"

She looked him up and down pointedly. "Perhaps, not that you'll ever find out what it was."

"Is this the way the vacation is going to be, then?" Jesse asked.

"You should know right now, Mr. Riker—"

"Jesse."

She rolled her eyes and shook herself loose of his grasp. "Oh, you Americans and your casual 'Oh, please call me Kevin' and what not. You should know, *Jesse,* that I don't take too well to people talking down to me. I happen to be a very intelligent person. I'm at the top of my class and speak five different languages quite fluently."

Jesse was surprised at first, and then a smile crossed his face. "Touché. I look forward to the challenge."

Hilda threw a sarcastic smile over her shoulder as she turned and followed Paul and her mother out of the station.

"Welcome to Heidelberg."

Jesse watched her go for a moment, not quite believing what had just transpired, then dropped his head and gave a short laugh as he started after her.

⁓

Hilda climbed into the car and sat as far away from Jesse Riker as was physically possible. As Peter pulled away from the station and headed home, she thought back on all of the letters that Paul had written and the things that he had said about his American friend.

He's a good fellow. He really helped me adjust during my first few days. He's training to be a combat pilot, you know, and he's quite good. Jesse is such a polite young man, Mother, which is why I was wondering if he could come and stay with us in Germany for a time.

At the time, Hilda had thought that it would be quite exciting to meet an American combat pilot. If he were handsome, it would make the experience all the more thrilling.

Hilda almost snorted aloud as she looked out the window. Yes, he was handsome all right, and arrogant and rude and quite self-centered at that. She had been infuriated with the way that he had looked at her as if he knew all of her secrets with one glance into her eyes. Hilda sighed. Oh, his eyes nearly undid her. They were not a muddy brown like many she had seen, but rich, and so dark except for the slightly reddish-tinted flecks that made her think of cinnamon. Back at the station, she had nearly become lost in his unwavering gaze, but fortunately, her mother had finally spoken to break the crackling tension.

"I say, Hilda, are you all right? You've been staring out that window for the past five minutes," Paul said. He gave a mock frown. "You aren't wishing me away already, are you?"

Hilda laughed. "Of course not, Paul, but Dederick may not like the fact that you're back to boss him around."

"Ah, yes, how is Dederick? You did not write much about him in your letters, Mother."

Benedikta shifted in her seat. "Yes, well, the boy is only nearing fifteen, and he is all caught up in politics. He is absolutely fascinated with everything Adolf Hitler says. He spends the whole day with his friends, and all they do is listen to his speeches on the radio when they're not in school. Then, he comes home and talks nonstop about it."

Hilda turned her head to watch the scenery again. She hated when Dederick came home and started going on about Hitler. She vividly remembered the day she first set eyes on the Nazi leader, and it still gave her chills. It was as though a button had been suddenly pushed that set into motion the trials to come for the next month. Trials that she had hardly been able to handle.

As soon as the car stopped at the edge of the curb, Hilda quickly stepped out and hurried toward the house. She breathed deeply and tried to clear her head. Her thoughts were much too jumbled to sort through at the moment, and she let them dissolve as she stepped into the house. Her mother began giving out orders.

"Peter, come and help with these bags. Paul, you can take those, can't you? Splendid ..."

Hilda turned at the sound of a door closing above her, and Dederick appeared at the top of the stairs.

"You're home early," she stated flatly.

"Was I supposed to be home at a certain time?" he returned.

She shrugged. "No, you're just home earlier than usual. Did you finally get bored listening to the same yelling voice day after day?"

Dederick huffed indignantly. "One does not get bored listening to Adolf Hitler, Hilda. There is no speech on right now." He came trotting down the steps and stopped in front of her. "That's why I'm home early."

Hilda put her hands on her hips and stared down at him. "Your brother is home, in case you didn't know. He is outside with his friend from America, and if you have any manners, you will go out and greet him."

Dederick scowled. He did not like Americans. But he strode out the door and called his brother's name.

Hilda started up the stairs, but her mother's voice stopped her. She turned and saw her standing in the doorway with Jesse next to her. Hilda frowned as he flashed her a grin.

"Hilda, would you be a dear and show Jesse to one of the guest bedrooms? I'm just going to check on supper."

Before she could protest, Benedikta promptly turned and made her way to the kitchen.

A tense silence hung in the hallway. Hilda clutched the banister and stared down at Jesse, who leaned casually against the wall and stared back at her with a wry smile. She raised her eyebrow and eyed him a moment longer, and then with a flip of her wavy hair, she turned on the stair and started up again. After a few steps, she heard him pick up his suitcase and follow her.

Hilda hurried down the hallway and leaned against the doorframe of the guest bedroom, trying to look as nonchalant as he had. Jesse turned the corner and saw her, and that amused smiled appeared again as he ambled down the hall. Her eyes narrowed, and she gestured impatiently into the room. He stepped inside and looked around. It was a very nice room. Two large windows let in the sunlight with a bed between them. A nightstand, dresser, and bulky chair also furnished the room.

"The toilet is through that door," Hilda stated, pointing toward an unopened door next to the dresser. "Supper is at seven. Don't be late." She turned to go, her hand on the doorknob to close it behind her.

"So do you treat all of your brother's friends this way?"

Hilda stopped and turned back to him. He casually leaned his knees against the bed and opened his suitcase to unpack his clothes. She turned her head away, not wanting to appear rude, but she was anxious to leave.

"No. He doesn't have that many friends, really."

Jesse glanced up, confused. "Why not? He's a nice guy."

"It's complicated."

"Try me."

Hilda sighed and stepped back inside the room, shutting the door. She leaned against the wall and watched him across the room. "Because of Hannah."

"Who's Hannah?"

Hilda hesitated and slowly took her beret from her head. "Hannah Strauss. She and Paul are very close. We all grew up together."

"And that is a problem?"

"She is a Jew."

Jesse looked up, anger in his face that she would say such a thing. He threw down a pair of pants he was about to hang up and strode across the room toward her.

"Why? Why is there such hatred against them?"

Hilda turned away, taking a few steps to escape him. He was quite imposing, even if his anger was not directed fully at her. "I don't know. I'm afraid of what it could become. Don't believe that all of us hold the same point of view. Things have been hard enough on my mother."

Hilda saw the fire slowly leave his eyes, and the room seemed to brighten once again with the evening sun, as though encouraged by the tension leaving the room. She sat down on the edge of the bed and looked out one of the windows. Jesse joined her a moment later.

"I'm sorry about your father. Paul was devastated to hear about his death," he said quietly.

"Thank you."

"If you don't mind my asking, what happened?"

Hilda shrugged, but she did not turn to face him. "I don't know. He went out one night after supper and didn't come back. A week later his body was found. He'd been shot through the heart several times. The police report said it was a robbery."

She felt his hand on her arm, and it seemed to alleviate some of the pain in her heart.

"I'm sorry, Hilda," he murmured. "I didn't mean to … you were close to him."

Hilda almost laughed; it was so silly a comment. "He was my father."

Jesse stood slowly, moved back to his suitcase, and continued to unpack. Hilda allowed herself to turn and watch him. His back was to the dresser when he spoke again.

"How old were you when they adopted you?"

Hilda started at the question, and watched him turn around to face her.

"How did you know that? Did Paul tell you?"

Jesse did not answer her question. "You don't look anything like him or your mother."

Hilda gave a short laugh and moved toward the door. "Easy to spot when the rest of the population is the perfect citizen with blond hair and blue eyes."

"I don't know about that." Jesse smiled as he folded a couple of shirts into a drawer. "I've always kind of had a thing for green-eyed brunettes."

Irritation filled Hilda, and she tried to mask some of it as she spun around. He was watching her in the mirror on the dresser. A crooked smiled revealed his perfect white teeth.

"Does that actually work where you're from?"

He turned to her and leaned against the dresser. "Of course, but I'm extremely picky. New things interest me."

"Boys and their toys," Hilda muttered and turned to leave.

"So you've written me off already, have you?" Jesse hurried across the room and put his arm across the door. "I don't give up easily."

Hilda smiled and folded her arms. "Paul may be nice, but he is also quite protective. I wouldn't give yourself any more than you can handle this vacation."

Jesse laughed. "You think I don't know how to handle Paul? We spent two years living together while he studied in California."

"I'm sure you can handle him. But I don't know about Dederick."

"Your younger brother? Why not?"

Hilda moved away and leaned against the bed frame, trying to be as nonchalant as he looked. "Dederick will not like you. No matter what. He is … quite patriotic. It's rather ridiculous."

Jesse sighed and moved over to the window. She turned to watch him.

"That's too bad," he said quietly. "I was looking forward to getting to know all of you on this trip."

Hilda felt the guilt seep through her. There was genuine hurt in his voice. She regretted what she had said, and her eyes softened. She took a few steps toward him. "I'm sorry. I've not made you feel very welcome. This hasn't been a good time for my family. I don't know why Paul invited you."

"Because I wanted to meet you all."

Hilda was surprised at his answer. His eyes shone clearly with his joy of being in Germany, and she smiled, touched by his friendliness.

"C'est doux," she murmured.

He held up his hands as though warding off an attack. "What? Was that another insult?"

She laughed and pushed his hands down. "No. Not at all."

"So what does it mean then?" he asked warily, but she saw a smile peek through his look.

"You silly Americans."

"Yeah, right." He laughed. "Just what languages do you speak, so that I know in advance?"

Hilda thought for a moment. "Goodness, German obviously. English, French, Spanish, Russian … I'm learning ancient Egyptian."

"Ancient Egyptian? What for?"

She laughed and shrugged. "Because I can. I've always loved languages, and I'm a fast learner when it comes to that and culture. I hope to go to Paris to study, but Mother won't let me go until I'm seventeen."

Jesse looked at her, surprised. "Wait. How old are you now?"

"Sixteen."

He shook his head. "That's all?"

"Yes," she said. "You did not know that?"

"Well, no. You look so much older than sixteen."

"I know, and it doesn't help that Mother continues to baby me. She still sees me as a mere child, and not as a woman." Hilda looked over at him. He was still staring at her wide-eyed. "What?" she asked.

"You really are only sixteen?" he asked hesitantly.

"Yes," she said with a laugh. "Goodness, you make yourself sound so much older. You're Paul's age, right? Twenty?"

"Yes."

"See. You haven't reached the grave yet, so stop gawking at my age. I feel more like twelve," she said, pushing him lightly.

They laughed and Hilda moved to help him unpack. She grabbed his shoes and went to the closet. "Tell me about your family, Jesse."

"Well, there's not much to tell. I've lived my entire life in California. My mom and dad served during the Great War, as a nurse and a pilot."

"Is that what made you want to fly?" she asked.

He turned to her abruptly. "How did you know that?"

"Paul wrote about you often in his letters, and he mentioned that you were training to be a combat pilot," she said as she turned back to him. "Did you choose to do that because your father served as well?"

"Yes. He has been my inspiration since I was a boy. He and his best friend Luke. He died at the end of the war, tragically."

Hilda saw the pain in his eyes when he mentioned the name, and she came to stand beside him.

"How awful. Did he have any family?"

Jesse paused. "His wife, Allison. She passed the same day he was killed, giving birth."

Hilda brought a hand to her heart. "That's terrible. I'm so sorry, Jesse." She slowly folded a pair of pants. "What happened? To the baby?"

"No idea," Jesse murmured, watching her. "Mom said that after Allie died a nurse took the child, and she never saw her again. It's been hard on my parents, but they've left quite a legacy. My sister is still young, but she already wants to be a nurse just like Mom."

"Wow. That kind of loyalty ... I can't imagine it."

Hilda stared at the pants in her hands, but didn't see them. She had a troubled look on her face, but Jesse didn't disturb her. After a moment, she put them away and turned to him with a smile.

"So you have a sister."

Jesse smiled. "Yes. Christina. She's quite the little fireball—"

Her abrupt cry cut him off, and Hilda pulled a shocked Jesse roughly to the floor as a gunshot cracked into the silence of the evening.

2

Jesse rolled away from where he had fallen on top of Hilda and sat up cautiously. What on earth had just happened? One moment they had been talking amiably, the next moment she had pulled him down so hard that his arm was beginning to ache. He turned to watch her as she cautiously sat up and peered out the window. The light was such that he could not make out anyone on the street below them. Hilda slumped against the wall below the window and leaned her head back, closing her eyes. Jesse rose to his knees and crawled over to her.

"Are you all right?" he asked quietly.

She shook her head slowly, and he could tell that she was barely keeping her calm. He put his hand over hers where it rested on her lap.

"It's okay, Hilda," he said gently. "You have every right to be afraid. You just got shot at. That never happens to a girl like you."

Jesse was surprised when she shook her head. "Yes, it does," she said quietly. "Three times before, to be exact."

He straightened with shock. "What are you talking about, Hilda? This … this has happened before?"

Hilda opened her eyes. "It started right after my father died. We were walking through the park one evening when we heard a shot, and my arm started bleeding. Mother thought it was an accident. I was in the hospital for a week. The second time, I was at my dresser, and when I looked in the mirror, I saw a man with a gun aimed at my head. I escaped with a graze that time and told everyone I bumped my head. I was ready for it the third time and got away without a scratch."

With trembling fingers, Jesse reached up and gently smoothed the hair away from her face, revealing a thin white scar that trailed just above her eyebrow, over her ear and into her hairline. Hot anger such as he had never known filled him and threatened to burst forth in a tidal wave of turbulent emotions. He forced himself to calm down for her sake, and for his own.

"Why would someone want to kill you? Didn't you go to the police?"

Hilda shook her head. "I can't."

"Why not?"

She looked at him with sad eyes. "They're the ones who want me dead."

Jesse wasn't sure whether he should be angry or shocked. How was it that a young sixteen-year-old girl was able to go through so much pain? The loss of a father and escaping death multiple times seemed too much for anyone. Jesse shook his head to clear his thoughts. He put his arm around Hilda's shoulders and she instantly leaned against him.

"Talk to me, Hilda," he whispered into her hair.

Jesse heard her sigh deeply, and it seemed as though she was going to begin, but pounding feet sounded on the stairs, and he heard Paul's urgent voice calling her name.

Hilda stood up and straightened her skirt and blouse. Jesse stood as well, and when she turned to him, her face was unreadable. Their gazes locked for a few moments, and then Paul burst into the room.

"Hilda, are you all right?" he said, gasping. "I heard the shot. Do you know what it was?"

Hilda shrugged, the look of indifference back on her face. "I don't know. Probably a policeman who lost control of his gun. Nothing to worry about, Paul. No one was hurt."

Paul's shoulders sagged in relief. "Well, that's good to know. My, you would think the streets weren't safe anymore." He turned back toward the door. "You two coming to dinner? It'll be ready soon."

"We'll be down in a few minutes, Paul," Hilda called to him as he strode out the door. When he had disappeared down the stairs, she closed the door behind him and returned to the dresser, where she straightened some clothes that had been thrown in their haste to get to the floor.

Jesse saw that the vulnerable look was gone from her eyes, and she turned to him with her smile back in place. He shook his head firmly, not about to be deterred so quickly.

"You were telling me about your younger sister," she said lightly.

Jesse walked to her and took her arms. She looked up at him, her mask partly gone.

"Why do the Nazis want to kill you, Hilda?" he demanded quietly.

Hilda sighed and lowered her eyes. "Your guess is as good as mine," she whispered. "Please don't say anything, Jesse. It's no one's business but my own."

"You made it my business when I landed on top of you just now," he stated.

Her face grew bright red, and she pushed away from him. Striding to the door, she turned back with a look of irritation on her face.

"You will find, Mr. Riker," she said, "that your American mannerisms will not be warmly welcomed if you continue to shove your way into other people's private lives."

"Look who's talking about shoving," he said pointedly.

Hilda's eyes widened, and she gave a huff of indignation. With a quick turn, she opened the door and placed her hands on her hips.

"I will see you at dinner, Mr. Riker."

With that, she pulled the door closed behind her with a resounding thud.

September came and went, and the autumn leaves turned in the city, filling the cold streets with a warmth of color. Hilda slowly walked home, her arms laden with groceries. The past weeks had been interesting. Her relationship with Jesse seemed to rest on a teeter-totter. One moment, they were the best of friends, and the next she couldn't stand the sight of him. Paul had taken him out to the countryside, but Hilda wasn't sure when they'd be back. Secretly, she had wished to go with them, but her mother needed her at home.

She turned and glanced at Dederick, who walked tall and straight, hands in his pockets, proudly wearing the uniform of Hitler's Youth.

"So, Dederick, have you finally formed a better opinion of our American guest?"

He scowled. "I think he should go back home to his eccentric movie star neighbors and leave us alone."

Hilda expected such a response, and at the moment didn't feel like fighting him. She turned to look up the street, shifting the grocery bag. She could feel Dederick's eyes on her.

"So you like him, then." There was no question in her brother's voice.

Hilda turned to him abruptly. "What? I didn't say that."

"You did not say you *didn't* like him."

"Well, I ... I think he's polite. A gentleman." Even Hilda thought the words sounded ridiculous.

Dederick snorted and straightened his uniform. A group of children played in front of them, and when their ball came bouncing toward them, he kicked it back into the street.

"Oh, please," he said. "You've been fawning over him since he stepped off the train."

"I have not been fawning over him! I admire his ... pursuits."

Dederick laughed harshly and looked at her. "You mean being a pilot? Oh so loyal to his country? Isn't that what I'm doing? Why don't you admire *my* pursuits?" he whined.

"Because, Dederick, you're still a boy in school learning mathematics and grammar. Jesse Riker ... is a man. Who knows? You might change your mind—"

Dederick's face turned a fierce red, and his fury was evident. "I will never stop wanting to defend Germany! Look at how far our country has come under the guidance of Adolf Hitler! I will serve him to the end, even if it is my death."

Hilda feared at his words and tried to brush aside his serious sentiments. "Honestly, Dederick, aren't you a little young to be talking about death? It isn't becoming to the ladies."

Dederick straightened his uniform again, rather uncomfortable as they passed a group of laughing school girls. Hilda smiled when he looked back at her, but when he turned away, she grew concerned.

She was about to shift the bags in her arms when a black car suddenly pulled up to the curb near them. Hilda, startled, dropped her groceries, and Dederick straightened to attention as two officers stepped out followed by a man in a black trench coat. The Gestapo hurried up to a man walking toward Hilda and Dederick, and with very little ceremony they pushed him into the car and drove away as quickly as they had come.

The scene lasted less than thirty seconds, but Hilda felt frozen in time. She watched the car drive down the street and turn the corner. Most likely that man would never see the light of day again. Her hands trembled as she reached down and tried to clean off the vegetables. Her heart pounded so loudly she was afraid the entire neighborhood could hear, and she put one hand to her forehead, trying to calm herself.

"It's only dirt, Hilda. It will wash right off."

She glanced up to find Jesse kneeling down beside her, and he picked up the vegetables and replaced them in the bag. Glancing between them and Dederick was Paul, who stood not far behind. Hilda began to grow flustered, and had the feeling of a bird on display at the zoo. She tried to help Jesse clean up her mess.

"Thank you," she mumbled hastily.

Paul stepped forward. "What luck we ran into you two! We just got back and ran by the University before going home. Mother's been wondering where you wandered off to."

"Not too worried, I hope," Hilda said as she stood. Jesse helped her to her feet, her hand in one of his and the groceries in the other. His gentle yet firm grip helped her heart slow to its normal pace, and she regained her composure. "We were just enjoying the sunshine while it's still here. How was your trip to the University?"

"Fine," Paul answered. "Many new professors I did not recognize, but I was able to show Jesse around."

"It's very beautiful," Jesse chimed in. "Our campuses just don't compare."

"That's not the only thing," Dederick mumbled.

"Dederick!" Hilda was horrified, but Jesse just smiled.

"It's all right," he said. "I agree with him. There are several things about Germany that I have come to love." He glanced at her for a split second, and Hilda blushed all the way down to her roots.

Paul held back a smile, but Dederick scowled at the shared look. He stomped over and took the groceries Jesse was holding and strode purposely through their locked hands. Paul shook his head at his little brother and followed.

Hilda looked up at Jesse. He was watching her, a small smile on his lips. He beckoned with one hand.

"Shall we?"

Hilda returned his smile, and they started the walk home side by side. Paul glanced back a couple times, smiling, and then ran to catch up with Dederick. Hilda silently thanked her brother, even though she wasn't sure what she was thanking him for. Did she want privacy with Jesse? She looked up at him. Yes, she did.

"So who was that back there?" Jesse asked as they walked.

"Oh, the car?" Hilda stiffened but tried to appear relaxed. "Gestapo."

Jesse whistled low. "Oh. Don't want to get on their bad side."

Hilda shook her head. "No, but it's hard to figure out their good side sometimes."

He beckoned back to where they had just come from. "Does that happen often?"

Hilda shrugged. "Occasionally, though it has been getting more frequent." She shivered. "I hate it when that car pulls up. It always reminds me of ..."

Jesse looked at her when she didn't continue. "Of what?"

Hilda looked out into the street. She could still hear the children playing with the ball behind them. She remembered Dederick doing the same thing when they were children, just as he had on that hot summer day not so long ago.

Hilda suddenly took Jesse's arm and leaned in close, afraid of whom might be listening. She knew she could be arrested for speaking out, but would they arrest her for being afraid?

"I was twelve. My father was still alive, Paul was still here, the Nazis hadn't taken over Germany ... I was happy. Dederick and I were walking home one day, much like we just were. He was playing with this big red ball my father had gotten him on his last birthday." Hilda smiled. "It was his favorite present."

Jesse put his other hand over their interlaced fingers. "What happened?"

Hilda paused briefly before continuing, her voice growing softer. "Dederick had chased his ball out into the street, not too far, and I saw a car come speeding toward him out of the corner of my eye. I think my heart stopped, I was so afraid. I screamed so loud, and Dederick managed to jump out of the way. The car stopped just passed him, and in it was ... Adolf Hitler." Hilda breathed in slowly after the name. "He was campaigning in the city. He got out of the car and told Dederick to be more careful next time, and I couldn't help but get this cold feeling as I watched him pat my brother's head. Dederick was enthralled. He didn't really know who Hitler was, but he'd heard the name. He tells that story to all his friends now. But I can't even think about it without feeling sick." She glanced up at the trees and watched the sun filter through the leaves. "He scares me a little."

Jesse watched her. "Hitler or your brother?"

Hilda looked at him, a thoughtful expression on her face, and then she turned her eyes to her brothers walking ahead of them.

"Both, I imagine."

Hilda sat curled up in the parlor with a book in her lap. The darkness outside swallowed the entire street, but the lamps burned brightly throughout the room. Dinner had been a quiet affair, but she had looked up many times to find Jesse watching her. There was so much said in his gaze. Somehow, something had changed over the course of that afternoon. She didn't know how to describe it, but whatever it was had caused her to lose her concentration all evening. She shut her book slowly and leaned her elbow against the arm of the couch. Her gaze became lost in the lamp light, but only for a moment.

A door down the hall suddenly banged open, and the angry voices of her brothers could be heard throughout the house.

"I saw you with her again today!"

"Dederick, please. We are just friends. And what we do is none of your business."

"It is my business, as a member of the Third Reich, and you are *not* just friends!" Dederick insisted.

Hilda silently stood from the couch and went over to the door, leaning her ear closer. Her brothers' voices were clearly heard now.

"Why does it matter to you? You don't have to be friends with her anymore if you don't want to," Paul said. "But Hannah and I … she has lost so much lately, what with the Nuremberg Race Laws coming into being. She needs a friend right now, and I choose to be that friend."

"Those laws are in place for our protection, and you would just go off and allow those Jews to continue benefiting from us?" Dederick was shouting now.

Another door opened across the hall, and quiet footsteps hurried toward the voices.

"Boys, please." It was Hilda's mother. "Our guest is just down the hall. Please don't bring your politics into the house."

"Dederick thinks he knows exactly what he's talking about, Mother!" Paul exclaimed, very angry now. "He hasn't a clue what is going on. He's just a kid."

A scuffle was heard, and Hilda started as bodies thudded against the wall.

"Boys, stop it this instant. Dederick, let go!"

The scuffling stopped suddenly, but Hilda could hear their heavy breathing. She leaned closer to the door.

"Dederick that is no way for you to behave. Now you apologize to your brother this instant!" Benedikta said firmly.

"I will not, Mother! You still think me a child too. Well, I am not a child! I am the future of Germany. I am part of Hitler's Iron Youth!"

Hilda heard the slap, and she could easily imagine Dederick's cheek turning bright red from their mother's slap.

"Dederick van Ostrand, if you want to be seen as a man, then stop acting like a child! You will not act this way in front of me. Is that understood?"

Hilda felt the tense silence between the three of them, and then heard Dederick's feet stomp up the stairs to his room. Benedikta murmured something unintelligible to Paul, and he hurried down the hall toward the library. Hilda heard her mother's footsteps coming toward her. She hurried back to the couch and sat down just as her mother opened the door and entered, closing it softly behind her. She walked slowly to a chair in front of the fire and sat down. Hilda saw her hands shaking, and a few seconds later, Benedikta's shoulders dropped as she cried softly into her hand.

Hilda went over to her quickly and dropped to her knees in front of her.

"Oh, Mother, I'm so sorry."

Benedikta sniffed and lifted her head.

"No, it is not your fault, Hilda. I'm sorry for ruining the evening by yelling and screaming. I can't imagine what Jesse must be thinking. I sent Paul to him."

Hilda took her mother's hand and held it tightly. When she lifted her head, there were tears in her eyes. "Oh, Mother, what's happened to him? He is always so cold and hard."

Benedikta shook her head helplessly. "I don't know, darling. I don't know."

They sat together for some time and watched the fire burn down to coals. A brisk wind began to blow outside, whistling between the trees and stealing many of the autumn leaves away. It covered all other sounds, so they didn't hear anything until a loud knock pounded at the door. Hilda jumped. Benedikta stood quickly and went to the window as the knock came again. She turned to her daughter.

"Hilda, upstairs now."

Hilda nodded and hurried out into the hall, where she met Jesse and Paul coming out of the library. Without a word, Jesse took her hand and led her up the stairs past Dederick, who came to the top of the landing, curiosity in his face. They didn't say a word as they went into her bedroom and shut the door. Hilda heard Paul open the door, and the pounding of feet was heard in the hall downstairs. When she glanced at Jesse, he was watching her, bewildered.

"What's going on? Paul just told me to go upstairs when he heard the door."

Hilda sat down on the edge of her bed and clasped her hands tightly in her lap. She looked out the window and saw the black car parked along the curb.

"Only one person calls this late at night in Heidelberg," she said slowly.

Jesse looked at her in confusion, and she finally raised her eyes to his. "Our friendly neighborhood policemen."

He went to the window where she looked out, and she knew he understood. "That man this afternoon?" Jesse asked.

Hilda closed her eyes. "I've had dreams of it happening to me. Walking along the road one day, suddenly their car pulls up. No questions, just a hood thrown over my head and I'm dumped in the trunk ..."

Jesse sat down next to her just as footsteps came up the stairs, and Hilda grabbed his hand instinctively. He wrapped his hands around hers as they both looked toward the door. The doorknob turned, and Paul entered. Hilda let out the breath she'd been holding. Paul slowly walked over in front of her, holding her gaze with a slow nod.

"Gestapo. They're asking for you, Hilda."

Hilda jumped up. "I've said nothing, Paul. I swear!"

He took her hands gently. "Then you have nothing to fear. Don't worry. I won't let them take you away."

Jesse stood, concerned. "Take her away?"

Paul led Hilda to the door and squeezed her shoulders tightly. "It's all right, Hilda. It's going to be all right."

She nodded slowly, and walked out the door and down the stairs. Jesse started to follow, but Paul held him back. Jesse looked at him.

"She's only a kid. What could she have done?"

Paul stared back at him seriously. "The Gestapo is known for filling their prisons and work camps for the smallest of wrongs. I pray Hilda didn't say or do anything too serious, but she is independent and makes up her own mind."

Jesse thought about their conversation that afternoon, and the ones they'd shared in the past, then stared back at the door. Had they finally given up their feeble secret attempts to eliminate her? Too many questions ran through his mind at what could happen. He had never felt more powerless to do anything, and uncertainty filled him. He did not like either of those feelings.

⌒⅄⌒

Hilda smoothed her hair before entering the dining room slowly, her trembling fingers locked firmly in front of her. A middle-aged man sat at the table, still wearing his black coat. Two officers stood solemnly beside him, and behind them, her mother watched nervously from the corner. The man at the table smiled politely at her and beckoned to the chair opposite him. As she sat down, his words ran over her skin like ice water.

"Good evening, Fraulein van Ostrand. I hope we are not disturbing your evening."

Hilda gracefully clasped her hands in front of her, if only to stop their shaking, and smiled back at him. "Not at all. What can I do for you?"

"We are with the Secret State Police. We have a few questions for you. Papers please."

Hilda stood slowly and retrieved them from the buffet in the hallway. She handed them to the Gestapo agent and returned to her chair. Her heart pounded as the seconds passed in silence. The agent studied the documents, slight surprise on his face, then handed them to one of his officers, who began to look them over as well.

"Well ... everything seems to be in order," he said, straightening a bit. To Hilda, he looked as though he was trying to gain the upper hand in the conversation once more. "Your mother's name is Benedikta van Ostrand, of French ancestry, is that correct?"

Benedikta stepped to her daughter's side. "Yes, I am her mother. I am originally from Paris."

"Yes, yes, that is the name on your papers," he said impatiently as he took them back from the officer and studied them again. "And your father ... Frederick van Ostrand. He recently died, yes?"

Hilda tensed, and Benedikta put a hand on her shoulder. Hilda nodded slowly. "Yes."

"My sympathies. A tragic accident, I was told. A mugging, yes?"

Hilda nodded and dropped her eyes briefly. The agent smiled slightly as if he noticed her discomfort.

"You were adopted, isn't that right?"

"Yes," she replied.

"All the paperwork is in order," Benedikta insisted. "You can contact the convent. They will have all the necessary files."

He waved her back again. "Yes, yes, we know. Your biological father was of German ancestry, we understand."

"Yes. He served in the Great War," Hilda said.

"Admirable. One final question. Have you been in contact with any non-German citizens recently?"

Hilda paused and glanced toward her mother. Benedikta raised her eyes briefly to the ceiling.

"My brother ... he has a friend staying with us," Hilda said slowly.

"Yes, we know all about your American friend."

Hilda stood impatiently. "Well, you seem to know the answer to all the questions you've asked, so I think you've wasted enough of both our time." She turned to go.

"One moment, Fraulein. Please sit."

Hilda took a deep breath to calm her anger, and took her seat again. The agent slid her papers back to her, but paused as she reached out for them.

"Have you been in contact with any *other* foreigners?" he asked pointedly.

"No."

"Are you certain?"

Hilda looked at him. "Yes. Quite."

He stared at her for a moment, then leaned back and casually reached into his pocket and placed what looked to be telegrams on the table in front of her.

"Do you recognize these?"

Hilda shook her head. She did not even want to look at them.

"They're telegrams," he stated, tapping them with one long pale finger. "From the British Secret Intelligence Service in London. We intercepted them and wish to know if they are a viable threat."

Hilda was shocked. London? What did that have anything to do with her? She slowly touched one of them, but the officer snatched them up.

"I don't understand," she murmured.

"No? Your name is mentioned."

"What? My name?" Hilda could not organize the thoughts running around her head. Her name?

"This surprises you?" he asked, watching her.

"It does. Greatly."

"As it does us. Can you swear to those of us in the protection detail that you had no knowledge of these?"

"Absolutely," Hilda said firmly.

Her mother cut in again. "Sir, please, this is outrageous. My daughter is only sixteen. Why would she be communicating with London?"

He stood abruptly, causing Benedikta to take a step back. An officer handed him his hat, and he placed it on his head.

"A very good question, Frau van Ostrand. One we wish answered." He stared down at Hilda, and she clenched her hands in her lap. Here it came. They would pull out the hood any moment now. Her stomach turned into a knot. "Seeing as how your brother has such an outstanding record among our officers, we don't have a need to bring you in ... just yet, anyway. We will be in touch. Please stay in the city until we contact you. Good night."

With a click of their heels, they left the dining room, and Hilda heard Dederick let them out. Once the door clicked shut, she slumped down in her chair, her head in her hands. Her mother's arms came around her.

"It's all right now, darling. They're gone."

Hilda took a shaky breath and lifted her head to find Dederick in the doorway, arms crossed, with a small look of surprise on his face. He hadn't heard their conversation, but Hilda wanted to get up and kiss him for his service. She did not agree with him on his political views, but they had saved her tonight, and she loved him all the more for it. She began to shake as she thought of how much worse the situation could have been.

Paul and Jesse rushed into the room, and Paul took Hilda's hands warmly in his. "What did they want?" he asked.

"Nothing much. They asked about Mother and Father," Hilda replied slowly, still trying to slow her pounding heart.

"That's all?" Paul's question voiced her own confusion.

Hilda glanced at Jesse, who was watching her with concern, but remained a safe distance with Dederick in the room.

"They thought I might be sending telegrams to London," she said, shaking her head. "London!"

Benedikta glanced out the window as she watched the tail lights of

31

the car turn the corner. She looked back at her family. "Paul, they will probably come back."

He stood and put his arm around his mother. "I'll go to the station tomorrow and talk with them. I'm sure it's just a misunderstanding."

Dederick stepped forward, curious. "How come they didn't take you with them for questioning?"

"Dederick!" Benedikta admonished. "What a horrid thing to say!"

Hilda stood and faced her younger brother. "I have you to thank for that, Dederick." She walked slowly over and placed a kiss on his cheek. She turned, and saw the entire room staring at her, waiting for her to collapse in relief, or fear, whatever it was that swirled inside her. She sighed deeply. "I'm tired. I'm going to bed."

Hilda slowly walked out of the room and up the stairs. Paul, Benedikta, and Jesse followed her out. Jesse stood staring up long after Benedikta and Paul left, and Hilda had disappeared.

3

She ran down the dark street, bathed in light every now and then by the cold, steel street lamps. And always, the car followed at its slow, steady pace behind her, as though mocking her attempt to flee. The headlights flashed. She fell to her knees and closed her eyes and ears to what was coming.

"Daddy!"

And suddenly a strong hand was there. She raised her eyes to the man who held her, his deep green eyes comforting as he rocked her back and forth. It was a warm, familiar touch, and she breathed in deeply.

An explosion sounded, and the man looked up, concerned. Planes flew above them, old planes, broken and tired of holding the defenses. He looked back and grew sad, suddenly very far away.

"No Dad, no!"

The headlights of the car blinded her, and she lost sight of him in the bright lights. Only moments, and then he was gone ... taken from her forever.

The night was still and cold, holding the essence of the frosty autumn. The wind quietly whistled through the trees and the branches slid across the windows in eerie high pitched scratches. There was no light from the moon, for it hung low and yellow in the black sky. The bedroom was so dark, and the odd shapes of the furniture looked ominous in the shadows. The glow of the harvest moon fell through the bottom of the window and cast a dull light that offered little comfort for Hilda as she lay staring up at the ceiling. The clock downstairs chimed twice, and the small sound echoed through the large but hardly empty house. As it died away, the silence took over once more. Two o'clock in the morning. Hilda sighed. She had tossed and turned for the past two hours, but had not been able to fall back asleep. It was a good thing that tomorrow was Saturday, for she would never be able to wake up in time for school. The silence nearly rang in her ears, and then a new sound sent her upright.

Thump.

Hilda looked around, startled by the sound that broke the silence like a gunshot. She tried to calm her heavy breathing and listened for the sound to come again. But it didn't. She lay back on the pillows slowly, thinking she must have imagined it.

It came again.

Hilda bolted upright and out of bed. Someone was downstairs, but who? Possibilities ran through her mind, and she tried to shove them away. After the night's visit from the Gestapo, any suspicious noise sent her heart into her throat. She silently tiptoed across the room, not even bothering to grab her robe, and stepped into the hall. Hilda grabbed a marble bookend from the small table against the wall and gripped it tightly in her hand. With steadier feet than she thought she had, she quietly made her way down the stairs.

The hallway was pitch black, and the darkened doorways loomed like entrances to tombs. Her eyes fell on the dim glow that shone underneath the crack of the parlor door. Cautious, Hilda moved to the door and stopped. No sound came from within. She froze with a sudden rush of icy fear. Had the intruder heard her? Was he ... was he waiting for her? Hilda told herself to slow down. She was thinking way too fast. She reached for the handle and let the door swing open on its own. She raised the bookend and stepped cautiously into the room. The lamp burned low on the table next to the sofa, sending a soft glow in a three-foot circle. Everything else remained in the dark. The one large window on the wall brought little light from the moon. Hilda slowly turned and glanced around the room. The dead silence was unnerving.

The person in the corner with his back to her frightened her and she squeaked, ready to throw her weapon at him, when he turned and the lamp light caught his face. It was Jesse, a closed book in his hand that he had just pulled from the shelf. He took in her pale face and raised hand, bookend clutched in her fingers, and his eyes widened.

"Hilda, what on earth are you doing?" he asked quietly. He leaned over and turned up the lamp.

His voice in the now bright room shocked her out of her fear and sent torrents of emotions flooding through her. She nearly sank to the ground in relief but just managed to hold herself with the help of the wall.

"Good grief, Jesse. I thought you were a robber," she managed to get out.

He smiled and lifted the book. "I may be guilty of that. I was going to steal this up to my room for a light read."

"What are you doing up so late?" she asked.

Jesse wandered over to the sofa and plopped down. "I'm a light sleeper. The wind kept me up. You?"

She shrugged. "Couldn't sleep. Too many things running around my head."

He studied her. "Are you all right?"

Hilda slowly shook her head. She came forward and curled up tightly on the seat of the one of the large armchairs in front of the fire. "The Gestapo doesn't exactly leave you feeling warm and cozy, you understand."

Jesse leaned forward. "What did they really want? They could have found out what they asked you easily enough on their own, couldn't they?"

Hilda stared at the glowing coals. "I don't know. At first I thought they wanted to know more about you, but their snoopy informers already told them you were here."

"So much for privacy."

Hilda gave a short laugh and turned to look at him. "Privacy went out the window when the Gestapo took over the state police. As did ... what is in your American Constitution? Freedom of speech."

Jesse stood up and walked over to the fireplace. "There are a lot of good rights, that's true, but my favorite isn't written down." He held out his hand. "Stand up."

"What?"

"Come on. Give me your hand."

She stared at him, smiling a little before she allowed him to pull her up from her chair. He held her hand tightly as he led her over to the window. With his other hand he pulled it open and positioned her in front of the cool autumn breeze that blew in. Hilda felt goose bumps rise on her arms, and she rubbed the spots down.

"Close your eyes," Jesse said.

She turned to him. "Oh, Jesse, please ..."

"Just do it?" He looked pointedly at her.

She rolled her eyes and faced the window again, letting her lashes fall reluctantly. She felt Jesse lift her arms slightly, and suddenly he encircled her waist, coming in close behind her, and her heart leapt. She tried to take a deep breath and calm the butterflies in her stomach as he leaned in and put his lips close to her neck.

"My greatest freedom," he whispered, "is when I'm up in the clouds, there's not a soul in sight, and the breeze is blowing all my troubles away. There are no kings or commanders up there. Only God and the beauty of the skies."

Hilda smiled. "C'est doux."

Jesse laughed softly, and his warm breath heated the cool skin of her neck in a way that made her insides shudder with anticipation, hunger.

"Will you tell me now?" he asked.

Her smile widened. "That is sweet."

"Hmm. Well thank you. I do surprise myself sometimes," he murmured, "but it's true. No matter what freedoms they destroy, they can't take this one away. Just feel the breeze, Hilda. Let it carry your troubles away."

Slowly, very slowly, Hilda relaxed. She lifted her hands and rested them on top of his. The breeze blew in and out, ruffling her hair and cooling the heat at the center of her soul from his touch. She let her head fall back against his shoulder, and they stayed that way for a while. Jesse breathed in the smell of her hair and studied her face in the harvest moonlight.

Hilda didn't know what provoked her; maybe it was the gentle breeze calming her, or the feel of Jesse's arms around her, or perhaps it was both. Her head turned slowly toward him, her lips soft and ready for a kiss she knew was coming. She felt him lean closer, the warmth of his breath so close to her lips. Her heart pounded, and her knees went weak.

But it never came. Quite abruptly Jesse pulled away and released her. He walked back to the fireplace and stared into the coals. Hilda remained facing the window, but her heart broke. A tear escaped her eye, and she firmly closed the window. The resounding thud seemed to close the door on what might have happened, and it could not be opened again.

"I'm sorry, Hilda," Jesse said quietly from across the room.

She gripped the window sill and shut her eyes against the pain of his rejection. "Why?"

His voice was soft, yet broken. "This can't happen."

Hilda rested her forehead against the cool glass for a moment. "I know." She turned to him and leaned against the window. "But in my mind, it does."

Jesse looked at her, the passion in his eyes evident, but he was resolute when he spoke. "Hilda, I'm leaving soon, and after that you probably won't ever see me again."

She shook her head and walked over to him. "Don't say that, Jesse. Please, not right now. Let's pretend, just for a little while."

He nodded slowly and pulled her gently into his arms. She melted against him, drawing from him his aura of strength and security. In this moment, she wanted time to stand still, so that they could remain as they were, uncertain of the future, but knowing they had each other's strength. An understanding passed between them that could not be denied, could not be refused. She stared up at him, unmoving in his arms, unwilling to let go. He met her gaze.

Jesse's arms tightened around her. He knew that he would never again meet a woman quite like this one. She filled his heart and soul, bringing new adventures with her presence every day. Jesse knew that if he had a choice, he would come back and marry her. But as he held her, he could see the storm that was coming. All over Europe, darkness was beginning to fall. Softly he spoke into Hilda's ear.

"In another life, Hilda, I would love you," he said quietly. "I'm sorry. I'm so sorry."

Hilda's eyes filled with tears, and she stepped slowly out of the comfort of his arms. "I know."

She left the parlor and shut the door quietly behind her. Nothing could come of her feelings. Nothing ever would. But that did not take away the fierce pain of her love for him.

Benedikta watched her daughter with curiosity the next day. Her quick glances across the room and quiet murmurings with a certain young man in particular made her realize that sometime over the course of the night, her daughter had fallen in love with the young American combat pilot. She let this information sink in slowly, not very surprised at the turn of events, yet somewhat thoughtful. She had known of many young girls who claimed to fall in love at Hilda's age. Benedikta thought that her daughter had on her shoulders a head smarter than that. Hilda was not one to throw herself easily at anything, especially a man. If it had been any other German boy, she wouldn't have minded, for Hilda would have gotten over it soon enough—but it wasn't. It was an American soldier. With things being as tense as they were between Germany and the rest of the world, this kind of relationship would prove to be none too good for Hilda. Benedikta shuddered, not wanting to imagine her daughter somewhere in the future behind bars with a Nazi guard, or worse, dead with a bullet through her head. Hilda was only sixteen, too young to have experienced all of the trauma that she had. Benedikta knew that no matter how much she tried, she would not be able to shield her daughter from what was coming.

Hilda stood silently and solemnly against a backdrop of steam and scurrying people, not hearing the shouts and whistles around her. The day was bleak and cold, an accurate setting for her mood. She watched as Jesse approached her mother.

"Thank you so much for your hospitality, Mrs. van Ostrand. I've had a wonderful time."

"It won't be the same without you, Jesse. Do give our best to your family when you get home, and safe travels."

He gave her a hug, and Hilda could see that her mother was fighting back tears. Jesse had been such a wonderful gift in a time of sorrow. The entire family would miss him.

Jesse moved to shake hands with a stiff looking Dederick, who wanted to be anywhere but where he was at present. Benedikta had dragged him along to keep a close eye on him.

Jesse thanked him and moved on to Paul, with whom he shared a hearty hug and deep thanks for a long lasting friendship. Hilda knew that Paul was going to visit him soon. Unfortunately, Mother was not going to let her accompany him. Hilda was wondering how long it would be before she would see him again when suddenly he was in front of her, and Paul was herding his mother and brother a ways down the platform to give them some privacy.

Hilda glanced up at him, and knew that it was a mistake. His eyes were glistening, searching. She wanted to look away but Jesse captured her chin gently and forced her to meet his eyes. She swallowed back tears.

"The past few days have been ..."

She nodded when Jesse didn't finish and grasped the hand that held her. "I know."

Jesse slowly shook his head in quiet disbelief. "I thought this would be much easier than it has turned out to be."

Hilda lowered her head and broke his hold. "I hoped this day would never come."

He smiled sadly. "This has been the best trip I have ever taken, Hilda. I'm sorry it has to end."

"We knew it would have to soon enough." She glanced at her family, and then took a step closer. "I wish I could come with you."

Jesse took her hand and squeezed it. "Me too."

Hilda leaned into the hug he gave her, and he kissed her forehead quickly before turning to board the train. She watched him, and her heart clenched.

"Jesse!"

He turned back to her, and she knew in that moment that there would never be another like him. She smiled sadly.

"You'll always be the one that got away," she said.

His face changed slowly, and he suddenly walked briskly back to her, taking her in his arms once more. A smile spread across his face, and he took in her eyes, hair, and rosy cold cheeks. He memorized every feature.

"I didn't get away from you, Hilda, and you most certainly are not getting off that easy." And he lowered his head and kissed her passionately.

From where he stood, Paul glanced over Dederick's shoulder and smiled at the scene. Benedikta also noticed, but her face was thoughtful and uncertain at what she witnessed.

Hilda was powerless in Jesse's embrace as he deepened the kiss, but she quickly succumbed to the pleasure and wrapped her arms around his neck to meet his gentle, exquisite touch. His hands pulled her closer until she felt his heart pounding against hers. She was glad to know she wasn't the only one. Finally, they pulled apart to catch their breath. Hilda shook her head in disbelief.

"I've decided I can't give you up, sweet Hilda. I will see you again," he breathed into her ear.

She looked at him, still trying to rise out of the haze of his kiss. "How can you be so sure?"

He smiled and stepped away, but held onto her hand. "I've told you before. I'm a determined man, Hilda. And I think I'm falling in love with you."

He moved toward the train, but she would not relinquish his hand. She pulled him back to her and kissed him again, all her love going into their final moment together. Who knew where their paths would lead them in the future? Somehow, they had to find a way back to each other.

They parted as the final shrill whistle blew, calling all passengers to board. Jesse picked up his bag with one hand, not letting go of her hand as they walked to the car together. She clung to him even as he began to climb the steps.

"I love you, Jesse," she called.

He kissed her hand and disappeared inside the car, only to reappear at a window. He pushed it down, and even as the train began puffing its way out of the station, he yelled over the noise, "I will come back to you, Hilda. Wait for me. Wait for me!"

She raised her hand in farewell, with the promise on her lips and in her heart. He did not hear her answer, but she knew he understood. She would wait for him.

For a long time after the train had disappeared around the bend in the station, Hilda stood watching its smoke trail into the sky. She was numb to everything around her. Even as her mother placed a hand on her arm and led her back to the car, her mind was on Jesse and America and so many other things that she wondered how she would move forward after that moment. The ride home was a quiet one; no one had much to say, and Hilda was glad for the silence. When they reached home, Dederick disappeared into his room, Paul led his mother into the parlor, and Hilda slowly climbed the stairs to her room. She stopped and closed her eyes, drawing in a slow breath. Jesse's presence seemed to linger all over the house.

When she walked into her room, she noticed that there was an envelope on her nightstand with her name on it, and her heart quickened at the familiar handwriting. When she opened it and reached inside, the first thing she pulled out was a note. She slowly sank to the bed as she read.

My dearest Hilda,

There were so many things I wished to say to you and could not find the strength to, but I hope we may continue to correspond through letters if you would do me the honor of writing. I have enclosed my address, and look forward to hearing from you soon. You are always in my thoughts.

Affectionately,
Jesse

P.S. I hope you don't think me vain, but I've also included a photo. I consider you a dear friend and would be delighted if you kept it for me.

Hilda reached into the envelope and pulled out the photo. Jesse smiled at her in his uniform, looking every inch the man she loved. She smiled and held it close to her heart.

Soon, my love. We will be together again soon, God willing. I will wait.

"Nothing that is can pause or stay;
The moon will wax, the moon will wane,
The mist and cloud will turn to rain,
The rain to mist and cloud again,
Tomorrow be today."

Henry Wadsworth Longfellow

4

Heidelberg, November 1938

Europe was on the brink of war. Over the years, Hitler had slowly worked his way into the minds of the young generation of Germany. His power grew steadily as the Gestapo was placed above the law and his military was mobilized. In the fall of 1937, Hitler met with his military and foreign policy leaders and revealed his plans for expansion into Europe. This meeting, known as the Hossbach Conference, marked the turning point in the Reich leader's foreign policy. The Fürher wanted a full-scale war. By 1938, Hitler had moved his troops into Czechoslovakia.

Benedikta sighed and dropped her pen on top of the large stack of bills in the study. She was getting too old for this kind of pressure. If only Paul were around more often to help her, but his job at the bookstore down the street kept him busy working hard to earn more money. He did not return to California to visit Jesse, but stayed home to help pay the bills. Dederick was never home, as he was busily involved in the Youth Program. Benedikta was proud of his dedication, even if she hardly ever saw him.

And then there was dear Hilda. After dropping out of school three years ago, she had diligently helped her mother by getting a part time job at the record store in town. Benedikta wished that she had stayed in school, for Hilda was so remarkably gifted at learning. She should not be working in a record store. She had even given up her dream to go to Paris so that she could stay at home and help her mother. But all over Germany, families were struggling to get by in the floundering economy.

A door opened and closed at the back of the house. A few moments later, the study door opened and Paul came in toting an armful of heavy dictionaries and what looked like old school books. Benedikta smiled and got up, eyeing the books.

"Whatever are those for?" she asked as she received a kiss from her son.

"They're for Hilda. Herr Strauss gave them to me because he knows she would like them, and no one has borrowed them in years. Is she home yet?"

"No, not yet. I expect her to be here soon, though. I have already started supper."

Paul nodded and went back to the door. "I'll go wash up and be down in a minute."

"Take your time, dear."

Paul hurried from the study and Benedikta went back to the bills. Sighing, she picked up her pen.

⸙

"Hilda! Hilda, wait up!"

Hilda turned around and watched her friend, Hannah Strauss, hurry up the street toward her. She smiled and stopped to wait.

"Hello Hannah. Are you just coming from the book shop?"

"Yes. Father is locking up and told me to go on ahead." Hannah fell in step beside her, and the two continued up the street. "What luck that I should run into you."

"Really?" asked Hilda, smiling because she knew what was coming. "Am I to play the messenger again? You would think the two of you would get sick of each other, considering how often you are together."

Hannah laughed and her pink face grew more flushed. For the past couple of years, Hilda had delivered countless letters for her to Paul. The two were so in love they could not see straight, or so Hilda thought in amusement.

"Honestly," Hilda said with light humor, "he really should just come out and propose so that I can quit this part time job of postal girl. I'll get it to him, I promise."

Hannah smiled, and her eyes sparkled with a shy glimmer as she handed Hilda a very thick envelope. Hilda placed it inside her coat.

"So, can we still expect you for dinner tomorrow night? I hope it wasn't too spontaneous of us to change the date to the tenth," Hilda said as they continued on.

"Oh, no," Hannah replied. "Father and I are very much looking forward to it."

The two girls shared a bit more of the latest news and then parted ways when they reached Hannah's house. Hilda continued on and soon hurried up the steps of her own home. Just as she was about to open the door, she noticed a black car across the street. She glanced around but saw no one. It wasn't the Gestapo; of that much she was certain. The car looked English. She turned slowly after a moment and entered the house.

"Mother, I'm home," she called. She took Hannah's letter from her coat pocket before hanging it in the coat closet by the door.

Benedikta stood as her daughter entered the study and kissed her in greeting.

"How was work?"

"The usual. Is Paul here?"

"Yes, he's cleaning up and he'll be down for supper. He brought home some books for you. Herr Strauss said you were welcome to have them."

Hilda smiled. "I'll make sure to stop by and thank him tomorrow."

At that moment, Paul entered the room and kissed his sister.

"Hello Paul." She held the letter out to him. "This is for you."

He recognized Hannah's handwriting and quickly asked his mother to excuse him before he hurried from the room. Hilda smiled, but noticed her mother looking after Paul with an unreadable expression.

"I'll go and get ready for supper," Hilda said.

"All right, dear. Oh, I put your mail on your nightstand."

"Thank you, Mother."

Hilda hurried up the stairs and pulled out a dress for dinner. She washed her face, neck, and hands before applying fresh color to her cheeks. She then slipped on the dark blue taffeta dinner dress. The long, elegant sleeves buttoned at the wrist, and the material outlined her small waist before it flared out slightly, ending at the knee.

Seeing that she had minutes to spare, Hilda went to check her mail. A quick glance through the letters told her that none had come from

America. She sighed and stared at Jesse's picture on her nightstand. She had not heard from him for over a year now. Hilda tried to laugh at herself for being so silly. They had only known each other for a few months and half-heartedly meant what they said to each other. She wondered now if he even remembered her. She had last written to him several months ago. Perhaps she should stop wondering and just live with the fact that their brief romance was over.

Looking through the mail again, Hilda was surprised and curious to find an envelope that bore only her name on the front. She immediately opened it and pulled out a single sheet of paper.

> *Miss van Ostrand,*
> *I know who you are. I would greatly desire to meet with you and discuss a proposition. Come outside this evening; I will be waiting at ten o'clock. Come alone.*
> *A friend.*

Something twisted in her stomach, but it was not fear. Hilda was utterly bewildered. Who on earth would send her such a letter? It could not be the Gestapo. They would have made it clear to her what they wanted. So then who?

Her mind was suddenly drawn back to the car outside the house. Hilda slowly stood and went to the window. The car was still there, and this time, its owner leaned against the door smoking a cigarette. She could not see his face because of the hat pulled low over his eyes, but he looked young, perhaps in his thirties. He took one last drag on his cigarette and flicked it away. He glanced at the house, climbed into the car, and drove away. Her curiosity heightening with each second, Hilda made her way down to supper, knowing as she did that she would be meeting this stranger at ten o'clock that night.

Supper seemed an eternity. Hilda moved her food around her plate with her fork and waited as her mother finally came around to clear the dishes. Declining dessert, she excused herself from Benedikta and Paul, but before she could get out of her chair, the front door opened and shut very quickly and Dederick walked swiftly past the dining room.

"Dederick," Benedikta called.

The young man slowly returned to view. He was dressed smartly in his uniform and seemed reluctant to linger. Benedikta smiled at her son. When he did not return one, she asked, "Have you eaten? We have plenty of food."

"Thank you Mother, but I have eaten. Please excuse me. I want to get a few things done before bed." Dederick turned smartly and hurried up the stairs.

Hilda quickly stood, for it was nearing almost nine o'clock and she could not wait much longer for her anticipated meeting. She did not, however, miss her mother's hurt look over Dederick's behavior. Hoping to cheer her up a bit, she smiled as she moved toward the stairs. "When I talked to Hannah today, she mentioned that she and her father could make it to dinner tomorrow night, Mother."

"Lovely, dear, thank you for telling me. I'll be sure to make something special." Her mother's voice was laced with sadness.

Hilda nodded and hurried up the stairs. As she walked by Dederick's room, she saw him holding a small handgun, and he was loading it carefully. She leaned in the doorframe and folded her arms, watching him nonchalantly. "You know that Mother would have a heart attack if she saw you with that."

Dederick started, and Hilda jumped back from the doorway, putting her hands up in front of her in mock alarm. "Careful, Dederick, you don't want to set that thing off accidentally."

"That is not funny, Hilda."

"You know what you need? A little bit of laughter."

"Hilda, would you please just go to your room and leave me to my work?"

"Really, Dederick, you should—"

"Hilda!" Dederick shouted. "Leave! Now!"

Hilda walked a little further into her brother's room, completely serious now. "Dederick, what's wrong? Is something bothering you?"

Dederick tossed the gun on the bed along with a very stout long stick and a long metal pipe. Hilda stared at them. "What's going on, Dederick? What is all of this for?"

He turned toward her, his face angry. "Just stay out of it, Hilda. No one can stop what is about to happen, so don't think about it! Just go to bed."

Hilda stared at him for a moment before she quietly turned and entered her room. She did not have time to wonder about Dederick. She had her own troubles to worry about.

When ten o'clock rolled around, Hilda was dressed in a navy blue dress over which she wore a button-up black wool coat. She hoped the colors would help her blend into the dark night. She had felt her Gestapo shadow keenly for the past couple of days. She grabbed her black gloves and quietly stepped out of her room. The house was dark and quiet; the family had long since retired to their bedrooms and no light shown beneath any door. She tiptoed down the stairs, grabbed her scarf, and threw it over her hair before hurrying out the front door.

As she walked across the street toward the car, she didn't notice Dederick peering out at her from behind the drapes of his window. Instead, she was fully focused on the man who stepped out of the car and approached her with a small smile on his face. He nodded his head in greeting.

"You are not Gestapo," she said quietly, crossing her arms.

He shook his head with a small laugh. "Not at all, Miss van Ostrand. My name is Rolf. Jeffrey Rolf."

She had been correct; he was English.

"What do you want, Mr. Rolf? Why the intrigue?" she asked.

"I do apologize for the bluntness of my letter. It was necessary. You never know who might be watching."

"The Gestapo has been shadowing me for three years now. I know who is watching," Hilda said with a hard stare. She wondered at his purpose in Heidelberg. "You do realize that it is dangerous for an Englishman like you to be here?"

"I could say the same of you," he replied with a sly smile.

Hilda was growing more suspicious by the second. Perhaps this was not such a good idea. "I'm afraid I don't understand. If you will excuse me, I must go back inside." She turned to leave.

"Do come for a short drive, won't you? I don't know the city that well."

She turned back to him, her curiosity beginning to take over her misgivings. He gestured innocently to the passenger seat, but Hilda wasn't quite ready to give in.

"What do you want from me?" she asked slowly.

"Nothing. On the contrary, I have something for you."

Hilda folded her arms and stayed where she was. "I don't trust you."

Jeffrey Rolf shrugged. "Who can trust anyone these days? Please, Miss van Ostrand, just a short drive. Your brother is becoming suspicious."

Hilda started and turned around in time to see Dederick pull away from the window. She looked between Rolf and the house for a moment, weighing her options. Was there a choice? Her curiosity won out, and she slowly walked over. He opened the door for her and moments later, they pulled away from the curb and made for the outskirts of the city.

Not a word was spoken until he pulled off to the side of the road and shut off the engine. They were in complete darkness. A flame flared up as he lit a cigarette, the glow illuminating his face every time he drew on it. When he offered her one, Hilda shook her head. He took a drag and turned to her bluntly.

"Now I think you can drop the charade, Miss van Ostrand. I must say you are quite well known in London."

Confused, Hilda stared at him. "I can't see why. I have no idea what you're talking about."

Jeffrey looked at her with slight surprise and a touch of respect. "I understand that you don't want to admit openly you're a spy—"

Hilda cut in quickly. "A spy?!" Her surprise could not be more evident. "Mr. Rolf, I am not a spy. Why would I want to spy on my own country?"

He laughed and rolled his eyes. "Surely you're not going to lie about that as well?"

"Lie about what? What are you talking about?" Hilda could not believe this man.

Jeffrey looked at her pointedly. "We happen to know from a very reliable source that you are not German."

Hilda laughed at the idiocy of his remark and stared at him in shock. "Have you gone crazy? Of course I'm German. The fact that I'm adopted does not change that. You have the wrong person. I quit school when I was seventeen to work at a record store to help my mother pay bills. I just want to survive what's coming."

Jeffrey sighed and reached behind him for a stack of papers. He handed them to Hilda with a watchful eye.

"The source was your father."

Hilda stared at him, not believing what she heard, but there seemed to be nothing but truth in his eyes. Slowly she shook her head, a dazed look on her face.

"No, no that's impossible."

"He is the reason the Gestapo are watching you. He started to investigate your past. This was what he found."

Hilda glanced down in disbelief at the telegrams, photos, and letters in her hands. They all said the same thing—she was thought to be a spy, but it could not be confirmed. Her German descent was questionable, according to a visit her father had paid to the convent where she had been adopted. Hilda could not take it all in without feeling dizzy.

"My father ... the telegrams. They asked me about the ..." She put a hand to her head, unable to continue.

Jeffrey's voice came quietly. "The telegrams stopped before we could learn more, so we started intercepting messages from the state police. They believe you to be a spy. Apparently that is false, but it is not safe for you here." He awkwardly placed his hand on her back. "I'm sorry, we thought you knew."

"He never ... told me anything," Hilda murmured with a slow shake of her head.

After a moment, Jeffrey retrieved something else from the back of the car. He held a small box, big enough for two or three books stacked on top of each other. "This package was given to us soon after we heard of his death, with strict instructions that it was for your eyes alone and to be given to you at the appropriate time."

She looked at it absentmindedly, then up at him. "So I assume you've opened it already."

Jeffrey didn't answer. He placed the box in her hands. Hilda fingered the edges, then folded her hands on top of it and stared straight ahead.

"Take me back please, Mr. Rolf."

He watched her a moment longer, then nodded. The car started a moment later, the headlights flooded the empty road, and they sped back into the city.

The drive back was as silent as it had been leaving. Hilda stared out the window at the darkness and tried to comprehend everything that Jeffrey Rolf had just told her. So many questions ran around her head, but she couldn't possibly begin to answer them. It seemed that her entire world had lost its foundation with one conversation. She felt anger well up in her, not at Jeffrey, but at her father. Why couldn't he just leave the past alone? They had been happy, hadn't they? Why did he feel the need to uncover such an inconvenient truth?

As they drew near to the commercial streets of the city, a loud commotion drew Hilda from her thoughts. Everywhere, it sounded as though glass was breaking all around them. A glow appeared on the horizon, near the university.

"Stop here," Hilda ordered.

"Miss van Ostrand—"

"This is far enough," she said. "It isn't safe."

Jeffrey pulled over and Hilda scrambled out of the car, the package hugged to her chest. Jeffrey leaned over and caught her gaze through the window.

"Will you be all right?"

Hilda didn't answer. She closed the door and hurried down the street away from him, away from the painful truth he had just revealed. Tears began to run down her face as she turned the corner. But she did not have time to weep. When she looked up, chaos was everywhere.

5

Paul awoke to shouting down in the street. He rubbed his eyes and stumbled to the window. Surprised, he saw a glow in the sky. That could not be right. It was eleven o'clock at night. People were running down the street, screaming and pointing. To Paul's horror, he saw German storm troopers, Gestapo, and Hitler Youth chasing them down the street with clubs and guns. A member of the Gestapo caught one man and took him down with a blow to the head. The man was trampled to death as the Nazis ran over him. A storm trooper grabbed a screaming woman and ripped her dressing gown as she tried to escape his grasp. Paul turned away from the window and raced into the hall, turning up the lamps as he went. He pushed open the door to Dederick's bedroom and closed his eyes in silent agony. Empty.

"Paul!"

He opened his eyes to find his mother running toward him. Her eyes were huge and filling with tears.

"Hilda is gone, Paul!"

Paul took his mother in his arms and held her as she wept. He had a feeling that he knew where Dederick was, but Hilda? The girl could be anywhere. He pulled away and started back to his room.

"I'm going to find her."

"No, Paul!" Benedikta pleaded. "It is too dangerous for you to go." She hurried toward him. "I will not risk you getting yourself killed."

"But Hilda!"

"I don't want all three of my children missing!"

Paul saw the fear in his mother's eyes. She no longer had control, and when it came to her children, that frightened her. He put his arms around her. "What's happening, Mother?"

"I don't know, Paul. I don't know, but I hope that it is over soon."

Hilda turned the corner and felt that she had entered a completely different world. Houses were burning, people were screaming, and there were bodies strewn about the ground. Her eyes grew wide with horror as she walked in the wake of the destruction done by the Nazis. People moaned out to her for help; some did not move at all. Suddenly, a very familiar house came into view, and she ran down the street, filled with fear. The roof of Hannah's home had caved in, and only four charred walls remained of the once warm and comforting house.

"Hannah! Herr Strauss! Hannah, where are you?" Hilda called, panic in her voice. Burned furniture lay everywhere as she quickly went up the path. She looked around her, and what she saw made her heart drop to her stomach. A body was lying nearby on the grass. It was a man. Hilda slowly went over and knelt with resigned sorrow beside the body of Hannah's father. He was most assuredly dead; a bullet hole could be seen through his chest. Hilda covered it with her hand as if to stop all that had occurred, and she wept for the old man. He had been Hannah's only relative. Where would she go now? Where *was* she?

"Hannah!" Hilda yelled, tears in her voice. At the sound of running feet, she turned with new hope, but it dissolved when three members of Hitler Youth came running down the street toward her. Hilda immediately rose and sprinted around the corner that she had turned just moments ago. She could hear the pounding of their feet behind her. She raced up an alley and, seeing her chance, dashed behind a stack of several large crates that had been placed underneath a flight of stairs. A small gasp from the shadows made her jump, and she automatically put her hand over the other fugitive's mouth, though she could not see who it was. The footsteps turned the corner and slowed.

"What do you suppose, boys?" said a voice in the darkness.

"Let's check around and if she's not here, we'll head back."

Hilda held her breath and prayed that she would be invisible in the black night.

"Do you see anything?" called the first voice again.

Oh, God, please ...

Something touched her arm. She turned and saw that a hand had reached out of the shadows. It was holding a pistol with the butt facing Hilda. She slowly took it and held it against her chest, praying as she did that she would not have to use it.

Footsteps sounded, coming nearer to the crates. Hilda raised the pistol, ready for what would come around the corner.

Nothing could have prepared her for the surprise she got.

Dederick stared wide-eyed and still down the barrel of her gun. The shock reflected in both of their eyes, but Hilda's hand remained unwavering. Time seemed to stop as the two siblings weighed each other's options.

"Dederick! Anything back there?"

He visibly swallowed. Their eyes remained locked and they knew that the turning point had come. Hilda thought she might choke on the silence. After a long moment, Dederick backed up. He straightened, nothing on his face as he turned away.

"Dederick!"

"There's nothing back here. Let's go back and find the others. This is a waste of time." Dederick turned smartly and Hilda heard his footsteps and those of his friends fade away.

She couldn't stand anymore. The gun dropped to the ground and she sank to her knees, shaking. She told herself to breath.

A hand gently squeezed her shoulder. Hilda turned and looked up to find Hannah, her dress ripped, her hair in disarray, and her face tearstained.

"Hannah! Are you all right? I saw your house and was so afraid."

Hannah broke down beside her. "Oh, Hilda, it was horrible. I heard glass breaking and when Father and I went downstairs, the living room was on fire. Father tried to save some of the furniture, but it spread too fast. He told me to go out the back door and run as fast as I could and not look back. I got out, but I hid in the bushes, and when he went outside he tried to fight them, and they ... they ..." Hannah broke into sobs, and Hilda immediately wrapped her arms around her.

"I know," she said quietly. Hannah cried for several minutes, and Hilda held her and tried to speak soothing words.

"I must go to him," Hannah said brokenly, but Hilda stopped her.

"No, Hannah, it is too dangerous. We should stay here until it is over."

Hannah suddenly glanced at Hilda, then at the gun that still lay on the ground. Hilda followed her gaze.

"Would you have done it?" Hannah asked quietly.

Hilda did not hesitate. "No, I wouldn't have."

Hannah nodded. She picked up the gun and returned it to her pocket.

"We should get some sleep," Hilda said with a sigh.

The two lay down and tried to get comfortable on the hard ground. There was silence for a long time.

"Hannah," Hilda whispered, "would you have done it?"

There was a long pause, and Hilda thought that she must have fallen asleep. But then, amidst the far off shouting and gunfire, Hannah's quiet voice said, "Yes."

Something was tickling her foot. Hilda slowly opened her eyes and glanced down. With a squeal, she quickly kicked the mouse away and stood, shaking herself. She glanced at Hannah. The girl was still sleeping peacefully, and Hilda was not about to wake her. The dawn was just creeping over the city, but it was not a pretty sight to Hilda. Everywhere, smoke rose in huge billowing clouds high into the sky. Hilda walked out of the alley and down the street. All around her, buildings burned and dismal flames sputtered and finally died. People were everywhere. Wails filled the air as families wept outside the remains of a once beloved home or synagogue. Some were cradling bodies that lay still in the street. Hilda shivered, and not only from the cold. She slowly made her way down the street, careful not to step on broken glass or burning wood.

"Hilda! Hilda!"

At the sound of the familiar voice, Hilda looked up, and relief filled her as she ran toward Paul. He took her in his arms and held her as though he would never let go. He touched her face and arms in search of injury.

"Are you all right? No one hurt you?" he asked, concern etched in his face.

"I'm fine, really Paul," she said, trying to calm his fears.

He looked past her and his eyes grew wide as alarm spread across his face. Hilda turned and saw Hannah feebly walking toward them. Paul ran to her and pulled her into his arms. By the tears on her face and the way she was gesturing, she was recounting her story to Paul. Hilda turned and continued up the street on her way home. She knew that her mother would be very worried, and she wanted to lay her fears to rest.

As she walked, one question remained in her heart. Why would anyone want to attack innocent people in the middle of the night? The Nazis weren't that vicious, were they? She had never liked them to begin with, but she had accepted the fact that they were going to be in power for a while. But this?

Nothing made sense. Hilda shook her head as she hurried up the path and into the house.

"Mother!" she called urgently as she raced up the stairs.

A door burst open, and Benedikta raced along the hall and met her daughter half way. They clung to each other for a long moment, content to just know that the other was safe.

"Oh, Hilda, are you all right? When we heard the shouts and saw that you were gone, I was so afraid. I prayed so hard that you would be safe. Oh, you didn't get hurt, did you?"

Hilda smiled in an attempt to lighten the mood. "I'm fine Mother, but I didn't get much sleep. Would you mind if I went to my room for a while?"

"Of course not, dear. I'll make you something hot and bring it up."

Hilda smiled her gratitude and moved toward her room. She entered slowly, went to her window, and stared out at the destruction around her. Carefully, she laid the package from Jeffrey Rolf on her desk and tried to sort out the events of the night. She pulled her journal out of the drawer of her nightstand and wrote furiously, thoughtfully, and slowly. The night weighed heavily on her, and she thought perhaps writing about it would take away some of the stress.

She did not turn around when she heard the door close behind someone. It wasn't her mother with the food; she couldn't smell anything. Hilda slowly closed her journal.

"You weren't supposed to be out last night." His voice was uncertain.

She turned to face Dederick, who stood just to the side of the door. His uniform showed little dust and was not wrinkled. His face was as hard as stone, but his eyes were sad and cold. Hilda pitied him. He always put on the look of a strong soldier, never letting on the feelings of his troubled heart. There were times when one could see, just beyond his eyes, the face of a confused and broken boy. Dederick was not all iron. He would never admit it to anyone, but she knew. He was first and foremost loyal to his country, but his heart knew the difference between what was honorable and what was cowardly.

"Who was he?" Dederick asked.

Hilda shrugged, not wanting to give him any details. "An old friend of Father's. He won't be back, though." She walked over to him, intent on the matter at hand. "Dederick, what is going on? I will persist until you tell me what just happened," she demanded with a firm look on her face.

"Justice."

She sat on the edge of the bed and beckoned to him, like she always had when he needed her as a child. "Tell me."

He looked at her with resignation, and then sat down. "Do you remember a few weeks ago in the paper reading about the member of the German Embassy in Paris who was killed?"

Hilda nodded, not quite sure where this was leading.

"It was done by a Jew," Dederick said, spitting out the name in disgust. "For his crime, they received just punishment."

Hilda stared at him in horror. For one man's crime, the Nazis had punished a whole race? "Dederick," she whispered, anguish in her voice and eyes, "what have you done?"

He jerked away from her and off the bed. His voice was strong when he spoke, but there was pain in his sharp tone.

"I did what was just!" he cried, his face beginning to turn red. "For years, the Jews have been nothing but a thorn in Germany's side. And now, finally, the Fürher has declared that he is going to take care of this problem."

Hilda stood up and faced him squarely. "They are not a problem, they are people. How do you think one man is going to take care of thousands of Jews? It can't be done. It is impossible. These people are not harmful, Dederick. They lead normal lives, like you and I. They are like any other person."

"No, Hilda, they are not!" he said. "They are more different than you realize, including that little friend of yours, Hannah."

"She used to be your friend too," she said quietly.

Dederick stopped and stared at her. He came close to her face and leaned in. Hilda did not back down from him.

"Is that who you were protecting, Hilda?"

She stared at him. "Excuse me?"

"Someone was with you last night. Was it that Jew?"

Hilda saw the determined light in his eyes. What was going on in his mind? What would he do if she told him? What would he do if she didn't? She took a deep breath and shook her head.

"If you had known, would you have given us away instead?" she asked carefully.

"Maybe I should have. Next time I will not be so merciful," he warned.

Hilda could not bear the hatred in her brother. She shook her head, tears coming to her eyes.

"There will not be a next time, Dederick."

He stared at her for a long moment, and then casually pulled out his gun. He felt the weight of it in his hands, then brought it up to her eye level. His eyes did not move as she raised hers to his gaze. A tense moment passed.

Dederick's voice came in a whisper. "How does it feel, dear sister?"

Hilda didn't move. He was scared; she could see it past his cold eyes.

"You won't do it, Dederick," she whispered.

The gun lowered a fraction of an inch. He was weakening. But not that much.

"Would you have?"

Hilda was about to answer him when a slight movement outside her door drew her attention. Benedikta stood in the hall holding a steaming tray. By the look on her face, she had not heard the conversation nor could she see the gun that Dederick held at his sister's heart.

With the shift of her eyes, Dederick knew that someone was behind him. In a second the gun was back in his coat, and he turned swiftly and walked out of the room.

Hilda watched him go. In the following moments, she did not remember her mother setting her tray down on the bed, or her asking if she needed anything else. Her mind raced with thoughts and warnings. For the first time, she realized the danger that she was putting her entire family in. Somewhere along the course of her life, something had happened. She didn't know what it was, but she had a feeling that the answers lay somewhere inside the package she carried.

Germany was no longer safe for her. She had to leave the country. As she thought back to what Dederick had said and the way he had acted, she realized that though he had a love for his family, his loyalty was first and foremost for his country. Though he often regretted his actions, he would continue on for Germany, the Third Reich.

Tonight, she would learn the truth, and with it would come the foundation of her future. In the years ahead, all of her actions would be based upon the information that she found.

₰

Paul slowly opened the front door and trudged into the hall. Peter took his coat, a concerned look on his face. Paul had finally managed to settle Hannah in with a friend of hers who was not touched by the destruction. The shock was still in her face, and he wondered what her reaction would be when she finally was back to herself. He closed his eyes and settled on the bottom step of the stairs, too tired to carry himself up to bed. Out the window, smoke still rose, a nasty reminder of the events of the night before.

The house was quiet; Mother and Hilda had probably already gone to bed. He had no idea where Dederick was, and right now he wasn't ready to face his brother.

"Sir." Peter stood above him. "Shall I get you a cup of tea before bed?"

Paul waved him away. "No, no thank you, Peter. You may go home when you wish."

Peter lingered for a moment, uncertain, and then gave a slight bow. Paul heard him take his hat, coat and gloves from the closet, and the front door shut silently behind him.

Silence dominated the house, and Paul was thankful. Too much suffering had been voiced that day. He needed peace from it all, if only for one night.

The stairs creaked above him, and he looked up to find Dederick on the landing staring at him. Surprisingly, he wore a plain white shirt with brown slacks. His suspenders hung down around his legs. To Paul, he looked more normal than he had in years, like the brother he remembered before he left for America. But it was his expression that caught his eye. Serious and uncertain, for once. He seemed slightly at a loss.

"Paul, you need to see this," he said quietly, then turned and climbed the stairs.

Paul stood, feeling every ache in his body, and followed his younger brother up the stairs. He thought he was going to show him something in his room, but instead he passed his own door and proceeded on to Hilda's room. The door was closed, and no light came from underneath.

"Dederick, don't disturb her, she had a long night—"

Dederick only shook his head and let the door swing open as he turned on the light. Paul could only stare in astonishment. The room had been cleaned thoroughly, and the bed looked as though it had never been slept in. Not a single book of Hilda's was in sight, something that Paul had never seen. He stumbled over his words, trying to figure out what happened. Dederick opened the closet.

"Her suitcase is gone. So are most of her clothes," he said.

Paul looked at him, bewildered. "Well, where did she go? She wasn't planning a trip was she? Dederick, did she say anything to you?"

His brother shook his head slowly. "I came back this evening and found it like this."

Paul slowly walked through the room, wishing this was a dream and he could wake up. But he knew it wasn't, and the pain hit him like a knife. A piece of paper sitting on her desk caught his eye and he picked it up. After a moment he held it out to Dederick.

"Did you see this?" he murmured.

Dederick took the note and held it up to the light.

To my dear family,
*   Please do not try to find me. I love you all so much.*
*   Hilda*

Dederick looked up and saw Paul watching him. He laid the note back on the desk and moved to the door, Paul behind him. The elder paused in the doorway and took in the room that looked as though no one had ever lived in it. He shut off the light and closed the door.

"Don't tell Mother until tomorrow."

Hilda lay on her bunk, swaying back and forth with the rhythm of the train. Nothing but darkness flashed past the window. She stared at the papers and package in front of her. Jeffrey's documents had come in handy; they included falsified identification papers that she had used to gain passage out of Germany. The French countryside now surrounded her, and she felt herself relaxing slowly with each mile. The pain of her leaving, however, would remain for a while.

The brown wrapped package seemed to stare up at her from her bed, and she leaned forward to study it. The London address was something she could use when she arrived. Slowly, she unwrapped the paper and opened the box. A fat, worn book lay in front of her, and when she opened it, she gasped, tears coming to her eyes. She would recognize her father's handwriting anywhere. It was his journal. As she flipped through the pages, telegrams and notes fell out. She carefully placed them in a pile and turned to her father's final entry, dated two weeks before his death.

I alone know the truth. I don't know who to tell of this secret I carry. Perhaps one day, if I can, I will tell Hilda, but not now. I hope I can be there to protect her. All I can do now is pray. God protect us all from what is coming.

Hilda stared at the page. What truth was her father talking about? Was it to do with her ancestry? Had he found something that would endanger her life? Whatever it was had cost him his, it seemed. She flipped through the other entries, but he never mentioned anything about his secret. He wrote of telegrams to London and a visit to the convent, but she could not find anything pertaining to his discovery. She picked up the telegrams and looked through them. The first one told of how they were going to look into the 'matter that you spoke of.' The second one verified her father's belief that she was not of German descent.

So it was true. Jeffrey Rolf had been right. Her father's theories had been correct. She was not German. So then where did she come from? France? Poland? Russia? Questions plagued her, and she felt irritation begin to set in. Was no one going to tell her anything? Was she to be kept in the dark about everything? She had to know, and if these papers couldn't help her, she would probably go mad.

The final note was old, much older than the other documents. It had yellowed with the years, and there were tears around the edges. It was covered in bloodstains, making the beautifully scripted words harder to read. The handwriting was unlike anything she had ever seen, so gentle and rich with swirls. Hilda would never forget it; it was so elegant. She wondered where her father had come by such a document. She held it close to her face, and the words came into focus.

To the receiver of this note:

This baby girl was born on November 4, 1918 to Luke and Allison Pendair, Americans who fought bravely for their country and died defending it. Please love her as your own and raise her in Christ's love, which binds us all.

M.R.

61

6

London was enormous. Hilda watched from a street corner as cars inched their way along and pedestrians bustled across the road. The ones that stood out most to Hilda were the soldiers and nurses. They were everywhere, and many of them seemed to be her own age. Their uniforms looked clean and smart as they walked down the street in groups, laughing and embracing and chatting.

After watching them for a moment, Hilda looked down at the address in her hand, and then across the street—this was the building she wanted. Located right on the Thames, it was a beautiful location. Hilda carefully crossed the street and glanced at the plaque next to the door. Once she stepped inside, there was no going back.

A secretary looked up at her entrance.

"May I help you?" she asked as she eyed Hilda from behind big, black-rimmed glasses. Her English accent was heavy, and Hilda immediately switched her brain from German to English.

"I, uh, am looking for Jeffrey Rolf. Is he in?" Her voice was steady, but her insides were shaking.

"He is. Do you have an appointment?"

"Actually," she said carefully, "he's not expecting me. This visit was rather spontaneous."

"Ah." The secretary looked at her with growing suspicion. "And what is your name?"

Hilda hesitated for a moment. "I would rather not say. I'm sorry, but it is very important that I see him."

"I see."

It was quite obvious to Hilda that the woman did not trust her at all. She didn't blame her. A strange woman walking into British Intelligence asking for one of their officers and not giving a name would raise suspicion. She only hoped that Jeffrey would agree to see her. She watched quietly as the secretary called up to him and told him the situation. Hilda nearly sagged with relief at his ready reply to see her.

The secretary told her how to reach his office, and Hilda set off with a determined stride. She wasn't quite sure what she would say to him and in her mind, her thoughts jumbled together in a great mess that she could not comprehend. Should she reveal the truth? How much did he deserve to know? She swallowed hard and found herself praying for guidance as she stopped before the door leading to Jeffrey Rolf and a future that held many uncertainties and surprises. By stepping into that office, she marked herself as a traitor to her own country, and with that came the ever present risk of losing her life. A risk she knew well already.

Could she risk losing all that she had grown up believing in? Could she leave all that she had known for something strange and unfamiliar? Hilda knew her decision would determine what she believed in the deepest, most secretive parts of her soul.

With a firm resolve, she raised her fist and knocked determinedly on the door.

Jeffrey Rolf could not have been more surprised when he opened his door to find Hilda van Ostrand. She was smartly dressed in a dark green traveling habit complete with hat, under which her long dark hair had been pinned firmly into a bun. Her bright green eyes shone brilliantly, more than he remembered, for it had been quite dark on their first meeting.

He quickly ushered her inside after a moment, closed the door, and locked it behind him. He watched as she glanced around the room, briefly taking in her surroundings. Jeffrey hurried around her to the front of his desk.

"Miss van Ostrand! This is quite an unexpected surprise." He faltered. "I'm afraid I ... don't ..."

She smiled, and with irritation Jeffrey found his heart tripping over a few beats.

"I'm sorry that my coming was so abrupt, but I have only been in London for a few days and I had no way to contact you," she said apologetically.

"It's quite all right, I assure you, it's just that when the secretary said that you did not wish to give your name, I expected ... well, I expected anyone but you."

"Were you expecting someone else?"

"No, no," he said hurriedly. "It's just that ... I have gotten calls of this nature many times, and the last person I expected it to be was you. Why, the Prime Minister could have walked in and I would have been less surprised!"

Hilda laughed at this, and Jeffrey felt himself tingle all the way down to his toes at the sound. *Stop it. You barely know her.*

"So, Miss van Ostrand, what brings you to London?" he asked with the appearance of calm.

"A very serious matter," Hilda replied, her smile now gone.

Jeffrey sobered immediately. He gestured toward the chair in front of him and went around the desk to sit in his own chair. "Has something unexpected come up? Nothing could have brought you to London so soon."

"Something of that nature," she said. She leaned forward and clasped her hands in her lap. "It involves the package you gave me, which I'm sure you opened."

He held up a hand. "This may actually surprise you, Miss van Ostrand, but we didn't open the package as a matter of fact. We felt it might be disrespectful to your father's memory."

Hilda stopped, clearly expecting a different answer. "So you don't ..."

Jeffrey let her gather her thoughts for a moment. He knew that he had been correct in his thinking that she was English, but had not expected her to come personally to tell him that. He studied her. "Was there something else you wished to tell me?"

Hilda continued slowly. "Well, having found out that I'm not of German descent, I have been floating around in limbo really, if you'll excuse my metaphor. I suppose I was ... I was wondering if I might be able to offer some assistance to you."

There was an underlying meaning in her words, and Jeffrey had a feeling he knew what it was. "You want to become an agent?"

Hilda looked up and met his eyes for the first time since explaining her coming. She nodded slowly.

Jeffrey held her gaze for a long time. Then he got up and came around the desk. He took her arms and lifted her from the chair. They were standing inches apart.

"Are you sure?" he asked.

Hilda gave a small smile. "I seem to already have that reputation, so I might as well."

"It's dangerous, Hilda," he said seriously. "Far more dangerous than you realize. Everywhere you go, you don't know the difference between your friends and your enemies. Your life is at risk every day."

"Do you say that to every person who wants to be a spy?"

"No."

She shook her head firmly. "I know what it is like to have one's life at risk all the time. I grew up with it. Mr. Rolf, I have nowhere else to go. I can't go home for danger of being arrested. I have already put my entire family under suspicion by my actions. My own brother would betray me for the good of his country." She stepped away from him. "I know what I am doing."

He wondered what she was speaking of. Her life beyond what little he knew was a mystery to him. She stood before him offering him what he had been hoping for since he had returned to London, yet now that the moment was here, he felt doubt seep in. What could he say?

"You'll become a traitor among your friends and family, Hilda."

"I already am."

Her eyes were determined. She stood straight and stiff holding his gaze, not relenting to the dangers he had told her of. The green in her eyes was deep and held the secrets of her life, past and present. He would not push her; he could not. She would not let him. He shrugged, resigned.

"Okay."

Hilda stared at him, almost confused. "Just like that?"

He nodded.

"Why so easily?" she asked.

Jeffrey shrugged. "Well, you obviously aren't going to give in, so I won't waste my time fighting you."

She sat back down, suddenly nervous. "When do I start?"

He smiled. "Right now."

65

The training was harder than she had imagined. After her first day, she woke up the next morning sore. When Jeffrey asked her how it was going, she merely groaned. He laughed and told her it was like that for everyone the first few days. There was so much running and target practice and learning to send coded messages that Hilda wondered if she had been crazy to volunteer. Then she would think back to that horrible night when so many had lost their livelihoods to the Nazis, and she kept going. Kept fighting.

And on those lonely nights in the small flat that she shared with two other girls, she would think of Jesse. During the short months that they had spent together, he had once told her about the training that he had had to do to become a combat pilot.

"It was very hard," he said. "It was every man for himself, and the instructors would not help you either. It was not an experience I would like to repeat."

She lay there in the dark, the memory of him closer than it had been in a long time. That they both struggled and sweat for a good cause made her feel that they were somehow connected, sharing the same experiences. She felt she understood him more than she ever had even when she was with him.

And it was during these times, when all was quiet and her thoughts came alive, that she ached for him. It had been three long years and still he consumed her dreams, the kiss they had shared at the train station very vivid on her lips and in her mind. She loved him more than that day on the platform when they had said their good-byes and she had promised to wait for him. She had thought that apart from him, the love would diminish and they would go back to their normal lives, but the flame in her heart had only been kindled over all of the nights that she had spent dreaming of him and crying over his picture.

Did he still think of her? She had not heard from him in ages, and for all she knew, he had completely forgotten about her. The thought made her stomach clench in her gut, and she pushed it away. She so much wanted to write to him again, but she knew the danger in which she would put both herself and Jesse was too great. She turned over on her side and tucked her hands beneath her cheek, close to sleep. But one question still plagued her tired thoughts.

Did he still love her?

7

Benedikta stirred her tea quietly in the parlor, content to be where she was for the first time in a very long while. Sitting across from her was her best friend, Elsa van Thof. They had gone to university together in Berlin and had been inseparable ever since. If Elsa had ever married, their children probably would have grown up destined to marry each other. They shared their deepest sorrows, their greatest joys, and their darkest secrets. When Frederick had died, Elsa had been there to comfort her and help her out of the pit into whose depths she had fallen. Though she had never been married, she had known love only to have it taken away far too soon. Benedikta and Elsa felt more like the sisters each other had never had than friends.

Now as they sat together catching up on each other's lives, Benedikta smiled, content and feeling as though the world was finally back to normal.

"I've been hearing strange things, Benedikta. I didn't want to assume anything until I had spoken with you personally," Elsa said in her quiet direct way.

Benedikta put down her cup and stared at her friend. "What do you mean?"

"I can understand why you would be reluctant to talk about it," Elsa continued in a low voice. "It's been talked of all over town, and I wasn't sure what to think."

Benedikta leaned forward. "What have you heard?" she murmured.

Elsa hesitated a moment, then said slowly, "It's been going around that ... that your Hilda has fled Germany ... turned her back on her country ... become a traitor. Do you know what they are calling her?"

Benedikta stood up so fast that Elsa jumped. She walked quickly around the table and took her arm. "Elsa, come."

Elsa barely had time to put on her coat, scarf and hat before they were outside walking briskly in the snow. They hurried down the street, saying quick hellos to friends passing by. Benedikta turned swiftly down a small side street toward the church at the edge of the city. When they were finally at the low fence surrounding the stone building, she slowed down to a walk, and finally stopped. Benedikta turned to Elsa.

"I'm sorry, Elsa. I did not mean to be so abrupt."

Elsa shook her head. "Don't apologize, dear. It was cruel of me to bring up such a disturbing subject."

"No Elsa, you don't understand." Benedikta stepped off of the road and wandered into the churchyard some ways away. Elsa did the same.

Benedikta took a deep breath. "I ... cannot deny the claims, but I can't acknowledge them either. I don't know all that occurred, but the day after Kristallnacht ... that awful night ... she left suddenly. There was a note but it told us nothing of her whereabouts."

Elsa studied her friend. "Benny, that was months ago. Has she really been gone that long without contacting you? It seems like a strange act for her, don't you think?"

Benedikta pressed her fingers to her temples. "I don't know what to think anymore, Elsa. Ever since Frederick died, I feel like the entire family has just fallen apart. Everyone wants to go off and do his or her own thing. Hilda's run off, Dederick's obsessed with serving his country. Paul is the only one who seems content to stay home. Of course, I don't know how long he will be with me. He is very attached to young Hannah Strauss."

"The Jewess?" Elsa said, cautiously surprised.

"Yes. You know of her? I didn't know you were acquainted," Benedikta replied. Her voice was distant, and she did not notice Elsa's alert gaze. "I want my family back Elsa," she continued, her voice broken. "I feel like I'm sinking and I can't find anything to hold onto. I must do something. I have to!"

Elsa placed her arm around her friend. "I know how you feel, dear. I remember when all of the chaos started and I didn't know what to do. I felt so alone and I considered leaving Germany to stay with my cousin in France."

"Yes, I remember when you said that. You were having lunch with Hilda and me. Julian Rousseau, right?"

"Yes, that's him." Elsa paused, and Benedikta studied her. She seemed to be pondering what she was going to say. Finally, she spoke.

"Benny, after all that has happened, what are your thoughts on what the Führer is doing in Germany?" she asked slowly.

Benedikta tilted her head thoughtfully. "Honestly, when Frederick was alive, I didn't pay any attention to Hitler's actions, but what I've heard from Dederick and what I see with my own eyes makes me very disappointed." She looked at Elsa. "Why do you ask?"

Elsa looked at her slowly. "Can I trust you with something, Benny?"

"You know you can."

Elsa took a breath of crisp air. "Well, I have never agreed with what Hitler does, and I am very sorry to be a part of a country so torn apart." She held her friend's gaze. "I thought that I had nothing holding me here. I thought that I should get out while I could, maybe go to America, somewhere safe. But then something happened back in February that made me change my mind."

"What?"

"I had a friend of mine come to me, asking for help."

"Help?" Benedikta asked, confused. "For what?"

"She is a Jew. She was affected by Kristallnacht greatly, and was unable to pay for the damage done to her store. She came to me, terrified of what the Nazis would do to her and her family. She asked me to help her, so I ... I took her in."

Benedikta stared at her, not quite understanding her meaning.

"I'm hiding her, Benedikta," Elsa said finally.

She let that information sink in. It dawned on her that Elsa, in a way, had become a traitor much like Hilda. When Hitler had threatened the Jews in one of his speeches back in January, she had felt the threat personally. She started acting strangely around Hannah, and Paul had been terribly hurt by her actions.

Benedikta looked at Elsa and saw the determined look on her face. Elsa knew what she was fighting for, and she had the courage to tell her, even though she did not know what Benedikta would do with the information. Could she do any less? Benedikta did not believe in neutrality; there were only two sides, and she had to choose. She did not agree with what Hitler was doing. So was she a traitor?

Hannah glanced up and smiled gently as the sun peeked through the clouds and blue sky appeared. Very slowly, spring was coming back to Heidelberg. She felt her heart lighten for a moment, and she quickened her step. She thought about the lovely time that she had spent with Paul last night. They had strolled down the street and simply talked, but the most wonderful moment of all was when he had taken her in his arms, kissed her, and told her he loved her. She sighed as she thought fondly of the memory. Would they ever get more than just a stolen kiss beneath the stars? Would they get to share a future together? The future was so bleak and unsure that she did not know. Since that horrific night nearly six months ago, she had prayed every night that God would allow her some happiness with Paul, however brief it may be.

Hannah shook herself out of her reverie as she heard a voice call her name. She saw that it was Judith, a young Jew who lived in Hannah's neighborhood. She hurried toward her, coat flying. Hannah grew concerned when she saw the tearstains that made trails on Judith's cheeks from her red, swollen eyes.

"Hannah, I'm so glad I found you!" she exclaimed, relieved. She quickly took her arm and led her down a smaller street toward the quiet community where most of the Jews resided.

"Judith, whatever is wrong?" Hannah asked breathlessly. "You look a sight! Is everything all right?"

"Oh, Hannah!" Judith cried, fresh tears coursing down her face. "It's awful!"

Hannah took her hands and squeezed them encouragingly. "Tell me, dear."

Judith sniffed. "Well, you know of the news that Hitler has taken Czechoslovakia."

"Yes."

"Well, my aunt and uncle live there."

Hannah felt a sense of dread fill her at the underlying tone. "Yes?"

"They were ... killed, Hannah. Because they were Jews. Innocent citizens, and they were murdered!"

Hannah held the weeping girl tightly and stroked her dark hair. Judith was only nineteen, and her young eyes had not seen the last of the terror beginning to surround them. She felt the anger begin to boil hot in the pit of her stomach. How could one person be so cruel to the innocent? Could Hitler really hate so much?

Hannah escorted Judith home to the waiting arms of her mother, and then strode purposefully back up the street. She had to see Paul.

He had never been more frustrated in his life. Paul threw down his coat on his bed and sat down at his desk. The rejection was getting harder to take. He dreaded going out; being spurned by people who were once his friends cut him deeply. Why couldn't they see what he saw? Were they so blind? Hannah was the most beautiful, innocent, fun-loving woman he had ever met, and no matter what anyone said, he was going to marry her.

An urgent knock on the door below startled him. It was the middle of the day; no one would be calling at this hour. The knock came again, and Paul hurried down the stairs just as Peter opened the door. He was very surprised to see Hannah hurry in the door. Peter began to protest her entry, but Paul stopped him.

"She can stay, Peter."

Hannah looked up at his voice and relief filled her eyes. She met him halfway on the stairs and flung herself into his arms. Paul held her gently and out of the corner of his eye, he saw Peter slip discreetly away.

Paul gently disentangled himself and kissed her forehead, his hold firm on her arms.

"Sweetheart, what is the matter? Are you okay?"

Hannah raised her tearstained face and wiped her nose with the handkerchief that Paul handed her. He led her down the rest of the stairs and into the parlor. Hannah stared out the window at the bustling street in a daze.

"I'm scared, Paul. I don't know what's going to happen. I'm afraid to go out into the street. I'm afraid to stay inside. I don't feel safe anymore." She laid her head against his shoulder. "Only with you."

Paul put his arms around her and sighed. He wanted so much to protect her but did not know how he could. He could not leave her to the lions and flee to save his own skin.

Hannah turned her head to look up at him.

"I ran into a friend of mine, Judith, a few minutes ago. She told me that her relatives were killed by the Nazis," she said flatly.

Paul stared at her, and saw the torment storming in her eyes. There was so much pain, so much uncertainty. Her beautiful face should not be creased with worry as it was now. Paul held her hand tightly. "Marry me."

Hannah started. "Excuse me?"

"I love you, Hannah. I love you more than anything and I want to care for you and protect you from everything bad in this world," he said softly, his breath caressing her face.

The look of awe and gentleness in Hannah's eyes made a glowing warmth steal over him.

"Are you sure?" she whispered.

"I've never been more sure of anything in my life."

Hannah walked a few steps away. "I don't want you to do this because you think that you have to protect me."

Paul went to her side and turned her so that she was facing him. "Hannah, before any of this happened, I loved you. Before your father died, I loved you. Before you lost your livelihood, I loved you. I love you still."

Tears pooled in the corner of her eyes, and she smiled genuinely for the first time since that horrible night. "Yes, Paul," she whispered. "I will marry you."

Paul's face lit up with joy. He gathered her in his arms and swung her around, and her laughter floated to the ceiling.

"You have made me the happiest man in the world," he breathed before his lips touched hers.

Paul had kissed her before, but very modestly. Into this kiss he poured his love, protection, and passion. The emotion buzzed through him like electrical currents. Her arms held him firmly around the neck, and she was only too happy when he deepened his embrace. Paul had never wanted anything more in his life than this woman who stood before him. She represented everything that was good and innocent, and he loved her.

Paul's senses were muddled, and all that he was aware of was Hannah. That was why when he heard voices in the hall, he did not let her go. When they entered the parlor, he did not pull away. Vaguely, he heard exclamations of astonishment, one soft and embarrassed, the other loud and furious.

"Oh! My goodness, I ..."

"Paul! What do you think you're doing?"

They finally broke apart, Paul with more reluctance than Hannah. Her cheeks were stained with embarrassment. She turned toward the door and gasped. Paul followed her gaze, and his face slowly drained of color at what he saw.

Benedikta and Dederick stood in the doorway.

"Choices are the hinges of destiny."

Pythagoras

8

Los Angeles, California
December 1939

*E*verything was on fire. Glass broke under his feet as he scrambled blindly through the street looking for her. People ran past him, screaming in terror. They did not notice him; no one did. Where was she? His eyes and mouth filled with ash and stung. He couldn't breathe. His entire body was hot, so hot. He was burning.

There she was. He would recognize her anywhere. He gave a cry of joy and ran toward her. She kept getting further away. Stay still, my love! I'm coming! She moved away again, toward the flames. No! Come to me! I'm here! She became a shadow against the flame, glorious and brilliant.

Jesse woke slowly and watched the early morning light peer through the window. He hadn't had a decent night's sleep in days. Hilda haunted his dreams constantly, and he couldn't understand why she had simply stopped writing and disappeared. It wasn't like her at all. But all of his theories went out the window with Paul's letter.

Jesse got up and threw on his clothes for a quick run on the beach. He had taken to exercise to relieve his stress, especially after long nights like the one he'd just had. Hilda's face came to his mind and he increased his speed, feeling the sea breeze blow his sleep away but not his anxiety. Today was different. Women watched him run the length of the beach and back, smiling and talking behind their hands, but he didn't notice. Today was different.

As he walked back up the path to his house, he saw his father Danny sitting in one of the wicker chairs, a cup of steaming coffee in his hand. He waved as Jesse came up the steps.

"Join me?" he asked.

Jesse sat down in the other chair and leaned his head back, wiping sweat off of his face. He took a deep breath and tried to slow his breathing.

"Rough night?" Danny asked, a watchful eye on his son.

"What? No."

"Jesse, I'm your father. I'm supposed to know when you're upset, and I know now. You're upset. What is it?"

Jesse sighed. "I'm just worried."

"About Hilda?"

Jesse got up and leaned against the porch railing. The sun warmed his face as he hid his discouragement from his father.

"We were exchanging letters, but I haven't heard from her in over two years. I think something happened to her, Dad."

Danny shook his head. "You don't know that, Jesse. Think about what is going on over there right now. Maybe she can't write."

Now it was Jesse's turn to shake his head. He turned around and pulled a tightly folded letter from his pocket. He handed it to Danny, who opened it curiously.

"It's from Paul," Jesse said quietly as his father began to read.

Dear Jesse,

Well, I suppose you have heard all of the news. We are at war. Life has been very uncertain ever since. Hitler thinks that he can take on the world, but I doubt it will amount to anything.

Mother is trying to take it as well as she can. She just wants life to seem normal, but she has been acting odd lately. Dederick is in the military, no surprise there. Last we heard, he was stationed somewhere in Poland. Mother is proud of his loyalty to Germany, even if he is a bit extreme. I'm worried for him. He is getting into things that could end in disaster.

As for me, I'm taking life as it comes, which includes marriage! Congratulate me, old boy! I got married to the love of my life, Hannah, last spring. It was rather sudden, actually. You see, she is a Jew, and not very well liked, if you know what I mean. But we are happy, and

Mother appears to be quite content with it all. Hannah is expecting; the child should arrive sometime in March. She is absolutely glowing. I hope you get to meet her soon. You will love her.

We have not heard from Hilda in quite some time. I was wondering if she had sent you a letter at all. She has been gone for nearly a year. She left the night after the Kristallnacht raids, and left no hint as to where she was going. I know that she can take care of herself, but Mother and I are very worried all the same. If she has contacted you at all, please let me know. You know how to reach me, I'm sure.

I hope you are well, and please say hello to your parents for me. Don't become a stranger, Jesse.

Your Friend,
Paul

Danny sighed and folded the letter carefully. Jesse's face was filled with pain.

"I'm sorry, Jesse. She's a strong woman. You told me that."

Jesse sat down and ran his hands through his hair. Danny could tell his son had something on his mind. When Jesse got to thinking about something, it was impossible to change his mind. Danny was apprehensive to hear what his son was thinking, but knew it was coming. Jesse looked up at him, serious and determined.

"I'm going to look for her, Dad."

"Now Jesse, just think about this for a second."

Jesse shook his head, his gaze firm. "No, Dad. I'm going to find her, no matter what it takes." He paused and looked out at the palm trees blowing in the ocean breeze. "The Royal Air Force is asking for volunteers to cross the pond and fight. I've been recommended. All I need are the certified flight hours. I wasn't sure if I was going to accept, but now ... I've decided. I'm going, and I will figure out what happened to her."

"Jesse, please. You must think about this. Think about your mother, your sister," Danny tried to reason.

"I have thought about it. And I can't get her out of my head. I just ... I need to be sure that she is okay," Jesse finished, pain behind his words.

"Is she really worth risking your life over?" Danny asked pointedly.

Jesse raised his eyes to his father without hesitation. "Yes."

Danny stared at his son. It was there. He recognized it clearer than a California summer day. He smiled softly and sipped his coffee. "You really love her, don't you?"

"What?"

"I've seen it before. That confused, concerned look on your face. The way you look when you talk about her."

Jesse sat down and leaned forward. "I just ... she's the most amazing, beautiful person I've ever known. And I need to know that she is safe." He watched his father for a moment. "Dad, how did you know Mom was the one?"

Danny smiled, remembering. "I had been injured in a training accident, and she was on duty that night. When she came rushing into the room with that worried look on her face ... you know it."

Jesse laughed. "How could I not? I've seen it plenty of times."

"That's the one. It was then that I knew. She was the only one I would ever love."

They sat there silently together for a moment. Danny relished these moments with his son, when they sat in silent unity where words were unnecessary.

Jesse thought of the last time he saw Hilda, waving from the platform and promising to wait for him. It seemed cruel to him now, what he had asked of her, when he knew their relationship would be difficult. But God help him, he loved her. He had to find her. Somehow, he had to.

"That's what I want, Dad. More than anything," he murmured.

Danny leaned forward and placed his hand on Jesse's shoulder.

"You'll know. When the time comes, you'll know."

Jesse could not help but smile as he stepped down from the plane and saw his friend Joshua Sauders standing there, a cowboy hat perched on his head. The two had met at training camp several years back and since then, they had been inseparable. They remained fast friends and continued to correspond, often flying to visit each other. Jesse had been looking forward to this vacation to Texas for weeks, and now he felt conflicted in his thoughts. It would be good to confide in Josh.

"How's life, cowboy?" he asked as the two shook hands with a smile.

"Scooping cow pies isn't anywhere near as fun as flying planes," Josh said. "Mom says I make more of a mess of it than a pile."

"I thought you graduated from that job when you were twelve," Jesse joked.

"Being away for months at a time doesn't put me too high on that woman's list," Josh said dryly. "Maybe with you around, she'll loosen up. She's already cooking up a feast for you."

Jesse laughed. "Well, I wouldn't want to keep her waiting. Besides, it was a long trip."

The two men walked out of the airport and headed toward Josh's Ford. A group of young teens twittered as they walked by. Josh smiled.

"I forgot about the advantage of having you in town."

Jesse smiled but said nothing. He hadn't told Josh about Hilda, mainly because her role in his life was complicated. So he kept his mouth shut as he got in the car and they drove away from the airport.

Jesse grew silent as they drove. Somewhere, amid all of the chaos of the war in Europe, was Hilda. Was she all right? Jesse had gone through countless possibilities of what happened to her. And what of Paul, and his mother and brother? Were they safe?

"You are a million miles away right now, Jesse."

He shook himself as Josh's voice broke into his thoughts. "Just thinking."

Josh studied him as they drove. "You have that look in your eye, like you've decided to do something and nothing's going to stop you."

Jesse did not speak for a moment, wondering how much he should reveal. But it was Josh, and he would appreciate his volunteering to cross the pond and fight.

"I've decided to go to England as a volunteer with the RAF," he said slowly. "They're looking for pilots."

Josh stared at him for as long as he could without drifting off the road. The surprise on his face was easy to read. "Why didn't you tell me this sooner, Jesse?"

He shrugged. "I hadn't made a decision until two days ago. I begin training right after New Year's."

Josh whooped and slapped the steering wheel. "Jesse that is great! You'll get to experience some real action."

"Yeah, it should be pretty great," he answered, his mind far away on thoughts of Hilda.

"Hey, you think I could volunteer too?"

Jesse turned to stare at Josh. "I don't see why not."

Josh's face was full of excitement. A plan whirred in his brain, and while Jesse knew it would be nice to have a friend with him overseas, he didn't want to detract from his other mission—finding Hilda.

⌒*∕*⌒

Mari sat quietly, legs tucked underneath her as she sat on the couch, her forehead resting against her fingers. It was late, and one lamp shone on the end table and illuminated the picture of Luke and Allison Pendair in that small church in London where they were married. The house was quiet and she dwelled on the memories that they had shared in the silence. She often wondered what would have happened if they had lived, if they had all come back home, and their children had grown up together. They would have been neighbors, grown old together, and watched their children get married.

The cushions sank as Danny sat down beside Mari. His fingers gently caressed her cheek, and she turned to him and smiled. They shared a lingering kiss and Danny drew her into his arms.

"I miss them so much sometimes," Mari whispered.

"Me too."

She shifted in Danny's arms, and there was an understanding silence for a moment.

"What do you suppose happened to her?" she asked quietly.

"Who?"

"The child."

Danny had wondered this many times, and every time, he simply ended up with more questions. "I pray that she is somewhere on this earth, leading a simple, quiet life."

"I hope you're right."

There was more silence.

"What do you suppose she'd be like?" Mari questioned.

"As beautiful as Allison and as smart as Luke."

She smiled and kissed Danny again. "I love you," she murmured.

"The feeling is mutual, I assure you."

Mari laughed, and then suddenly grew quiet. "Jesse seemed out of sorts before he left for Texas. Do you suppose it is the war in Europe? He does have friends over there."

Danny sighed and tightened his arms around her. "He received a letter from Paul van Ostrand a few days before he left. Hilda van Ostrand has been missing for a year apparently. There's no sign of her anywhere."

"Oh how awful. I can't imagine what he must be thinking." Mari leaned into her husband, but sensed Danny was not finished.

"Mari darling, there's more. Jesse has been offered ... that is, he's accepted a volunteer position with the RAF. He'll begin his flight certification hours at the beginning of the year."

Mari sat up and looked at him, the pain in her eyes poignant and real. "Danny, how could you keep this from me? My son, going overseas to volunteer in a war that is not our own? I won't have it, I won't!"

"Sweetheart, please. You must understand. He is a grown man and will make his own decisions. He's like us, Mari. He's not afraid of a fight if it is something he believes in. You were a volunteer once too, remember? I distinctly recall your parents having a fit over your decision to leave little Jesse with them. Was that not a harder situation than this?" Danny took her hands and held her gaze. "A higher purpose is taking Jesse to Europe, I know it. And all I can do is have faith that there is meaning to all this."

Mari's eyes filled with tears and she looked down at her hands, still clasped in her husband's. "I'm not standing in his way," she whispered, "but I'm not happy that he's going."

"He just wants to serve, Mari, like you and I did. Christina is doing the same thing as a nurse. We've taught our children the loyalty that we have and served for, and now they are taking up that duty."

Mari sniffed, and Danny raised his arm comfortingly around her shoulders.

"It's all the same signs. Just like the beginning of the Great War. Do you think we'll be dragged into this one as well?" she asked softly.

His arm tightened around her. "I think it is inevitable. No matter what anyone says, we can't remain neutral forever. Someone is bound to force us into this war. It could be any time."

Mari felt herself shiver uncontrollably. "Why do you think so?"

"Well, Hitler seems to have the outrageous plan of trying to take over the world, and Canada is already involved. The entire world is getting drawn into this. It won't be long before we are, too."

"And Jesse," Mari whispered.

Danny gently pulled her against his chest and held her. He knew that very soon, Jesse would be caught up in the war going on in Europe, but not just to fight. Hilda van Ostrand was caught right in the middle of it, and Danny knew his son well enough to know that he was not about to leave her in the midst of war. He would go to England, and would find her at all costs.

9

June 1940

J esse waved to his parents one last time from the ship's railing. His mother had tears in her eyes as she waved her hankie and Jesse smiled reassuringly. His uniform had been pressed and he stood smartly as the ship sailed out of the harbor. He watched as the New York City skyline slowly receded. God only knew when he would return and see his family again.

After years of waiting and wondering, he was finally going back to Europe. It had been much longer than he hoped, and he knew that many things would be different, but he was going back.

As the ship began to pull into the Atlantic, Jesse went to the bow and stared out at the vast sea, wondering what awaited him in England. He did not regret his decision to volunteer; not only would it bring him closer to Hilda, but he genuinely wanted to join the fight against Hitler. Josh had written him saying he would follow him soon to volunteer as well, but for Jesse, it was personal. He had seen firsthand the terror the Nazis had brought to the people, to Hilda, and the thought made him angry. He wondered how Paul and his new wife were coping with the discrimination and hoped they were able to share happiness together, especially with the coming of their new baby.

As the sun set in the west, Jesse felt its warmth slowly fade from his back. The journey would be less than a week and hopefully without incident. His mother had written to Dr. Holden, their close friend from the time of the Great War. The good doctor and his family would host him in London before he reported for duty. And while he stayed with them, he would search for answers to Hilda's disappearance.

Jesse took the elevator down to his cabin to unpack his bags and settle in. A half hour later, he walked along the deck and watched the dark chilly evening fall around the ship before he went to dinner. There was a frigid wind blowing and he rubbed his hands together for warmth.

"Excuse me, would you mind directing me to my cabin, I seem to have lost ... oh, I'm sorry, I've mixed you up with somebody else."

A young woman stood in front of him looking very lost. She was dressed in a fine dark blue traveling suit that buttoned all of the way up to her chin in two rows. A white cap covered her shining blonde hair, and blue eyes sparkled up apologetically at him.

But that was not what made Jesse turn around. The distinct German accent drew him like a magnet, and he studied her carefully. It was very strange to find a German woman anywhere near the United States. He gave a nod of his head. "It's quite all right."

"I mistook you for a steward. Your uniform threw me off, I'm afraid." She smiled at him. "I'm sorry."

"No need." He held out his hand. "I'm Jesse Riker."

"I am Tanya Berezovsky," she said, shaking his hand.

"It's a pleasure. Are you on your way home?"

Tanya nodded. "Yes. To Germany."

"Interesting," Jesse said with a smile. "I have a few friends in Germany."

She laughed slightly, as though the idea of him having friends there seemed rather absurd. "Do you indeed? Where in Germany?"

"Heidelberg."

"Ah yes, lovely city. I considered the university there for a time. I come from Berlin, Mr. Riker."

"Call me Jesse."

His kind manner made her smile widen. "Only if you will call me Tanya."

"I'm sure that I would butcher trying to pronounce your last name anyway."

They both laughed at his comment before he continued. "Your name is Russian, Tanya. How is it that you live in Germany?"

"You are quite observant, yes. Actually, my father is Russian and my mother came from Berlin. I am only half German but I have lived there my entire life." She studied him up and down, taking in his uniform. "You are an American," she said, no question in her voice. "But you are going to Europe for the war?"

He shrugged, not sure how much information he should reveal. "I am, yes. I am sorry if that bothers you. I haven't been in several years, so I don't quite know what to expect."

Tanya sighed. "Yes. I'm afraid to know how changed it will be."

"You haven't been home since it began? That is a long time to be away," Jesse said.

"I've been studying in New York for the past few years."

"Really? My friend in Germany studied in California. He stayed with me and my family."

"Yes, the abroad education has become quite popular," she said with a smile.

Jesse could not help thinking how odd their conversation was. Technically, they were enemies, and here they were talking about education. War was a strange thing. The dinner bell rang suddenly, and Tanya sighed with annoyance.

"That's my bell, and I still haven't been able to locate my cabin. Until then, I won't be able to change for dinner." She shrugged and turned. "Well, I suppose I'll see you around for the next few days, Jesse."

"Wait, Tanya. Perhaps I may be of service to you." He stepped forward. "Where are you located?"

She looked at him with a smile. "Thank you, Jesse. It's D Deck, Cabin 323. I just can't find my way around here at all. I probably won't make it to dinner on time either."

"Then would you allow me to escort you?" he asked courteously.

"Why, I would like that, Jesse. Thank you."

Tanya gazed at herself in the mirror of her small bathroom and added just a bit more rouge to her cheeks. She wore a slim fitting gown of gold satin and a brown fox fur draped over her shoulders. Her white gloves were spotless and on one wrist, three strands of diamonds glittered against the fabric.

The dress and the fur had been gifts from her father several years ago. She had not seen Nicholas Berezovsky since that day when he had left Germany for the last time and gone back to the Soviet Union. After his promotion into the higher ranks of the NKVD, he never returned to Berlin, and Tanya preferred it that way. She had always hated her father's work in the secret police. Trips to Moscow felt more like trips to prison. When her mother died a few months after her father left, Tanya immediately applied to go to America to study and left before he could send for her. Since that day years ago, she had not seen or corresponded with her father at all.

Tanya gave her image one last critical look before she switched off the light and hurried out into the sitting room to grab her purse just as a knock sounded on the door. She opened it to find Jesse Riker standing there attired in his dress uniform. She smiled at him.

"You look very handsome, Jesse," she stated.

"The same must be said about you, Tanya. Does your cabin suit you?"

"I am thankful enough for the fact that I found it. Thank you again for your services earlier."

Jesse smiled. "I'm glad I could help. And now," he said as he offered his arm, "shall we go?"

"Yes. Let's."

He led her up to B Deck, where music greeted them the moment they stepped off the elevator. A string quartet sat just inside the restaurant and people milled about everywhere, some in uniform, some not, with cocktails in their hands. The tables were nearly full with laughing parties as Jesse escorted Tanya up to the maître d, who bowed.

"Captain Riker, we have your table all prepared for you. Right this way."

Tanya smiled at the waiter who took her wrap and sat down across from Jesse in the elegant dining room. Crystal chandeliers sparkled from the ceiling, candles glowed from the middle of every table, and beautifully scripted menus were given to them. Tanya settled herself in and waited until Jesse had ordered champagne before opening up the conversation.

"So, as America is not a part of this war, you must be coming to Europe as a volunteer."

"Yes, I am. I feel it is my duty."

Tanya nodded. "I respect people for knowing exactly what they fight for. It shows character."

"Thank you." Jesse looked at her with open curiosity. "If I'm not prying, where do you stand in this war? Being of two opposing countries must be difficult."

Tanya laughed. "Fortunately, I have not had to face that predicament yet. I honestly don't know what to expect when I get home. My father probably already knows that I'm coming and is waiting to haul me off with him to the Soviet Union. I didn't even write to him."

Jesse looked puzzled. "Then how would he know?"

She fingered her napkin absentmindedly. "He is ... um, he works for the NKVD. One of the higher officers."

Jesse was surprised. Her father had a high place in the Soviet secret police, and her mother was German? "That is quite a predicament."

Tanya smoothed her napkin in her lap. "If I may be honest with you, my loyalty has always been to Germany. I spent my happiest years growing up in Berlin with my mother."

"I respect that. I know of a woman like you who also struggles with her loyalty. These are difficult times we live in, no denying it."

At that moment, the waiter returned with the champagne. He poured some into each glass and left the bottle beside the table.

Jesse and Tanya raised their glasses with a smile.

"To ... what should we toast to?" Jesse asked.

"To this moment, where there is no war, just friends," Tanya said quietly, a wistful smile on her face.

"Cheers."

"Cheers."

Tanya sipped her champagne delicately. "This friend of yours, how has she handled her loyalties with the war now here?"

Jesse twirled his glass slowly. "Honestly Tanya I don't know. She ... actually disappeared before the war broke out. No one knows where she went."

Tanya brought a hand to her heart. "Oh Jesse, I am sorry. I have heard similar stories however. Many people left before it became too dangerous and fled west."

Jesse leaned forward, a hopeful look in his eye for the first time that night. "Really? So it might be possible that ..."

Tanya nodded. "Entirely possible. Many of my friends wrote me not to come back because of the danger."

Jesse's eyes narrowed in confusion. "So then why are you returning?"

Tanya took another sip of champagne. "I guess I just ... am hoping that what I've heard is exaggerated. I have such happy memories of home, and I pray that not that much has changed. It may be naïve of me, but ... it's all I have. Hope."

Jesse smiled softly. "That's all any of us can do Tanya, is hope."

It was the fourth day into their journey. The ship was expected to arrive that night, and Jesse and Tanya enjoyed one more walk around the deck.

"I cannot think of a time where I have enjoyed myself more, Jesse," Tanya commented as they stood at the stern looking out at the wake.

"It has been fun. Are you all prepared for after you leave port?"

"Yes. I make the Channel crossing late tonight." She turned to him. "I wish you the best of luck, Jesse."

"The same to you, Tanya. I hope our paths cross again sometime."

"As do I." She gave him one last smile before going to the stairs and down to her cabin. Jesse watched her go and then turned back to watch as the sun slowly sank lower toward the water. Hilda's face came to mind. He wondered where she was at that moment, if she was watching the same sunset, and if she was safe. So many unanswered questions came to his mind and he tried unsuccessfully to shove them away. He had constantly kept her in his prayers over the years, and once again he gave her over to God and asked Him to protect her and bring them together again. Jesse wondered if, like her country, Hilda too had changed. Would he recognize her? So much had altered during their separation, the war being the greatest of them all. Her views on it could change their relationship forever. Jesse sighed and pulled his collar up tighter around his neck. His conscience told him not to worry, but a deeper gut instinct spoke otherwise. Pray, it said. Pray.

Tanya moved along with the throng of people hurrying toward the cabs lined up along the curb. As much as she tried not to get jostled, she had to hold on to her things tightly. She was about halfway to the street when she noticed two men in dark long overcoats with stern faces studying the crowds. Tanya ducked behind one tall man and pulled her hat lower over her eyes as the crowd moved along the row of cabs. She dumped her bags into one of them and scrambled in. She tried to catch her breath and said hurriedly, "Terminal Four please, and quickly."

The driver turned, and Tanya let out a startled yelp as she faced a similar looking man as the other two outside. She threw open the door and practically jumped out, only to be confronted by the men she had seen earlier. One of them stepped forward. He took her arm and when he spoke, she felt her heart sink at the thick Russian accent behind his English.

"Miss Berezovsky, you will accompany us quietly please."

Jesse's eyes were tired from searching the crowded port for his host. He sat on a vacant bench and glanced at the clock. The ship had docked almost two hours ago. Where was the doctor? He sighed, tucked his hands into his coat and closed his eyes.

Hilda walked toward him, her eyes pleading with him to listen. He shook his head, and her eyes filled with tears. Behind her, from a great distance, he saw Paul with a young woman. She was thin and ghostly white, and Paul held her with all his strength. He looked up and met Jesse's gaze. Jesse wanted to help them, but he couldn't reach them. Hilda fell before him and grasped his hand tightly.

"Jesse, please ... please ..."

"You're the very image of Danny."

Jesse woke with a start when a hand touched his shoulder. A wrinkled smiling face looked down at him.

"Dr. Holden?" Jesse asked as he stood up. He absolutely dwarfed the man.

"Jesse, I presume." Dr. Holden laughed. "I see you inherited your father's height as well." He gestured behind him, and Jesse noticed the two women with him. "My wife, Mary."

The older woman came forward, a sparkle of awe in her eyes. She had aged very well, and a gentle smile came upon her face as she said quietly, "It is so good to finally have you with us, Jesse."

"Thank you, Mrs. Holden."

Dr. Holden led the other woman forward. "And my daughter, Grace."

Grace had inherited her mother's beauty. Her glistening blonde hair was pulled back in stylish waves. Jesse smiled as he shook her hand.

"It is a pleasure," he said warmly.

"Indeed," she replied shyly. She lowered her eyes with a small smile.

"My car is over here," Dr. Holden said, leading the way. "I'm sure that you will want to get settled and rest. Was your trip all right?"

"Fine, fine," Jesse replied as he took the seat offered him next to the doctor.

"Very good. You can never tell with all of these war ships about."

"John!" Mary scolded lightly. "I am sure that Jesse does not want to hear about the war right now. Let him catch his breath!"

"Of course. Forgive me dear boy, but some days it feels like I am consumed by it."

"Daddy, you know how many times Mum and I have told you to take a break from the hospital. You work too much," Grace piped up from the back seat.

"Yes, I know my dear, but I can't seem to stay away."

"Where is the hospital that you work at, sir?" Jesse asked.

"Near the edge of town, closer to the airfields. It is the same hospital that your mother worked at when she was here. Would you like to see it sometime?"

"I would, thank you."

The drive was a scenic one, and Jesse kept getting turned around since the English drove on the left side of the road. They drove passed Buckingham Palace and Kensington Gardens, and Jesse knew that he would be doing a great deal of sightseeing in the days ahead.

Dr. Holden pulled up to a narrow yet quaint white house that was surrounded by several others like it. Jesse glanced around as he entered. It was smaller than the van Ostrand home, but not by much. There were no servants, but he did notice a cook scurrying across the hall to the kitchen. The house smelled of a mix of stewed turkey, carrots, and onions, and reminded Jesse of how hungry he was. The hallway was very long and narrow, quite a contrast to the spacious archway in Hilda's house. There were more rooms by far, but each was very small. Grace led him up a very tall staircase to a guestroom on the second floor. It was comfortably furnished with a double bed, dresser, nightstand, and a stuffed chair. Jesse set his suitcase down and looked around. There was a window that opened up to the back, and he pulled aside the curtain, watching as a stray dog chased a cat through the backyard. Jesse sat down in the chair and sighed. There was a good deal of exploring to do, but right then, he just wanted to sleep.

It was a lone figure that stepped out of the cab that night. With hat pulled low and collar up high, it was hard to tell who the person was. The only noticeable thing in the thick blackness of the night was the blonde hair that peeked out from underneath the hat. The figure hurried along the street, keeping a quick pace toward the center of London. No late night owl bothered to stop and say a greeting. The wind picked up and glancing at the sky, one could see that a storm was coming. Passing quickly by several rows of houses, the figure hardly noticed the single light on at the back of one of the homes. The breeze grew steadily stronger, blowing the overcoat in all directions. The moon appeared for but a split second and revealed a pale face. The coat swirled open once again just before the moon disappeared. Underneath, there was blood everywhere.

10

Jesse awoke to a bustling house the next morning. Sunlight spilled in through his window and he rubbed his eyes against the light. He glanced at the clock on the dresser. It was nearing nine o'clock. He threw off the covers and dressed in a pair of tan slacks and a white shirt. When he looked out the window and saw the clouds darkening the sky, he grabbed his jacket, hat, and scarf and hurried down the stairs to breakfast.

"Well, good morning, Jesse." Mary greeted him with a smile as she entered the dining room with a steaming tray. "I hope you slept well. I reheated breakfast for you."

The smell of eggs, ham, toast, and coffee came to his nose and he sighed with contentment. "Thank you, Mrs. Holden," he said gratefully as he sat down at the place that she set for him.

"Now now, we'll have none of that. While you are with us, you're family. You may dispense with the formality. Mary is sufficient."

Jesse smiled as she gave him a small nudge. He knew he would like this woman.

"Now," she said as she bustled around, "John has gone to the hospital once again, and Grace is spending the day with friends. I'm afraid that there is no car that you could use today and I know that you wanted to see the city."

Jesse laughed. "It's quite all right, I assure you, Mary. I'm sure that if I did have the use of a car, I would not make it past the lunch hour. I would like to walk, thank you."

Mary glanced out the window with worry. "It does look like rain is on the way, you know."

He smiled. "That's never stopped me before." He quickly finished his breakfast and got up to put on his coat. "I don't know when I will be back, so don't worry yourself."

"Do you know the way back here?" she asked with a grin.

"I'm sure that I can figure it out. See you later, Mary."

Grace peeked out from behind one of the mannequins as Jesse Riker passed by on his way to the center of town. She knew that she would never get tired of looking at that man. The Lord must have had something special in mind when He chiseled Jesse. She sighed dreamily as she watched him cross the street.

"Grace? Grace, are you even listening to me?"

Grace turned with a start and almost knocked over a hat rack in close proximity. "Oh! Oh, I'm sorry, Abigail, I'm afraid my mind was elsewhere. Um, what was the color that you liked?"

Abigail stared at her quizzically and then shrugged her shoulders. "What do you think of the pale blue? Do you think it goes with her eyes?"

"Oh, anything you put on Susan makes her look absolutely lovely, Abby. After all, she takes after you, dearie."

"Oh, well, thank you." Abigail walked up to the counter and placed the dress in front of the clerk.

"Is that all miss?" he asked.

"Yes, thank you."

Abigail paid the amount and together, she and Grace walked out and down the street.

"I could use some lunch, Grace. I'm not quite used to rations yet. There's a darling little café down the way with a fireplace."

"Mm," Graced murmured, her thoughts elsewhere.

"So, what was it that completely caught your attention in the store?" asked Abigail.

"What? Oh, it was nothing." Grace said quickly.

Abigail laughed. "Of course, nothing. Come now, Grace, I haven't seen you wear that face since we were in school. Who is the man?"

"Abby!" Grace exclaimed.

"Well, that was obviously what you were looking at in the dress shop!"

Grace sat down in one of the chairs when they entered the café and took a table in the corner. She threw her coat, hat and gloves on the rack next to them and sighed.

"My parents have very good friends who live in the states, and their son has come to stay with us for a while before he volunteers with the RAF in the Eagle Squadron."

"Ah, a man in uniform. And American. That answers many questions," Abigail said with a small smile.

"Oh, Abby, I'm hopeless," Grace said with a sigh. "I'm well past my prime and still living with my parents, working for the newspaper and not anywhere near getting married."

"Now now, dear, there is a plan for everyone and for some, it does not include marriage. You shouldn't feel that you have to throw yourself at every man that comes your way."

"You should see the man," Grace muttered under her breath as their waiter came with water.

The young ladies ate lunch over light conversation. Abigail spoke of her husband, Peter, and of her small daughter, Susan. Grace tried to pay attention, but her thoughts wandered endlessly and very soon, Abigail was calling her name from across the table.

"Honestly, I can't keep your attention for two seconds, can I?"

"Forgive me once again, Abby. I must appear very dull to you."

"Darling, you're supposed to be having a good time today, remember? It's your day off. Enjoy yourself!"

Grace smiled. "Yes. Shall we continue our shopping day?"

Abigail eagerly got up and took Grace's arm.

"Lets."

Jesse stood, hat pushed back on his forehead with his hands in his pockets, and watched as several Royal Air Force pilots soared above him. The sun moved constantly behind endless clouds that came closer and closer. At some points, it shone down on the road where he stood, which led to the pristine white hospital surrounded by lawns on which wounded soldiers wandered while others were pushed in wheelchairs by volunteer nurses. He went up the steps to the porch and was about to open the door when a voice called to him from his right.

"Enjoying your day, son?"

He turned. Dr. Holden walked toward him, having just finished examining a patient who was reclining on the porch. He smiled and nodded to him.

"Good day, sir."

"Have you simply been walking around the city?" the doctor asked.

"Yes. I've heard so much about it from my parents. My mother sent me with a list of things that I had to see. Just walking through the city eliminated about half of them."

Dr. Holden laughed and turned Jesse out toward the lawn. He pointed. "Is that on the list?"

Jesse followed his finger and found himself staring at a very large tree. It stood slightly separate from the others. "No. What about it?"

"Come with me." Dr. Holden led him out on to the lawn and paused in the shade of the branches. "It was many a day when I would stand on the porch and watch your mother and father out here. This seemed to be their special spot."

Jesse walked closer and put his hand against the cold bark. His fingers touched an inscription and he looked closer. They were initials. *A.W. & L.P. 1917*. Dr. Holden noticed his curiosity and stepped up beside him, his eyes on the etching.

"Allison Winter and Luke Pendair. They were married here in London and died only a year later. A tragic story."

"Yes, my parents have told me about them," Jesse said quietly. "They were the best of friends, weren't they?"

The doctor smiled. "They were inseparable." His face looked sad, as though picturing a memory in his mind. Jesse watched him.

"You miss them, don't you, sir?"

"There is a hole in my heart where they were, yes. Sometimes I sit out here and just remember them in happier times. Well, different times."

Jesse nodded. Yes, very different times indeed. And yet history seemed to be repeating itself.

"Dr. Holden!" a nurse called from the porch.

"I must go, Jesse. Duty calls. Feel free to come in and look around whenever you like."

Jesse smiled. "Thank you."

The doctor went back into the hospital, and Jesse moved out from under the shade of the tree. While the sun shone brightly through the clouds that morning, the cold was stronger, and more clouds gathered threateningly. He put his hands in his pockets. A soft drone sounded above him and Jesse looked up to see more RAF planes flying high above the hospital as they ran through drills. That would soon be him. Excitement and a nip of fear grew in his stomach.

"Going to join them soon?"

Jesse turned to the new voice and saw a man walking toward him. He was not very tall but had broad shoulders, wavy blonde hair and dark brown eyes. He was dressed casually in a suit but also wore a long coat with a scarf up to his chin. Jesse smiled.

"That's the plan."

"You're American," the stranger said, small surprise in his voice. He held out his hand. "Jeffrey Rolf."

"Jesse Riker." He shook the proffered hand and stared at him casually. "So, does your young lady volunteer here?"

Rolf laughed. "No, I was visiting a friend."

"Wounded in the war?"

"Yes, but not so bad. Sure to be right as rain soon enough."

"That's good to hear."

Rolf studied Jesse. "You are a volunteer?"

"Yes. Arrived a few days ago."

"Well, we could definitely use the help, thank you."

"It's an honor," Jesse said.

Rolf looked at the sky, and then shook Jesse's hand once again. "Well, it was a pleasure meeting you, Captain Riker."

"And you."

"Maybe we'll run into each other here again sometime."

"Perhaps, though hopefully not for anything too serious," Jesse said with a smile.

"Yes, let's hope. Good day."

Jesse watched as the man walked away and decided as he did that the people in London were nicer than he expected. He chuckled to himself. Feeling the cold again, he drew his collar closer to his neck and hurried back toward the center of town.

⌒❦⌒

Grace said her final good bye and left Abigail on her doorstep after thanking her for the lovely day. Then she turned and quickened her step toward the hospital. The rain was just starting to fall when she looked up from her brisk pace and nearly slammed into Jesse.

"Miss Holden!" he exclaimed.

"Captain Riker!" Grace suddenly realized her tone sounded terrified, and she cleared her throat, hoping to make herself sound more normal. "I'm sorry, I did not see you there."

"Where are you off to in such a hurry?"

"Oh, well, I was going to see my father, but I do believe the rain will catch up with me before I get there, so I may just make my way back home."

"Would you like me to get you a cab?" he asked politely.

"Why, that is very kind of you, Captain, thank you."

"Please, Grace. It's Jesse."

Grace watched, speechless, as he took her arm and led her to the curb to hail a cab. Her "thank you" came out as a whisper and her voice caught at the end. She felt her face flush as Jesse smiled and told her that she would see him shortly. She nodded meekly. After the door was shut, the driver had to ask her three times where they were going and she gave the address quickly.

Halfway through the ride she shook herself and came to her senses. She was horrified as she looked back on the way she had behaved. Briskly fanning herself, she looked out the window and tried to calm her nerves. She quickly paid the man when she reached home and hurried up the steps and into the house. Shutting the door quickly, she leaned against it with a hard breath. "Mother, I'm home!"

Mary called from the kitchen. "I'm just working on supper dear. Oh, and a telegram came for you."

Grace found it lying on the table in the hall and she picked it up quickly, still trying to calm her heart. She felt like a silly schoolgirl. How ridiculous.

The telegram was from her superior at the paper. She opened it as she climbed the stairs, and a moment later all thoughts of Jesse Riker were erased from her mind, and she slammed back to reality in one swift exciting leap.

Angelis Chevalier was back.

11

Jesse had never felt so at home walking the streets of London. The past week had blown by like a breeze, gentle and comforting. He had been able to forget his worries for a time and simply enjoy the history that surrounded him. He now sat in a small café along the street, eating a muffin as he wrote a letter to his father.

Dear Dad,

My time here in London has so far been one of relaxation and enjoyment. Dr. Holden, Mrs. Holden and Grace have been very kind. They have helped me through London and I have only gotten lost a few times. A few days ago, I went to the hospital and saw that famous tree that you and Mother used to sit and talk under. Dr. Holden told me a little about Allie and Luke Pendair as well. Anyway, I wish that you and Mom were here to tell me all about your times here and show me around. I'm still keeping my eyes open for Hilda, just in case she might have left Germany for safety. There is a very small chance however, and I'm not getting my hopes up.

My training with the Eagle Squadron has gone well. Josh arrives in a week to join me. Though the excitement is still there, it is a serious kind of thrill now that I am actually here. Was it that way with you? I feel somehow unprepared, even though I had excellent training in the states. I know I did the right thing Dad, even though I am hesitant now that I am here. Keep me in your prayers and send Mom and Christina my love.

Your son,

Jesse

Having finished the letter, Jesse folded it and put it into an addressed envelope. Finishing his muffin, curiosity bade him look up when the bell above the door jingled merrily. He was surprised to see Grace walk to the counter and order a coffee. She appeared to be antsy, yet in an excited way. She accepted the drink gratefully, turned from the counter, met his eyes and stopped. Jesse smiled.

"Hello," he said.

"Hi." She appeared suddenly nervous. Her eyes darted around constantly.

Jesse cleared his throat and tried again. "Would you like to sit down?"

Grace glanced at the chair opposite him for a moment and then replied, "Thank you."

She set her drink down on the table and sat down with a glance at the letter. "To your father?"

"Yes," Jesse replied. "I try to write to him as often as I can."

"I've heard my father speak of him often. He thinks very highly of him," Grace said.

"As do I."

Grace was silent again, and Jesse tried to break her obvious tension. This must be the way British girls kept their feelings to themselves. He liked it much better than the girls back home who constantly stared at him.

"So, your father tells me you're a journalist," he said casually.

Grace smiled, and the passion she had for her work seemed to relax her a little. "Yes, I write for the war column of the post. Most of the time it's just an update on what is going on, but I love to write about the Underground Movement."

"Really? Isn't that a little ... risky? You never know who is reading it."

"Of course we only get limited information, and we don't write anything that would risk lives, but it cheers people to hear about their successes."

"How do you manage to get the information?" Jesse asked. "I can imagine they would be pretty tight-lipped about it all."

97

"Yes, they are, but a friend of mine works in the Intelligence office, rather low down on the chain of command, but he is able to give me tidbits of news. I've actually just received a tip from my superior that I need to ask him about."

The bell above the door jingled again, and they both turned. The person who came in looked very familiar to Jesse, and when Grace called to him, he remembered where they had met.

"Well, as we speak ... Jeffrey, hello!" Grace called.

He turned and caught sight of the two. He smiled and came over to where they sat.

"Well now, isn't this a merry party. Hullo, Grace." Jeffrey turned to Jesse with recognition in his face. "Captain Riker, how good to see you again so soon, and still in one piece I see."

Jesse smiled and shook his hand. Grace looked back and forth at the two of them.

"You two know each other," she stated with surprise.

"We met briefly at the hospital," Jeffrey said mildly.

"What were you doing at the hospital?" she asked.

"I hadn't seen your father in a while, and I thought I would stop by and say hello."

Jesse looked at him with veiled surprise. Why would Jeffrey lie to Grace about why he was at the hospital? It seemed quite silly to do so to someone who was such a good friend of the family.

Grace went on without looking at Jesse, who sat with a slightly confused look on his face. "Jeffrey is the friend I was telling you about, who works in Secret Intelligence, and he is such a dear, letting me in on little things for my article." Grace smiled.

Jesse nodded, realizing now why Jeffrey had misled Grace. His "friend" in the hospital must have been a wounded agent. Only so much information could be revealed, and if Grace worked for the newspaper, it was very important to keep most of the facts to himself.

"Is it true Jeffrey, the rumor going around?"

"What rumor, Grace?" he asked lightly.

"That Angelis Chevalier is back?"

Jeffrey stared at her and shook his head with a smile. "You newspapers never stop, do you?"

"So it is true!"

"Now Grace, you know I am not allowed to reveal anything without the approval of my superior."

"I knew it was true!" she exclaimed, ignoring his remarks.

"Who is Angelis ... Chevalier?" Jesse asked, interested.

"She began as a courier in France, but she has since become one of the greatest assets we have, and is talked about all over London." Grace leaned in. "They call her ... the Turncoat Spy."

"Have you ever met her?" Jesse's curiosity had peeked suddenly.

"Goodness no, a very rare few have. No pictures have ever been seen of her, but I've done articles following several of her successful missions."

Jesse found himself engrossed in the story of the mysterious Angelis Chevalier. "Are you well acquainted with her?" he asked Jeffrey.

"To an extent, yes, but she is away so often, and I am usually engrossed in paperwork in my lowly spot in the basement."

Jesse suddenly got an idea in his head. "I say, how hard would it be for you to find someone, Mr. Rolf?"

"Not too hard, usually. Why?"

Jesse met Jeffrey's eyes with a hopeful gaze. "I have a friend. We met several years ago, but I haven't heard from her in a while and her family is very worried."

Jeffrey nodded. "What is her name?"

"Hilda. Hilda van Ostrand."

Something akin to surprise flashed across Jeffrey's face, and Jesse was not surprised. It was probably much harder to find a German woman than anything else.

"Hilda van Ostrand, you say?" Jeffrey's voice sounded careful.

"Yes."

"I will try. And now, I must be going. It was a pleasure, Jesse. Good day, Grace."

"Will we see you at the theatre benefit tomorrow, Jeffrey?" Grace leaned forward excitedly. "Father and Mother and I have obtained excellent seats."

Jeffrey smiled. "I wouldn't miss it. Cheerio." He gave one last strange look at Jesse and then left the café.

"Theatre benefit?" Jesse asked after the door closed behind Jeffrey.

"Oh, heavens, I forgot to mention it. The theatre is having a benefit for those involved in the war effort, and we are all invited because of Father's work at the hospital. We would love for you to join us, Jesse."

He smiled. "Sure, I would love to."

The next day, Jesse was second guessing his decision as he stared at himself in the mirror. He awkwardly adjusted his tie. He had never been to the theatre and now he was not sure that the experience would appeal to him. He was dressed in his spotless shade 84 service dress uniform, his hair slicked back. Jesse sighed.

A knock sounded on the door. "Jesse, are you nearly ready?" It was Dr. Holden.

"Yes, sir," he replied hastily, giving himself one last look before he opened the door. Dr. Holden was dressed in a fine black tuxedo and to Jesse's relief, seemed just as uncomfortable as he did.

"Never was one for these things," the doctor muttered on the way down the stairs. "But the ladies enjoy them to no end."

Jesse smiled. They stepped into the entry hall and were greeted by the women. He stopped short. Grace stood there in a glittering white evening gown that fell to her feet in shimmering folds. Her hair was pulled back into a wavy bun, which was elegantly adorned with a diamond flower hairpiece. Pearly white gloves stopped just above her elbows. She wore jewelry, but she certainly did not need it.

Grace smiled and stepped forward. "You clean up quite nicely, Jesse."

He cleared his throat. "I'm afraid that next to you, I will look a bit dull."

Grace laughed nervously. She accepted the wrap that her mother put around her shoulders and took the arm Jesse offered her. Then they were off.

The drive through the city was something that Jesse had never done at night. Though several stores were closed, restaurants, nightclubs and theatres were brilliantly lit, and elegantly dressed ladies and gentlemen walked along the street enjoying the evening. Jesse momentarily forgot about his discomfort and watched the people milling about.

When they stepped out of the car in front of the theatre, Jesse was amazed at the sight. There were soldiers, pilots, sailors, nurses and countless others, all adorned in their best dress uniforms, and the ladies sparkled like the jewelry they wore under the bright lights. Reporters hovered outside the theatre along with photographers, their cameras at the ready. Jesse gave a low whistle.

"I've never been to an event quite as ... overwhelming as this," he murmured to Grace as they walked inside. The lobby of the theatre was adorned in red velvet with high ceilings from which dangled massive glimmering chandeliers.

"I know," Grace said, gripping his arm. "It's all really an encouragement for the people to boost their confidence in our fight. I think it's a nice diversion for all the soldiers, personally. They love good entertainment. Keeps their mind off the next battle."

Jesse looked around and took in all the high ranking uniforms he saw. "Who all is here?"

"Everyone. Many important government people. Even Winston Churchill is supposed to be here somewhere. But it's mainly for the soldiers."

The bell in the lobby chimed, signaling that the show would begin in a few moments. Jesse looked around. "I wonder where your parents went off to. They have the tickets."

"Yes, I thought I saw them over on the other side of the lobby."

The two moved across the room and skirted through groups of military personnel moving into the theatre to find their seats. Jesse, being quite tall, used his extra height to search the room for the gray head of Dr. Holden.

A small gathering at the end of the lobby caught their attention. A group of several men and women were talking quietly amongst each other. One of the women in particular caught his eye. She held herself in such a manner that Jesse could not stop staring. Her golden blonde hair was intricately coiled atop her head and was studded with many tiny sparkling diamonds, and more sparkled from her fingers and wrists. Pure white gloves ran up her arms and a midnight blue dress hung in dazzling design from her shoulders. She seemed to stand apart from the other women and from her blonde hair, Jesse thought eagerly that it might be Tanya. Perhaps she had decided to stay in London. He turned suddenly when Grace gave an excited gasp and pointed.

"Jeffrey, hello!" she exclaimed. "What a delightful surprise!"

One of the men turned to them and smiled, and Jesse recognized their friend. He waved, but when Jeffrey saw him standing next to Grace, his smiled faded and a disturbed expression filled his face. He glanced back at his party, appearing slightly out of control to Jesse. Having heard the greeting, the woman in the blue dress turned.

At that moment, time seemed to stop. Jesse could not move, and his heart thundered in his ears. Her features were older, but to Jesse she had never looked so beautiful. It had been years, but there was no mistaking it. The woman across the room was Hilda.

"The course of true love never did run smooth."

Shakespeare

12

Music and voices filled the theatre with a magical sound, signaling that the performance was ready to begin, but Jesse was oblivious to everything around him. He only saw the woman who stood only a few feet away gazing back at him in shock. He could not tear his eyes from her. Her hair was no longer brown, but a beautiful blonde. But her eyes, oh he had forgotten how green her eyes were and how quickly he could get lost in them. All of the memories that he had of the time they had spent together so long ago crowded back into his mind and he took a step forward.

Just as quickly as her surprise showed on her face, it was covered up by a composed expression as though everything were exactly as it should be, and she turned toward the door. Jeffrey wasted no time in ushering her away from them and into the theatre. Jesse followed after him, leaving Grace wondering what just happened.

"Jesse? Jesse are you all right?" Her voice seemed to come from far away.

Jesse was seconds behind them as they disappeared inside the dim theatre, but the usher at the door stopped him.

"Sir, may I see your ticket?"

"I don't have ... I just need to speak to that woman," Jesse said urgently as he tried to find Hilda in the darkness beyond.

"I'm sorry sir, but without a ticket you can't enter."

"Please! I just need a minute!"

The usher held his ground and glanced around for any security. Jesse was becoming frantic when Grace came up behind him and put a hand on his arm, concerned.

"Jesse, come. Mother and Father are waiting at the other door with our tickets. We'll see Jeffrey after the performance."

Jesse stared into the theatre but he could not make out anyone in the dark, and he reluctantly allowed himself to be dragged away. His brain could not understand what just happened and he felt the pain of hurt and confusion swell inside him.

The Holdens and Jesse entered their box and sat down just as the lights went out and the performance began. As the stage lights came up, Jesse spotted Hilda close to the front.

Jesse tried to see her face as he watched her. She looked calm and composed as she watched the production, occasionally leaning to either side of her to share a comment with the men next to her. She never glanced his way again after their first shared look in the lobby. Jesse clenched the arms of his chair. She was not at all how he remembered her to be, but then what had he expected to find? The young intelligent and carefree teen that he had fallen in love with as a young man was replaced with a very serious woman who seemed to have forgotten all about the man in America whom she had promised to wait for. The ache in his stomach grew tighter and stronger until he felt on the verge of screaming. A gentle hand touched his arm and he turned to find Grace giving him a concerned smile.

"Jesse, you look like you're about to be sick. Are you all right?"

He gave her a forced smile. "It's the uniform. Think I tied the tie too tight. I just need a little air."

Grace nodded and turned back to the performance. Jesse rose quickly and went as fast as he could without running into the lobby. If he had turned around, he would have seen Hilda carefully glance back, searching for him.

Jesse slumped down onto one of the sofas against the wall and loosened his tie. In misery he leaned forward, his head between his hands. If he thought anymore about her face when she first saw him, he was sure his heart would crack. A simple fun evening had, in the blink of an eye, turned into a nightmare.

Jesse was so unaware of everything around him that he did not hear someone calling his name until a pair of feet came into view. He looked up to find the usher who would not allow him entrance to follow Hilda. The usher handed him a folded piece of paper, what looked to be the playbill.

"Sir, a note for you from the lady."

Jesse stared at the note for a moment, then slowly took it from him. His name was clearly written on the front. Confused, he looked around. The lobby was completely empty save for him. As the usher turned away, he opened the playbill. On the inside cover was a hastily scribbled note, and the handwriting was achingly familiar.

Dear Jesse,

It must come as a great shock to see me here in London. I apologize for my behavior this evening, but please believe me when I say it was necessary. What I have to say to you cannot be told in this letter. Please meet me in the park next to the hospital tomorrow at one o'clock. There is so much I must say to you, and some things I can't. Please trust me. My actions will be explained in good time. And please burn this note.

Sincerely,
Hilda

Jesse's hands shook as he finished the letter. Nothing was making sense in his head. Something was very wrong. Jesse did not know what, but in the pit of his stomach he felt the fear begin to rise in him. Not for himself, but for Hilda. Paul's letter ran through his head. *She left the night after Kristallnacht, and left no hint as to where she was going. Mother is very worried, as am I.* Jesse closed his eyes. He was worried too. He knew he would not be able to concentrate on the performance, nor would he be able to talk to Hilda. Jeffrey, it seemed, wanted to keep a tight leash on her. The next moment Jesse got, he would have words with that man.

Jesse stood slowly and waved the usher over. He came at once.

"Would you please inform Dr. Holden and his family that I have returned home? Nothing for them to worry about, just a headache."

"Indeed, sir."

The usher hurried away to do his bidding and Jesse took his coat from the woman at the checking counter. As he walked out into the cold, he knew he would not sleep a wink that night. Tomorrow held too many questions.

❧

The frost bit into the morning air as Jesse walked aimlessly through the park. He had been up before Mary, eaten a quick breakfast and had been wandering around since eight o'clock that morning. His mind was busy with possibilities of what Hilda would say to him. Wringing his hat in his hands, he finally sat down on a bench facing the hospital across the street, that dear old tree bending with the weight of it stories from the past. For a moment, he wished he could have stayed twenty years old. Life had held so much promise then, and he had been happy because then, Hilda had been there too. Now he was lost and confused, not quite sure where he was going. He put his head in his hands and tried to block out everything around him.

Jesse didn't know how long it had been, how many footsteps had gone past, when a dainty but determined step halted in front of him.

"Jesse?"

He glanced up and found Hilda staring down at him with loving concern in her eyes. It was a gaze he finally recognized from the old days and he leaned back to take in everything about her. She wore a spotless gray suit and a matching hat covered her neatly pinned hair. Very little makeup was on her face for she did not need much, and in her hands she clutched a small purse.

Hilda sat down next to him hesitantly. Her green eyes were dark and somewhat sad. Neither of them spoke for a long time, just sat and pondered the thought of at last being together again.

Finally, Hilda broke the silence.

"This is my favorite place in the whole of London," she said quietly. "I used to come here every day to walk, to get away from town and see the sky for a moment. Something just seemed to draw me here."

It went quiet again after she said this, and she sighed with exasperation. "Jesse, please say something."

Slowly, Jesse looked up at her and stared into her eyes. Hilda could not look away. She so desperately wanted to take hold of him and never let go, to have him kiss her like she remembered from so long ago. She had ached for his strength and now that he was finally here, she could not grab hold of it.

"What did Jeffrey say when you left?"

"He is not my keeper," Hilda answered firmly.

Jesse's gaze traveled over her, the gaze of a stranger. "You've changed."

Hilda looked pointedly at him. It had been almost five years, or had he forgotten already? She turned away and stared up at the cloudless summer sky.

"Your hair's different," Jesse said softly.

"Yes."

"Did you ever get to Paris to study?"

"No." Hilda paused. "Not to study."

Jesse watched her for a moment, then with a sigh he took her hand. Hilda closed her eyes and held on tightly.

"Of all the ways that I imagined us meeting again, I never expected it to be like this," he said with a flat tone.

A single tear escaped from her eye and made a trail down her cheek. When they kept coming, Hilda could not contain herself any longer. She leaned forward, her need so evident that Jesse's arms were around her before her hands had left her lap. Her tears fell silently as he held her and they were both quiet for a while.

Hilda's voice suddenly came from where she rested on his shoulder, sad and soft.

"I want to go back," she said. "I wish things could be the way they were before. When my father was alive, and there was no Hitler. I just want to forget everything."

Jesse ran his hand slowly up and down her back and gently kissed her forehead when she pulled away. "I was just thinking the same thing a few moments ago."

Hilda put her head in her hands. "You can't possibly imagine what's happened," she said miserably.

Jesse hesitated. "No, I can't," he said. "Not unless you tell me."

Hilda looked up at him, and he was surprised at the look of sadness and desperation. "I ... I can't ... tell you."

"Hilda, I promise everything is going to be all right. Part of the reason that I came here was to look for you."

"Oh, you don't understand Jesse!" she exclaimed. "There is no possible way that you could know what I've been through."

"Then why don't you tell me," he insisted earnestly. "If this has something to do with the war, I'll understand. I've seen it too. I know where you stand."

Hilda's tears fell harder. "You could never understand." She lifted her head and met his gaze. "I was there, Jesse. I was there when the Germans marched into Paris. I was there when their tanks rolled down the street. I was there ..." she stopped, uncertain.

Her reluctance to confide in him made him irritated. "That must have been a thrill to see," he said dryly.

Hilda's head jerked up and her green eyes sparked fire. Her hand shot across his cheek as she slapped him harshly. Jesse was only partially surprised to see anger in her face when he looked at her. He immediately regretted his words and the hurt look on her face deflated his frustration.

"How dare you. How can you even say such a thing? You don't know what my life has been like." She shook her head. "You don't know me anymore."

"You're right, I don't," Jesse replied, his voice raising a notch. He leaned forward and looked hard into her face. "Who is Angelis Chevalier?"

She looked startled and some of the blood drained from her face as she glanced around the park nervously. "How do you …? Jesse, please. You must not use that name. You don't realize the danger."

"Good heavens, Hilda! I go away for a few years, come back and look at you! A new face, a new name ... what else do I need to know?"

She blanched and brought her fingers to her mouth with a slow shake of her head. Jesse saw that he had scared her and reached for her hands. They were trembling.

"Hilda," he said gently, "Hilda, I'm sorry. I'm just so confused. I can't seem to think straight."

She shook her head and wiped her eyes. "It's not you, Jesse. It's me. You're right. I am different, very different from what you once knew me to be." She hesitated, and a slight grimace came to her face. She pressed a hand to her stomach, and she was having difficulty going on. Jesse squeezed the hand he held to comfort her. A short breath escaped her before she continued.

"Jesse, a few years after you left, I met—"

"My god, Hilda!" Jesse's eyes were full of fear and concern. "Your hand!"

Looking down at her hand, she saw with horror that it was covered in blood. Jesse took it in his own and pulled her toward him as he searched for the cut. She doubled over in a cry of pain.

"Hilda!" Jesse exclaimed, supporting her as she fell forward.

"It's nothing," she gasped.

"Lean back," he instructed.

"No!"

"Do it!"

"Jesse, I have to go!" she said as she struggled to rise.

Jesse looked in horror at the circle of blood about six inches in diameter that steadily grew over her stomach. Like a shot he was up.

"Hilda, what happened?" he cried.

"Nothing!" Now she sounded like she was having trouble breathing.
"I'm not an idiot!"

"Jesse, please stop shouting," she pleaded, clutching her stomach. Her
face was pale, and she swayed unsteadily on her feet. She felt lightheaded
and heat rushed to her head as blackness closed around her. Before she
hit the ground, she felt Jesse's arms catch her up against him. There was a
roaring in her ears, and then there was nothing but empty blackness and
thick silence.

⁓

Jesse lowered Hilda slowly to the ground, in shock at what had just
happened. Quickly he pressed a handkerchief against the bleeding. His
hands shook and he told himself to calm down. All of his training came
back to him in a rush and he lifted her gently in his arms, crossed the street
carefully, and hurried toward the hospital.

"Hilda ... honey stay with me, please. Please Hilda! Help! Someone,
please help!"

A nurse came running out onto the porch, her eyes wide at the sight
she saw. She took a few halting steps forward and stared at the blood before
Jesse's voice snapped her back to attention.

"Dr. Holden. Quickly! Tell him there is a woman who needs his help
right away. Go!"

The nurse nodded and stumbled back through the doors, yelling as she
ran. Jesse held tightly to Hilda as he tried to make his way up the steps.
He lost his footing and broke their fall, bringing her carefully to the floor,
where he rocked her in his arms. "Hold on, honey. Hold on."

It seemed like eternity but was only moments later when Dr. Holden
rushed out, an orderly and a nurse behind him toting a stretcher. His
face was serious and professional as he knelt beside them and studied
the wound. He peeled away Hilda's blood soaked clothing and lifted the
bandage underneath.

"Gunshot," he said practically, not seeing Jesse tense at the word.
"Rather poorly taken care of by the looks of it. No wonder she started
bleeding." He glanced at Jesse. "Do you know what happened?"

Jesse shook his head and felt his hands begin to shake once more. Shot?
"I don't know ... she just collapsed. She was turning pale and couldn't ...
breathe very well."

"Let's put her on the stretcher." Dr. Holden and the orderly lifted her gently and hurried into the hospital, Jesse close on their heels. He had seen his share of wounds, but knowing that it was Hilda made the situation entirely different.

"Dr. Holden," he said from behind them. "She will ... be all right, won't she?"

"I won't know the full extent of the damage until I get her to an operating room. But I'd say a higher power was on your side today. How did you just happen to be across the way? Any more time lost and she may not have made it to the porch."

Jesse paled at the thought and sent up silent thanks that Hilda had chosen that spot to meet him.

"Now, Jesse, you must go," the doctor continued. "I promise I will find you the moment I know the outcome of the surgery."

"Doctor, please. This woman ..."

"I know Jesse. I know."

Hilda's pale, lifeless form turned the corner and disappeared, and Jesse sunk down to the floor against the wall, his head in his hands. He could not stand the idea of finding her again, only to lose her forever.

Dr. Holden carefully pulled his stitch closed as the nurses cleaned up around the operating table. The only noise that could be heard was the loud ticking of the clock in the hallway. He patiently sewed up the wound, intent on keeping his work clean. Hopefully there would be very little scarring when it fully healed.

The door opened and Mary entered, coming up beside her husband to watch his progress.

"John, I heard what happened. Is she all right?"

"She'll be fine as long as there is no infection. Have you seen Jesse?"

"He's still outside pacing in the hall. He is extremely upset. I didn't realize he had such a close friend in London."

"Neither did I."

Mary sighed and turned her eyes up to the young woman's face. She froze, unable to move her gaze anywhere else. She could not push words past her lips as she stared in shock at the incredible resemblance.

"John ..."

"There," he said as he finished the final stitch. "Darling, would you mind calling in a nurse to bandage her up?"

"John."

"What?"

Mary never took her eyes from the woman's face, and John wondered what on earth she could be so entranced by. "Have you noticed how much she looks like ... they could be twins ..."

Dr. Holden finally took off his glasses and wiped his eyes before glancing down at his patient's face. He started as he took in the smooth jawline, elegant nose and high cheekbones. He sputtered for a moment and glanced at his wife. They shared a bewildered look.

"It can't be," he tried to reason. "The child died ... didn't she?"

They both tried to consider the possibility and glanced down at the young woman again for a long moment. A low moan came from her lips and her head jerked on the pillow. The morphine that Dr. Holden administered had not quite set in yet.

"No ... no," she moaned. "Have to get out ... they'll find me ... nowhere to hide ..." Perspiration beaded on her forehead as the girl was bombarded with dreams. "Hide me ... hide me ... oh Mother, hurry ... he's coming ... betrayal ... betrayal! Oh, Dederick, why? Why?"

13

Poland

Tanya woke with a start as the train jerked to a stop. Through bleary eyes she looked out the window at the bustling train station. Fog hung low everywhere and it was fairly hard to see. Turning back, she saw two men sitting opposite her in the compartment. She immediately recognized them as two of the agents who had nabbed her in London. Since then, time had seemed to blend together as the endless hills had flown past. Occasionally they would pull into a station, but the stops did not mean anything to her.

With caution, Tanya asked in German, "Where are we?"

One of the agents nodded to the other, and they stood and began to take down the suitcases from the rack above.

"Are we stopping here?" she asked.

The third agent, apparently the leader whose name she had found out was Yuri, entered the compartment and muttered in Russian, "We just crossed the Polish border. It is no longer safe to be on this train."

"Why?" Tanya inquired.

He slowly turned to her. "Germany and the Soviet Union have divided Poland and it is not safe to take this train anymore."

"Bet the Polish aren't thrilled about that," she muttered under her breath as she stood and reached for her coat. When everything was prepared, Yuri turned to her once more.

"Now, Miss Berezovsky, your cooperation is needed in this instance, unless of course you would rather become a prisoner of the Germans."

"I'm not quite sure which is worse," she said dryly, and then followed them out the door.

They exited the train quickly and went down the street at a swift pace toward what looked to be a very old hotel. It seemed as though they were about to enter when suddenly, three German foot soldiers came through the front door. Yuri made a swift turn down an alley and they followed it for what seemed like ages. Tanya's feet were aching by the time the alley finally opened up. They were at the edge of the town, and a green meadow lay before them. Beyond it, a vast forest was barely visible through the thick fog that hung very low. Yuri conversed in a low voice with his comrades for a moment before they all nodded. Tanya eyed them suspiciously. This was clearly not a part of the plan.

"The mist will hide us, but it will probably lift very soon. We must hurry," Yuri urged. They began to move forward, but Tanya dug in her heels.

"Absolutely not," she stated firmly. "Walking out into open fields in occupied territory is a very stupid idea. Besides, you all stick out like sore thumbs anywhere." She crossed her arms in determination. "Absolutely not."

Yuri looked at her for a long moment, and then turned to the others and nodded. "We will wait for nightfall," he said flatly.

Tanya nodded, but underneath her composed face her mind was working frantically to form a plan. If there really were soldiers patrolling the tree line, she might have the chance to escape. There was not much time left in her window of opportunity and she had to work fast.

It was getting very cold when they finally stepped out of the alley. The lights from the town behind them illuminated very little, but Tanya knew that even then they could be seen. She glanced around several times as they entered the dark meadow. The waist length grass rustled softly in their wake. An animal scuttled away to their left. She followed the sound with her eyes, watching the grass sway with its movement. The line of trees could hardly be made out in the darkness. Her eyes began to adjust and as they did, she noticed flashes among the trees. Her eyes narrowed in concentration.

German soldiers were patrolling the tree line.

Tanya's brain began working frantically and in an instant, she had an idea. "I have to use the lavatory," she said softly as she turned to Yuri.

"Now?" he asked, exasperated.

"Yes!"

"You can wait until we reach the trees."

"It cannot wait," she pleaded.

He turned to her in frustration and crossed his arms. "Then go."

"I can't with you staring at me!" she said with irritation.

"Fine!"

Yuri waved her away with a huff and whispered fiercely in Russian to his companions. Tanya hurried toward the tree line, and she could feel their eyes on her back. Time slowly ticked by as she allowed herself to disappear in the shadows. She slowed hesitantly as she came to the edge. Broken German whispers were coming from just inside the tree line.

"… shoot?"

"No … just a girl … wait …"

"Hello?" Tanya called out quietly in German.

A dark form detached itself from the shadows just outside of the trees. One hand lay against the bark; the other held a pistol. "Who are you?" asked the man.

"Please," she said as she stepped closer. "Some men were trying to assault me in town. Will you help me?"

He beckoned her slowly forward with one hand and grabbed her arm roughly. Tanya tried to conceal her alarm.

"Your papers?" he whispered.

She produced them quickly. He swung a flashlight over them before giving them back.

"You are lucky Fraulein, that I am as nice as I am. I could have shot you where you stood."

"I was willing to take my chances," she said.

He glanced over her. "You are going somewhere?" he asked, taking in her traveling clothes and bag.

"I am on my way home to Berlin," she stated.

"What were you doing out so late at night?"

"Is that really of consequence?" Tanya said hurriedly. "They will be coming soon."

He hesitated, then took her arm again and said something harshly in German to someone in the trees. Then he led her toward the town. As the light grew she saw that the man was very young. He could not have been much older than herself. She tried conversation as they walked.

"Do you come from Austria?" she asked.

"Germany," he said shortly.

"Near Berlin?"

"No."

"How long have you been in the service?"

"A couple of years now."

"What is your name?"

"You may address me as Lieutenant, Fraulein."

"You seem rather young for a lieutenant ... Lieutenant," she commented, watching him. "How old are you?"

"Old enough," was his short reply.

Tanya shrugged. "I guess communication isn't one of your strong points."

"Words mean nothing unless they are acted upon."

"Oh, so you're a philosopher too!" she exclaimed with a smile. "I like that. If words mean nothing without action, what have you to say about God, who created the universe by merely speaking?"

He stopped and looked at her pointedly. "Fraulein, you waste your time and mine. I am a man of action. Words mean little to me unless I see them brought about. That is why I believe in the Third Reich and in Hitler. He doesn't simply promise things. He acts upon those promises. And that is why we shall win this war."

She stared at him, curious about this boy, or man, or whatever he said he was. As she caught his gaze she saw something change in his eyes, as though the hard shell protecting him from feeling was slowly melting. She smiled softly and continued to walk.

"How patriotic of you." She cleared her throat. "Well, your parents must be very proud of your service."

He grunted and quickened the pace. Within minutes, they reached the train station.

"The next train to Berlin leaves early tomorrow morning," he said. "Is there somewhere you can stay until then?"

Tanya thought of the hotel that Yuri had avoided. "Yes."

"Very well then." He turned and began the walk back down the street.

"Thank you," she called.

He stopped and turned. His shoulders had lost some of their stiffness, and she could see that he was softening slowly once more. "Maybe we will see each other in Berlin sometime, Fraulein. I will soon be transferred there."

Tanya smiled. "I would enjoy that."

He turned back, but she stopped him once more. "Am I not to know the name of my rescuer, then?"

He met her gaze, and Tanya felt her heart jump when his teeth flashed against his dark face as he smiled.

"Dederick van Ostrand."

When Hilda opened her eyes, she cautiously took in her surroundings. She did not recognize the room that she was in or the bed in which she lay. Nor did she recognize the young woman next to her. She tried sitting up but it hurt too much. The woman, who had been asleep, jumped up and gently laid her back against the pillows.

"You need to rest, miss. You have been very weak."

Hilda shook her head. "I have to go. They'll be looking for me."

"No, miss. You have been very weak," she repeated. "The doctor will see you in a moment."

"Doctor? Am I in a hospital?"

"Yes. My father is the doctor here. He will come shortly."

Hilda glanced at her. "How long have I been here?"

"Nearly four days. There was a chance you would not make it through the first night."

Hilda narrowed her eyes in concentration and suddenly, everything came back in a rush. The walk in the park, the pain, being carried somewhere away, and then sleep. Blissful sleep …

"Jesse," she murmured.

"He went out to the airfield this morning. He should be here soon, though, and you can see him then."

"No, no," Hilda said hastily. She tossed back the blankets and stood up slowly, dizzy as she swayed on her feet. The young woman grabbed her arms in alarm.

"No, you mustn't!" she exclaimed. "You'll hurt yourself! Please!"

"I must go," Hilda murmured. Even in her state of health, she was stronger than the other woman, so with minor difficulty she broke free of her and went out into the hall.

"No! Come back!" called the woman as Hilda stumbled down the pristine white hall. An ache began in her stomach, but she continued on.

"Help! Father! Father!"

A door opened next to her, then another.

"What in the world …?" came a woman's voice.

"My god …"

Hilda glanced toward the voices and saw faces peering out of doorways along the hall. In front of her a door opened, letting in a chilly breeze, and footsteps ran toward her. The swift turn of her head made her dizzy and she felt herself falling forward toward another black abyss. Vaguely, she heard the screams and shouts around her. The floor rushed up to meet her and she closed her eyes to enter the oblivion, but strong hands caught her under her arms and lifted her against a solid chest. It did not take much for her to realize that the person holding her was Jesse, and she wrapped her arms around him and closed her eyes as she laid her head against his jacket.

"Don't let me go," she whispered.

"I won't," he promised.

⸻

Dr. Holden came slowly back down the hall to the waiting area where he found Jesse and Mary sitting together on the couch. Jesse jumped up when he came into view, concern on his face, but the doctor waved it away.

"She's resting," he said confidently.

Jesse took a deep breath and walked a few steps away from the two. The whole incident had sapped the strength from him, more than any time that he had spent at the airfield. His brain felt heavy with burdening thoughts and all he wanted to do was sit down and sleep.

He had never run so fast in his life as when he had caught Hilda before she hit the floor. His heart pounded as he held her until the fear in him gradually receded. Jesse closed his eyes and heaved a sigh. When he turned back, John and Mary were staring at him.

"Is something wrong?" he asked.

Mary glanced at John before clearing her throat. "Uh, well, John and I were just wondering about your friend, Jesse."

Jesse swallowed and felt himself slowly getting nervous about this progressing conversation.

"She is a lovely girl," John stated.

"Yes she is, sir."

"How do you know her?"

Jesse shifted in his chair. "Uh, we met a few years ago when I was in Europe visiting her brother."

"Ah," John said with a glance at Mary. "What is her name?"

"Hilda." The name came out even before Jesse had time to think about the question.

"So she is German?" Mary asked.

"No. Yes." Jesse shook himself and cleared his throat. "Um, I mean, yes, she grew up in Germany."

"Interesting," mused Mary. "She looks fairly young. Is there anyone we can contact who knows her? Where are her parents?"

Jesse lowered his head. "Her father is dead and she has not heard from her mother in a long time."

"Oh," she said softly.

There was silence in the room for a long time. John finally cleared his throat and got up. "Well, my dear, I must do my rounds."

"Of course, darling." Mary kissed him goodbye and walked with him a ways down the hallway. Jesse heard their soft murmurings, and then a door opened and closed. A few moments later, Mary came back to the waiting area. She smiled at Jesse.

"Do not worry about your friend, Jesse. She will be just fine, you'll see."

Jesse sat unmoving for a long time and pondered the short conversation. Why had he felt the urge to twist the truth about Hilda? He knew she had something to hide, and he had almost lied about something he did not even know! She had come to him for help and had not even told him what she needed. Questions kept coming up that did not make sense. Why the false name? And where had the gunshot wound come from? Had it been another one of her narrow escapes from death that she had told him about so long ago? Had she been afraid to go to the hospital?

Something clicked in the back of his brain. Meeting Jeffrey at the hospital, and then seeing him again in the café ... what had Grace said? He wracked his brain. Jeffrey worked for the Secret Intelligence Service. He failed to mention he knew Hilda when Jesse brought her up. And that intriguing name ... the Turncoat Spy. Jeffrey had not been pleased to see Jesse at the benefit, and he was beginning to understand why. Things were coming into focus, but Jesse had to be certain. He had to speak with Jeffrey Rolf.

Jesse entered the building hastily and after several moments, he found Jeffrey's secretary sitting as straight as a board at her desk. She looked up and watched him like a hawk from behind her black-rimmed glasses.

"May I help you?" she asked shortly.

"Yes. I would like to speak with Jeffrey Rolf."

Her brows rose at his accent and her eyes narrowed. "Do you have an appointment?"

"Uh ... no, but it is very important."

"So they all say," she muttered. "Your name?"

"Jesse Riker."

She reached for the intercom and announced him. Jesse thanked her and hurried by, ignoring the face she made no attempt to hide as he passed.

Jesse pushed open the door and saw Jeffrey sitting at a desk piled high with papers and files, many of which were stamped across with the word "confidential." The room was sparsely furnished with a file holder, a bookcase, and two chairs in front of the desk. Jeffrey looked up from his work, surprise dawning on his face.

"Captain Riker!" He got up and went around the desk to shake his hand. "This is a pleasant surprise. Is there something I can help you with?"

Jesse nodded. "I need to ask you some questions."

Jeffrey motioned him to sit, and then he took the chair opposite him. "I will do the best I can to answer them," he said.

Jesse sat forward and began. "First of all, what is your connection with Hilda?"

Jeffrey's eyes widened. "Well, you certainly get down to the core of things, don't you?" He sighed deeply. "I had a feeling you would come see me after the benefit."

"How do you know her?" Jesse pressed.

"I was acquainted with her father when she was younger. We met a little over a year ago."

A year ago.

Jesse leaned forward and looked him straight in the eye. "What did you do?"

"I beg your pardon?" Jeffrey looked shocked.

"Her brother wrote to me saying she disappeared without a word over a year ago," he stated.

Jeffery glanced down at his hand. "I know what you want, Jesse, but

119

what you are asking me to say would present dangerous risks to many, including yourself."

Jesse stood up. "Mr. Rolf, you don't understand. This is more than just curiosity. This woman ... she ... I know her better than almost anyone. Probably better than you."

Jeffery narrowed his eyes. "I doubt that."

In an instant, Jesse had him by the lapels and was inches from his face. "Listen to me," he said through clenched teeth. "You have no idea how hard it's been. Her business is my business. And so help me, if you have forced her to do anything—"

"She has done everything of her own accord!" Jeffrey cut in. "I have forced her to do nothing."

"But you no doubt have encouraged her!" Jesse grimaced and abruptly let go of Jeffrey's coat. He ran his hands through his hair as he turned away and gave a deep sigh as he supported himself against the back of the chair. "Who is the Turncoat Spy?"

Jeffrey stared at him for a moment and straightened his jacket. "I would be breaking a million rules telling you that information. But it's not that difficult to figure out. Whoever coined the phrase has no imagination."

"Give it to me straight, Rolf. Is Hilda the Turncoat Spy?"

Jeffrey sighed and folded his arms. "Now that would be impossible, wouldn't it, considering that Hilda van Ostrand is not even German by blood."

Jesse lifted his head in shock, but Jeffrey calmly sat down and placed his hands on his desk, his look sympathetic, as though comforting a lost little boy. "Jesse, listen to me. You apparently know Hilda quite well. If you care for her as much as you imply, you will leave now and keep your questions to yourself. And," he added with emphasis, "stay away from her."

Jesse stared hard at him for a long moment before turning abruptly and leaving the office. He had to get out. Now.

Jeffrey watched him leave tensely. As soon as he was gone, he picked up the phone on his desk and dialed a number. Riker was getting too deep, and too many questions almost always led to disastrous consequences. One thought pleased Jeffrey more than the others. Jesse Riker did not know Hilda as well as he imagined.

When the voice came on the other line, Jeffrey said, "I need you to have a man ready for me right now. The hospital. I have a pick up."

Jesse wandered in the park all afternoon musing over the day's events. Hilda, Angelis, whoever she was, was somehow connected with Jeffrey Rolf, which meant that she must also be somehow connected with the SIS. A dark thought entered his mind. What if she was a spy for Germany, passing along military secrets? Would she really do that for her country, even if she did not respect the leader? Jesse remembered when Hilda had told him how much she wanted to serve. Was this where her loyalty had led her?

He found himself at her bedside moments later. Never taking his eyes from her face, Jesse sat down in the chair next to her bed and watched her even breathing. She seemed so peaceful outwardly, but he knew a torment of emotions raged within her.

"What secrets have you kept from me, my love?" he whispered. "Why did you not confide in me?"

The most shocking news was that Hilda was not German by blood. Where had Jeffrey come by that information, if it was even true at all? Had he simply said that to shake his faith in Hilda? Where did she belong, if not in Germany? *She belongs with me, who loves her.*

Jesse was determined to learn the truth from her the moment she was strong enough. Something was not right. Not only about Hilda, but about her father as well. It was strange that Jeffrey knew of him. Had her father in some way been involved in this whole mess as well? Jesse shook his head and looked up as Dr. Holden entered quietly.

"Mary just rang," the doctor murmured. "Supper's ready. She's in good hands, lad. Don't you worry. You'll see her tomorrow."

Jesse took a deep breath and tried not to think about what the next few days would bring. Instead he got up and kissed Hilda's forehead lightly, then followed Dr. Holden out the door. He knew that even if he tried to plan a way to bring the subject into the conversation, it would not go any way he imagined. No matter, the questions would soon be answered.

But it was not to be. When Jesse returned to the hospital the next morning, the bed was made, the room was completely clean and not one mark remained of someone having been there. Hilda was gone.

"Where is she?"

The courier pointed to a door on his left in the dim hallway. Jeffrey entered and shut the door behind him. The room was dark and the moon shone in through the window onto a bed where Hilda lay, pale as the sheet over her in a restless slumber. He knew that she would be startled awake by anything so he quietly whispered her name. Her eyes jerked open, but she did not move.

"Jeffrey?"

"Yes?"

"Is it all right?" she asked, staring up at the ceiling.

"Yes."

She sighed. "And your man?"

"He was just supposed to locate you and bring you here."

Hilda turned her eyes to him then. She looked angry, but it was a pitiful anger to him.

"I was going to come back soon," she said shortly.

"The longer you stayed there, the more danger you put them in."

"They wouldn't let me leave!" she insisted.

"You could have found a way," Jeffrey returned.

"I was trying!"

They stared at each other for a long time before she finally turned away and stared out the window. Jeffrey waited a few moments and then sat down in the chair next to her bed.

"How do you know him?"

Hilda turned to him. "Excuse me?"

"How do you know Jesse Riker?"

She hesitated for a long moment. "Why do you wish to know?"

"It's important."

Hilda sighed. "He is a friend of my brother. We spent a few months together in Germany. I have not seen him in several years."

Jeffrey waited for her to go into more detail, but she simply closed her eyes once more.

"Tell me the truth, Hilda."

"That is the truth."

"Not all of it."

She turned her head sharply toward him and her eyes flashed. "Why can't you just leave it alone, Jeffrey? It is in the past. I am here now and it's over."

Jeffrey leaned forward. "Hilda, I need to know."

"No you don't. It is none of your business."

The silence could be cut with a knife. Jeffrey knew that he would not get any more out of her on the subject, so he cleared his throat. "How is your wound?"

"It would have been fine if your doctor had treated it properly."

"You were up too soon."

"Wasn't it you who thought it would be good for me to get out and be seen at the theatre?"

"I only thought that it would be wise for you to be seen as healthy," Jeffrey said.

"Well I'm not, am I?"

More silence followed.

"You don't need to worry, Jeffrey. I will not be seeing him again."

He sighed and stood up. "You are a good agent Hilda, and to lose you would be a great tragedy. You must be very careful." He opened the door and was about to step outside.

"I know what I'm doing, Jeffrey."

"I know you do, but I don't want you to get hurt again."

She pierced him with her stare.

"I won't."

14

The sun hung low in the sky as Hilda aimlessly walked the streets of London. A few wisps of blonde hair blew freely in the wind and she tucked them underneath her navy and white hat. Several formally dressed couples walked past on their way to elegant restaurants before attending the theatre. She sighed deeply as she continued on toward home where she knew Jeffrey would be waiting for her. She had invited him over to dinner that night after finally easing the tension between them. She passed through Kensington Garden and paused in front of the statue of Peter Pan.

Hilda sat down on a bench and placed her hands in her lap. It had been several weeks since she had last seen Jesse and since then, she had felt as imprisoned as a bird in a cage. His face had remained constantly in her mind and she wondered if he was okay. She knew that he had come to join the Eagle Squadron as a volunteer. Having visited the hospital often, she had seen the dangers that it presented. Throughout her time as an agent for the SIS, she had faced several dangers and learned to cut herself off from any emotion during an assignment. When the danger involved a close friend, however, she could not help but be afraid.

Hilda still loved Jesse. She knew that without a doubt. There had been a time when she thought that she did not love him anymore, that their time together had been nothing more than a silly romance, but seeing him again after so many years had only intensified the feelings that she hid for so long. Hilda also knew the extreme danger that she put him in should her enemies find out. She had to keep her distance. Letting Jesse close could mean his death. And hers.

❦

Jeffrey stood as Hilda entered her apartment. Without a word, he came over and hugged her. She knew that there was so much to be said in that embrace, but he could be so hard to read sometimes.

"I was beginning to worry," he said.

"I just took a few minutes to wander in the park for a bit."

They sat down on the couch and Hilda picked up the tea that Jeffrey poured for her. "What is my new assignment?"

Jeffrey leaned forward. "We're sending you back to France. We think you can do the most good there."

"Paris?"

Jeffrey pinned her with his gaze. "Yes Hilda, but you must be careful. You remember what happened last time. You nearly got killed because of your folly."

Hilda turned her eyes to meet his. Her face was full of pain. "I couldn't stand by and watch while those Nazi devils rolled down the street," she whispered. "Speaking out was the only weapon I had against them. I wasn't the only one who was angry."

Jeffrey put his arm around her and sighed. "I know. But it nearly got you killed. I can't lose you. You're too important."

"As what, an agent?" she said dryly.

"No!" he said. "You're important to *me*, Hilda. As a person. I ... I care about you."

Hilda met his gaze with a start, her eyes wide. "I ... I'm not sure I know what you mean."

"You mean a great deal to me, Hilda. You must know that. I've come to care for you more than anything. Every time we send you into the field, I'm so afraid that you won't come back." Jeffrey sighed heavily and ran his hands through his hair. "Hilda, I'm falling in love with you and I can't stop it."

Hilda could only stare at him in shock. The thought had never registered that another man might love her. She had heard men say she was beautiful, but only Jesse had ever loved her. Her breathing grew shaky as his hands cupped her face.

"I ... I can't stand it anymore," he said huskily.

"Please, Jeffrey ..." she whispered, her eyes closing in torment.

"Let me, Hilda. Please, let me."

His lips met hers tentatively and she trembled at the touch. His arms encircled her and pressed closer and closer until there was not even air between them. He was so gentle, and it seemed to Hilda that he could not be serious. Jesse had been so passionate in his affection that day they said good-bye and she did not know anything else. She had been thrilled with his love, but she also knew the danger of it. Comparing the two men, she knew Jeffrey was the safer, more predictable one.

But she had given her promise.

Abruptly, Hilda pulled away. Jeffrey immediately released her, but remained close. "I'm sorry, Hilda. I could not help it. I have wanted to do that since the day I met you."

She turned to him. "Jeffrey, please. I ... I'm very flattered, but ... I can't."

He sighed and nodded. "I understand, Hilda. But I can wait. I will wait."

Wait for me, Hilda. Wait for me.

She shook herself and stood up. "No you won't. You love the woman you know, but there is so much more that you will never understand." Hilda turned away from him. "I'll stop by the office tomorrow and pick up the files. Thank you for telling me."

Jeffrey stared at her with a small look of pain in his eyes. She hated to hurt him, but she had to be alone and sort her thoughts before her mind lost control.

He stood and took a small step closer. "Hilda ..."

He was cut off by a distant rumbling sound that grew louder with every second.

"What on earth?" Hilda went to the window. Pulling back the curtain, she looked out toward the channel and saw several dark shapes flying toward London.

"Jeffrey?"

"Yes?"

"Does the RAF run drills this time of day?"

He slowly made his way over to her side and followed her gaze. "My god," he whispered.

Hilda realized it at the same moment. They bolted into the hallway and started pounding on other doors.

"Get underground!" Hilda yelled as families in the middle of supper opened their doors. She heard Jeffrey screaming at people in the lobby and on the stairs. She raced through apartments looking for anyone who might still be inside. People, seeing the planes, were screaming as they raced down the stairs to the basement. Women grasped their babies to their bosoms and older teens led their younger siblings with a firm hand. Outside, sirens began to wail a warning of the coming attack.

"Hilda!" Jeffrey was fighting the downward flow to reach her. "Hilda, come on!"

Hilda ignored him as she reached the last few rooms. She threw open a door and stopped in her tracks. A little boy no more than five years old stood alone in the middle of his living room and stared up at her wide-eyed. Behind him, the huge window filtered brilliant evening light onto the floor and silhouetted in the light, the planes slowly got bigger and bigger, so big that she could see the pea green color and the swastika painted on the tail wing. She grabbed the child tightly and turned around to find Jeffrey standing in the doorway. His eyes widened and he yelled, "Get down!"

Hilda dropped to the floor with the boy beneath her mere seconds before a loud explosion split through the air and the window behind her shattered, scattering thousands of shards of glass in every direction. Some pieces bit into her back, but she ignored the sharp pain as she struggled to get up. Jeffrey took the child easily and led them down the stairs where they joined the others huddled in the basement. A relieved mother came up to collect her child and thanked them through tears.

"He just slipped away in the confusion," she stammered as she clutched the boy to her.

"He'll be all right," Hilda said with a smile. She and Jeffrey were able to find a corner away from the others in the crowded basement. Above them, the bombs continued to drop on London, beginning the first of many long nights of destruction from the German-filled skies.

As they sat in silence, some trying to sleep, Hilda wondered if Jesse and his friends were all right. They had to be preparing for a counter attack. She wondered about her mother and brothers. Ever since she left, she wondered about them and kept them close in her thoughts and heart. God only knew what was truly going on in Germany. The only home she had ever known.

Hilda did not notice Jeffrey staring at her until he murmured her name and she turned to him. He looked at her strangely.

"What?" she asked quietly.

He took a breath, but did not let it out for a long time.

"Jeffrey?"

He took her hands and finally asked, "Do you know how your father died?"

Hilda started at his question. She felt his hands tighten on hers as she looked away in slight confusion. She had always had her suspicions about her father's death, but she had eventually put them aside to move on with her life, and then she had met Jesse and they had all faded away.

"Do you?"

She shook her head hesitantly. "No. Jeffrey, I'm not sure I like where this is going."

"You need to know."

"Know what?"

"The truth."

"Father, supper is almost ready. Mother says Cook made your favorite."

Frederick van Ostrand looked up from his desk as Hilda came running into his office. Her curly brown hair was tied back with a bright red ribbon that matched her skirt perfectly. She ran over to him and hugged him tightly before hurrying out of the study at her mother's call. He heard her yell upstairs for Dederick, then the pounding of his youngest son as he ran down the stairs. Frederick smiled softly and sat back in his chair. Paul had been in America for more than a year and he missed his strong quiet presence. There was a void in his heart that could only be filled by his son. Of course, he was not the only person to be missing him; the entire family felt his absence, Hilda especially. The two had always been very close and she relied on him for so much.

Frederick sighed and closed his eyes. Thinking of Hilda brought him back to the torment he had faced for little more than a year. He thought back on the day he had gone to the convent to meet with the mother superior. He could understand her uncertainty in giving him the note that had accompanied the child. Now with the suspicion of the Nazis hanging over him, he had to be more careful than ever. He knew that his life was already on the line for corresponding with British Intelligence, but he knew that they were the only ones that he could trust with his daughter's past. The Nazis were on his tail, so close that he could feel the muzzles of their guns against his neck. Every time he went out, he felt their eyes burning into him, drilling holes into his back that he felt would soon be there. There was no escaping what was to come, and he knew it.

"Father?"

Frederick looked up and saw Dederick standing in the doorway. "Father, we are all waiting for you."

Frederick stood and smiled. "Of course, Dederick. I'll be right there."

His son disappeared from the doorway and Frederick turned back to his desk to examine the pile of papers, the incriminating evidence that would be the death of him. It had all been such innocent curiosity at first, yet how quickly it had spiraled out of control. He only hoped he had not put his precious daughter in danger.

Frederick took a small box from his desk and put the documents inside. After a moment's thought, he took his journal, placed the documents within the pages and wrapped the entire package in brown paper. He scribbled an address on it and hid it inside his jacket. He shut off the light, closed the door to the study, and locked it behind him. Sending up a prayer, he turned to go to supper. The night held many things that would determine his future, and Hilda's.

Something was bothering her father. Hilda had been able to tell when she had come into his office telling him that supper was ready and then he had hardly touched his food during the meal. Even though he had joined in the conversation around the table, his eyes had been distant and distracted. Now as she sat in her bedroom at her desk, the bothering feeling came back to her. It had happened several times. Her father constantly stared at her when he thought she was not looking. Every time he did, she noticed the look in his eyes. It was one of sadness and longing, and yet there was also a sense of great pride and joy at what he saw. He had so much on his mind lately, with Paul gone and Dederick engrossed in his involvement with the Hitler Youth. He was worried about many things beyond her understanding. Her concern for him growing, she pulled out her journal and turned to a fresh page.

February 5, 1934

Hannah wasn't at school today because she has been sick, so I sent her a box of my homemade cookies. I still miss Paul very much, but he continues to write to me as often as he can. I am quite intrigued by his American friend, the pilot. Paul says that he might even be able to arrange a visit. It would be so exciting to meet a real American. I can't wait for him to come home.

Father has been acting very queer lately. When he thinks I am not looking, I see so much despair in his eyes, and sometimes I even hear him crying. I hope he is all right.

Hilda laid down her pen, prepared to go find her father. Before she could move, she heard the front door close quietly below her. Turning her eyes to her window, she saw the figure of her father going down the pathway. His shoulders were slumped and his hat was pulled low over his eyes. Her heart sank. He would probably not be back before she went to bed. As she turned from the window, she noticed something else. Another figure had detached itself from the shadows and was following her father slowly as he walked down the street. Hilda wondered at this for a long moment and she tried to think of who it might be. But she was so tired and could not think straight. Father would be fine. He knew how to take care of himself. Tomorrow morning, bright and early, she would ask him what was wrong.

Frederick quickened his pace as he walked down the street. A quick glance over his shoulder told him that the man was still behind him. The night seemed to close in around him and choke him in its black clutches. It was like a warning. A threat.

He never wanted to get into any of this. All he wanted was to grow old and watch his children get married and have their own kids. He sat down on a bench and put his head in his hands. He was done. He did not want any more to do with any of it. He wanted Hilda to grow up like any other normal child and live to a ripe old age with no Nazis breathing down her neck. He just wanted her to be happy.

Footsteps sounded closer. His shadow, he knew. Frederick was about to look up when he heard an engine come roaring down the street. This was it. He took a deep breath and made a quick decision. He pulled the package out of his coat and scribbled a quick note on the back. No one, not even the British, could know its contents. It had to be Hilda. He dropped it softly underneath the bench he sat on, where it blended into the darkness, just as a car pulled up to the curb and two officers hopped out followed by an inspector. The footsteps of his shadow quickly faded away.

The inspector stepped forward as Frederick stood up. They seemed to size each other up for a moment. Frederick was much taller and broader, but the inspector also had his officers.

"Herr Frederick van Ostrand?" the inspector asked coolly.

"Yes," Frederick replied.

"You will come with us, please," he stated, gesturing to the open door of the car.

Frederick stared at that door for a long time and studied the inky blackness that waited beyond it. He began walking toward it as if in a dream. He did not feel any part of his body. He was watching himself from a distance as he got in the car that he knew led to his death. There was no emotion, no despair or hysterics. Just ... nothing. He was completely calm as he was led into the Nazi headquarters and brought before a panel of officials who sat in full regalia. The inspector sat him in a hard wooden chair before the table and Frederick waited. Waited for the inevitable to be said. Waited for the pointing finger that held the ultimate accusation. Waited for the long, long, short walk down the dimly lit hall that haunted the nightmares of every person who dared to go against the Reich. Frederick took a deep breath and let it out quietly.

"Herr van Ostrand," began the official that sat at the middle of the table, "you have been brought here to answer to accusations made by several members of the Third Reich. Your actions have been reported and are as follows: operation under cover with unnamed foreign countries, fraternizing with intelligence personnel of the United Kingdom, and conspiring against the German government. You are hereby charged with high treason against the Third Reich, a sentence that carries the death penalty. Do you have anything to say in your defense?"

Frederick remained calm as he looked up at the man, whose face and voice had remained blank during the entire charge. "Is there any hope for me should I give one?"

The official raised an eyebrow. "I doubt it."

Frederick nodded as if in understanding. "Then no, sir, I do not have anything to say."

The official looked surprised for a moment and then shook himself. "Very well. Herr van Ostrand, you are guilty of treason against the Third Reich and will this night be executed by firing squad. Take the prisoner away."

The two officers brought him to his feet and began to follow the inspector out, but Frederick turned back to the table once more. "Please, sir, my family does not know of my dealings and I would be grateful if it was kept that way." With that, he turned and preceded the officers through the doorway. He was led down the dim hallway and out to the closed in yard. Frederick thought of the others who had been led to this point, this wall in their life that blocked them from what might have been. There was a time in every person's life where they had to choose, and Frederick had made his choice.

He was not afraid as they stood him against the wall, only sorry that he had put his innocent child at risk from his own curiosity. He was not afraid as he heard the squad march in front of him, only hoped that his shadow would find the package and deliver it one day to his dear Hilda. He was not afraid as the officer called out his orders, only felt peace and held a prayer in his heart for his precious family. He prayed that they would prosper and that Hilda would live to know the truth and understand his love for her. A final command was shouted, the guns fired, and Herr Frederick van Ostrand fell to the ground, dead.

"Years, following years, steal something every day;
At last they steal us from ourselves away."

Horace

15

August 1940

J esse had never seen such serious faces on the men of the Eagle Squadron as they prepared their planes for flight. Not a word could be heard on the still air of the autumn evening as tanks were filled, guns were loaded and planes were brought to life. Somber officers stood by as the pilots hurried to their planes. Jesse joined the flow of men and ran to his plane. When he was given the all clear, he headed for the runway. Behind him, his wingman and friend Josh Sauders followed. Jesse's hands clenched as he followed the other planes into the sky. The London bombing had been severe, killing many and leaving families homeless and without food. Worst of all, he did not know if Hilda was all right. He had not seen her since she disappeared from the hospital and though he had tried to find her, it was obvious that she, mostly likely with Jeffrey's blessing, had no wish to be found. At this point, Jesse would be happy just to know that she was alive.

The planes grouped into tight formation as they flew through the overcast English sky and across the Channel toward Germany. They were going to Berlin. And they were going to bomb it.

Hilda watched the rain fall on the streets of London from the hospital porch. Even from where she stood, the smoke could still be seen rising from the debris of the city.

She had known that something like this would eventually happen. Germany was capable of many air attacks; they had already carried out raids on various RAF airfields and radar stations. But now it seemed they were determined to see the morale of London shattered in ceaseless bombings. Thousands were homeless and fires still burned threateningly throughout the city. Hilda shut her eyes tightly and sent up a prayer for Jesse. Wherever he was, the RAF's response to this attack would be swift and brutal, and no doubt he would be a part of it. Her heart clenched at the thought of him in danger. His capture, or worse, death, was not something she wished to consider.

Germany's attack triggered many new avenues of retaliation, and the SIS had taken all into consideration. Hitler obviously presented a tough challenge from the air, but what they did not know was if the Germans could invade by land. It would all depend on what they were told.

Hilda sighed and touched the back of her shoulder gently. The nurse had told her that the stitches would come out within the week, but to be careful. She laughed shortly. Be careful. She was going to France in mere days and that was anything but careful.

The evening was settling in as she put on her coat and prepared to go back home. A cab waited for her at the curb and the driver waved at her. She hurried over, climbed in, and closed the door against the rain. Turning, she discovered Jeffrey sitting next to her. Their eyes met. She could not say anything.

"Hilda, please ..." he began.

"What are you doing here?"

"I had to see that you were okay."

"It's only a few scratches, Jeffrey. Nothing to be worried about."

"Hilda ..." Jeffrey stopped, unsure of how to continue. He looked down at his hands for a moment, and Hilda turned to look out the window.

"There is nothing for us to talk about, Jeffrey." She sighed and closed her eyes against the pain. "I have nothing to say to you."

"What more can I say than I am sorry?" he asked miserably.

"Six years," she whispered. "For six years I have wondered, had my suspicions." She turned to him, her eyes full of anguish. "How could you know and not tell me?"

"I ... I wanted to protect you." Jeffrey's eyes pleaded with her. "It was your father's wish, Hilda. He didn't want you to get hurt."

"Didn't want me to get hurt? Jeffrey, I was shot at four times within a year of my father's death. I was under the constant threat of being arrested by the Gestapo. I lived and breathed danger long before I met you." She stopped and leaned her head back against the seat. A single tear slipped down her cheek. "I didn't even get to say good-bye."

Jeffrey's arm was around her in an instant and they were both quiet for a long time. Hilda's tears fell silently down her cheeks and the emptiness that she had felt when her father died returned painfully in that moment. She felt her heart clench in her stomach from the agony of not being able to give her father a hug and tell him she loved him. She thought she would break from the torment of it all.

"I'm sorry, Hilda," Jeffrey whispered. "I'm so sorry."

The cab pulled up to the curb next to Hilda's building, mercifully spared from extensive damage during the air raid. She stepped out without a word and closed the door. From a distance she heard the cab pull away, but her mind was blank. She stared absentmindedly at the note on her door from the landlord telling her that her rent was overdue. Her suitcase lay on her bed in the process of being packed. Her window was covered with plastic wrapping, as it had broken during the bombings. In just a few days she was going to France, and she would be able to forget all about the conversation with Jeffrey and focus on her work. She could forget it all.

But the dawn of her departure arrived, and Hilda lay in bed wide awake and watched as the sun rose slowly over the city. She had not slept a wink the whole night. Her brain was cluttered with thoughts that would not go away and they had plagued her to no end. Her father's death had never held so much pain as it did now. She was angry, yes, but there was more sorrow than anger. In the past, she had been able to think about that awful time without being extremely affected. Now that she knew the truth, she got an ache in her gut at the mere mention of him.

Jeffrey was another problem. Hilda could hardly look at him anymore without feeling pain. Ever since he had told her of his feelings, she always felt as though she was walking on eggshells around him. So much changed after that night and she did not think their relationship could ever be as it was before.

And Jesse ...

A very distant rumbling broke into her thoughts and she sat up quickly.

The sound was very soft, so soft that anyone who was sleeping would never hear it. She turned to her window and saw, very far away, a contingent of planes making their way toward the airfield on the outskirts of the city. Hilda sighed with relief. The bombs had been dropping on London every day since the first raid and caused no end of terror and confusion among the citizens. But these planes were clearly RAF, and from the way they slowly limped above London, they were returning from a mission. She watched them for a long time.

Jesse was most likely among them. Hilda wondered if he too felt the strange effect of the first battle, as she had returning from her first mission. Was he queasy, as she had been? Her first kill had been even worse. Jeffrey could not talk sense to her for nearly a week. Shedding another human being's blood, whether in the service of king and country or not, changed a person forever. She had friends in Berlin; had they suffered from the recent raid on their great city? And what of her family? Were they safe? There was no end to the thoughts running around her head as she rubbed her face and turned to the new task at hand. Her identity cards lay on the dresser, ready to make Hilda van Ostrand disappear as she once more returned to France.

It seemed a miracle to her that she managed to retain a grasp on reality despite the barrage of personas she took on. Hilda van Ostrand, Angelis Chevalier, Hilda Pendair ... each name shook her to the core and questioned where she belonged. And as she glanced at herself in the mirror, she did not think she would ever find the answer.

There was absolutely no excuse to be inside on that fine afternoon in Paris. While the air still emanated a chill, the sun was shining from a cloudless sky and not a breath of wind stirred the trees. Angelis Chevalier ran her finger around the rim of her teacup and casually turned her glance over the people walking up and down the sidewalk. The street side café was bustling with people, but she still managed to find a corner to herself where she could see everything. Down the street, the Eiffel Tower loomed high up into the clouds, the glory of Paris.

Carefully studying the men and women that sat around her, Angelis wondered how they could be so oblivious. They went on with their daily lives, unaware of the control over them. They were puppets that waited to be moved, ready to wave as more Germans marched into Paris. She twisted a piece of dark rich red hair around one finger and took a sip of her tea. The change in her disguise had been necessary after the failure of her last mission. Full red lips were accented against her pale skin and sharp green eyes closed discreetly, as if mesmerized by the taste of the drink. Her dark green suit was spotless and her hat was pulled low over her eyes.

Angelis was well aware of the man who sat down opposite her even before he entered the café.

"Do you mind?" he asked, gesturing to the chair. "Everywhere else is full."

She shook her head.

"It's fairly warm today, don't you think?" he asked casually.

"It's not bad, considering the time of year," she stated before she took another sip of tea.

"How long have you been in Paris?"

"A few days now."

He casually pulled out a box of Camels. "Cigarette?"

"Thank you." She took the cigarette he offered her, but did not light it.

He lit his own cigarette and then stood from his chair. "Well, enjoy Paris," he said with a smile. Leaning forward, he added softly, "Cheerio."

Angelis acknowledged his departure with a nod of her head and a smile. A few minutes after he left, she dropped some money on the table and continued down the street. After a few moments, she stopped at a bench in the park to sit for a while. It was off by itself and after a quick lowered glanced around, she pulled from her purse the cigarette that the man had offered her. She removed the thin white veneer and pulled a piece of paper out of the tiny metal tube beneath it:

Hitler planning invasion of Britain: Operation Sea Lion. Not absolute. Report to contact.

Angelis studied the note for several seconds. Casually, she took a matchbox from her purse and another cigarette. This one she lit and with the lingering flame, she burned the message and the white veneer. With that, she stood and made her way back to her flat.

The evening was cool and crisp when Angelis left several hours later, now dressed in a black sparkling gown and mink. The ball at the Embassy was the place to be that night. Everyone who was anybody in the government would be there. It was the perfect opportunity to meet with her contact. So many people around would make them unnoticeable and there was always the possibility that she could hear other news.

Angelis let the servant take her mink and entered the ballroom. Several officers turned their heads as she walked to the refreshment table for a drink. She had leaned toward dangerous and mysterious tonight. Her red hair hung partly free in thick curls and her make-up was dark and richly colored. Her dress was daringly low and emphasized her curves. Sparkling diamonds glittered at her throat and wrists.

After lingering a moment longer she left the ballroom, took the stairs to the second floor and went out onto one of the balconies for some fresh air.

"Ravishing, my dear, simply ravishing."

Angelis rolled her eyes and turned her head to look at the speaker. His French was smooth and rolled off his tongue like honey.

"Jacques, this is a business meeting, not romancing time."

"Ah, you're no fun, Angelis." He laughed and came up behind her. His arms teased around her waist and he kissed her neck just below her jaw.

Angelis turned around and pushed him away. "Do stop. There are more serious matters at hand." She wiped her neck and turned back to the railing. Jacques joined her.

"Hitler is planning an invasion of England, code name Sea Lion. It's not definite, but the plans are being processed."

Jacques lit a cigarette and inhaled thoughtfully. "I leave for England tomorrow night," he said. "I can get it to SIS. They have a man who's on top of it. He'll take care of it."

"How can you be sure?" she asked, irritated at his confidence.

"How can anybody be in this business?"

The music and laughing voices from the ballroom flitted out of the windows below them, and Angelis turned discreetly and checked the doors to the balcony, but not a soul was in sight. A few couples drunkenly danced out into the garden below, and the girls laughed as soldiers pulled them awkwardly toward the shadows. Angelis felt nausea begin to build in her stomach.

"How do they stand it?"

"Ah, my dear, but that is the way of the French. Adaptable, accommodating, survivors to the end," Jacques murmured, drawing on his cigarette. "Rather like me."

"You are a fighter, Jacques."

"Am I?" His eyes glanced thoughtfully down on the scene. The merriment continued and Angelis looked away. She did not understand her contact; she never had from the moment they first met. But then, how could she when she did not even know his real name?

"The higher ups have sent word," he continued suddenly before he took another drag. "You will be based outside of Versailles as a contact. There is a small contingent there whose leader has just been killed. He did not talk, so they are still relatively safe to continue their work, but you will be taking over."

"How long?"

Jacques shrugged. "They don't tell me the details. You'll receive word when you are scheduled to fly out. Until then, you're staying with an old family friend, Julian Rousseau."

Angelis stared at him. "Rousseau? But that could be traced back ..."

"Don't say another word," he interrupted. "I don't want to hear it. You've got a problem with some connection to your real life, you take it up with the big boys. I'm just your contact." He gave a resigned smile. "Au revoir, mon cher, and good luck."

Jacques flicked his cigarette over the balcony, turned promptly, and disappeared as quickly as he had arrived. Angelis watched him go with pity. Jacques had nothing to live for, so putting himself in constant danger was just another part of his day. His heart was not in his job, but he was equally unafraid of death. Her heart clenched as he disappeared. So much depended on the information he carried.

Angelis sighed and went downstairs to collect her coat. Her work here was done. Versailles awaited her, and whatever happened after that ...

As she took her coat from the maid, she was aware of a group of men in dress uniforms smoking and talking just outside of the ballroom. She caught a bit of their casual conversation.

"Yes, the regiment in Poland should be on leave soon."

"They've been there so long, they deserve some time in our great capital."

Angelis tried so hard to hear what came next, but they moved on to other topics. On leave from Poland. Dederick had to be in Berlin, then. She walked slowly out of the Embassy. She had not thought of her family in a while, especially her younger brother. She wondered if Paul and Hannah were married, or if Dederick had a lady friend. She laughed softly at the thought. He was still such a boy in many ways, though he would not admit it. She doubted he allowed himself time for romance.

It took her much longer to get home than it had to reach the Embassy.

Angelis wandered, looking in shop windows and walking through the parks. Her hands were beginning to turn cold, and she dug them into her warm coat pockets. The cool autumn nights were in full swing. Whatever danger they brought remained to be seen.

16

November 1940

Dear Dad,

It's hard to explain how different things are here than back at home, but then you would know. As you have probably heard, London has been the target of endless air raids over the past few months. There is so much fighting. Sometimes we won't go a day without going up. It gets very tiring sometimes, but then, it is war.

We're going up again this afternoon, though I can't say where. Pray for us, Dad. It's really hard sometimes.

Still no word from Hilda, but I know she is in God's hands, so I cannot be afraid.

Send my love to Mom and Christina. I love you all.

Your son,
Jesse

"Hey Jesse, you about ready?" Josh asked as he grabbed his goggles.

"Yes," he replied, folding the letter and putting it in an envelope. He stood up and grabbed his goggles and jacket. "Let's go."

The two ran out to the planes. Josh glanced at the coordinates as they went and Jesse could see he was nervous. He knew that Josh still struggled with each mission and he was ill at ease more often than not every time they took to the skies. Jesse smiled and smacked him lightly on the shoulder. "No worries, Josh. It's just the same as any other mission. Remind me of the coordinates of the artillery factories again." Anything to get his friend's mind off the danger they were flying into.

Josh was good with numbers and maps, and it calmed him down as they climbed into their plane. He taped the coordinates to the control panel in front of Jesse. All around them, men were shouting orders and waving the planes to the runway. Within minutes, they were taxiing alongside their comrades and then they were in the sky.

With each mission to Germany, the crossing seemed faster to Jesse. Before he knew it the order came to prepare the artillery. Josh glanced at him and gave a quick nod before scurrying to the back of the plane. In mere minutes, the noise around them was deafening.

The loud explosions from the ground artillery rose up as the bombers flew over Berlin. Jesse tried to keep the plane steady as Josh found the targets below. All around them, bombs whistled as they fell to the ground and ripped into the artillery factories and airfields that surrounded the city. Josh locked onto his target and reached for his controls.

"Bombs away!" Jesse yelled into the radio.

"One away! Two away! Three away!" Josh shouted over the noise.

Jesse's ears drummed with each explosion, and he watched as a plane on his right was hit and went down, crashing into one of the factories in a ball of flames. He jerked his head away and focused on his own flying.

"Bombs away!" Josh yelled.

"Bombs away, copy!" he affirmed.

At the signal, the planes turned to return to base, their bellies empty of their destructive cargo. Jesse was beginning to breathe easier when a last blast of artillery fire ripped into their right wing and took out one of their engines.

"We're hit!" he cried.

"Hold her steady!" Josh called from the back as he scrambled to the cockpit to join Jesse. "Get up in the clouds!"

Once they were a safe distance from the city, Jesse lowered their altitude and took in the damage. The engine sputtered in and out before going silent. He grabbed the radio and spoke quickly but calmly.

"Mayday, mayday. We're hit. Our right engine has failed. Mayday." Jesse turned to Josh. "Where are we?"

Josh grabbed the map. "Nearing Frankfurt." He checked the gages.

"Fuel is dropping, slowly. We might be able to make it to the coast. I don't know."

Jesse checked the gages himself and gripped the wheel. The two men glanced at each other and Jesse took a deep breath, searching the sky. "Okay Josh, no more radio. We need to be as invisible as possible. Check our fuel cans; see what we have." Josh shook his head slowly but crawled toward the back of the plane to do his bidding.

An early autumn darkness fell around them, and Jesse pushed the very present danger away and let himself dwell on the never too far thought of Hilda. He knew that she was working undercover, but his real question was how she had gotten from Germany as a simple young woman to England as a spy. He sensed that there was some motive that had pushed her to where she was. She obviously had not told anyone about it, including her family. For all they knew, she could be dead. Hilda was hiding something, and it was more than just espionage. He had known it from the moment she met him in the park.

Jesse's thoughts continued to dwell on her and he remembered all of the times that they had had together so long ago. Life had seemed so much simpler when he had visited Germany. Now he was afraid of what he would find should he ever set foot there again. His hands trembled. Each mission over Germany left him with a sick feeling and he prayed the van Ostrand family was somewhere safe. He thanked God that no mission to Heidelberg had ever been planned. He would not make it to the plane, even if someone forced him.

Josh interrupted his thoughts a few moments later and took the seat next to Jesse quietly as he reached for the map once more. "All the cans in the back are empty."

Jesse nodded. It had been a far reach to believe they would have extra fuel. Supplies were thin as it was. The plane sputtered and coughed, and Jesse glanced down at the gages.

"Pray we reach the coast and soon, or we'll be in a pretty sticky situation."

Josh threw the map down and looked out the window of the plane before dropping his head for a second. He looked back at Jesse, his calm beginning to waver.

"Yeah. We'll be dead."

Angelis hurried to the stove when the kettle began to whistle. She took the pot off the fire and poured the hot water into two mugs to prepare the tea. She hummed to herself as she listened to the rhythm of the wind on the little cottage. The door opened, bringing in a gust that whipped at the candles and fire, along with Julian's hunched frame. He quickly shut the door and hung up his coat, scarf, and hat.

"How was it in town?" she asked.

"As blustery as it is here. Not much activity at all." He dropped a bag on the kitchen counter. "The carrots you asked for."

Angelis smiled. "Thank you. I have some tea to warm you up."

"Ah, you spoil me, girl." But he laughed and took the cup she offered him. He settled down in a chair next to the fire with his newspaper and read as she prepared the evening meal. "I'm surprised that there is any air activity today," he stated as he read.

Angelis looked up from where she was putting the carrots in boiling water. "The planes went up today?"

"All afternoon, actually. Going somewhere east of here."

"For a mission?"

"What else?"

Angelis went silent after that, but her mind was still working. Was Jesse up there, right now? Was he safe? Not a day went by that she did not think about him. The constant fear within her came not from the danger that she put herself in, but the thought of not seeing him again. She shuddered.

In a few minutes the soup was ready. Supper was a quiet meal and went by fairly quickly. Julian thanked her politely before going back to his paper.

"I'll be back late tonight. Don't wait up," Angelis said as she put on her coat, gloves and hat.

"Be safe," he called from his chair.

"I will."

Angelis stepped out into the howling wind and climbed into the old truck parked outside. After a couple of false starts, the car finally ran smoothly and she pulled away from the cottage and out to the road leading into the city.

The wind pressed against Jesse's back as he plowed through the trees away from the main road. Josh moaned against him, and the gash on his leg grew darker with blood by the second. Headlights flashed through the trees and he ducked, bringing Josh down with him, but the dim moonlight revealed the lights only belonged to a farmer's truck. He shut his eyes tightly and gulped in a shuddery breath. The shouts of the Nazi patrols echoed in the night, far away near the site of their crash. Jesse could only credit it as a miracle that they managed to escape the wreckage before soldiers were on the scene.

"Jesse," Josh mumbled. "You can't drag me all the way to England. You go; find a way home."

"Any more words like that out of your mouth and I'll punch you in the nose, Sauders," he whispered harshly. "You and I are both getting out of here, understand? Now stand up. You can do it."

With a slight groan, Josh raised himself up and Jesse supported his friend as they continued their rush through the trees that covered one side of the main road. His words seemed to spur Josh on, but inside, Jesse's heart sank. How in the blazes would they make it out of there? Nazis patrolled every road and they were only miles from Paris, one of the biggest German headquarters in Europe. Theirs chances were slim to none.

The wind sliced around them and whipped branches in their faces, but Jesse counted it a blessing. Josh could not keep his walk quiet if his life depended on it, and it did. The wind's high moan was a Godsend.

"Lord," Jesse murmured, "I know You're watching up there. We could really use a good Samaritan right now."

"Did you say something?" Josh asked halfheartedly.

"Get down!"

Not ten feet in front of them, the trees thinned and revealed a small cottage. A single lamp burned in one of the windows, but other than that the house was dark. Jesse's eyes narrowed. There were too many questions. He knew it could not be a Nazi residence; they would not be stationed so far from the city. But dealing with the French presented just as dangerous a risk. Before he could consider his options, headlights flashed up the tiny road leading to the house. Jesse crouched behind one of the trees and Josh huddled in a ball at his feet, trying to stifle the pain in his leg.

A truck slowly pulled up to the front porch, but it was not a Nazi vehicle. The man who lived there must have returned. A moment later, the driver door opened and a hunched figure wrapped in a heavy coat hurried up the steps and into the house. Jesse was no great judge of body language, but he felt slightly comforted by the sight of the small country man. Perhaps he would take pity on a couple of wounded airmen, and maybe even have connections to return them to England.

Before Jesse could move toward the cottage, two more sets of headlights appeared on the small road. He shrunk back, heart pounding, as the cars pulled up next to the truck and half a dozen Nazi soldiers poured out of one, while a high ranking official stepped from his own car. Jesse guessed him to be a major by the looks of his uniform. The major barked orders to the soldiers, who climbed the steps and pounded on the door.

Jesse tried to calm his breathing and glanced down at Josh. His eyes were closed, but his face was tight as he tried to remain silent. Jesse looked back up at the cottage, but ducked quickly as a couple of soldiers meandered toward the edge of the forest and lit cigarettes, chatting amongst themselves. As they casually glanced into the trees, Jesse had the horrible feeling that they were searching for certain downed enemy pilots. He swallowed and molded himself to the tree.

It took several moments for the cottage door to open, but when it did, the soldiers' attention was drawn away from the woods and Jesse cautiously watched the scene. Judging by the size of the man who stood in the doorway, he could not be the same one who had only moments ago hurried into the house. Without waiting for an invitation, the soldiers pushed their way inside and the door slammed shut.

The next few minutes were agonizing. Jesse could hear them ransacking the cottage as they looked for any sign of enemies of the Third Reich. He slid to the ground quietly, an arm on Josh's shoulder to keep him quiet. Possibilities ran through his brain, but in every one of them, the outcome was blurred and risky to say the least. They could not move from their position; the slightest noise would send those guards into the trees with guns they would waste no time in using. He was thinking so hard that he did not notice Josh's touch until his friend nearly punched him. He looked down.

Josh was pointing at the cottage, where the Nazis were just now appearing on the porch. The guards at the trees threw their cigarettes into the bushes and hurried to attention. As the engines rumbled, Jesse leaned down and spoke low in Josh's ear. "Are you crazy? What if we go in there and there are swastikas hanging on the walls?"

"Risk we have to take," Josh mumbled. "Those guards won't be back for a while at least now that they've searched the place. We have no other choice ..."

Josh grimaced and dropped his arm to the ground. Jesse watched the cars drive away, and soon the only sound was once again the moan of the wind. He shook his head and tried to think of another option, but none presented itself. Josh could not continue the way he was going. They needed help and the risk would be high no matter where they went. As soon as the lights turned the corner, he grabbed Josh under the arms and hauled him as quickly as he could to the house and up the steps. Before he could reconsider his plan, he knocked soundly on the door.

The silence within was unnerving, and Jesse glanced at his friend slowly. "He won't answer. We should move on."

"Once more ..." Josh said quietly.

Jesse sighed, but knocked one more time. Josh grew heavier by the second. His leg needed attention now, or else he would not make it another mile. He sent up a silent prayer, and his gut lurched as the door slowly swung open. The big man appeared, quiet shock on his face as he glanced over his shoulder and then past them, as though checking to make sure the soldiers were really gone. His eyes gave Jesse a sliver of hope.

The man opened the door wider and without another thought, Jesse stumbled inside. The Frenchman quickly shut the door behind them and led them to a pair of chairs. Jesse dropped Josh in the one closest to the fire and bent down to study his leg. It looked much worse, dark and sticky with blood. He glanced up at the old man, whose eyes darted from the two pilots to a door on the opposite wall. He appeared as nervous as Jesse felt.

"Please sir, we need shelter for the night," Jesse gasped quickly. "Will you help us? Help?"

The man appeared to understand that word, for he nodded quickly and ran to the stove, where he poured two cups of steaming coffee. Jesse dropped into the chair that the Frenchman had offered him. His feet felt like lead from all of the running that he and Josh had done. His hands were grimy from crawling in the dirt and his face was scratched from the branches that had whipped his face as he ran. Looking at Josh, he saw that his friend was in the same position. Josh had sunk to the floor next to the fireplace. He was so still that he could have been mistaken for dead. Jesse shuddered at the thought and thanked God for their escape from death. But how many more times would there be? How many more days? How many more hours? Jesse was not afraid to die, but afraid of what would remain unsaid should his life be taken.

He came out of his thoughts as the Frenchman brought him the cup of hot coffee. Jesse nodded his thanks. He drank deeply and let the warmth roll over him. The hot cup sent tingling sensations through his fingers. Jesse closed his eyes, too tired to keep them open. He wondered, once again, how they were going to get back to London. God only knew how much English the man understood, and he and Josh spoke absolutely no French. Nevertheless, he had to try and at least communicate with him. Jesse lifted his heavy lids and glanced at the man, who was sitting at the kitchen table with a newspaper, which he did not seem to be reading, though he was looking at it. Awkwardly, Jesse cleared his throat and stood. His feet cried out in pain as he walked uncertainly over to the table. The Frenchman looked up, and his eyes darted across the room before meeting his.

"Sir," Jesse began.

The man looked up at him as if in hesitation and tilted his head to one side. After a moment, he pointed to himself and said quietly, "Julian."

Jesse glanced over to where Josh was now sitting up. He was grinning, despite the pain in his leg. Jesse tried again.

"I'm Jesse. Please, my friend, he's wounded. Can you help?"

The man's eyes narrowed in confusion. He shook his head and pointed again to himself. "Julian."

"Is there a way out of here? Some way safe?"

Julian did not answer, just shifted his glance between Jesse and the door on the far wall.

"This is going nowhere," Jesse groaned.

"They should give us French lessons before we do these missions," Josh said with a slight grimace.

"If only we had someone who could interpret, this would be a whole lot easier," Jesse said.

"I can."

The soft voice came from the door that now stood open and appeared to lead down into a cellar. It was an unforgettable sound, even if he had not heard it for months. He turned slowly and saw her standing there in the doorway, and his heart leapt at the beautiful sight of her. He now realized it was she he had seen pull up to the cottage and hurry inside.

"Hilda."

She started at the sound of his voice. "Jesse! Oh, I didn't recognize you in the shadows." She took a step forward. "What ... what are you doing here?"

He came over and stood in front of her, gently touching her now dark red locks that glowed in the firelight. "How are you?"

Hilda smiled softly at his reference to her wound. "Much better, thank you." She suddenly realized the situation. "Jesse, you can't stay here. You put yourself in too much danger already."

Jesse gently took her hands. There was so much to be interpreted from his look. He did not care about the danger. Indeed, a sense of relief had come over him.

"It's so good to see you, Hilda," he said softly.

"I've wondered about you," she said.

Josh cleared his throat, and Julian began speaking rapidly to Hilda in French.

"Is there a way out of here tonight?" Josh asked.

Hilda shook her head. "Julian says the soldier were here looking for you. The roads are being watched. You cannot leave tonight."

Jesse sighed deeply. "We put you in danger by staying here."

"It is dangerous everywhere. Besides, your friend needs medical attention." She said something to Julian, who nodded and promptly went to a cupboard against the wall where he pulled out blankets.

"I'm afraid you will have to bear the floor tonight, gentlemen, but you should stay quite warm by the fire," Hilda said.

The men watched as she neatly arranged the blankets in front of the fireplace. Outside, a steady rain began to fall, driven by the wind. Once all was arranged, Hilda beckoned Josh to lay down once more by the fire, and he could not protest to the soft blanket. The moment his head hit the pillow, his eyes closed in exhaustion. Hilda murmured something to Julian and the man disappeared.

"He's fetching some pillows and bandages," Hilda said before she focused on the wound in front of her. "Jesse, please bring me the hot water on the stove top."

Jesse hurried to do the task before he sat on the other side of Josh's prone body and watched her concentrated movements as she deftly cleaned away the dried blood and dirt to see the extent of the wound. Her green eyes glowed in the firelight and set off the reds in her hair. The color reminded him of the danger that was still very present.

"Hilda," he said, "what are you doing here?"

"Julian is an old friend," she stated simply, not raising her gaze from her work.

"Hilda ..."

"Jesse, please," she begged, and looked directly into his eyes for the first time, "don't ask me questions you know I can't answer. You put yourself at risk."

"So do you," he persisted. "Those soldiers tonight could just as easily have been looking for you."

"Oh, Jesse, why do you have to make it so difficult!" Her hands reached up and framed his face. "I want to tell you," she whispered. "I do, but I can't. I'm sorry."

The rest of the night was torture for Jesse. Hilda put on her show, becoming Angelis, especially when Josh came to as she tightly bandaged his leg. His heart clenched with every fake smile she gave, and he ached to understand her hushed conversations with Julian.

Later, when they had all retired, Josh managed to tiredly voice his opinion. "I don't know, Jesse. I just feel uneasy about it all. How do we know they aren't waiting to hand us over to the Germans in the morning? I don't trust that man, and who is she?" he asked.

Jesse lay with his hands linked behind his head and stared up at the ceiling. "She's a woman who has gone through more than we could possibly imagine."

Hilda sat in bed and listened to the sound of the rain. She would not be surprised if a few snowflakes began to fall. The chill of winter had been in the air for a while now.

Dominique had not shown up to the meeting that night; something must have gone wrong with his mission in Berlin. When she asked Marie about him, the young woman simply began to weep. She had not seen or heard from her brother in over a month and she feared the worst. Hilda was worried too. It could only mean two things. Either he was in hiding ... or he was dead.

Buried deep in the floorboards were documents that if found on her person, could get her killed. The Underground's success depended on her getting them to her new contact, and their next mission could not fail. But the danger was imminent.

The Nazis' arrival had been unexpected and terrifying; she usually knew of their raids in advance and could adequately prepare. But when the first knock sounded in the house, her heart stopped. When the major had entered the cellar where her hiding place was located, she breathed a sigh of relief that he left only with a bottle of Julian's favorite label, and not dragging her out kicking and screaming. When had she come to be so terrified of her own people? The reason she joined the SIS in

London was because she knew their ways so well; it was all she had ever known. But suddenly Germany had changed, and these ruthless men she now witnessed where nothing like the carefree and hopeful boys she remembered growing up. Dederick came to her mind, but she pushed that thought away roughly.

She tried not to think about the man in the other room. She had thought that he would be gone forever once she left London. Though she had not told Jesse, the mission she was on did not intend to return her home in one piece. Even Jeffrey had tried to give her leave of the mission, but it had been no use. She left tomorrow for Paris with Marie to begin an assignment that would be more dangerous than any she had undertaken. There was a very slim possibility that she would come back. Julian did not even know the danger involved.

Filled with a sudden need, Hilda got up and went into the front room where Jesse and his friend slept. She curled up in Julian's chair and stared into the fire, grateful to simply be near the man she loved. She thought back on the times when she and her brothers had been children, naïve and exuberant, just happy to be together. More than anything now she wished that she was with them, just as they had been. So much had changed so quickly, and she knew that things would always be different between her and her family, no matter how the war turned out.

"Can't sleep?"

Hilda jumped at the voice and looked down to find Jesse staring up at her. He propped himself up on his hand, dark against the fire light, but his eyes were so piercing, so understanding, that she found her own filling with hot tears. In a second she was on her knees in front of him and her arms wrapped tightly around his neck. He returned her embrace and Hilda felt safer than she had in a long time. She shook with the strength of her emotions and felt weak as Jesse gently pulled her down next to him, cloaked in the safety of his arms.

"I'm here, Hilda," he murmured. "I have always been here, and I always will be."

She raised her eyes to him and tried to convey what she did not dare say. "Jesse, you know I can't confide in you, but you trust me, don't you? After our last conversation in London, I was afraid you thought ..."

His arm tightened around her shoulders. "Forgive me for what I said. I was afraid and confused. I didn't know what to expect after Paul wrote me of your disappearance."

She sat up. "He wrote to you?"

"Yes. Told me you up and left Heidelberg without a hint as to where you were going. Your family was very worried about you. It was part of the reason I joined the Eagle Squadron."

She nodded slowly and lowered her head to his chest once more. "I'm glad he was able to reach you. And that you came to London. I was not sure what to think when I saw you. After the years of silence, I didn't know what to expect."

Jesse forced her eyes to his. "What happened, Hilda? I wrote you as often as I could, but after a while, you just ... didn't respond."

"But I did, Jesse! Nothing changed for me," she murmured earnestly. "I thought you had met some American girl and forgotten about me."

"Never," he said adamantly. "How could you even think that of me? I feared you saw me as the enemy when the war seemed imminent."

Hilda sighed and shut her eyes slowly. "Whatever it was, this awful war changed everything, didn't it? How could it have become such a horrible mess? It seems this whole thing was doomed from the start."

"Don't say that," Jesse said, and the fear was evident in his voice. "I love you, Hilda. No matter what happens now or in the future, I will never forget you. Even if the entire world falls apart because of this war, you will always be close in my heart."

Hilda felt the tears fall down her cheeks. He still loved her. She did not realize how much she missed those words until the ache in her heart consumed her. She swallowed the pain and burrowed deeper against him. "And you in mine," she whispered. "I made you a promise."

"Then I will pray every day for God to give us a second chance, with no war and no secrets. Just like it used to be."

Hilda felt her doubt creep in. Nothing would ever be as it used to and Jesse was a fool to think otherwise, but where his steadfast faith stemmed from in such a time, she could only wonder. The world was lost and confused in its rage and destruction, but somehow he seemed to remain unchanged by the war. She clung to him, wishing some of his strength would seep into her bones and give her the courage she so desperately craved to fight on.

They held each other for a long time. For Hilda, it could be the last embrace she ever received. But that thought did not deter her as a strange peace filled her being and her eyes fluttered closed.

The next morning, Hilda woke to the soft sound of birds outside the window. She lifted her head slowly. The sun's light filtered through the trees as it climbed gradually into the sky. She sat up quietly, not wanting to disturb Jesse. As she moved to the sink to prepare coffee, she saw Julian standing in the doorway staring at her. His look showed nothing as she turned on the faucet.

"Now what?" came his low question.

She put the water on to boil and moved past him. "I need the trunk from the attic."

When Jesse and Josh finally woke from their needed sleep, Julian and Hilda had procured a trunk that looked very old, but its contents were of the latest fashion. She removed several shirts and pants, clean but old. They both walked over, bleary eyed as she began to lay out their outfits.

"This is going to hide us from the Nazis?" Josh asked, now quite recovered and quite skeptical.

"No," replied Hilda as she straightened from the floor. "But this will." She held up a bag that looked to be full of sheep's wool.

"How is that supposed to help?" Jesse asked.

"You'll see."

An hour later, he did see. Hilda carefully put the finishing touches on his white moustache and beard. The glue made his face itch. Glancing over, he saw Josh doing several double takes in the mirror at his own transformation. He looked back at Hilda. Her face was so close, her eyes so focused, and he suddenly stayed her hand with his own.

"Why are you doing this?" he asked.

She searched his face. "What do you mean?"

"We are the enemy, Hilda. I was flying home after bombing your country. We fight against everything and everyone you love. Why would you help us?"

"Do I not do the same?" she argued. "I too, fight against what once meant everything in the world to me. Do not pretend to think you know me."

"I once did, and last night I thought I found the girl I loved," he said earnestly. "What happened, Hilda?"

She held his eyes for a long moment, heartbroken. "Last night was a dream. And now morning is here." She stood up and went to the sink to wash her hands. She and Julian exchanged a few words and then he went outside. She looked completely composed when she turned from the sink.

"Okay, listen carefully," Hilda said. "We can take you as far as the west side of Versailles, and Julian's connections are prepared to take you to the coast. While we are going along the road, you are not to speak at all. When we reach the guards, I will do the talking. You will say nothing. Is that understood?"

"How do we know this isn't a trap?" Josh questioned, his eyes narrow.

Hilda turned to him. "Would you rather stay and be killed?"

This silenced him. After a moment, Hilda reached for her coat, hat and gloves, and then motioned them to follow her outside. Julian sat in the car waiting. Hilda slid behind the wheel and started the engine. Josh and Jesse climbed into the backseat. Soon they were on their way down the road, toward what they could only guess.

Within ten minutes they were approaching a guard post. Jesse held his breath as the car slowed to a stop and the guard, a young man, came to the window. Now they would find out if their disguises did the job.

"Where are you headed?" the guard asked, though his question seemed rather rehearsed. Jesse had the feeling that he was new to his post, if not the military all together.

Hilda smiled warmly up at him. Jesse tensed.

"I'm taking my uncles into town for a shave. They haven't been to the barber in months," she said with an innocent laugh.

The guard glanced back at them, taking in their heavy beards, and nodded. He stepped back and opened the blockade. Hilda blew him a kiss.

"You're a dear," she murmured as they drove though.

Jesse and Josh both released the breaths they had been holding. Maybe their disguise really did work.

"Is it that simple?" Jesse asked, leaning forward.

"Quiet."

The second blockade was not as easy as the first. The officer drilled Hilda with questions, his stern gaze roving over the car. Without missing a beat, she answered each question with calm composure, her French flawless. She fluttered her lashes over innocent, wide eyes as the guard slowly began to relent under her charms. After several long agonizing moments, the officer grudgingly let them pass. Jesse looked at Hilda's hands. They were white and trembling.

They drove for several minutes just outside the city until she turned onto a smooth dirt road that ran off into the horizon. This road they continued on for about an hour, and the sun was high and brilliant when she finally pulled off the road and stopped the car.

"This road continues on, but a few miles from here you'll see a yellow house that looks like Julian's. That's where you want to go. They will know who you are," Hilda explained as they got out of the car.

Jesse and Josh got out and looked down the road. Nothing was in sight.

"I'll get our stuff," Josh said, and he went around to the back of the truck.

Jesse and Hilda did not move; they simply stared at each other.

"Thank you," he said.

She laughed slightly. "Just doing my patriotic duty." Hilda pushed a hair away from her face and stared down the road for a moment. "Jesse, I ..."

"Here, Jesse. You about ready?" Josh asked as he handed him his pack.

"Yeah," he said. Jesse turned back to her and gently brought a hand to her cheek. "It's all right, sweetheart," he murmured. "I know."

Hilda shook her head slowly and her eyes betrayed her carefully placed thoughts. Clearing her throat, she stuck out her hand. "Good-bye Jesse, and good luck."

Without taking his eyes away, he pulled her to him and kissed her deeply, passionately, as he had done so long ago at the train station. He broke away after only a moment, but Hilda was still unsteady on her feet. He put his lips to her ear and whispered, "Good-bye, Hilda."

He and Josh turned and made their way along the road. The sun in front of them made them all but disappear, and Hilda felt her heart clench as she lost sight of Jesse in the morning sunshine.

17

Paris was lit up as brilliantly as day that night. Everywhere, couples in fine attire strolled down the sidewalks on their way to evening events. From her chair, Angelis could watch everything very easily. Across the table from her sat a man that she knew nothing about, only that he would play a vital role in the mission's success. She thanked the waiter who brought her dessert and lifted a small forkful of chocolate mousse to her mouth. The sinful sweet held no taste for her. Her entire focus centered on the man across from her. He did not know her name; she did not know his, but they were both there for the same cause. She stared at him closely. It was very possible that by the end of the night, one of them would end up at the bottom of the river. She fluttered her eyelashes and took his hand.

"I've had an absolutely wonderful time tonight, dear," she purred.

He smiled seductively and led her outside to a nearby alley after paying the bill. Once there, he pulled her to him and kissed her mouth with intense passion. She responded with the same intensity, all the while hoping that anyone passing would think them simply two lovers unable to part from one another's company.

Angelis felt his hand slide up her back to the top of her dress. He slipped a small folded paper down her back before pulling away.

"It's been fun," he murmured, wiping her lipstick from his mouth. "Good night."

She nodded in acknowledgement. He disappeared from view and she never saw him again.

After waiting a few minutes, she went out to the street and got into the car that was parked along the curb. The minute she got in, it pulled away.

"So, how did it go?" Marie asked.

"Fine. Drive."

Now in the shelter of the car, she unzipped her dress and stuffed it and her shoes into a bag. Marie produced a suitcase and from it, Angelis pulled a trench coat and hat. These she pulled over her undergarments quickly, then sat back in her seat, the note securely in her bodice.

Marie was tense.

"What is it?" Angelis asked.

"Someone's following us."

Slowly, Angelis looked back. A black car followed behind them, and it was getting closer. She tried to think back to where they could have gone wrong. The whole evening had gone flawlessly.

Too flawlessly.

With sudden realization, Angelis pulled out the note. Opening it, her worst fears were confirmed.

Your contact is dead. And soon you will be too.

She crushed the note in her fist.

"What do I do?" Marie asked.

Angelis took a deep breath. "Somebody talked."

The two shared a look. Their lives depended on the next move Angelis decided to make.

"Pull into this alleyway up here," she instructed.

Marie did so, and Angelis sighed with relief when she saw that it went through to the next street. Maybe, just maybe, they could get out of this alive.

Marie stopped the car, and the two jumped out. Angelis opened the trunk and pulled out four handguns.

"Who?" Marie asked quickly as she pulled her collar up around her face.

"Not sure," Angelis said. "Could have been the new contact, could have been someone in London. It doesn't matter now. Ready?"

Maria nodded. They split the guns between them and dashed down the alley. The rumble of cars grew steadily louder and voices shouted behind them. Tires screeched to a halt, and the two women heard a loud crunching of metal. Angelis dared a look back, and saw their car blockade had done the trick. About half a dozen Nazis poured out of the car and ran after their dark shadows. Angelis fired one shot and an officer stumbled and fell into the gutter of the alley.

Marie took the next shot, downing another with one bullet. Officers continued to fall as they chased the spies down the narrow alley, but more and more continued to appear. Sweat streamed down Angelis' back and face. It stung her eyes and with the darkness, she could not see very well.

A close cry turned her head. Marie fell next to her, a dark spot growing on her upper back.

Angelis caught her up and tried to carry her. "Come on Marie, you can make it. We can make it."

"No Angelis," she gasped. "You must go. Take these ..." Marie weakly pushed her weapons toward her.

"No! Marie please, we can make it."

"Tell my brother ... that I love him." Her breathing was shallow now.

"Marie!"

"Go while you have ... the chance."

And then she was gone. It was all so sudden and so horrible that Angelis was held in shock for a minute. She grimaced and leaned her head against Marie's chest for a moment, but the sound of gunfire brought her to her feet and she sprinted toward the other end of the alley. The Seine waited on the other side, if only she could make it. Air burned in her lungs as she ran for her life.

Angelis broke free of the alley and charged across the street. She made it to the middle of the bridge before she heard their whistles in the open air. People along the river gasped and ducked to the ground. Angelis climbed over the railing and took a huge leap away from the bridge. A shot rang out just before she hit the water, and then everything went dark.

It was a cold morning. Snow was soon to fall, he was sure. Nobody was out, and for good reason. Five o'clock in the morning was not the happening hour. The man pulled his coat collar up higher to hide the long scar that ran the length of his cheek. The recent addition to his features was still red, and that, along with being back in Paris, could get him shot. His hat pulled low, he walked the length of the river. There was no way he could get to Versailles yet to contact Marie, and getting out of Paris would be difficult enough. The river's currents swirled below him, and he glanced down.

There was a body floating near the steps.

He stared for a split second before springing into action. He hurried down the steps. Red hair floated lamely around a pale face with blue lips. Sitting down on the steps, he lifted the woman gently from the water and into his arms.

Her toes, fingers and nose were tingling. Blood and heat rushed into them with intensity. Slowly she felt herself begin to shake. Her stomach quivered as warmth slowly encompassed her, and she realized her shoulder was throbbing painfully. She opened her eyes and had to blink because everything was fuzzy. The room slowly came into focus and she found herself in a small flat, the hustle and bustle of Paris beneath her. She was lying on a couch that had been pulled near the fireplace and a man was adjusting several blankets that covered her. He glanced up and caught her gaze.

"Welcome back," he said with a smile.

"Dominique," Angelis scratched out of a throat unused.

"Well, you haven't lost your memory, that's good." Dominique felt her arms and head. "How are you feeling?"

She glanced around. "Have I been sick?"

"Pneumonia. That and the bullet in your shoulder gave you an infection. I wasn't sure you would make it. But you always did prove to be stronger than the rest of us," he said with a smile. He turned to the fire and his features caught the light.

"Good heavens, Dominique," she said weakly. "Your face ..."

"I know," he said impatiently. "Not right now. Angelis, what happened?"

She swallowed. "Assignment went bad. It was a trap. We were doomed from the start."

"We?"

"Marie and I. There was no way out."

Dominique held his breath. "Where is she, Angelis?"

She met his eyes and shook her head sadly. "I'm sorry, Dominique."

He nodded slowly. There was nothing to be done now. He could not dwell on it, and Angelis knew Dominique would remain professional in front of her. Now, all that mattered was getting out of France. The whole operation was compromised, and there was no one left they could trust.

London was their only option. She was not sure what the SIS would say, but there was nothing more she could do.

✕

It was well past midnight, and Dominique and Angelis were in their private compartment on the train to Normandy. She sat in a chair in her nightgown and long socks with a wool overcoat around her. Even though it was warm inside, she felt more secure with it on. She gingerly rested her injured arm against her body. Dominique sat on his bunk in his pajamas and bathrobe, reading. After watching him for a moment, Angelis posed her question.

"Are you going to tell me what happened?"

The book came slowly down to reveal his blank face. His scar was vibrant against his pale skin. He set the book aside and laid back, his gaze toward the ceiling

"I got caught trying to get into Berlin. Two weeks in their rotten prison with torture. I swear I'll kill the man who gave me this." He pointed to his scar. His voice stayed monotone, but in it was all the emotion that he kept hidden in his gut. "Do you know what he said to me before I escaped that night? He said that this was good exercise for him before he went out with his girlfriend." Dominique laughed harshly. "That night, they were getting ready to move me to one of their camps up north. I managed to slip out of the truck and since then, I've been making my way back to Paris. Then I found you." He looked at her. "What about you?"

Angelis sighed and settled deeper beneath her coat. "Marie and I were given orders to meet with our new contact in Paris. He had information on German naval activity and we were going to make an exchange. Whoever he was, he talked and got himself killed. We walked into a trap. We tried to get to the river, but Marie ... she didn't make it. I made a jump for the water and that's when I must have been shot. I don't really remember."

"No doubt they probably thought you would drown in the river. You got lucky, just like me," he commented as he placed his book beneath the bunk. Leaning back, he closed his eyes and sighed.

Angelis watched him feign sleep. She understood his pain. His sister had been his only family in the world, and now she was gone and he was alone. She felt her eyes begin to water. She was to blame, and she knew it. If only she had paid more attention, been more focused. She should have known something was wrong. But she had been oblivious and now her friend was gone forever.

Getting up, she went over to where Dominique lay and sat down on the edge of the bunk. Gently she touched his hand. "I'm so sorry, Dominique."

His hand gripped hers tightly. "She was all I had," he murmured, pain in his voice. "I can't do this, Angelis."

"You're strong, Dominique. You *will* pull through." She pulled him up so that he met her eyes. "We'll help each other. No matter what happens, all right?"

He nodded slowly, and she pulled him into a fierce hug. They would make it through. They would.

⌇

Jeffrey sat at his desk and stared at the papers in front of him, but he could not concentrate. He had thrown himself at Hilda, and then she had left without a word. He knew that she had not taken his feelings lightly and he appreciated that, but her lacking response worried him. He had taken a chance by telling her of his feelings, and now he was not sure whether he was right to do so. The cold London air seeped through his window, and he shivered.

There was something between her and that pilot Jesse Riker. He did not know what, but he intended to find out what past history the two shared and how it affected Hilda now. He sometimes caught her alone, crying silent tears or staring off into space. Captain Riker had a hold on her that no one else did. Jeffrey felt the jealousy begin to well up inside him. And he hated it.

Without warning, the door to his office opened and two tired and ragged looking figures stepped inside. They both wore long overcoats with up-turned collars and had hats pulled over their eyes.

"Excuse me," Jeffrey said with indignation as he rose from his chair. "What on earth makes you think you can come barging in without permission?"

One of the figures looked up, and green eyes sparkled out from underneath. "We didn't want to be announced. I hope you don't mind."

"Hilda," he whispered. Like a shot, he was out from behind the desk. He hugged her fiercely.

"Okay, Jeffrey. Okay. Okay, I can't breathe," she gasped after a moment.

"Are you all right?" he asked, concern in his voice. Suddenly confusion was on his face. "What are you doing here? You're supposed to be in Versailles."

The other person stepped forward, a hand on Hilda's shoulder. "They were betrayed. It was no longer safe to stay."

"Jeffrey, meet Dominique," Hilda said quietly.

The two men shook hands and sized each other up. Jeffrey flinched, but just a little. "What do you mean, betrayed?"

"The contact you set up in Paris. He was caught and must have talked. They knew right where to find us."

Jeffrey went to his desk and shifted through some files. "I'll talk to my superior," he said. "We'll set it up and get you back."

Dominique and Hilda shared a look.

"Did you not hear what she just said?" Dominique exclaimed. "He talked. Lord knows what he told them. It's too dangerous to go back. My own sister was killed!"

"I'm very sorry, but that is not something I can worry about right now," Jeffrey said.

Dominique slammed his hands down on the desk. "You may think it's difficult to sit here at your desk and try to save the world from destruction, but you have no idea!"

"*I* have no idea!" Jeffrey leaned in close to Dominique. "I'm here every day trying to save your sorry backsides. Do not tell me what is difficult!"

"Stop it," Hilda said firmly. "Your bickering will get us nowhere. Honestly, the two of you are behaving like children."

The men stared daggers at each other a moment longer before straightening.

"Dominique is right, Jeffrey. For now, it is too dangerous to go back to Paris. You still have plenty of contacts there who aren't blown. Use them," Hilda urged.

"What about you?" he asked.

"We need to let this settle. Then we'll think of something."

He nodded slowly. He could not fight with her. By putting her at risk, he went against his own feelings, and he could not do that.

An awkward silence followed and the three of them simply stood staring at each other. A minute later, a knock came on the door.

"Um ... sir?" The secretary poked her head through the door. "Someone to see you in the lobby."

Jeffrey turned with some difficulty and forced a smile. "Of course. Thank you."

He looked back, gave the two spies an abrupt nod, and left the office.

Grace sat in the café and stared blankly at the cup of tea in front of her. Christmas had been wonderful, but it had gone by far too quickly. Her father was back at the hospital again and Jesse was busy at the airfield. Life was back to normal and she was back to her old lonely self.

She had fallen for Jesse Riker, and hard. She would never admit it to a soul, but it was the truth. He was far out of her reach, but she could not help it. It was useless to fight it.

"Hullo, Grace."

She looked up. A smile split across her face. "Jeffrey. It's been far too long."

"May I join you?"

"Of course."

He sat down across from her and stared at her for a moment. "Are you all right?" he asked.

Grace paused for only a moment. Jeffrey watched her with kindness in his eyes and she sighed, then dove in. "Have you ever felt like someone is so close and in your reach, but you know you will never really have them?"

He looked up, startled at this, and nodded with deep understanding. "Yes, I know exactly what you mean."

Her surprise was evident. "You do?"

"Yes."

She sighed and looked back down at her tea. "It feels horrible, doesn't it?"

He nodded and took her hand. "Yes, it does."

They sat that way for a moment. After a while, Grace smiled and laughed softly. "So, would you like to join me in a cup of tea and my misery?"

Jeffrey smiled and was about to answer when a loud explosion interrupted them, followed by another down the street. Jeffrey frowned and looked out the window up at the dark sky. His eyes narrowed, and he grabbed Grace's hand and pulled her up and out of the shop. The wail of the air raid sirens filled the streets, loud and dreadful.

"Come on!" Jeffrey shouted.

As planes flew above them, Grace held on to Jeffrey's hand for dear life as they ran to the nearest shelter. Several other people were running for the shelter as well. Jeffrey helped her down the steps and they found a corner to sit in.

"Are you all right?" he asked her gently. She nodded her head and looked down at her hands.

"I'm sorry I was so abrupt a moment ago," he said.

"It's all right," she stated with a gentle smile. "You were only protecting me."

Their eyes found each other and held. The kindness in them turned questioning. The moments drew on like an endless eternity of floundering in a warm pool.

Grace looked away quickly. She and Jeffrey were friends, nothing more.

Right?

~%~

Jeffrey stared out of his window at the falling snow. The New Year had come and gone, but 1941 did not bring the changes he wished for. Things were getting out of control. He could not handle all of the pressure being put on him, and his emotions were starting to take hold.

The door to his office opened, and Jeffrey turned. A content smile spread across his face. "You're on vacation. What are you doing here?"

Hilda smiled and walked over to his desk. Her cheeks were flushed from the cold and a small pile of snow covered her furry cap.

"I just feel a little lazy, I guess. The last mission seems so long ago. I miss Julian a little, and Dominique went back to France last week, so ... it's just me."

"After your last scare in Paris, I would think you were ready for a break." He glanced at her shoulder. "How is your wound?"

"Much better. Dominique did a decent job, considering he's not a surgeon."

Jeffrey came around to the other side of the desk and leaned against it, studying her. She gave him a quizzical smile and leaned next to him.

165

"These past two missions ... I'm amazed at your strength," he murmured. "It's been a rough time."

Hilda grew serious and her gaze seemed far away. "Yes. Marie was a dear friend. I wish I could have done something to save her."

Jeffrey laid his hand on hers gently. "There was nothing you could have done. Don't let yourself get down on that thought. It's a new year, with new beginnings."

She smiled at him. "Yes, and you weren't supposed to be here. It was supposed to be a surprise. What are you doing in the office anyway?"

He shook his head and ran his fingers through his hair. "Just feeling ... overwhelmed. A lot of life not going the way I want it to. Things I don't really understand. It's a whole bloody mess." He looked up and met her eyes. They sparkled with concern for him. His heart beat faster, and hope shone in his eyes. "Hilda ..."

"Jeffrey, please," she said, her face full of pain. She struggled to find the words to say. "I can't. We can't." She leaned away and pulled a small package from her bag. "Here. For you. I'm sorry I didn't get it to you before the holidays."

Jeffrey gave a small smile and took it from her. "Thank you."

"Open it now," she said excitedly. "When I saw it I just had to get it for you."

He laughed and tore off the wrapping paper. He took the lid off the box and pushed aside the tissue. A silver watch sat inside.

"It was in the window of the jewelry shop, and I knew it would be just perfect." Hilda looked at him when he did not say anything. "Do you like it?"

"I do ... very much," he said.

"Oh, good! I knew you would. And now, I must be going, Jeffrey. I'll see you soon?"

Jeffrey nodded, his eyes on the watch. Hilda hurried out of the office and passed his secretary as she came in with a package. Jeffrey studied the present in his hands and sighed knowingly. Watches were given to good friends, and that was all he would ever be to Hilda.

"Sir, this just came."

He looked up. His secretary held a small narrow box in her hand with a note on top. She put it on his desk.

"Uh, thank you."

After she left, Jeffrey glanced down at the box. The note had Hilda's name on it. With a frown, he picked it up. Not many people knew that name. He opened the note and read the short message.

For the days I will never forget.
Love, Jesse

For a long time, Jeffrey stared at those words. He did not like them; he disliked the writer even more. He was about to slide the box into his drawer when his door opened suddenly again, and Hilda's voice sailed in.

"I'm so sorry, Jeffrey, I forgot to mention ... oh, what a lovely package! Who is it for?"

Jeffrey stammered, unable to answer, as she walked over and looked down at the note.

"For me? Jeffrey, that is so sweet of you!" Hilda opened the note and read silently, her face losing its cheer. She slowly looked up at him. "Where did you get this?"

Jeffrey tried to form words in his mouth. "I ... it just came in, right after you left. Honestly ..."

Hilda ripped off the brown paper and opened the blue velvet box. A dazzling necklace lay on the narrow cushion. Tiny, exquisitely cut diamonds and sapphires were elegantly woven into a shining silver chain. Hilda's eyes were pained and hurt when she looked up at Jeffrey.

"Why were you hiding this from me?" she asked, anguish in her voice.

"Hilda, I'm sorry," he said, but he knew deep inside he wasn't. And so did she.

"What you are is jealous! You've wanted to ruin our friendship from the moment you met him!"

"That note sounds to me like you two are more than just friends," he said, irritated now.

Hilda slapped him harshly and fled the office, clutching the necklace. Jeffrey watched her go and slumped into his chair when she disappeared. Any hope he had fled with her.

"Oh, god."

⁓

Hilda hailed a cab and within minutes, she was at the edge of the airfield. Paying the man quickly, she raced into one of the hangers.

"Jesse!" she cried.

A few pilots sitting at a table playing cards glanced up. She cleared her throat.

"I'm ... looking for Captain Riker."

They all turned to look at a lone pilot who sat by himself, reading. The pilot stood and she recognized him as the man who had been with Jesse in France. She noticed his arm in a sling, and her hopes dimmed.

He recognized her as well.

"You ..."

"Captain Sauders! Please, where is Jesse?"

Josh motioned her to follow him outside. Once the door was closed he turned to her, his face serious. "I never did thank you for saving our lives back in France."

"Captain, what's wrong?" she asked with dread.

After a moment's hesitation, he replied, "Jesse told me that if you came by the airfield, I was to give you this." He pulled a folded piece of paper out of his jacket and handed it to her. His eyes reached sadly into hers. "I'm sorry, miss. I'm so sorry."

Hilda watched him go back inside, not quite believing what she held, what she heard. Sorry? For what? With dread, she looked down at the note in her hand. Her eyes stung with tears as she opened it.

January 2, 1941

Dearest Hilda,

I wrote this note knowing of the possibility that something might happen to me. I wanted nothing more than to spend the rest of my life growing old with you, but God has seen fit to take me home to eternity. I will always treasure our last good-bye.

Never forget who you truly are, Hilda. You have a strength that many have lost in this war. Always hold on to that, and to the belief that God has a higher purpose for your life. Remember that even in the darkest of nights, He is faithful and will light your path to the truth.

All my love,
Jesse

Hilda slowly dropped to her knees and doubled over, silent tears falling from her cheeks. She would never get the chance to tell him the truth, and every moment she had let slip through her fingers came back to her like a knife digging into her heart. Jesse's prayer for a second chance would never be answered.

Hilda clutched his letter, his final words of love and encouragement, against her breast. A single sob broke from her lips and echoed into the still, quiet sky around the empty airfield, wrenching with the pain of what had been so precious and was now lost forever.

"What a cruel thing is war: to separate and destroy families and friends, and mar the purest joys and happiness God has granted us in this world; to fill our hearts with hatred instead of love for our neighbors, and to devastate the fair face of this beautiful world."

Robert E. Lee

18

Berlin, August 1941

The summer evening was the perfect temperature as Tanya strode out of the magnificent State Library on her way home to her flat. The sun still stood brightly in the sky, as it would for another hour before night set in. She dodged a military truck as it went speeding by, carrying a group of young soldiers to their barracks.

Germany had changed drastically in her absence. Tanya almost cried when she arrived and was immediately searched and interrogated by the customs officers. It was not the home she remembered, but it was the only thing she had left. Moscow had never been a home to her, only a prison, and if this was her only other option then she had to be content with it. After the first initial weeks had passed, she was able to obtain a job at the library, allowing her to fill her days with a task she enjoyed, as well as make friends with Doris, another librarian who worked with her and did not seem to live and breathe the Nazi regime, as did all of Berlin. She was a welcome friend in a very changed city.

Tanya stopped at a flower vendor along the street and chose a bouquet to brighten up her flat on the lovely summer evening. She buried her nose into the flowers and thanked the vendor as she paid him.

"Celebrating something?"

At first Tanya did not recognize the voice. It was deep and strong, with a light air to match the warm day. She turned and her face split into a surprised smile. Her rescuer from Poland, Dederick van Ostrand, stood on the corner, straight and tall in his uniform and wearing that beautiful smile she had first managed to coax out of him months ago. He took a step toward her and Tanya's eyes twinkled as she slowly shook her head in happy disbelief.

"This fine summer evening," she murmured, "and happy reunions. I see you made it to Berlin in one piece, my dear knight in shining armor."

"As did you," Dederick replied. They shared a look and after a moment, they both laughed.

"I can't tell you how good it is to see you again, Dederick."

"And I you, Tanya."

She tilted her head, and her smile grew. "You remember my name."

"Of course," Dederick stated. "It is my duty and in this case, my pleasure, to remember all those who cross my path."

While Tanya laughed at his words, something inside her questioned them. She was very happy to know another face in the city, but cautious to get close to him. When Dederick held out his arm to her, however, his charm won her over at that moment and she stepped forward.

"May I walk with you to wherever you are going?" he asked, then looked around suddenly. "Unless there's another fellow about ready to steal you away with his charms."

Tanya took his arm firmly. "No, I am quite content to have you in my company, Dederick. Very happy, in fact."

He looked down at her and she once again saw the softening of his gaze. There was something about him that from a distance made him seem rather ruthless, but when she saw the look in his eyes and the gentle way he led her on, it all seemed to fade away. There were two sides to Dederick van Ostrand. Tanya had seen the soldier he was very clearly in their first encounter, but she was curious to know the man who lay beneath the steel, and what secrets he held from the world.

The door could not have slammed more loudly in his face as Paul walked dejectedly from the Berlin headquarters of the State Police. He looked up at the towering stone as the sun disappeared behind the city. A red hue traced the sharp cruel edges, as though taunting his attempts to reason with the Gestapo. After five trips to the headquarters in Heidelberg, he had finally come to Berlin, but it seemed there would be no success in the capital. He buried his hands into his suit pockets and slowly made his way down the street back to his hotel. The pain of his failure threatened to choke him and not for the first time, he felt the sting of his freedom while his dear mother sat in prison, the victim of the Nazis' suspicion hovering over his family.

He was surprised they waited so long to make an arrest. He had a strong feeling that Dederick's loyalties to the Reich had something to do with their delay, but when they finally did come it was his mother, not him, that they dragged away. Her defense was not heard, nor was a trial held. She was simply thrown into a moldy cell, where she remained until Paul could figure out a way to free her. He knew the van Ostrands had been observed carefully by the Gestapo going back as early as his father's death; Hilda had written her suspicions to him while he was in America. What he did not understand was why. Why? Every single action by Hitler's strict regime seemed to boil down to that question. Why? There was no logic behind what was happening in Germany and yet with only a few words, the Führer managed to hold the puppet strings of an entire nation in his hand. The world had gone mad. Completely mad.

Paul looked up briefly before crossing the street and almost ran into a young woman, and the flowers in her arms tumbled to the ground.

"Oh, I'm so sorry Fraulein ..." he mumbled as he scrambled to help her.

"It's quite all right," she said next to him.

They both looked up at the same time and she seemed startled for a moment, but Paul did not have time to dwell on it, for another voice caught his attention, much more familiar to him.

"Paul?"

He glanced up, just as shocked as Dederick, who turned from the taxi and stared at his older brother. It had been years. Paul could see the way his brother had grown in more ways than one. His body had filled out with muscle, a few scars on his face, probably from his posting in Poland. But he mostly noticed the protective look in his eyes as he bent down to help the young woman up. No wonder the poor girl had been startled; despite the difference in their age, Paul and Dederick were like twins, with the same blonde hair, blue eyes, facial structure and stature.

Paul slowly rose to his feet, his eyes glued to his brother. For a moment, neither of them could speak; they only sized each other up, taking note of each other's differences. Paul knew that Dederick was noticing his slimmer figure, due to the lack of rations they came by. All the while, the young

173

woman looked between them and after a few seconds, she shifted the flowers in her arms and stepped forward.

"Hello," she said with a smile, and stuck out her hand.

Numbly, Paul shook it. As if offended that she reached out to him, Dederick pulled her gently back and moved her toward the taxi.

"Get in the car, please," he murmured softly, though Paul heard him.

She began to protest, but Dederick was firm. "Please Tanya, get in the car."

The woman called Tanya glanced between the two of them once more before slowly getting into the taxi. Dederick shut the door and turned to his brother. Paul was uncertain what was coming until the last thing he expected happened. Dederick hugged him tightly, then led him a short distance from the taxi.

"It's good to see you, Paul."

"Is it? I wasn't sure," he replied with a glance back at the car. "Was that little show for your lady friend?"

Dederick didn't reply, but it was an answer to Paul. He brushed it aside, refusing to let his anger rule the conversation. It was Dederick, after all, who had kept the Gestapo at bay when Hilda was under scrutiny and when their sister's disappearance put the whole family in a suspicious light.

"How have you been?" Dederick asked lightly.

Paul thought before answering. "To be honest, I am happy. There have been many tribulations since you left for Poland, but I have my family to be thankful for." He looked at his brother. "Have you heard what happened to Mother?"

Dederick stiffened and stepped slightly away from his brother. "No ... what?"

"She was arrested shortly after you left. I've been trying to negotiate her release, but I've had no success." Paul sighed and ran his fingers through his hair. "I didn't think it would be her. Honestly I thought it would be me. I couldn't believe it when they took her away."

"There must have been some cause," Dederick mumbled.

Paul gawked at him. "How can you say that? How can you say that of your own mother? 'There must have been some cause.' Was there, Dederick? Because I don't recall ever really knowing what the hell was going on!" Paul's voice was yelling by the time he finished.

Dederick lifted his hands and tried to calm him. "Paul, get a hold of yourself. Do you want to be arrested too?"

Paul shut his eyes tightly for a moment and Dederick led him a little further down the street. Not a soul was in sight, but he still glanced around as Paul took a deep breath.

"Dederick, what is going on? I have no control over what is happening. There must be something you can do for Mother," he begged. "Maybe they will listen to you."

His younger brother looked away once again and his eyes narrowed. Following his gaze, Paul saw the young woman, Tanya, standing next to the taxi, a hand on the open door and a concerned look on her face. Dederick's voice dropped low.

"There is only so much I can do, and this is not in my power, Paul. I'm sorry." He turned and started back toward the car.

Paul watched him go, his faith crumbling at his feet. He should have known Dederick would do nothing. He was surprised he had let himself believe that his brother might show some compassion and fight to free their mother. But no. Dederick would always be loyal first and foremost to his country. Nothing would ever get in the way of his loyalty. He was the poster child for the Nazi regime in Paul's eyes.

"Dederick."

His brother turned back once more, the look in his eyes slightly irritated. Paul stared back evenly. "You're an uncle. Hannah had a baby last year." He watched Dederick's face change, morphing from shock to anger, from disgust to confusion, to a sudden understanding. "Just thought you would want to know. It's a girl."

Paul turned on his heel, rounded the corner, and disappeared from sight.

A book slammed onto the counter and startled Tanya out of her thoughts. She mumbled an apology and quickly checked out the desired volumes to the customer in front of her.

She could not get the scene between Dederick and that man out of her head. They had to be brothers; they looked so alike, it shocked her. She had not heard most of their discussion, only the last thing that the man had said as Dederick walked back to the taxi. "You're an uncle."

Dederick had been very silent during their ride to the restaurant they had decided on. Tanya did not try to coax anything out of him; his thoughts seemed too far away for her to reach, or even understand. But the incident had been on her mind constantly since then and now, she couldn't concentrate on anything. She hastily set the clock to the time she would return and put it on the counter, and then hurried down to the small employees lounge.

Doris was the only one there when she arrived, a cup of steaming coffee on the table in front of her and a cigarette between her fingers. She smiled when Tanya came in.

"Why darling, hello! Do sit down for a moment if you have time."

Tanya smiled and took the chair across from her, but her eyes betrayed her thoughts. Doris studied her curiously. "You look like you're a thousand miles away, Tanya. Care to come back to the land of the living?"

Tanya sighed and laced her fingers together in front of her. "I'm sorry Doris. I can't seem to keep my thoughts straight right now."

Doris smiled and took a sip of her coffee. "I don't think I would be able to either if I had such a handsome officer escorting me to work."

"Oh, you saw that did you?"

"Darling, all the ladies were twittering about him from the moment they saw him. I daresay the cleaners had a time getting all the oil off the windows from their noses pressed against them watching you together." Doris leaned forward. "So tell me, who is he? Is he stationed here for long?"

Tanya smiled. "I don't know how long he will be here. We met in Poland, where he rescued me from a rather ghastly situation."

Doris gasped. "He rescued you? Oh darling, do tell all."

Tanya laughed and brushed her away. "The details are not important, Doris. But he was quite a knight in shining armor. I'm surprised he remembered me. We only met again yesterday. His name is Dederick van Ostrand."

Doris grew quiet and stared at her. Tanya was surprised to see her normally carefree friend wearing such a serious expression. "Why, Doris, whatever is wrong?"

Doris did not speak for a moment and leaned back to take a drag on her cigarette. She finally blew it out after a moment. "Don't you know who he is, darling?"

"No, not really. We've only met twice. Doris, whatever is the matter?" Tanya was beginning to worry.

"My boyfriend told me that Dederick van Ostrand is the talk of the barracks. A better Nazi could not be found. Blonde with gorgeous blue eyes, loyal to his country and ready to die for the cause. He is the perfect Aryan."

Tanya shrugged. "And that is such a bad thing? So he has devotion."

Doris shook her head. "My dear, don't you understand? His loyalty to Germany is placed before everything else. Friends, girls ... even his family."

Tanya could not take her eyes from Doris. She remembered the man on the street and swallowed her growing unease. Doris cocked her head, pitiful compassion in her eyes as she took another long drag on her cigarette before smashing it into the ash tray.

"The rumor is ... the boys in the barracks say that ... Lieutenant van Ostrand turned in his own mother."

Tanya tried to close her ears to what she heard, but it fell on them painfully anyway. She shook her head adamantly.

"No ... no, that's all it is. A rumor. He would never do something like that." She stood. "I've seen him, spent time with him. He's ... different. He would never do such a thing."

Doris looked up at her sadly. "It's like you said, Tanya. You've only met him twice."

Tanya turned angrily and left the lounge, not wanting to hear any more of Doris' ugly lies. For that was all they were. Lies, lies, lies.

19

Heidelberg, September 1941

Hannah glanced down at the yellow star on her jacket and sighed as she turned away from the store. The sign spoke for itself—JEWS NOT WELCOME. She had seen them everywhere and unfortunately, had gotten used to it. At first she had wanted to rebel and fight back for her freedom, but then she learned that staying out of the way and keeping her mouth shut kept her out of trouble.

Hannah walked home slowly and enjoyed the time she had to be with her thoughts. Ever since their marriage, life for her and Paul had been difficult. Though kept relatively secret due to the Race Laws, many of their friends shunned them and going out together in public was near to impossible. Surprisingly, Benedikta had warmed to the situation quickly and they had become very good friends. They spent as much time as they could together—until that horrible day.

Hannah looked away as three young officers passed her. One of them whispered something to the other and they laughed boisterously. The third spit on her shoes before moving along with his friends. Hannah felt the rage begin to boil in her stomach, but she took a deep breath and pushed it down. She would only get herself into more trouble, and Paul would not be happy to see her coming home with another black eye, especially on the night they were going out. Elsa, who had remained a true friend, had

178

promised to look after Maria while they were gone. She sighed with relief. Finally, a night of peace.

Hannah reached the complex and hurried into their flat. Giving her husband a kiss, she said with a small smile, "I'm afraid we will have to survive one more day without milk, my dear. The store was not feeling very hospitable."

Paul sighed. "I'm sorry, Hannah. No trouble other than that?"

"No," she said, not feeling the need to tell him about the officers.

"Good," he replied. "You're going to have to be quick. Our reservations are at six, and Elsa should be here any minute."

"Of course." Hannah hurried into the bedroom and greeted Maria, who giggled with delight when she was lifted into her mother's arms. "How's my darling girl?" she said with a big smile. "Yes, that's you. My, you are growing so fast."

"Ma, Ma," Maria chirped with a giggle.

"Oh, my beautiful girl! If they could see you now, they would be as proud of you as I am."

Laying the baby back in her crib, Hannah stopped suddenly, thoughtful as she unbuttoned her coat. "Paul?" she called.

"Yes, dear?" He appeared in the doorway.

"Do ... do you ever think about Hilda?" she asked, hesitation in her voice.

Paul's face turned sad and remorseful. "Yes," he said quietly. "All the time." He came over and helped her unbutton the back of her blouse. "Why do you ask?"

"It ... just came to my mind suddenly. Sometimes I miss her so much."

Paul put his arms around her waist and kissed the top of her head. "I know. I do, too."

"Do you think she's all right?"

"She certainly knows how to take care of herself. I'm sure she's fine."

Hannah moved to the wardrobe and pulled out her dress. "I still often wonder why she left," she mused as she slipped it over her head.

"I wish I knew. So much could have provoked her." Paul let his eyes glaze as he thought of his sister.

A knock at the door turned their heads.

"That will be Elsa," he said, making for the door.

"I'll get Maria," Hannah said as he disappeared back into the living room. Turning to the crib, she saw Maria's deep sky blue eyes watching her. "Come on, beautiful. Be good to Elsa." She wrapped her in an extra blanket and put a small wool hat on her head.

"Well, haven't you grown into a beauty!" Elsa exclaimed as she entered.

Hannah smiled at her dear friend and let Maria flap her way into the older woman's arms.

"Now, now, we'll have none of that," Elsa reprimanded with a stern look. "Give your mother a kiss good-bye."

"Ma, Ma," Maria cried excitedly and turned her head toward Hannah. Her little hands came out, clenching and unclenching, beckoning her to come. Hannah laughed and planted a kiss on her tiny lips.

"I love you, darling," she cooed.

She stepped back as Paul kissed his daughter, and then they led Elsa to the door and waved as she went out to her car.

Paul placed his arm around his wife with a little squeeze. "So, now that we're alone," he said with a smile as the car disappeared around the corner, "our reservations are actually at seven."

Hannah laughed and gave him a quick kiss on the cheek. Paul was so good to her. He had endured so much for her, suffered relations with his brother and friends, and been ridiculed by the entire community. All because he loved her.

Hearing a car pull up at the curb, they turned. A contingent of cars was coming down the street. Nazi officers, machine guns at theirs sides, hurried past them and into the building. One of them, a major, stopped in front of them.

"Are you residents here?" he asked.

"Yes," Paul replied, his arms wrapped protectively around Hannah.

"We are evacuating this building. Your papers, please," he said matter-of-factly.

With a glance at each other, they removed their identification cards and handed them to the major. After a moment, he glanced up at Hannah. "You are required to pack your belongings and accompany us, if you please, madam," he said. Turning away, he spoke with another officer.

"What of me, Major?" Paul asked loudly.

The major turned and looked at him, surprised at his question. "You are free to do as you please," he said indifferently.

"Then I will accompany my wife," Paul replied firmly, even when he knew his words doomed him.

Slowly, the major turned back, his eyes narrow. "As you wish," he said between clenched teeth.

Paul nodded and then turned and led Hannah back up to their complex.

"Don't do this, Paul," she whispered as she stuffed some of her clothes into a suitcase.

He grabbed her hand. "I won't leave you."

"What about Maria?"

"Elsa will take care of her until we get back."

"But when *will* we get back?" she asked as tears began to fall down her cheeks.

Paul wrapped her in his arms and held her. "Soon, darling. Don't worry about anything. We're going to be fine."

Hannah nodded slowly against his shoulder and wiped her eyes. He returned her wobbly smile and led her out into the hallway to join the other families filing out of the building. Officers were everywhere guiding people onto the trucks. Hannah looked at the hand that an officer offered her for a moment, and then took it hesitantly. His grip was hard and cold and she shook herself loose as soon as she was seated next to Paul. The officer gave her a playful smile and winked. With disgust she turned away.

Within thirty minutes, the motors were rumbling and the trucks jerked as they rolled into motion. As Hannah and Paul watched their home fade away, they wondered to themselves at their hopes. Each began to doubt the optimism that they displayed on their face. Safety was behind them and uncertainty lay before. They could be going to their death for all they knew.

Hannah laid her head on Paul's shoulder and fingered the lapel of his jacket. Even with all of the torment she had heard of Jews experiencing, her worry lay with Maria. She hoped with every breath that she would stay safe. She was in good hands; Elsa would make sure she stayed out of danger.

The Lord Almighty held them in His hands. Now all they could do was wait and wonder.

⁓

Hannah sat with her husband's head in her lap and listened to the train wheels clack over the rails. He had fallen asleep almost immediately after they got on the train. The car was very crowded, but they managed to find a spot in a corner next to a very small crack between the wooden beams. She watched as the desolate landscape flew past. Trees were bare and their leaves blew lamely in the wind. The grass, tall and brown, gave shelter to nothing but a breeze that blew between the swaying stocks. Hannah ran her fingers through Paul's hair and kissed his forehead. She loved him so much that she felt she would burst with it. She had been so thrilled at the thought of growing old with him, watching Maria become a young woman and get married. A tear slipped from her eye. They were supposed to live to see the end of the war, when the family would be reunited. But that future grew distant with every mile the train clattered over the tracks.

"Oh, Elsa, please take care of Maria," Hannah whispered. "Lord, why? Why does it have to be like this? You were supposed to protect me. Where is the Messiah? Because now would be a great time for him to come." She shut her eyes in frustration. "Why us, Lord? We trusted You to protect us. Where are You? Where?"

"Hannah?"

She opened her eyes to find Paul staring up at her.

"Are you all right?" he asked quietly.

After a moment, she shook her head sadly. "I'm so sorry, Paul. I'm sorry that you got dragged into this." The tears flowed freely now. "You never should have married me."

"No, no," he said quickly as he sat up and took her in his arms. "Marrying you was the best thing I have ever done. It is a day that will always be with me."

"Oh, Paul, how can you say that?" she cried, angry at his calm. Her composure wavered. "We are going to our deaths. You know that, don't you? They'll lock us away and kill us!"

Paul slapped her. Hannah's head whipped to the side and she saw dozens of other faces staring wide-eyed at her.

"Stop it," he whispered harshly. "You don't know what you're talking about. You're out of your wits. Now calm down."

Hannah stared at him with a blank face and sadness in her eyes. She was hurt at his actions, but knew that they were necessary. She was becoming hysterical and he was the only person keeping her mind sane.

"Paul, I'm scared," she whispered, broken.

"Oh, darling," he said with anguish, and pulled her to him. She cried silently for a long time. Paul understood her fear. The train took them on into unknown territory, and everything they knew would be challenged by what lay ahead.

A few hours later, Hannah woke with a start as the train jerked and began to slow down. She sat up from where she leaned against Paul's shoulder and looked through the crack in the boards. Tall, dreary buildings rose above them to the sad sky. People were everywhere, moving huge stones or carrying buckets and buckets of dirt. Blank faces stared as the train came to a slow whining stop in the center of all of the camp.

Paul put his arm around her protectively. "It's okay," he whispered. "I will always be with you, no matter what happens."

She nodded and gripped his other hand tightly. "I love you," she said, gentle tenderness reflected in her tone.

"I love you too, so much," he returned with a smile.

They shared a lingering kiss, basking in a moment that would remain etched in their memory.

The heavy door was pulled open with a screech and soldiers began shouting, pointing, and herding them out of the train. People were everywhere, covering every square inch of grimy dirt. Hannah clutched Paul's hand; she had never been so terrified in her entire life. They followed the throng of people that moved toward a line that led into a long building. Hannah glanced around. Older men and women hugged each other through silent tears. Little children stared wide-eyed from their parent's sides. Babies slept contentedly in their mothers' arms. No one talked, and yet the noise was deafening. She turned into Paul's shoulder when a straight-backed officer came striding past.

Abruptly, she was pulled away from Paul and pushed into a line of sullen women. Ahead, their clothing was removed and placed in piles according to the garment. Hannah cringed, repulsed. Turning, she searched frantically for Paul. He was in a similar line. When she got to the table, she was ordered to remove all of her clothing and jewelry. She glanced down, her face red as she hurriedly unbuttoned her dress and chemise.

Oh, Lord, could it get any worse?

Once again, she was pushed ahead to where three lines were forming. A scream behind her turned more than one head. Two officers were struggling with a young woman who refused to give up her jewelry. She frantically clasped her prized possession as she was dragged out one door. A few minutes later, a shot rang out. Everyone around her jumped. Hannah was hit hard over the head and an officer yelled at her to move into the middle of the three lines. Shaking, Hannah moved with the other women. They were sent into freezing showers and then handed scratchy blue and gray dresses. She slipped into the uniform silently and proceeded outside to where groups of women were being led to different barracks by several officers. She searched for Paul.

There he was! Being led to the barracks with a large group of men.

"Paul! Paul!" she screamed.

He turned and saw her, but shook his head hard. An officer turned toward her.

"Paul!" She tried to fight against the flow of women coming from the building, but she was pushed back farther and farther. Paul grew smaller.

"Paul!"

Something hit her head with a sickening thud, and everything went black.

Her wedding ring was gone.

That was the first thing Hannah realized when she woke. Where was it? She could not remember the officers taking it from her. Why not? They had taken everything else.

It was dark and soft breathing could be heard all around her. She sat up with a start. She was in the barracks on a narrow bunk with two other women. It was hard and cold, with just a flimsy blanket covering her. Tears came to her eyes and she lay back down, crying out to God in her heart. *Why?*

She was completely alone.

20

December 1941

T anya applied the last touch of deep red lipstick to her mouth and smacked her lips. Her red dress glinted in the lamplight of her apartment and her hair hung thick and wavy around her face. She smiled and winked at herself in the mirror of her vanity.

"You look great," she murmured. With that, she grabbed her fur coat and purse and went out into the brisk evening.

The night was alive with activity. Young people wandered everywhere on their way to dances and parties across Berlin. Tanya waved when she saw Doris passing by and they stopped to chat quickly.

"How are you, Doris?" Tanya asked.

"As well as one can be in the midst of a war, but we get by," Doris said with a chuckle.

"I know what you mean," Tanya replied. "This has been a very strange year."

"I'll see you at work on Monday?"

"Of course," Tanya replied.

"Until then, darling," Doris called as she continued down the street.

As Tanya walked on, she realized how true her previous statement was. The past year had been very strange indeed. Her time in America seemed like a dream now. Those memories had been overrun by the flood of events that had taken place from the moment she stepped off the boat in England.

85

Her uncertainty over her father's reaction to her arrival, then being nabbed by the NKVD. She smiled at the thought of her rescue in Poland. From then on the happenings in Berlin had kept her busy and content. She had met so many new people and the uncertainty she had felt in returning was completely gone. Now she wondered how she could have been so nervous. This was her home, where she had grown up with her mother, safe and happy within the magnificent city.

She frowned slightly as she continued to walk. Was she safe even now? She was surrounded by friends, but beneath it all there was a lurking suspicion. Any one of them could be a traitor and in a time of war, even close friends could not be trusted. She had yet to tell anyone that she was Russian, let alone that her father had a high office in the NKVD. Her life could be at risk by the slightest hint of suspicion. Tanya's mother had made sure that the truth of her husband being a socialist was kept hidden. And her father had his own personal political reasons for keeping his daughter a secret. That her Russian identity safely remained in the dark made her sleep easier at night.

The night brightened as the moon glowed down on the happening streets. Tanya slowed her steps as she came upon one of the finest restaurants in the city. Couples milled about, laughing and talking as if they had not a care in the world. It was one of the few times that Tanya felt slightly jealous of their easygoing lifestyle. To go through a day with nothing to worry about was a luxury that she had not had in some time.

An ache came to her stomach as she witnessed a loving father across the street sweep his daughter off her feet and into his arms. Their laughter came to her ears, and she almost put her fingers in her ears at the surprising pain it invoked.

"Hello there, beautiful."

Tanya turned toward Dederick's warm gentle voice and let her eyes say what she had to hide in public. She smiled. "Hi. I was wondering where you were."

Dederick glanced over her, love in his eyes. "Right here, waiting for the prettiest woman in Germany to arrive."

Tanya laughed. "That's sweet, but surely not true. However, I'll take the compliment."

He offered his arm. "Shall we?"

"Indeed."

They strolled into the restaurant and ignored the stares that were sent their way. It was not considered gentlemanly to meet a young lady for an outing, but Tanya had her reasons for asking Dederick to meet her at the restaurant. She did not want him to know where she lived or what she did with her free time. There were some things that he just could not know about her.

She stopped her thought process and smiled as he held out her chair for her. "Thank you," she said as he sat down across from her. "This is lovely."

"Hardly worthy of a woman like you."

She laughed at his flattery. The waiter arrived and Dederick ordered champagne. Light music played in the background and a few couples were dancing. Tanya slowly began to tap her foot with the rhythm.

"How was your day?" she asked.

"Relaxing," Dederick said with a smile. "It's been nice to get up and not worry about going out on patrol."

"Well, you deserve a time of leave after all you've done," Tanya murmured proudly.

"How is work at the library?" he asked.

"Oh, sometimes all I do is categorize and stack more and more books. It's all right, I suppose."

"Maybe I will come steal you away for lunch sometime."

Tanya smiled. "That would be nice."

They stared at each other for a long moment. She could not believe how much she loved him. Dederick had been a little rough around the edges when she had first met him, but as they grew to know each other during their time in Berlin, she could see that there was so much more to him than what was on the surface.

Tanya suddenly remembered. Pulling her gaze reluctantly away, she reached into the pocket of her coat and retrieved a lavishly decorated package. "Here. I could not wait to give this to you, so it's an early birthday present."

"Thank you." Dederick accepted the gift with a smile.

Opening the box, he pulled aside the tissue paper. Inside was a sleek pair of black leather gloves lined in soft wool. Dederick slowly pulled them out and fingered the fine leather.

"I ... I wasn't sure how much longer you would be here and I figured you might need them when you go ... well, wherever you are going," Tanya stated quietly. "Hopefully they'll remind you of me, and how you swept me off my feet."

"No more than you swept me off mine."

Dederick caught her eyes and held them for a long moment. So much was said without words in that gaze. Tanya had come back to Berlin unsure and afraid, without a single friend. In fear and darkness, Dederick had come and saved her from an uncertain future and had given her confidence. He, in turn, had changed from being a cold and lifeless soldier to believing in something again and slowly coming back to life.

"I love you," Dederick said quietly.

Tanya stared at him, every hope she had ever felt coming to life in her eyes. Her heart soared, as light as a bird and warm as a summer breeze. She leaned across the table, took his face in her hands and in front of the whole restaurant, she pressed her lips to his.

In a world that had gone mad in its desire for power, the kiss was the only thing that seemed real. The restaurant, the people, and the city faded, and left nothing in its wake but quiet and peace. Dederick's gentle touch swam over her, stealing her breath and her heart. She was lost in a sweet sense of tastes and smells that overcame all the fears and doubts.

Slowly, reluctantly, Tanya pulled away. Her eyes could not help but betray the overwhelming love that was bursting in her heart. His hands cupped her face, traced the outline of her jaw, as if memorizing every feature.

"I love you, too," she whispered.

He sighed as though in disbelief that she had truly said those words. "I don't know what happened, but somewhere along the way, I lost myself."

Tanya smiled. "Maybe you'll find yourself out on the dance floor."

They stood together and made their way to the center of the floor. Their minds saw themselves alone, locked in body and soul, a glow that penetrated the uncertainty and fear. The world outside raged with war and loss. Inside soared with hope and love. Tanya sighed.

"You are the most wonderful, compassionate man I've ever met," she whispered.

Dederick smiled, but as she leaned back against his chest, she missed the painful expression that crossed his face. He stumbled slightly and tried to right himself.

"Darling, are you all right?" Tanya asked.

"Oh. Yes, darling, just ... just tired."

She smiled up at him as they continued to sway to the music, lost in the tingling warmth of the evening's discovery.

Dederick's eyes lingered as long as they could on the woman he loved as she walked down the street into the night. At the corner she turned back, glimmering in lamplight and fog. The street was almost deserted, and he sighed and lifted his hand in farewell as she gave him a smile.

He turned toward home as Tanya disappeared into the darkness. Dederick had never been as happy as when he had first met her. When he had been in the lowest depths of despair and hope had gone, she came and rekindled the forgotten joys of life. His thoughts of loneliness drove him to the difficult remembrance of life before Tanya. A time when he had been driven by betrayal and anger, a time when he had committed the worst act of deceit he possibly could have, for nothing could ever hurt more deeply or terribly than betraying someone who loved him.

It was his fault that his mother was in prison. He alone was to blame. The entire episode could have gone unnoticed, but he had chosen in favor of his country. Now his mother was in jail, all because of those letters.

Dederick found them in his mother's dresser while home for a few days on leave. He had been cordially invited and, as any good son would, he had accepted. He still remembered with stark clarity the shock that ran through him as he stared at the United States postmark on the envelope. *Treason.* The word resonated through his mind as clearly as it had then. He did not think. He simply acted. And those actions had cost him dearly.

As Dederick walked slowly down the street, he let the cold seep through and hoped that it would harden the thoughts that flowed through his mind. But the image of his mother, pale and thin sitting against the cold hard wall of a dank cell, forced its way before him. It hit him like a fist in the gut and he clutched his head as if in pain.

"Why?" he shouted at the dark, lonely sky. A man across the street stared at him for a few seconds before walking on.

"Why do you torment me?" Dederick's eyes were wide, as if wanting to take in some unseen force above him. "I did what was right! For my people. For my country. Anything less would have been betrayal, just like they did to me! Should not justice be done? Why don't you answer?" he roared.

The wind was the only reply and a few minutes later, the snow began to fall. Dederick stared up at the flakes that fell softly on his face. "Leave me alone," he whispered. "You will not make me turn."

"Lieutenant? Are you all right?"

He turned to find one of his officers watching him from a few feet away, a confused look on his face.

"Uh, yes, I'm fine." Dederick struggled to put his emotions back together for a moment before turning fully to face the soldier. "It there trouble?"

"Only minor. We've got some night clubs to break up."

It hit the newspapers that morning with a bang. Everywhere in the city, people were talking about it, excitement in their voices, wonder behind their words. Tanya studied the dramatic headlines over her morning cup of tea as she sat by the window in one of the bakeries that lined the street. Japan had bombed the U.S. Pacific fleet and air bases in the state of Hawaii. She knew without a doubt that this meant war for the United States. Hitler would most certainly drive full force against them as well.

Tanya could not help but feel pain. Over 2,000 lives were lost. For many, a son, a father, a brother, a friend was not coming home. Her mind moved to Jesse Riker, the man whom she had met on the ship. Did he know the turmoil that his country had just plunged into? If he was still alive, he must know. Wherever he was, Tanya hoped he was well.

"Good morning, darling."

Tanya looked up from the paper in her hands. Dederick smiled down at her, his eyes filled with the love that had been so evident the last time she saw him.

"Hello," she said quietly.

He took the seat next to her and covered her hand with his. "Are you all right?" he asked, concern behind his voice.

Slowly, she turned the paper toward him, the headline there for him to see as clear as the winter day. "Have you seen this?"

"Yes. Quite a birthday present, huh?" He laughed a little.

Tanya narrowed her eyes and frowned. He took in her consternation, the way her hand was unresponsive under his. He moved his chair closer to her and took her face between his hands.

"Tanya, what's wrong?"

She lowered her eyes and freed herself from his alarmed gaze. "Dederick ... have you ever met an American?"

His hands froze where they had begun a slow descent back to his lap. She captured his gaze, pleading, hoping, wondering what he would say.

"I have," he replied slowly. "Why do you ask?"

"I met one once, coming home," she said quietly as she looked out at the busy street but did not hear the noise. "He was a nice man. A gentleman." Tanya turned back to him. "What did you think?"

Dederick was taken aback. He had not expected that he would ever have to think about Jesse Riker again. The relief that encompassed him after the man left had been short-lived. Hilda had moped around for months, checking the mail every day and writing letters almost as often. After she had left home, he had quickly let himself be removed from the atmosphere that had been suffocating him for years.

And now the man had been brought back to his mind again.

"Dederick?"

Tanya was staring at him, waiting for his answer. Dederick cleared his throat. "He was, uh ... polite." The word sounded dead to his ears.

She sighed, a soft smile on her lips. "Yes, they are nice, aren't they? They seem so ... alive, and happy. That's probably a silly description."

Dederick leaned toward her. "Tanya, why are we talking about this?"

He eyes were pained and she took his hand. "Why would anyone want to hurt them? What did they ever do to make Japan angry?"

He sighed and leaned back in his chair. "It's war. That's the way it goes."

"I hate it," she whispered. "I hate this war."

"Tanya, be careful what you say," Dederick warned. "There are those who would turn you in as a traitor for speaking those words."

Her eyes jerked to his, shock and hurt on her face. "You would, wouldn't you?" she said, anger behind her words. It was more a statement than a question.

Dederick was shocked at her resentment. "What are you talking about?"

"Rumors travel fast. I've heard things, Dederick. You would turn in your own mother on the slightest suspicion of treason. For what? A promotion?"

Anger boiled deep in his stomach. He slowly stood. "You don't know what you are saying, Tanya," he said, trying to calm himself.

"Don't I?" She sounded weary, and her eyes looked suddenly tired as she gazed up at him. "Who can be trusted? Who is a friend? You don't even know me, Dederick. I hardly know you. Our personal lives are so secretive." Tanya stood and grabbed her purse and newspaper. "We all have something to hide, Dederick. It's going to be hard, what we have. I hope that somehow we can fight through it." With that, she turned and made her way out of the bakery and down the street.

Later that night, the radio crackled in Tanya's apartment as she sat in front of the fireplace. She stared into the flames, her thoughts on what she had said that morning. She had spoken out, yes. Perhaps too much, but she had long ago lost the fear she had in coming back to a war torn country. Her heart was broken, she knew, but she could rise from the damage, unafraid of the challenges and obstacles that waited.

She listened quietly as the number of casualties from the Japanese attack was read off. She had read them many times, but it still pained her to think of the young sailors lying at the bottom of the harbor. She felt suddenly alone, lost and depressed.

A light snow began to fall and she watched it feather through the darkness from her window. It would be fresh on the ground tomorrow, covering up the dirty mush that was now in the streets.

Tanya turned off the radio, banked the fire and crawled into bed. A slight wind whistled outside and sent the snow drifting past. She closed her eyes against the exhaustion, the sorrow and the uncertainty. There was going to be plenty of time to deal with them. She would start from scratch, not only on her thoughts, but in her heart as well. After all, tomorrow was a new day.

Standing quietly on a busy street corner near the center of London, Grace watched the endless line of American troops march through the streets. Thousands of people lined the sidewalks, waving and cheering, grateful for the assistance that the United States was sending. After the attack on Pearl Harbor, the inevitable had not been long in coming. The Americans, along with Britain, declared war on the empire of Japan. In turn, Germany declared war on the United States, and so it began. Little over a month had passed and thousands of soldiers were pouring into England. The war had taken a dramatic turn.

Grace felt a familiar presence next to her and she turned to find Jeffrey watching the crowd wave to the troops in the street. She quietly folded her arms and turned her eyes back to the soldiers.

"So, they are coming at last," she said, no emotion in her voice. "It is finally their war as well."

"We will need them, Grace. We have a chance now," Jeffrey replied.

She sighed and nodded reluctantly. "I know Jeffrey, I don't mean to be critical, but I just wonder that maybe if they had come sooner, maybe all those men who died … maybe they would still be here."

"I know." He turned to her and carefully studied her face. "How are you doing? It's been a year."

Grace dropped her eyes and turned away from the street and the cheering crowds. The two of them slowly made their way toward the quieter London streets.

"It still seems so surreal. I know that he is dead. I've told myself that every day. But I always look up expecting him to walk through the door, like he always used to." She looked at Jeffrey. "How is your friend taking it? I saw her at the memorial. I know they were close years ago."

He nodded slowly and put his hands into his pockets. "It's been hard on her. I myself did not realize how close she was to him until he died. It was a bit of a wakeup call for me."

"For me as well."

They stopped and stared at one another for a moment. An understanding passed between them, but it broke quickly as Jeffrey cleared his throat. Grace looked away and clasped her hands.

"Well, I must be getting back to the office. I'll see you later, Grace," Jeffrey said. "May I hail you a cab?"

"No, don't be silly. I'll be seeing you, Jeffrey. Good-bye." She turned and walked briskly down the street without looking back.

Ten minutes later, Grace's cab pulled up to her house. She paid the fare and slowly walked inside. From the kitchen, she heard her mother puttering around preparing for the midday meal. She tossed her coat and bag on the hall buffet and found her favorite chair in the living room. She flipped on the wireless next to her and for a moment, simply listened to the low static.

Since the news of Jesse's death, life had trudged on slowly, quietly. Her father had taken on the responsibility of writing to the Rikers, hoping he could express his deep sorrow to them in more comforting tones than the military. Life had gone on. Though she had rid herself of the feelings she once harbored for him, there still remained a low, deep ache in her gut at the loss of her friend. He had filled the house with laughter and joy, and the silence that now lingered seemed unnatural, unreal.

The radio crackled again, discussing the coming of the American soldiers. Grace touched her hand to her head and reaching over, she flipped off the wireless. She could not stay in the house. Her thoughts grew dreary when she was idle and she needed to get out.

"Mother," she called as she stood and moved toward the kitchen. Mary appeared in the doorway.

"Yes, dear?"

"I'm going out for a while. I don't know when I'll be back, so don't worry yourself."

Mary studied her daughter. Her concern was evident as she studied the somber face and sunken cheeks. She went to her and gently laid her hand against Grace's cheek.

"Are you all right?" she asked softly.

Grace knew her mother was giving her the chance to answer as she felt. She smiled gratefully. "I just need to get out of the house for a while. Do something to take my mind off of ... things."

Mary nodded in understanding. "Well, since you're going out, would you take some food to your father for me?"

"Certainly." Grace followed her mother back into the kitchen where a basket sat on the counter.

"And while you're there, maybe you could help him with anything he needs. You know how he enjoys your company," Mary encouraged.

Grace smiled and took the basket. "Perhaps I will."

Mary walked her to the front door and handed her the coat and bag she had just discarded with the urge to have a good time. When the door closed behind her, Grace stood on the step and stared out at the bustling London street. Despite the dreary weather that had accompanied the new year with a vengeance, the city was always busy. She slowly started down the steps, the basket clutched in her hands. Somehow, she had to forget about the loneliness of the past year.

When Grace reached the hospital, she hurried up the walk and onto the enclosed porch where several wounded were lounging in deck chairs. Some had bandages over their eyes; many had lost limbs, and all stared with dull eyes at the dark sky. Her gaze faltered when a young man turned sad eyes to her face. Going through the door, she nearly ran into her father.

"Grace!" he exclaimed, surprised.

"Father! Um, Mum asked me to deliver this food to you, and I wanted to see if you needed any help. You look very crowded," she commented as she looked around.

"Well, thank you, dear," he said with a smile. "Help is always needed." He took the basket from her. "I'll put this in the lounge. If you will, there is a man waiting to have his head bandaged in the ward down the hall."

"All right." Grace kissed his cheek and started down the hall to the room he had indicated, removing her hat and coat.

She entered quietly. The room was dim, and all of the soldiers were asleep. The only sound was their even breathing. Grace stared at them, compassion and despair mingling in her eyes. How many men would have to be hurt, would have to die, for this war to end? Maybe this was not such a good idea. Painful memories pressed against her heart at the sight of the wounded men. Her eyes began to fill with tears and she wiped at them uselessly.

"Looking for someone?"

Startled, Grace looked around for the voice. It had come from a handsome young soldier who was sitting in a chair against the wall next to the door. No wonder she had not seen him when she came in. His uniform was dirty, torn in some places, which made it difficult to see his branch of the military, and above his left eye, a gash about three inches long had been stitched together, leaving a thick clean red line. His hands had bloodstains on them, probably from where he had reached up to the wound. His piercing eyes found hers and she forced a kind smile on her face.

"You, I believe," she said in answer to his question. She moved to the sink and washed her hands before opening a cupboard and removing a white rolled bandage.

"You don't look like a nurse," he stated, assessing her attire.

"And you don't sound English," she returned.

"Touché."

Grace laughed. "My father is a doctor here," she answered. Holding the cloth to the back of his head, she slowly wrapped it around the wound. "How did you get this?"

"Training accident. Pretty stupid, actually. I butchered a landing and bashed my head against the stick," he said sheepishly.

"You're a pilot," she commented with a slightly pained smile. "Don't worry. You're not the first." She studied him. "Where in America are you from?"

"Texas. Beautiful country. The best in my opinion."

Her smile grew full of laughter. Securing his bandage, she stepped away and held out her hand. "I'm Grace Holden."

"Joshua Sauders," he answered as he shook her hand.

She looked at him curiously. "That sounds familiar. We haven't met before, have we?"

"I highly doubt it. I've been so involved in the Eagle Squadron, and this is only my second trip to the hospital and hopefully my last," he added with a smile.

"The Eagle Squadron. I had a friend in the Eagle Squadron. He was killed about a year ago," Grace said quietly.

"Wait. Holden? Your friend wasn't Jesse Riker, was it?" he asked.

Grace stepped back, shocked. "It was."

Joshua stood and stepped toward her. "That's why your name is familiar. We flew together in the states, too. We were as close as brothers up there in the clouds."

She smiled softly at his description. "He was a good friend, wasn't he?"

"The best."

They shared a quiet moment, memories wrapped in the silence of the ward. Grace finally looked up at Joshua and caught him watching her, a smile on his face.

"I'm glad to have met you, Grace," he murmured.

Grace reached a hand up and touched his bandaged head gently, letting her smile widen.

"And I you, Joshua."

Grace walked home with a lighter step that afternoon. She felt like she had accomplished something of value for the first time in months. She hummed as she walked and greeted everyone she passed. She had just decided that she would go back to the hospital tomorrow when a voice in front of her called her name. Her heart began to race and butterflies winged through her stomach as she looked ahead and saw Jeffrey walking quickly toward her.

"Jeffrey, um ... hello," she said softly, her heart pounding above her words. She felt heat rise up her neck as she noticed his intense gaze. "Is everything all right?"

"Grace, what luck! I was just at your house and your mother told me you went to the hospital. I was just on my way there," he said with a soft smile.

"Yes, I was helping my father for a while. Why were you going to the hospital?"

Jeffrey shifted on his feet for a moment before replying, "I wanted to see you."

"Oh," she said after a second. "That was kind of you. Thank you."

Grace started a slow steady walk up the street, wondering, hoping he would follow. She wanted his company desperately, but felt it improper for her to convey it.

Please, Jeffrey, walk with me. Stay with me.

He fell in step beside her, and Grace turned her face toward the opposite walk to hide her joyous smile. Bells began to ring in her heart and she could not stop them.

Somewhere along the way, things had changed. Grace and Jeffrey had been friends for years, but suddenly they had taken a turn along the road, and the feelings were quite different now, she knew.

"So," he said, "how have you been?"

She turned back and looked at him as they walked. "As well as I can be since you saw me a little while ago."

"Yes, well, I realized I left rather rudely and, well ... we haven't spent much time with each other over the past several months. I guess I just ..."

Grace waited for him to continue. A slight touch against her hand made her look down. His fingers rested lightly against her palm, waiting for an invitation. She smiled softly and intertwined her fingers with his. Jeffrey clasped her hand tightly. She looked up at him. His eyes held something she had never seen before, something he had saved just for her.

"I've missed you, too," she murmured.

They walked on for a time, content to be together for the short time they had. They laughed and talked about memories they had of the past, enjoying the afternoon.

"Do you remember when we were in the café about a year ago, talking about how miserable we both were?" Grace asked.

Jeffrey laughed. "Yes."

"I don't see how I could ever feel that way now. I thought I would never get over him when he died, but I guess I knew all along that I could never have him."

"Jesse Riker?" he asked.

"Yes."

Jeffrey looked thoughtful as they continued on. "It's funny how life seems to blind us to what's right in front of us until the right moment, and we realize exactly what we've been missing."

They shared a long look. Grace had been in love with Jesse. And Jeffrey had been in love with Hilda. And all the while, the two had been in love with each other. Life worked in strange ways sometimes.

They arrived at Grace's house a few minutes later. Jeffrey walked her to the door, but did not relinquish her hand. She looked at him, only slightly surprised.

"May I call on you again?" he asked softly.

Grace smiled and reached up to plant a light kiss on his cheek.

"You can take that as a yes," she murmured.

21

Dederick crouched as he ran to the shelter of the overturned military truck. Everywhere around him, the ground troops slowly advanced closer and closer to Sevastopol. The heavy fire had not let up for days and every bone in his body ached with weariness. He took a sip from his canteen before turning to the soldier next to him.

"This siege will never end!" Dederick groaned loudly above the gunfire.

"I believe that's why they call it a siege, sir," the soldier said.

Dederick gave him a look. "No kidding. How old are you?"

"I'll be eighteen in August, sir," he replied. His eyes darted around, not quite believing that he was having this conversation with his commanding officer.

"Eighteen," Dederick muttered under his breath. "Those were the days."

"Sir?" the soldier asked, confused.

"Look out!"

The nearby loud cry rose above their conversation. The soldier looked up, and his eyes grew wide. In a quick move, he shoved Dederick several feet away seconds before a shell hit the truck that they had just been hiding behind. Dederick was thrown back and he cried out as pain bust into his lower arm. Holding it to his side, he looked around. The young soldier lay on his back, staring wide-eyed up at the smoke-filled sky.

"No," Dederick gritted out, moving to his side. "Medic! Medic!"

He carefully placed the boy's head in his lap with his good arm. "Come on, come on," he pleaded softly. "Hang in there ... you're fine."

Dederick's hand fell away from the boy's face, unable to accept the sacrifice. It should have been him. He should have remembered what easy targets vehicles made. But he had not.

A medic appeared at his side.

"He's dead, sir," the medic said in a flat tone after feeling for a pulse. "The troops are moving toward the harbor. They hope to take them by surprise from the south."

Dederick could not answer. His eyes were glued to the pale dirty face in front of him. So young. Why did they have to be so young? A life that could have been lived so quickly ripped apart at the hands of war. When victory came, the boy would not return home.

"Sir, your arm!" the medic exclaimed. He took it for closer examination.

Pain like a knife seared through Dederick so badly he grew nauseous. Spots danced before his eye and a heated darkness consumed him.

The fields and hills of Poland flashed by as the train raced over the rails toward Moscow. Tanya gazed out of the window as they went along. Her fingers absentmindedly traced the bottom sill, her eyes open but not seeing.

The past months had been long and uncertain. The arrival of the American Forces in England had spurred the Germans into greater action. The air raids on Britain had been frequent, and German offensives had begun in both the Crimea and the Gazala Line. The assassination of SS leader Heydrich had been avenged, but at the loss of thousands of innocent lives in the liquidation of Lidice. A new wind was blowing.

Tanya pulled a letter out of her bag that Dederick had sent her over a month before. Since the clash they had had in December, she had not expected to hear much from him. His letter was brief, but there was so much to be taken from it. Her hands smoothed the paper as she read.

Dear Tanya,

We are being sent to Sevastopol. We leave in two days. I don't expect you to be at the station, but I would very much like to see you. I am sorry about the silence I have kept these past few months. Know that it is not your fault. I have been struggling with my thoughts lately.

I hope to see you at the station but if not, I will understand.

Yours,
Dederick

Tanya regretted not going to the train station every day. It had only taken her a second to realize how much she really *did* want to see Dederick. A few days later, she did something she thought she would never do.

She contacted her father.

A letter of reply came a few weeks later, a note of surprise hidden beneath the much more evident business tone. He had agreed to see her safely to Moscow. Two escorts would be waiting for her in Poland.

Tanya now looked across at the two stone-faced men. They were not the ones who had tried to take her forcibly a few years back, but they looked as though they would in a heartbeat. Tanya started second guessing her plan. She had put herself into her father's power by writing to him. Was the captivity worth it for a chance to see the man she loved? Dederick's face swam before her mind. Yes, anything to see him smile and take her in his arms. Tanya replaced the letter in her bag and leaned back against the seat. Her eyes drifted shut, and she fell asleep to the rocking of the car.

When she awoke, the sky had grown noticeably darker. She rubbed her eyes and tried to get the crick out of her neck. Standing up, she stretched her aching limbs.

The door to the compartment burst open, and her escorts charged inside.

"What are you doing?" the taller one demanded in Russian.

"Stretching," Tanya replied, irritated. She placed her hands on her hips. "Do you mind?"

He turned to the other and they muttered together. The second nodded and hurried out.

"You know I can understand you," Tanya said sarcastically.

He sat down, much more calm than he had been moments before. "Sergei is bringing you some food," he said, motioning for her to sit.

She did, but kept an annoyed eye on him.

"We were sent to protect you, Tanya," he continued. "We wouldn't want anything to happen to you."

She sighed and leaned back, staring out into the darkness. "Don't worry. I'm not going anywhere."

"We will be arriving in Moscow tomorrow morning," he stated as he took a book from his satchel. "I suggest you sleep some more. You will want to be well rested before you see your father."

Tanya almost jumped at the word. Her father. Did she even think of him as such? Hardly. She could count the times she had spent with him on one hand. The last time she saw him, she was a teenager. Several years had passed and she knew that he might not recognize her. It did not matter. She would not be staying long. She was there to see Dederick, and then she was going home. And nothing was going to stop her.

Tanya stepped out of the cab and stared up at the tall foreboding building. Though she had a plan in place to find Dederick and escape, she had a horrible thought that if she walked into that building now, she would never come out.

Her heart pounded as she walked between her escorts into the lobby and started up the stairs. With each step, Tanya grew more nervous at the meeting ahead of her. Deep within her, beyond the fear of seeing her father again, was the hope that he would be happy to see her. She was his daughter. He must harbor some love for her.

They walked into a small lounge that was filled with plush chairs. A secretary sat at the far end of the room typing away at her desk. She looked up at their entrance.

"We are here to see Nicholas Berezovsky," Sergei stated.

She stood, her manner looking as stiff as her starched black suit. "He is in a meeting, but he should be finished any minute. Please sit down."

Tanya took a seat that faced the door they had entered by. It was her one escape, the one that was so close and yet so far. She felt the pressure begin to suffocate her as her escorts took a place on either side of her. They were not going to give her the chance to run. She tried to breathe normally and put on a nonchalant air. Her hands trembled as she placed them in her lap. She had tried to avoid this moment at all costs. Yet here she was.

Glancing around the dim room, Tanya noted wryly how well the atmosphere matched the personality of the Soviet Union. She remembered winters in Moscow as a child. It had been even drearier then, and everywhere she went felt like prison. Nothing had changed.

The door behind her opened with a slight click and muffled laughter came from inside the room. Tanya stiffened. *Oh, Lord, help.*

The heels of the secretary sounded across the floor and soft voices were heard. A moment later, all noise ceased. Tanya closed her eyes and silently pleaded for strength, then slowly stood and turned.

An old man stared back at her. Dressed in a black suit of the finest quality, Nicholas Berezovsky studied his daughter. His graying hair brushed his collar and his dark brown eyes refused to leave hers as he slowly walked toward her. His hand reached out and Tanya told herself not to flinch. He noticed her discomfort as he touched her cheek very lightly.

"Yes," Nicholas murmured. "Just like your mother."

He turned and waved his agents away as he led her into his large office. The secretary went back to the work at her desk and Tanya watched her disappear as the door closed behind them, and let out a slow breath. Her last escape had just been cut off.

Tanya glanced around. The room was entirely furnished with none but the highest quality of dark wood. She decided to be one step ahead of her father in the conversation.

"I see the Soviets have decorated you nicely for your service," she commented as she sat down in one of the dark red velvet chairs.

Nicholas eyed her as he sat down. "It is customary with the office I hold."

"Of course," she remarked. Tanya slowly folded her hands in her lap. A slight look down told her they were trembling.

Calm. Don't let him see you're afraid.

After several moments of silence, Nicholas digressed. "I must say Tanya, that your letter came as quite a surprise," he stated, staring at her as though he would pierce into her darkest secrets. She turned her eyes away and focused on the massive bookshelves lining each wall.

"I know," she said. "Do you enjoy reading?"

"Excuse me?" he asked, a bit taken aback.

Tanya smiled. She had managed to catch him off guard. "I was just noticing the extraordinary amount of books you have and wondered if you took a fancy to reading." She turned innocent eyes to him.

Nicholas looked lost for a moment. "Well, yes, I suppose on some occasions when I have the time," he finally answered.

"I enjoy reading as well," Tanya continued, careful not to allow him another chance to speak. "Do you think I might borrow some from time to time?"

"Well ... I suppose that would be all right."

"Oh, wonderful, thank you." she said. She stood quickly and went over to study some of the volumes. Her eyes saw the words but did not comprehend them. She needed space to breath. Space to fight her war of wits against him.

"Tanya," Nicholas called, and she froze. She knew what was coming.

"I've been meaning to ask you," he continued even though she did not turn to him. "Why, after such unwillingness to return a few years ago, did you suddenly write and say you were coming to Moscow?"

She was ready with a reply. "I'm surprised that with your high position you don't already know, Father." Tanya added the last word with emphasis.

Before he could reply, the secretary opened the door and placed Nicholas' mail on his desk. They both watched her leave.

"Does she know?" Tanya asked.

"Yes."

She raised an eyebrow at his indifferent answer. Did he realize what that meant? Coming back over, she sat down and leaned toward him.

"So, you managed to keep your office and still tell everyone that you had a half German daughter living in Berlin who was coming to visit you?" she questioned.

"No, I managed to keep my office by telling everyone that I had a full-blooded Russian daughter in occupied Poland who was coming to me for safety," he answered.

Tanya sat back, amazed at his bluff. "Well, well," she murmured. "Here I am thinking that I caused such a stir because I might have revealed your dark secret by sending you my letter. How did you explain the German postmark?"

"I did not have to," he replied. "She only puts it on my desk. She does not look at it."

"Clever you are, Father. I suppose that comes in handy with your job."

Nicholas stood slowly. Tanya stared up at him, and fear pinched at her gut. She had pushed too far.

"I did not invite you here to interrogate me, Tanya. You're behaving like a spoiled teenager. Perhaps you start behaving less like a child and more like my grown daughter."

Tanya stood as well. "Perhaps you start behaving less like a businessman and more like my father."

They stared at each other, their challenging words hanging between them. They had finally rid themselves of all former pretenses and were truly showing their feelings. They each had the willpower to take the other down a notch and they were ready to pull out their most painful weapons to triumph.

Finally, Nicholas spoke, his voice low and calm. "Why did you come?"

Tanya's eyes faltered. It had come to it at last. What she said would determine whether she walked freely from the office or went through Moscow with escorts for the rest of her life. She stared hard into his eyes, and her heart prayed that he would believe her.

"Why do you think I came? Simply because I chose to remain in Berlin after Mother died does not mean that I hate you, or that I don't wish to be with you. You are the only family I know." She sighed and leaned back, hoping the effect would help win him over. "The air raids in the city were getting more frequent and worse, so I felt it was time for me to leave. You were the only one I knew I could come to."

When she finished, she stared at him with what she hoped was an innocent look. Her father's eyes seemed dark and hard as he weighed her answer.

"Was there another reason?" he questioned.

She acted surprised. "What other reason would there be?"

He shrugged. "Well, it is possible that you came here to spy on me and report to someone in Berlin."

She stood, insulted. "Father!"

Her rage must have appeared very real, for he looked apologetic.

"You must understand my curiosity, Tanya. I have not heard from you since your mother's death, and your letter was such a shock that I am quite overwhelmed and unsure as to why you are here."

"I just told you," she said softly, looking down.

Nicholas was quiet as he contemplated her words. Tanya kept her eyes on her hands, but her heart pounded so loudly in her ears that she was afraid he could hear. He had to believe her. He had to.

After a moment, Nicholas buzzed his secretary. "Call for a taxi."

"Yes, Comrade Berezovsky," she said through the intercom.

Tanya looked up, confused. His eyes met hers.

"I've arranged an apartment for you not far from here. You should be comfortable there," he said flatly.

She stared long and hard at him. Was he really letting her walk away? She was free to go? Nicholas sat down and began to shuffle through his mail. Instinctively, Tanya went around to his chair and placed a light kiss on his forehead.

"Thank you, Father," she murmured. He did not say anything, so she turned and walked slowly to the door. She opened it, but turned back for one final look. Nicholas remained at his desk, opening his mail. She slowly went out the door and walked passed her two escorts, who were sitting just outside the door, and took the stairs down to the lobby. The cab was waiting outside and she got in. The driver knew exactly where to go and she arrived a few minutes later at a nice apartment building near the commercial area of Moscow. The landlord led her to the second floor, where a finely furnished two-room flat awaited her.

When Tanya was finally alone, she went to the window and cautiously looked down at the street. People were everywhere, most of them in ragged old clothing. The glory of the Soviet Union. Glancing around, Tanya saw no lone figure standing around the entrance of the building. No one had followed her. Perhaps her father trusted her after all.

With the first meeting over, Tanya felt more confident that getting to Sevastopol would not be too difficult. She had not doubt that it would fall to the Germans and once she arrived there, she would be safe from her father's grasp. And she would be with Dederick.

The mere thought of the man she loved made her ache inside. It had been far too long since she had last seen him and she suddenly wished she had a picture of him. At least that would ease her pain somewhat. For now, all she could do was wait and hope for the day of their reunion to come soon.

Forgive me, Dederick, for being so stubborn. I was a fool to let you go. I'm coming, my love. I'm coming.

⤚

Nicholas threw aside his mail. Tanya's kiss had left him unsure of her true intentions for a moment, but he soon remembered who he was. He did not know why she was here, but he was going to find out.

"Tell Sergei to come in here," he commanded over the intercom.

Nicholas knew Tanya was lying when she said that she had come to see him. She had administered her wiles, but they had no effect on him. He was surprised that she had fallen so easily for his scheme. Was she that gullible? Or had her relief over their first meeting so engulfed her as to blind her to his true intentions? Whatever it was, he did not think she would so easily tell him why she was really in Moscow. It did not fail to confuse him as to her motive. She knew no one in the city. She had only been to Moscow once as a small girl. Nicholas had been building up his career then, so he had never let her or her mother leave the apartment unless he was with them. There was no possible person she could know.

Nicholas stood and paced behind his desk. What factors would come into play when he found out what Tanya was really about? For all he knew, she could have truly come to him for safety from the air raids. And yet he did not think that was the reason. She had always been a strong-willed girl. Nothing had stopped her from going to America when her mother died. He could not picture her running to him, of all people, for protection. Something was wrong. There were endless possibilities to account for her coming to Moscow. It would be difficult, yes. But he would find out all the same.

A knock sounded on the door. Sergei entered and came forward. Nicholas put on a business like attitude and came to sit in his chair with a regal manner.

"You and your comrade did well in escorting my daughter here," he said formally. The agent nodded his thanks.

"Your services are required once more," Nicholas continued. "You received the information I sent you about the apartment?"

"Yes, Comrade Berezovsky," Sergei replied.

"Good. Her intentions here in Moscow must be revealed. You understand?"

"Yes, Comrade Berezovsky."

Hannah slowly trod back to the barracks. She was alone, cold and tired. She had been at Auschwitz for nearly a week now. The transfer to the camp had been horrendous. The smell had been so bad that she fainted, awakening to the shouts of the soldiers as they pulled into the camp. They had been herded once more through the lines and showers, once again given scratchy frocks and led to barracks. Hannah was surprised she had survived for so long; the past year felt more like ten. Despite all of the atrocities and pain, she had forgotten how to cry. The last time she had let herself was when she had secretly met with Paul several months ago. The endless weeks in the camp had not been kind to him. The agony of seeing him looking pale and gaunt had been too much for her to bear. He had been so strong and handsome and now, because of his love for her, he had allowed himself to be beaten and transformed into a man she no longer recognized. Hannah had never felt such anger boil within her, even when her father had been killed. That night, she had cried herself to sleep for the last time. She went through the motions of the manual labor and forced herself not to think about Paul, or where he might be, if he was even still alive. She knew she would break down if she did and she could not show them that she was defeated.

Hannah's feet dragged as she continued on down the long line of barracks. Far away down the road, the searchlights shone bright along the wall and flashed in her face every now and then before moving on. Guards walked around their outposts, laughing and talking. Hannah could not remember the last time she had laughed. Perhaps it had been the day she had said good-bye to her precious daughter, on that hopeful night so long ago. Hannah sighed and closed her eyes to put out the memory.

Suddenly, a hand shot out from between two barracks and grabbed her arm. She was yanked into the shadows and a hand covered her mouth to prevent her from screaming. Eyes wide with terror, Hannah glanced around, blind as her eyes adjusted to the darkness trying to see her attacker. Through the gray shadows she saw Paul's face appear, a finger to his lips in a warning for silence. Hannah immediately stopped struggling as relief flooded over her. The moment he removed his hand from her mouth, she threw her arms around him and held him like a lifeline that had been thrown to her just in time. She breathed him in, content to have this moment, however short it was. She felt his arms come around her, embracing her with the same intensity. Hannah felt her eyes begin to grow wet, and she fought the tears back with a vengeance. She had to be strong for Paul, show him that she was all right.

"Oh, I was so scared," she whispered. "I didn't know if they had moved you as well." She leaned back and framed his face. "I've missed you so much."

Paul covered her hands with his own. "I've missed you, too. I'm sorry it took so long to see you."

"I don't care," she said softly. "You're here now and that's all that matters."

He sighed and kissed her with passion and longing. Hannah felt her heart begin to race. How she had missed being with him! The emptiness in her heart was like a huge chasm she felt she would never be able to cross. If this was all she would ever have, then she would take it. Her arms went around him again, and she returned his kiss with all the love she held inside. How she needed this. Wanted this.

After several moments they finally drew apart, breathless. Hannah let her head fall on Paul's chest, and his arms held her as they simply listened to the closing night. Tomorrow would begin another day of torture, resuming the nightmare they lived in, but right now he was here.

"I need you," she whispered shakily.

"I know, darling," he replied. "When all this is over, we will go home to our little girl and we will never be separated again."

Hannah lifted pain-filled eyes to his. She wanted to believe him. So badly.

"What will happen to us?" she asked.

Paul shook his head, defeat in his face. "I don't know, Hannah. Every now and then I hear something about the war, but it's been quiet for several months." He put his hands on her shoulders and shook her slightly. "No matter what happens, stay strong. You must stay strong."

"I'm trying, Paul," Hannah said quietly. "It's just so hard sometimes."

"I know," he replied. "Don't worry. They can keep us apart, but I will protect you."

She smiled softly up at him. "I know you will. I love you."

"I love you."

They shared another lingering kiss, and then just as quickly as he had appeared, Paul was gone in the shadows. Hannah let herself breathe for a few moments before carefully glancing around. She quickly stepped out and resumed her slow, dragging pace to her barracks. Inside, her heart beat lighter. Somehow it would be okay. After seeing Paul, she knew they could make it. Together.

Hannah tried not to pay attention to the harsh yells coming from the guard a few feet away. She continued with her steady pace as she pushed the wheelbarrow back over to the massive pile of stones waiting to be carted away. She kept her eyes down as she knelt next to one of the women around the huge mound. As she began to load more stones, she made sure not to make eye contact with anyone around her. The despair in their eyes only served to make her feel all the more trapped.

Sweat clung to her back as she moved the heavy stones. Though no one in the group spoke, the noise was deafening. All around them, machinery groaned, guards yelled, hammers pounded and every now and then, a gunshot rang out. Hannah though of the prisoners led to the gas chambers or taken outside the walls and executed. How many knew they were going to their deaths? How many begged for mercy? How many were defiant to the end? Was that what they were all working toward? Ultimate pain and death. Some of the stories she'd heard were horrifying. Women cut in half? Disabled children strangled in attempts to "help" them walk again? Hannah grimaced. What had the world come to? Who could allow such evil to endure?

Her tormented thoughts took her mind away from her work and she dropped a heavy rock on her foot mindlessly.

"Ouch!"

"Oh, are you all right?" a soft voice asked.

Hannah turned. The small woman next to her gazed at her in astonishment.

"Oh, my ..."

"Judith?" Hannah whispered in disbelief.

"Hannah ... I can't believe it! I didn't think I'd ever see you again!"

Hannah embraced her dear friend from home with a small cry. She quickly pulled away when she noticed the guard begin to turn in their direction. They both went back to their work.

"When did you get here?" Judith murmured.

"A week ago," Hannah replied as she continued to fill the wheelbarrow with stones. "And you?"

"I've been here for about three months."

"Where were you before?"

"Dachau."

"I've heard that with the deportations beginning outside of Germany, many Jews have gone into hiding," Hannah said quietly.

"Yes. They were the smart ones."

Hannah laughed bitterly. Knowing the Nazis, they would weed out as many people as they could. They were ruthless unrelenting scavengers, and always would be.

"Judith," she said quietly. "Do you every wonder why the Messiah hasn't come?"

Judith turned to her, eyes alight with a new fire. "He has come, Hannah."

At Judith's words, she put down the stone abruptly and stared at her.

"What?" Hannah whispered. The possibility that the man for whom her ancestors had waited centuries for had finally come put such a hope in her heart as to make her chest begin to ache. "How ..."

"He is Jesus," Judith whispered, radiant with joy.

Hannah almost laughed aloud at her absurd answer. "Oh Judith, don't tell me you're turning into one of those ridiculous Christians."

"But it's real, Hannah," Judith urged. "He really is the Messiah! When I was in Dachau, I met a man there who showed me the truth. It's all in the book of Isaiah, everything we ever wanted. It was all right in front of us the whole time. At first I didn't believe him but after I read it, I felt such peace. I knew it had to be true."

Hannah stared at her as if she did not know her. "Judith, have you gone mad?"

"Hannah, I promise. Have I ever lied to you? Jesus Christ is the Messiah!"

"You don't know what you're saying," she muttered, piling more stones.

Judith was quiet for a minute, then said softly, "He's real, Hannah. All you have to do is accept him and you can escape this hellish nightmare." Glancing around, she pulled several rumpled, dirty pages from inside her shirt and slipped them to Hannah, who had no choice but to take them as the guard looked toward them. She quickly hid them in her own shirt.

"Read it, Hannah," Judith whispered before she returned to her work. "Read it, and you will see the truth."

Hannah didn't answer. She wouldn't.

She couldn't.

That night as Hannah fell into bed, she noticed that over half of the bunks across from her were bare. The Hungarian gypsies that had occupied them were gone. Hannah lay down on her side, a cold chill in her bones. Outside, a cruel wind whistled through the silent camp. An occasional dog barked but other than that, nothing stirred. With the scratchy blanket pulled up to her shoulder, Hannah tried to breathe as quietly as she could, fearing that if she even sneezed, a guard would come crashing through the door and drag her away to be killed.

At Auschwitz, the value of life stood precariously on a tight rope. One false move and she could be stomped out like a flame on the ground. The thought made her head spin and she closed her eyes and tried to calm herself. She had to take it one day at a time. The Nazis had shown their colors on the value of life. For all she knew, one day could be all she had.

♫

A few days later, Judith did not appear at the rock pile. Hannah knew better than to ask anyone around her of the young woman's whereabouts, but the strange churning of dread within her could not be ignored. Women who disappeared never came back.

Her spirits lightened later in the day. She was helping an older woman whose wheelbarrow had overturned. As they hurriedly retrieved the rocks before any guards saw, Hannah glanced up for a moment. There on the dusty hill above her, bathed in the late afternoon glow, was Paul. He stood calmly, watching her. She could not see his eyes, but she knew that his gaze was for her alone. She stood slowly and let the rocks in her hand fall into the growing pile. Paul slowly put a hand to his lips. Anyone watching would have thought he was stifling a yawn, but she knew. She softly touched her own lips to receive the kiss he blew her. Her heart felt lighter than it had in days. Even so, the sadness she felt radiating from him made her want to take him in her arms and comfort him. Hannah knew that he and several others had been forced to dig massive graves to accommodate thousands of bodies. The turmoil he must experience every time he threw a lifeless man, woman or child into the pit made her heart clench.

Stay strong, he had said to her. She would be. For him, she would be.

As she fell into bed that night, Hannah prayed. She prayed harder than she ever had. She prayed for Paul and for all of their friends suffering through the same horrific experience. She hoped dearly that the torment would soon end and they could all return home. She prayed that the war would come to a close, and that the world would know the reality of all that had occurred. When they were released, they would not keep silent. They could not. Every nation would realize the brutality that coexisted with the perceived peace that tried to make them blind to all else. Yes, they would see and know.

And they would remember.

♫

True to Hannah's prayer, the world was beginning to see and realize just what was going on behind the neat regime of Nazi Germany. In England, the British House of Commons had been informed of the mass executions of the Jews occurring throughout Nazi controlled Europe. After British Foreign Secretary Anthony Eden's account of these killings, the United States declared that the atrocious crimes would be avenged. Soviet troops were moving west, slowly penetrating controlled areas. Though the Nazis were intent on destroying all traces of the death camps, their attempts became more and more unsuccessful.

The world would know. For all of the voices that had been and would be silenced, they would live on in the testimonies of others who would come forward, and those who came and witnessed the atrocities, and by these witnesses, the world would never forget.

"There are things that we don't want to happen but have to accept, things we don't want to know but have to learn, and people we can't live without but have to let go."

Unknown

22

London, December 1942

Dr. and Mrs. John Holden
Request the pleasure of your company
At the marriage of their daughter
Grace Elizabeth Holden
To
Jeffrey Alexander Rolf
On the seventeenth day of December
In the year of our Lord nineteen hundred and forty two

Hilda glanced at the invitation once again as she put the final touches on her hair. She still couldn't believe it. The same amazement resided in her as it had the day the invitation arrived at her door a few months ago. At long last, Jeffrey was getting married.

Hilda looked in the mirror one more time and assessed her appearance. She wore a burgundy colored dress with a black sash at the waist and black trim around the hem and sleeves. She put her hand to her hair, which she had intricately twisted and braided until it lay in a thick figure eight against her head. She picked up her hat and pinned it to her head so that it was fashionably cocked to one side. She gave a deep breath and grabbed her coat from her bed and hurried out the door. It would not be polite to show up late to her good friend's wedding.

Hilda stepped out onto the street and hailed a cab. She bundled herself inside against the cold winter weather. The driver made his way expertly through the afternoon traffic, and as they went, she allowed herself to think back on the past two years.

Hilda felt nothing but emptiness after Jesse's death, unsure of where to go and what to do. She no longer felt the thrill or desire to go out into the unknown, into the danger. Something inside her had died with him that day, the passion and loyalty they had shared for their country, that dear country that she had never been able to tell him about. And she had lost the chance forever. Now she was not even sure to whom she belonged. The family she had always known had disappeared, the country she grew up loving had betrayed her, and the one man who had changed her life was gone.

She looked out the window, above the rooftops of London. Hilda's heart clenched in pain as she thought of the joy that Jesse had felt every time he was in the clouds. He would never know that feeling again, the exhilaration and freedom found in the skies.

The cab stopped in front of a small church on the quieter side of London.

"Thank you," she said as she paid him the given amount.

She hurried up the steps. There were several people still talking in the lobby and ushers were trying to lead them to the pews, which were already quite full. Hilda glanced around; she knew no one in the crowd. People were murmuring and laughing lightly as they waited for the ceremony to begin. She silently slipped into the ladies room and removed her coat and hat. As she did so, she noticed that gradually from extensive washing, her rich brown locks were beginning to show once more. The fading reds and blondes revealed a piece of the girl she remembered. A slightly wistful smile appeared on her face. How she wanted to go back to those wonderful days in Heidelberg when she never pretended to be anyone but herself. Hilda knew that her time as an agent was soon to end. Intelligence had not required her to return to duty; she had a feeling that Jeffrey had said something to them in her favor. There was no reason for her to stay in London any longer and for the first time, she considered the possibility of going home.

Hilda went back into the lobby and thanked the usher who handed her a program as she came to the door. He led her to a seat about two-thirds of the way back. Coincidentally, she found herself being seated next to a pilot. When he looked up, she knew the shock was evident on her face, because she saw it reflected in his. Joshua Sauders slowly stood and allowed her into the pew. An awkward silence passed between them before he spoke.

"Hello."

"Hello again," she said softly.

"It's been a long time. How are you?" he asked.

"Um, doing fine, thank you."

The pews were almost full, and for a moment they glanced around and watched the other guests.

"Bride or groom?" Hilda asked as she casually took in the people around them.

"Bride. She bandaged my head. You?"

"Groom. He's a friend."

More silence passed between them and Josh looked seriously at her. She saw his firm gaze and knew what he was about to say.

"I'm sorry about Jesse, ma'am. His loss was felt very deeply among the pilots. He must have been a good friend," he murmured.

Hilda smiled as she thought of happier times in Heidelberg. "He was a good friend to both of us."

"Believe me ma'am, he didn't go down without a fight, I guarantee you that," Josh said firmly.

She nodded, turning toward the cross at the front of the church. "I know."

"Sorry ma'am, but Jesse never did introduce us."

Hilda turned to him, suddenly unsure of how to respond. The look in Josh's eye was one of thanks and innocence. He could not know what she had done, who she had become. But that was all behind her now. "My name is Hilda."

Josh shook her hand with a smile. "It's a pleasure. Joshua Sauders."

Hilda smiled. "Yes, I know."

The sound of music broke into their conversation, and they both turned to the back of the church. A young girl entered carrying a basket of flowers, which she scattered here and there as she moved down the aisle. Hilda glanced at the program. Her name was Susan Spencer. Her mother, Abigail, was the maid of honor. A few moments after Susan entered, Abigail appeared in the doorway, dressed in a forest green gown that whispered as she walked. As Hilda watched her flow down the aisle, she felt her eyes grow slightly wet. She had dreamed of this many times. How often she had pictured Hannah walking down the aisle in pale blue silk. Then the music would start to play, and she would make eye contact with Jesse and slowly walk toward him, beginning their lifelong journey together.

Hilda wiped her eyes and stood with the rest of the guests as Grace began the walk toward the front of the church. Jeffrey stood there looking nervous, and yet seemed in awe at the vision walking toward him. Grace had pulled her hair lightly away from her face, leaving a few wisps curling here and there. Her white gown fell in shimmering folds and trailed about five feet behind her. No veil covered her face, and everyone could see the glow radiating from her. Hilda smiled softly. There was not a happier woman in all of London.

She turned her eyes to Dr. Holden. He looked so joyful for the happiness that his daughter had found. He smiled and nodded at his guests, every now and then turning a loving glance toward Grace. He suddenly turned his head and found Hilda's eyes. A strange look came to his face, and his gaze made Hilda feel like she was under an x-ray machine. Faltering, she lowered her head and waited until they had passed by. *Odd.*

Jeffrey accepted his bride with a beaming smile, his eyes never leaving her face. Dr. Holden stepped back after giving her away at the pastor's question and the ceremony began.

"Friends, we are gathered here in the sight of God to witness the joining of this man and this woman in holy matrimony," the pastor said with a smile, his voice commanding yet kind. "Now marriage is not a thing to be taken lightly. There will be hardships and sorrow along with the joy and laughter, and it will be up to you both to see each other through. You have committed yourselves to each other forever, in love and devotion." He opened his Bible and read from the first book of Corinthians. "Love is patient and kind; love does not envy or boast; it is not arrogant or rude. It does not insist on its own way; it is not irritable or resentful; it does not rejoice in wrongdoing, but rejoices with the truth. Love bears all things, believes all things, hopes all things, endures all things." He closed the Bible and stared at the two people before him. "Take these words and keep them with you always. When you are angry or troubled, look to them as your guide. Just as the Lord gave us the laws of our lives, so He gave us the ways of love. Marriage is sacred and holy in His sight and He rejoices at the union of His followers." He smiled and asked them to turn to one another. "Jeffrey, would you repeat after me please?"

As the vows were read, Hilda watched as though from far away. She never thought she would see the day when Jeffrey got married. She smiled, even as she felt her heart begin to break. She was losing the only friend she had left. She felt truly alone.

Jesse had been dead for almost two years and the ache still held fast in her heart. There was no one left in the world that she could turn to for comfort, for love. She thought for a moment. What had the pastor said about love? It was not arrogant or selfish? A nagging thought poked at her brain. For so long, Hilda had secluded herself in her own self-pity, mourning because there was no one left to love her the way she wanted to be loved. She hung her head in shame. She had been so naïve as a young girl, so wrapped up in herself. Dederick had often commented on how she had moped around in misery after Jesse left. She had not wanted to face it then, but she now realized how she had only wanted everyone to please her, including Jesse. She had blamed him so often back then for making her wait for him for so long. Hilda wanted to sink into the floor at the thought.

Jeffrey and Grace exchanged rings, their eyes remaining on each other. Hilda wanted that. She wanted it so much. The kind of love that she could always run to for help and support. She felt despair fill her. In his last letter, Jesse had told her to be strong, but with his death the last of her strength had seeped from her. Her only chance at that love was gone.

The pastor's wife stood up and sang a hymn, and when she finished, Jeffrey and Grace turned to face their guests. The pastor beamed as he announced, "Ladies and gentlemen, it is my privilege to introduce to you Mr. and Mrs. Jeffrey Rolf, man and wife. You may kiss your bride, Jeffrey."

They turned to each other. Jeffrey leaned slowly toward her and took her in his arms. Grace's smile never left her lips as she closed her eyes. He kissed her softly, tenderly, and Hilda wondered how Jeffrey ever could have fallen for another. Grace was everything a man could hope for. She was young, gentle and innocent. Her vibrancy radiated wherever she went, and she had left such a wonderful impression on every person who knew her.

Loud applause resonated through the church as the new couple made their way back down the aisle. Hilda gathered her coat, prepared to leave for the reception as soon as the bridal party was on its way. She did not plan to stay for long, only to say hello to Jeffrey and wish him congratulations.

A slight nudge next to her made her turn. Joshua was staring at her with a smile.

"Since we seem to be the oddballs, how would you like to stick with me at the reception?" he asked.

She faltered and tried to form an excuse to flee. Finally she gave a weak smile and nodded. "Sure."

They got up and followed the crowd out to where several cabs lined the curb. She and Josh slid into the back seat and took the short ride to the reception hall. Hilda stared out the window. The sun shone brightly, but a brisk temperature had taken hold. She did not mind; Jeffrey and Grace were happy and that was all that mattered.

"So, how do you know Jeffrey?"

The question drew Hilda's gaze from the window to Josh's inquiring eyes.

"He was ... a good friend to me when I first arrived in England," she murmured.

"Really? You're not British?" he asked, surprised. "You could have fooled me. So are you French then?"

"No, I'm not."

Her blunt reply clearly stated that she did not wish to pursue the topic. Though curious, Josh acknowledged her desires.

"It was a lovely ceremony," he commented.

"Yes, it was," Hilda said with a smile.

"Makes me think about tying the knot as well." Josh looked at her thoughtfully.

"What?"

He was slow to answer for a moment. "Well, sorry if this is too painful, but ... if he hadn't been killed, would you and Jesse have ..."

Hilda looked out the window for a few seconds. "I don't know, Joshua. I always hoped so. He was the only man I ever loved, but our lives just ... didn't seem to match up anywhere."

"I'm sorry," he said sincerely.

"Don't be. Oh look, we're here."

The cab stopped at the curb, and Josh helped Hilda out and they followed the crowd up to the ballroom on the first floor. Many people were already milling about, glasses of champagne in their hands.

Josh hailed a waiter, who brought them two flutes. The two of them stood just outside the room and listened to the light music. There was laughter and talking all around them, but they both seemed to be at peace in each other's company. Hilda felt her heart begin to settle. There was still a dull ache deep within her, but the pain was no longer cutting her wide open. She turned to Josh.

"Thank you," she said.

"For what?"

"I don't know," she said quietly, "but I feel more content than I have in a long time. I think knowing you knew Jesse as a close friend ... well, it helps with the pain somehow."

Josh smiled slightly. They did not say anything more, but there did not seem to be a need for words. Hilda sipped her champagne and watched the cars through the window coming to and fro on the street leading to the center of the city. After a while, Josh asked, "Would you like to go in and get some seats?"

"I suppose I can stay for a little while," she said and followed him into the ballroom.

"Do you have an important matter to attend to?" he asked playfully.

She laughed. "No. It's just that social gatherings were never my forte."

He joined her in laughing as they both sat down near the back of the ballroom. Almost as soon as they did, Mary Holden called for everyone's attention.

"Ladies and gentlemen, the happy couple, Jeffrey and Grace Rolf!"

Loud applause ensued as the bride and groom entered. They made their way to the dance floor and the band struck up a slow song. The two flowed across the floor, their eyes only for each other. Hilda watched Jeffrey and could not believe that this same man had once professed undying love to her. She knew she had hurt him with her denial, but what had come of it had brought more joy than either could have anticipated, and she was glad for him.

The song continued for a few minutes and applause followed the dance. The couple made their way to the head table and soon the food was served. Joshua and Hilda were seated with several of Grace's old school friends, who chatted incessantly. They shared amused looks behind a hand or a glass. At one point in the meal, Hilda looked up and noticed that Jeffrey and Grace were beginning to go around and greet their guests. She gulped down some champagne, suddenly panicked. She wasn't sure if she wanted to face the man who had professed love to her and the woman who had tended her without knowing who she was. The situation looked to be very awkward and she stood quickly. "It's getting a bit stuffy in here, Joshua. I'm going to step outside for a moment."

He began to rise. "Would you like me to go with you?"

"No, no, don't trouble yourself. Excuse me."

Before another word could be said, she hurried out of the ballroom and stepped out onto the sidewalk. The sun was low in the sky and the crisp air felt refreshing against her hot face. Seeing a tree close by, she hurried over and leaned against the bark. Her eyes closed. She thought she could handle this. It seemed easy enough to sit back and watch her friend get married, but she had not counted on all of the memories that would be triggered by the event. She was ready to return home.

"Hilda!"

She opened her eyes to find Jeffrey running toward her. She sighed.

"I saw you leave," he said, stopping in front of her. "Is something wrong?"

"No, nothing," she replied. "It was just a little stuffy in there." She looked at him with a small smile. "Congratulations, Jeffrey. It was a beautiful ceremony."

His face beamed. "It was, wasn't it? Oh Hilda, I've never been so happy. I didn't think I could ever feel that way again."

"I'm glad for you," she said sincerely. "Tell Grace that I send my congratulations to her, as well." She turned.

"Wait. Where are you going?" he asked, dismay in his face.

"Oh, you know me and social functions, Jeffrey. Go on back to your reception. I'll be fine."

"Really?"

His question stopped her. She looked at him quizzically. "What do you mean?"

"You know what. For months, you didn't talk to anyone. You isolated yourself from everyone who cares about you. We all were very worried."

"I'm all right now, Jeffrey. Don't fret. Now really, you shouldn't neglect your guests on account of me."

Hilda gave him an encouraging smile at his doubtful look. After a few moments, he finally gave a compromising shake of his head and walked back slowly to the reception. He turned at the entrance. She gave him a confident wave, and sighed deeply once he disappeared inside. She turned and leaned her forehead against the tree trunk. She did not know what she would do, but she could not stay.

Hilda straightened her shoulders. Nothing remained for her in London. She knew who she was; she would search for the truth of what really happened that day, a day that had shouted victory for so many, and had cried despair for so few. She would find the only people who really knew the story of her real parents. And she would learn the truth.

But first she would go home. It would be risky, but she owed it to her family. An explanation to them was the only thing to do. She knew right away that she could not just write a letter. For one, it could fall into the wrong hands and put many lives in danger, and she knew that a simple letter would not put into words the pain that she had felt in leaving them. She had to go back.

As she began to slowly walk back toward the taxis, Hilda wondered at the change she would find in the city she had grown up in. Would she even recognize it? Would she be recognized? Several other questions ran around her mind and made her head pound. Instead, she focused on her plan to get there. She would need to use her forged papers from Jeffrey. She would once again travel as Angelis Chevalier, but not as an agent. She was so tired of the lies and deceit. No more pretending to be someone she was not. Hilda would send Jeffrey a letter of resignation and be gone. The war had become personal, and it had hit her harder than most in so many different ways. But it was time to forget what it had done to her. Time to leave it all behind and simply let the precious time she had be lived out. She could do no more. And no less.

Jeffrey checked the messages that his secretary had brought in one more time. No message from Hilda. His eyes narrowed with worry. She had not contacted him since the wedding nearly two weeks ago. He sincerely hoped she was okay. He had asked around several times. No one had seen or heard from her in many days. He knew that Hilda could take care of herself, but his concern did not cease. She could be anywhere. She had her tricks that enabled her to travel quickly and quietly throughout most of Europe. She could blend in anywhere with her knowledge of language and culture.

Throughout the day, Jeffrey absentmindedly sorted his files and read through confidential paperwork. His mind was not settled. Though Hilda had not been on assignment in almost two years, he still felt as though it was his responsibility to watch over her. He was the reason she had come to London in the first place. If he had not contacted her, she probably would still be in Heidelberg, safe at home within the comforting circle of her family.

But then she would never have touched his life like she had. He doubted that he and Grace would ever have come to the idea of marriage. Life would have gone on, yes, but at a much duller pace.

His thoughts were interrupted as his secretary entered.

"Yes?" he inquired.

"Sir, your wife just called and said that supper would be a bit late tonight, and this just came for you." She placed a plain white envelope on his desk. It bore his name and business address only.

"The post already came," he said.

"A delivery boy came by with it, sir." With a nod, she left just as quickly as she had entered.

Jeffrey glanced down. There was no return address on the envelope. Curious, he opened it and began to read. His eyes never left the page.

Dear Jeffrey,

By now I am far from London, as you probably have guessed. There was nothing holding me there any longer. I would like to officially give you notice of my resignation, though you probably realized that as well. I regret to say that I cannot divulge my location, even though you may eventually come to discover it. Just know that I am being well taken care of and you do not have to worry.

Thank you for being such a wonderful friend to me. I do not know when I shall see you again, but know that you truly changed me. I shall never forget your kindness to me and I hope we shall remain friends for a long while. Perhaps when we meet again, it will be under more peaceful circumstances. Until then, my good friend.

Hilda van Ostrand

23

H ilda stepped down from the train and simply stood there for a moment. Her heart pounded as the reality of where she was came crashing down on her. She was home. It had taken nearly five years, but she was finally home. People bustled through the station, hurrying to an appointment or event. Soldiers climbed on and off of trains, waving and smoking cigarettes to keep warm. She looked around. Nothing had changed. Everything looked exactly as she remembered it. And yet, she knew everything had changed.

"Miss, you must move along," came a voice behind her.

Hilda turned. A young soldier stared back at her. He was in a starched uniform, his face blank as he pointed toward the exit. Hilda moved slowly, as though her mind could not comprehend what her feet were doing. The reality hit her again. She was home.

A smile broke on her face, and she strode purposefully through the station, determined and confident in her blue traveling suit. Home. Hilda finally felt like she was in a place where she knew people loved her, trusted her. She almost broke into a run at the thought of them. Mother, Paul, Hannah. She couldn't wait to see them.

Outside, she hailed a taxi and gave him the address. Hilda could not take in enough as they drew closer to the house. People came in and out of shops that she had enjoyed going to as a child, and children running

225

around laughing made her think of the times she had spent doing the same thing with her brothers.

"Stop here," she directed as the driver came to her block. "I'll walk now. Thank you." She paid him and sent him on his way.

Clutching her bags tighter in her hands, Hilda made her way down the street at a quick pace. Children ran past her, giggling and shouting. Mothers told each other the latest gossip as they walked to market. Hilda's excitement grew. This was a place she knew and understood.

A few houses before her own, she paused for breath. Smoothing the hair under her hat, she put on a confident smile. Straight backed, she walked the rest of the way, hoping all the while that her mother would still recognize her.

What she saw made her smile fade. Hilda slowed to a shocked halt at the sight before her. A bleak, gray house stared like an ominous face onto a garden unkempt and overgrown with weeds. The path to the front door was no longer visible and broken beams stuck up from the once pristine white porch. Paint was peeling from the walls, and no light came from the ragged and dusty windows.

Hilda dropped her bags in quiet astonishment. Where was her mother? And Paul? Something was terribly wrong.

Footsteps along the sidewalk turned her head. An old man whistling a low tune was meandering along the sidewalk.

"Excuse me, sir," she cried as she hurried toward him.

He looked up in surprise. "Oh. Good afternoon, Fraulein."

"Sir, please." Her eyes were wide. "Do you know what happened here?"

He looked toward the house. With a slight chuckle, he said, "This dump? It's been abandoned for a while now. No one's lived in it for near three years, I think. Was on the market for a while, but nobody wanted it."

"What happened to the people who lived here?" Hilda whispered.

"Heard the son up and married some Jewish whore, and the mother just disappeared one day. Bad family history," he stated with a nod, as though he alone knew the truth. "That's why no one wanted the house. After a few weeks the staff left, and no one's lived here since." He looked at her suddenly. "Why do you inquire?"

"No reason," she replied automatically. "I was just ... curious."

"Suit yourself." With a tip of his hat, the man continued on down the street, whistling. If Hilda had not been so preoccupied with her pain, she would have noticed him cautiously look back at her through narrowed eyes before continuing on. But she didn't.

Taking her bags, she went through the gate and pushed her way through the weeds to the door. As she placed her hand on the doorknob, she closed her eyes and tried to prepare herself for what she might see. She had grown up in this house, and nothing would keep her heart from breaking at the sight of its demise.

Hilda took a deep breath and pushed open the door. It groaned loudly at her intrusion, and she tried to close it quietly as though not to disturb the peace that the rooms had been left in for so long. Putting her bags by the door, she straightened and glanced around. It was very dim and she picked her way across the creaking floor toward the parlor. If she remembered correctly, an old fashioned lamp would be on the table next to the couch. As she entered the room, memories assailed her. This was where Dederick had announced Germany's withdrawal from the League of Nations, where she had learned the news of her father's death, and where she had first felt the fluttering of love for a young American pilot.

Hilda's eyes slowly adjusted to the light and she noticed that all of the furniture had been covered in sheets. All of the trinkets that had been on the tables were gone.

Only the lamp remained on the side table, covered in dust. Managing to find a small box of matches in a drawer, she held the flame to the wick and a dim glow filled the parlor.

She moved back toward the middle of the room, only stopping when a startled mouse scurried from its hiding place to a hole in the wall. Hilda ran her fingers over the dusted sheets, not minding that her hands got dirty. Some pictures on the wall caught her gaze. She wiped the dust off of the glass and studied them. Her family's smiling faces stared back at her. The picture had been taken when she was ten. There she sat on her father's lap, beaming. Her brothers stood next to her, Paul looking handsome and mature at fourteen, and Dederick, happy and boyish at nine. They had been a family then, content, full of life. How much had changed since then.

The next picture caught her eye. It showed with stark clarity the change that had come over them all. Her mother sat in a chair, a sad smile on her face. Hilda stood next to her, looking quiet and lonely. Paul displayed a gentle smile from where he stood behind Benedikta. Dederick looked stern and unmoving on the other side of the chair.

She sighed. Hilda remembered that picture well. She had been eighteen then, an age at which she thought she would have traveled the world. Circumstances had kept her at home, however, and she had not gone any further than the town shoemaker. Yes, much had changed.

Room by room, she moved through the house, touching things here and there, remembering. At last, she came to the doorway of her bedroom. Looking in, Hilda saw more sheets covering her furniture. She walked in and dropped her purse on the desk in a puff of dust. Glancing into her closet, she saw that all of her clothes were gone. A look in her trunk told her that her books were gone as well. Everything was gone. Hilda glanced at her desk. Or was it?

Slowly, she stood from where she knelt by the trunk and went over to the desk. She pulled off the sheet and stared at the dark wood. Reaching up, she touched the picture of her parents that hung above the desk. No one had known. It had to still be there.

Gently, Hilda lifted the picture aside. There it was. The key hung just as it had in the years of her childhood. She took it off the nail and inserted it into the desk drawer. After some shaking and twisting, the lock clicked and the drawer opened freely.

It was all there. Her notes on languages, old photographs, letters, and most importantly, her journal. She sorted through them, smiling at some and remembering others. All was not lost. Some of her heart and soul still remained. Within the pages of her diary, there still lived a young girl who had been enthusiastic about life, excited to live her dreams, and loved by a family that had existed once. It was all here. In her thoughts. In her heart.

A slight creak below her made her start. Downstairs, someone was opening the front door. Hilda quickly began throwing the sheets back on the furniture. The creaking became louder as the intruder made his way up the stairs and down the hall. She grabbed her purse and scurried into the closet, closing the door just enough so that she could still see. From her purse she drew a revolver and held it at her side.

The footsteps stopped and hesitated before entering her room. Slowly, the intruder came into view. Hilda clamped a hand over her mouth to keep from gasping in shock. Her eyes grew wide with terror, with confusion, with wonder.

The man stepped into the room and glanced around, assessing the situation. He took in the poorly draped sheets and the dust that had not yet settled in her haste. He sighed, staring out the window, and yet Hilda knew he was not seeing anything.

"Hilda." It was a statement rather than a question.

Slowly, she opened the door and leveled the gun on him. Her eyes did not waver as he turned to her. "Take out your gun, slowly," she commanded.

He did so, holding it with the barrel facing him.

"Throw it on the bed," she said. He complied.

A long moment passed as they stared at each other. Much time had gone by, but it felt like just yesterday they had been in this same dilemma. Her eyes shone with disbelief.

"I thought you were in Berlin," she whispered.

Dederick shrugged. He looked every bit an officer in his spotless uniform. She noticed he kept one arm close to his body.

"I was," he answered. "After my leave was up, they sent us to Sevastopol. I was injured during the siege, so they sent me back to the hospital in Berlin and during my recovery, I decided to travel here for a time."

She never let her eyes wander from his face. "How did you know I was here?" she asked.

"An old gentleman came to headquarters and told us that a young woman was inquiring after this place, and considering the history, he felt it necessary to report you. I had a feeling it might be you, and I wasn't about to feed you to the wolves."

"Why would you do that?"

"You are my sister, Hilda. I'm not as cruel as you may think," he murmured.

"The last time we saw each other, your mercy had reached it boundaries. Even as a child, you put your country before everything, including your family. Why should that have changed?"

Dederick sat down on the edge of the bed, and Hilda immediately moved to take his gun further out of reach. Even as she did, though, she noticed brokenness around her brother that she had never seen before.

"Something tells me you've been doing the same," he murmured. "Believe me, Hilda, it hurts more than you know."

The agony in his voice sent her to his side. She sat down next to him, quiet for a moment before asking, "What happened to them?"

He looked at her, his eyes full of pain. She wondered at the emotions swirling through him. He looked so lost.

"Dederick?"

He gave a deep sigh. "Paul married your friend, Hannah, and they moved into the apartments near the university. No one would socialize with them, not even their own kind. Mother was always good to them, though. Last I heard of them was in Berlin. They'd been deported, sent to a camp up north."

Hilda's heart clenched. She had heard of the hideous camps that the

Nazis had built, bringing in millions of people for hard labor. The horrors of their methods of experimentation and execution had reached all the way to London. She was gripped with fear at the thought of her brother and best friend, two people so in love, thrown into one of those harsh camps. She swallowed hard and tried to appear strong in front of Dederick.

"And Mother?" she asked, afraid to know the truth after such horrifying news.

He was silent for a long time. Hilda noticed that his hands were trembling. She gently put her hand on his arm. "Dederick, what about Mother?"

Her quiet question seemed to startle him, but he answered slowly, "She was ... arrested."

Hilda's eyes narrowed in confusion. "What? What happened?"

He took a deep shaky breath. "Some fool found letters he thought were discriminatory to her, and ... he had her arrested under suspicion of treason."

Hilda felt anger begin to boil inside her. "Who would do such a thing? She never would have betrayed her country. Never!" She rose from the bed. "Do you know who it was, Dederick? God help me, I will find him!"

"He is here," Dederick said in a broken voice.

Hilda stared at him, not understanding, not *wanting* to understand. It couldn't be. It couldn't.

"You?" she whispered.

"I am the fool. I found letters in Mother's desk. They were addressed to you from Jesse Riker. My guess is Mother hid them from you to stop your romance with him. You knew she was afraid of what it would mean when war came. But in my zeal for my country, I was blind to her innocence." Dederick looked up at her unbelieving eyes. "I have never regretted anything more than when I turned her over to the authorities, Hilda. Do with me as you will."

She stared at him, the pain within her almost unbearable. Her brother deported, and her mother arrested on Dederick's orders? She could not comprehend all that he had said, all that he had done, and she felt herself begin to break at what had happened to her family. The gun rose, and for a moment she was blinded to everything but her anger. How could he? Benedikta had loved him more than any mother could have loved a son, and he had thanked her by turning her in as a traitor.

The next moment, Hilda saw how far her brother had fallen, how lost he was. They were not very different from each other. Her hand began to shake as she slowly lost her composure. She was alone once more.

"I can't ... I miss them so much ..."

The gun fell from her hand, and she broke down. At that moment she did not care if Dederick grabbed the gun and took her to the authorities. She deserved to be in prison. She was the traitor, not her mother. She did not deserve to be free.

Then the last thing she ever expected happened. She felt Dederick's arms encircle her. The two of them clung to each other in the middle of the room, frightened and alone. They were the only family each other had to turn to, and right now it just seemed right.

"I'm so sorry," he whispered.

"I'm sorry, too," she said as tears ran down her cheeks.

They slowly pulled away and stood silently together. This could be the last time they ever saw each other, and somehow they were content. They had finally come to terms with what they had done, and for now, it was enough.

"Where will you go?" Dederick asked quietly.

Hilda shrugged. "I don't know. I thought I would be safe enough here, but now ... I think the only thing for me to do is return to England for now."

He nodded slowly. "So that was where you went. We all wondered." He glanced at her. "What about Jesse?"

She gave him a single look. "He was killed."

"Oh. I'm sorry."

"What about you?"

"I go back to Sevastopol in two weeks," he said as he moved around the bed and placed his gun back in its holster. "I will probably be there indefinitely."

"Oh," she said.

Dederick moved toward her slowly and placed his hand on her shoulder. So much was said in his touch. "I hope you can forgive me for what I've done."

Hilda knew the moment had come, but when she thought back on his confession, the pain was too near, and she could not bring herself to say the words. She met his gaze. "We've all made mistakes in this war."

He nodded, a sad look on his face, and moved to the door. "Good-bye, Hilda. Maybe we will see each other again someday." He reached into his coat and pulled out a number of envelopes tied together with a string. "These are yours."

Dederick disappeared from view and she heard him go down the stairs and out the door. Then, the house was silent once again.

"Good-bye, brother," she whispered.

Hilda knew she must go. The Gestapo was alerted to her presence, and it was no longer safe. She glanced around the room. She wanted to stay, oh how much she wanted to stay.

Moving to the nightstand, she opened the drawer, searching for anything to carry her treasured papers, and was surprised to find her old Bible. Her father had given it to her when she was nine. She had stopped reading it when he died.

Slowly, Hilda lifted it out and shook the dust off of the cover. A piece of paper fell out from between the pages. It was an envelope, still white and neat from remaining between the pages. She picked it up and turned it over. Her name was written in fine script. It had been many years, but she still recognized it. The writing belonged to her father.

Her hands shook as she tore open the envelope. She wiped the tears from her eyes and began to read.

> *My dearest Hilda,*
>
> *If you have found this letter, then I have been torn from you forever. I'm so sorry, my darling, that it has come to this. It happened so suddenly, and I had no idea what I was getting myself, and you, involved in until it was too late. Hilda, you know you were adopted, and I have never regretted that action for a second. There are certain documents that I have hidden, and their content is vital to your identity. They must not fall into the hands of the Nazis. I have sent them to a safe place, and hope they will find their way to you.*
>
> *My dear Hilda, I only wish I could have seen you grow up into a lovely young lady. I am so sorry that my intense curiosity has come to such a fate. I only wanted to know more about my beautiful daughter. I love you so much. If you are ever in trouble, contact a man named Jeffrey Rolf in London. I know he was sent to follow me, and he can help you. Be safe, my dear. God only knows where this world is headed, but I pray He keeps you safe from its cruelties. And now, good-bye, Hilda.*
>
> > *Love always,*
> > *Father*

Hilda closed her eyes in agony. If only she had known sooner. She might have been able to ... what? Go to the police? They had wanted to kill her father, and her. Nothing could have prevented his death. She knew that now.

Sighing, she looked around the room. After only a glimpse, she once again had to leave the place she called home. Would there ever be a time when she could come back to stay? She hoped so. With all her heart, she hoped so.

Once more, Hilda found herself on the sidewalk outside the gate, holding her bags and wondering where she would go, and how she would get there. She did not have to wonder long. A soft call came from a few feet away.

"Hilda?"

She turned toward the voice. A middle-aged woman in a black coat with a scarf over her head was staring at her. A few moments later, Hilda realized who it was with a start.

"Elsa ..."

The woman beamed. "Oh, I knew it was you! Look at you! All grown up and beautiful."

The two shared a warm embrace, and then moved down the walk together. Elsa talked as they went.

"You truly have turned into a lovely young lady, Hilda. Why, your mother and I used to talk about you all the time, wondering where you were, what you were doing ... and, well, here you are!" she said with a short laugh. Hilda was silent. Elsa cleared her throat quietly. "I suppose you've heard the news?"

"Yes," Hilda murmured.

"A terrible thing," Elsa said softly. "What heartache she must be going through. Paul did all he could to help your Mother before he was arrested."

"It seems, in war, that the innocent are always the ones who get hurt." Hilda gave a sigh, then suddenly turned to her mother's old friend. "Elsa, I need help."

Elsa nodded with understanding. "I thought as much. I moved out of the city to an old estate about a year ago. I'll take you there."

233

Hilda sat at the dressing table in her room and brushed out her thick brown hair. The room was sparsely furnished, but clean and comfortable. Staring at herself in the mirror, Hilda realized how much older she looked than her twenty-four years. The war had hardened her beyond any possible repair.

A knock sounded on the door.

"Come in," she called.

Elsa appeared in the doorway. "Oh, good, you're done with your bath," she said. "As soon as you're dressed, come downstairs and you can meet the children."

Hilda turned in confusion. "Children?"

"Yes. Most of them have nowhere to go. They came home from school one day, and their parents were gone."

"How awful."

"Yes. Some of them are too young to realize it, but they still have questions. I do my best, but ..." Elsa sighed. "Well, come down when you're ready."

Hilda nodded, and Elsa closed the door behind her.

A few minutes later, Hilda came to the bottom of the stairs. Two little boys raced by her, shouting and laughing. Elsa appeared in the doorway of the kitchen wearing an apron. A little girl with dark curly hair stood next to her holding a wooden spoon caked in batter. Hilda smiled and came forward.

"Oh, good, here you are!" Elsa said. She turned to the little girl. "Lulu, why don't you keep an eye on the cake while I show our guest around?"

The little one nodded and skipped back into the kitchen. Elsa smiled as she removed her apron and hung it on a hook just inside the door. "Little Louise," she said with a laugh. "She's only four years old and determined to become a cook when she grows up."

Hilda's smile widened. To see young, innocent children enjoying life was like a balm on her heart. At least some of this world still knew the meaning of living.

Elsa led her through the house and stopped children from their play to introduce them. They all smiled politely as they said hello. Elsa sent them back to their play, and the two moved back to the front of the house, where three more children were jumping rope outside in the brisk weather.

"How old are they?" Hilda asked as they walked.

"The oldest is almost thirteen, down to the youngest who is two. They are all very sweet children. It's a pity they must live in a time like this,"

Elsa said quietly. "Here we are." She stepped out the door and began to call to the children.

As she did so, Hilda noticed a slight movement off to her right. The door to what looked to be a parlor was cracked open just a bit, and a pair of deep blue eyes stared into her own.

Those eyes ...

When she turned, there came a slight gasp, and the door shut quickly. With a slight glance at Elsa, who was still talking to the children, Hilda walked softly over to the door and opened it. Stepping inside, she noticed the room was not a parlor at all, but a library. The shelves were mostly bare, but the furniture was all of the finest quality. It had to be the most handsome room in the house.

Hilda saw then what she sought. A little girl sat on the window seat and turned from staring out at her entrance. She wore a light blue blouse under a brown pinafore, and black stockings made their way down to her shoes. Her light brown hair was in a single braid down her back and was tied with a light blue ribbon. Around her neck, she wore a chain from which hung a simple gold ring.

Hilda smiled and walked forward. "Hello."

The child did not say anything, only stared at her with wide innocent eyes. Sitting down next to her, Hilda tried again.

"What is your name?"

No answer.

Hilda wondered if this was how the entire conversation would ensue. She tried one more time. "Your necklace is very pretty."

A small hand came up and fingered the ring. Encouraged, Hilda continued. "It's must be very special to you."

The big blue eyes came down to where her fingers clasped the ring. "My ... mommy's."

Hilda came off the seat and knelt down to the girl's level. "It was your mother's ring," she stated softly. "I'm sure she is very pretty, just like you."

The little one nodded.

"She'd be glad to know that her ring is in such safe hands," Hilda continued.

Another nod.

Seeing she would get nothing else out of the girl, she rose. "It was nice to meet you."

The child had resumed her stare out the window when the door opened and Elsa appeared.

"Ah, there you are. Shall we continue?" she asked with a smile, but not before glancing between the two of them.

Hilda nodded and followed the older woman out of the room. The two went upstairs, and Elsa showed her the nursery and the schoolroom.

"What a sad looking child," Hilda said as they walked.

"Yes," Elsa murmured.

"Does she say *anything*?"

"Very little. And never to any of the other children."

"What happened to her parents?"

"Deported. Like most." Elsa stopped in the middle of the room. "Hilda, there is something you must know ..."

"What is her name?"

"Maria ... her name is Maria."

"How sad she looked," Hilda said. "For a child that young ... how old is she?"

"She'll be three in March," Elsa murmured. "Hilda ..."

"Three years old," Hilda whispered. "To lose your parents at so young an age ... what is it, Elsa?"

Hilda looked confused as Elsa clasped her hands in front of her. They were shaking.

"Hilda, there is something you must know about Maria," Elsa said slowly. After a slight pause, she continued. "She is Paul and Hannah's daughter."

Hilda stared at her, speechless. Slowly, she sat down in a chair she did not even know was behind her. Maria? Her niece? It didn't seem possible. Just when she thought her family was lost to her. Those eyes were just like Paul's. No wonder they had looked familiar. She could not find the words, and they stumbled out of her mouth.

"I have a ... I'm a ... my *niece*," she whispered.

"It's Hannah's ring that she wears around her neck. I found it ... in the folds of her blanket the night they were arrested. It must have slipped off when she handed Maria to me. The child won't take it off."

Hilda felt tears come to her eyes. So much happiness came with the birth of a child, and Paul and Hannah had only enjoyed it for a short period before they'd been torn away. She sent up a fierce prayer that they would return home safely. Maria needed her family.

"Hilda, there's more," Elsa said, kneeling next to the chair. "It is getting ... too dangerous for her to stay here. For any of the children to stay here. That is one of the reasons I brought you here."

Hilda looked at her, and understanding overcame her shock. "You ... you want me to ..."

"Yes. I want you to take Maria to England."

24

Hilda watched from her seat as Maria slept across from her. The child was sprawled across the seat of the compartment with one of Hilda's coats covering her. She had slept most of the way as the train sped across France toward Normandy. Hopefully, they would be in London within the next few days.

As she stared at the beautiful small face resting on the seat, Hilda still could not believe that Maria was her niece. Lovely, sweet, quiet Maria. Hilda could not stomach the thought of her loving brother and her kind friend being taken from what they had found together and thrust into a horrific reality that they might not survive.

Hilda turned to stare out the window. Every now and then the church steeple of a small village pierced the sky. How had the world come to this? Hannah's only crime was her heritage. And Paul's was that he loved her. Their sweet love had produced the miracle of Maria, and too quickly, she had been torn from them. Hilda was her only family. She felt too inadequate for such a role. She had never had to worry about protecting a three-year-old girl. In some ways, it seemed easier to worry about fighting someone twice her size than taking care of someone she could pack in a small suitcase.

Quietly, Hilda leaned forward and pulled the coat further over Maria's shoulder. Although she stirred at the touch, the girl slept on. Hilda sighed. Maria had said no more than two words throughout the trip. She had opened up more on the first day they had met than the rest of the time they had been in each other's company. Though she did feel some hurt over the girl's reluctance to trust her, Hilda could understand what was behind it. The parents she had been with for such a short time had disappeared, and she did not understand why. This new relative whom she had just discovered was dragging her across the continent to a country she had never been to with a language she did not speak and people she did not know. Yes, Hilda probably would not warm to that idea, either.

With a sigh, she leaned back. So much had changed in so little time. And yet Hilda felt as if something great had been accomplished. Her time with Dederick had been short, but full of understanding. Her brother had bared his soul for the first time in many years, and his embrace once again made her ache for the family she had lost. The family she might never see again.

Turning her eyes back to Maria, she saw the little girl's eyes open, and she gazed up at her. With a small smile, Hilda leaned forward.

"Hello. Are you hungry?" she asked.

Maria sat up and nodded slowly. Encouraged, Hilda stood and opened the compartment door. She hurried down the car and caught the trolley to buy a plethora of nuts and sweets for the two of them to snack on. As she walked back, she hoped that now, somehow, they could connect.

But when Hilda returned the compartment was empty. She dropped the snacks on the seat and looked out into the hallway. "Maria?"

There was no answer. The panic began to rise within her. "Maria!"

She ran down the car, opening doors and frantically asking if anyone had seen a small child. All shook their heads.

"Maria! Maria!"

In front of her, a compartment door opened and an officer stepped out. In his arms, looking scared and slightly confused, was Maria. The officer, his face kind, looked at Hilda.

"Is this who you are looking for?" he asked.

Hilda stared at him. His kind manner helped her smile at him, but she was shaking like a leaf beneath her suit.

"Yes," she answered breathlessly, her eyes wide with worry. "Thank you."

The moment he set Maria on the ground, the girl raced into Hilda's arms and clung to her. The officer smiled, trying to lighten the mood. With a nod of his head, he stepped back into his compartment and closed the door.

With a sigh of relief, Hilda carried the shaking child back to her seat and set her on her lap. When they were facing each other, Hilda said firmly, "Don't *ever* run off like that again. You scared me."

Maria wiped her eyes, which were beginning to tear. "I want to go home."

Hilda pulled the girl close and held her tightly. "It's too dangerous to go home, Maria. If it weren't, we would be home."

"Where are we going?" she asked in a voice muffled by Hilda's shoulder.

"To a safe place, darling. Don't be afraid. Everything will be fine."

Jeffrey had never felt so stifled in his office before. The light from the window seemed musty and suffocating. The past few weeks had been wonderful, but he felt as though he had seen more of the walls around him than he had of Grace. He sighed and rubbed his eyes. He was ready for the day to be over.

"Hello, Jeffrey."

Jeffrey looked up, startled at the voice. His eyes grew wide with disbelief. Hilda stood in the doorway, looking tired but content, her hair thrown across one shoulder in a braid. He stood slowly.

"Hilda ..."

Within seconds, he had his arms around her. How he had missed her. The nerve-wracking worry he had endured made him more haggard than he had been a long time. Grace had been worried about him, and her concern had only added to his plight.

"How are you?" he asked quietly.

She sighed with a small smile. "I've been better."

A slight noise made them turn. A little girl appeared shyly in the doorway. She looked to be no older than maybe four. A glance at Hilda showed him she understood his confusion.

"Who ..."

"Her name is Maria. She's my niece."

Jeffrey watched in amazement as Maria came forward and took Hilda's hand. The little one's eyes were wide and staring, but the fear was evident in her face.

"I need your help, Jeffrey. I have to get to New York," Hilda said, her voice quiet but determined.

He blinked. New York? Very few commercial barges dared their way across the Atlantic. "Are you crazy? Do you know the dangers that come with that kind of crossing? You could be killed!"

"The danger is worse here, and I will not send Maria off to the country with strangers. Please, Jeffrey, we must go. Will you help?"

He sighed and ran his hands through his hair. "How long have you been here?"

"We only just arrived this morning."

He looked at her for a long time. "Hilda, I don't understand ..."

"Jeffrey, please!" she begged. "I can't answer your questions. You're the only one who can help us."

Her eyes were wide and pleading. Next to her, Maria clung to her hand. Jeffrey stared at the two of them. They looked so lost and alone. He could not fight her. Their time together was over, and they had to take their separate paths. He was comforted that he even got to see her again. When he had received her letter, he had not known if he would ever have the chance.

Count your blessings, Jeffrey. She did come back, if only for a little while.

With a small sigh, he nodded slowly. Hilda smiled with relief and gave him a grateful hug. He kissed her forehead and gave her an encouraging grin.

"I'll make all the arrangements," he said as he moved around to his desk. "When to you want to leave?"

"As soon as possible," she replied. "I don't want to be in London for very long if I can help it."

He nodded again. When nothing further was said, Hilda led Maria back to the door.

"Oh, Jeffrey," she said. "I'd rather you not tell anyone about us."

"Of course not, Hilda."

As she turned to leave again, he stopped her. "Hilda, where you went ... did it go well?"

She gave him a sad smile. "Yes, Jeffrey, it went well."

He looked at her closely. "You went home, didn't you?"

She nodded silently. He did not need to ask her any more questions. Clearly, it had not been what she had expected.

"I'll be in touch," Hilda said. With that, she left as silently as she had arrived.

Jeffrey watched the two of them leave, and the door shut with a soft click behind them. So many people she loved had been taken away from her. He would not allow that little girl to be wrenched from her as well.

◆

A few days later, Hilda idly walked the streets of London. For the past few hours, she and Maria had been shopping for new clothes for their journey. Maria had next to nothing, and Hilda knew she did not have enough to last a month in America. When Jeffrey had contacted her to confirm their passage the following week, she had asked him about the fashions in the states. With a smile, he gave her a list of things to buy once they got to America. One item on the list was called *jeans*. She had looked at him, confused.

"What are jeans?"

He laughed. "They're a type of pants, Hilda. Didn't you ever see any western movies?"

"No. Is that what they wear?"

"Yes. It has become a popular fashion among the ladies."

A few minutes later, Hilda and Maria arrived at the gates of Kensington. She found an isolated spot amongst the trees with a small stone bench. Maria let go of her hand and wandered into the snow bank as Hilda sat down. Placing the parcels next to her, she sighed and watched the small girl begin to build a snowman.

After a moment, Hilda reached into her bag and pulled out the bundle of letters from Jesse. His handwriting stood out like a piece from the past. She traced the letters with a trembling finger. Untying the string, she lifted the first letter and opened it. It was dated May 29, 1936.

My dearest Hilda,

I still can't believe that it is nearing one year since we first met. My parents still are in disbelief over the fact that you've stolen my heart. They thought no one ever would. I wish I had a picture of you that I could show them. I've tried to describe you to them, but my words don't do justice to the face I see in my dreams.

I don't know when I will be able to come back. I will keep trying. Christina wants to meet you. She's heard so much about you and has not met you that I think she's beginning to believe you are just a fantasy. Did you know she wants to be a nurse? She reminds me much of you. She can't wait to serve her country.

242

Always hold onto your dreams, Hilda. Don't ever let anyone tell you that you can't do something. God has a plan for you, and all you have to do is trust Him.

I can't wait to hear from you. I love you, Hilda.

Always,

Jesse

As a small tear escaped down her cheek, Hilda looked up to find Maria standing in front of her holding an armful of sticks. She gave her a huge smile.

"For his arms," Maria said, looking toward the small round snowman behind her.

"They're the perfect size, darling."

Maria smiled and attempted to skip back to where she had been playing. She tripped, and fell into the soft snow with a laugh. She looked back at Hilda and gave an innocent giggle. It soared, pure and sweet, up through the trees. Hilda felt her heart clench. Maria made her want children of her own. Had it not been for the war, she might have.

As she continued to read through the stack of letters, she noticed the subtle changes that appeared in Jesse's tone. He sounded more formal and less in love as she went through each page. Hilda felt her heart break more and more with every word she read. By the time she reached his last letter, dated July 2, 1937, she felt more alone and lost than she ever had.

Dear Hilda,

First of all, I must tell you this will be my last letter to you. I am sorry that you have refused to return my letters, and I hope that it was nothing I said. Please know that though I am making the decision to break off our communication, I will gladly make contact with you should you so desire. I will always hold you in the highest esteem.

Hilda, I don't know what it is that has made your silence toward me occur, nor do I assume to know the reasons behind your decision. However, you can always rely on me to be here for you as a friend. Our time together meant so much to me, and I will always treasure it. Thank you for the memories you have given me. God bless you.

Sincerely,

Jesse

She frowned in confusion. How had he not received her letters? It didn't make sense, his final words, but as she put the letter aside, what lay beneath it made her heart wrench. Her own handwriting stared up at her. All of her letters to Jesse after their first year of correspondence sat in her lap, unopened and unread by the man she loved. Her mother had left out no stops, and it was too late now.

"Aunt Hilda?"

She looked up as Maria placed her hand on her knee.

"What now?" the little girl asked.

Hilda shrugged, trying to wear a smile after the devastating blow to her heart. She could not let the past darken what lay ahead of her. So much had been lost already, and she needed something to hold onto. Her next step would determine what it was.

"Are you ready to go back to the hotel?" Hilda asked.

Maria shrugged. She became preoccupied with the snowball she held in her hand and tossed it back and forth between her mittens.

Hilda stood and gathered their parcels together. She placed all the letters in her bag and took Maria's hand. They turned out of the little alcove and made their way down the path toward the far off gate. Between the trees to their right, Kensington Palace could be seen standing tall and beautiful in the surrounding gardens. During her time in London, Hilda had never gotten tired of walking through the trees, admiring the colors and splendor that went hand in hand. It had been her quiet sanctuary, the place she could come to get away from the lies and pretense that encompassed her life. She knew of no other place she would rather be.

Well, except one.

"Hilda?"

At the sound of the male voice, she looked up. Walking toward her, dressed in the smart looking uniform of a pilot, was Josh. A brightness that had been hidden inside her for months burst forth. She felt a huge smile spread across her face. Dropping everything, she ran to him and gave him an enormous hug. He laughed and returned her embrace with the same fervor.

"Oh, Josh, I've missed you!" she said with a laugh.

"Where have you been? I tried to look for you after the wedding, but it was like you just up and disappeared," he stated, confused.

"I left for a little while; I had some things to do."

"Are you staying in London, then?" he asked.

She hesitated just a moment. "Well, actually, we're scheduled to be on a ship to New York next week."

He stared at her, then looked beyond her.

"We?"

Hilda turned when his gaze landed on Maria. With an encouraging smile, she beckoned the girl forward.

"Joshua," she said as she placed the girl on her hip, "this is my niece, Maria."

Josh smiled, though there was slight surprise behind his eyes.

"I'm afraid we were just on our way home when you caught us," Hilda said quietly. "We've been out shopping all day."

Josh's face brightened, and he eagerly stepped forward. "Please allow me to escort you home. I could carry your bags."

Hilda's smile turned thankful. "That would be wonderful."

He hurried past them and collected the packages she had dropped, and they continued on down the path.

"So, you are leaving for America?" Josh asked, and Hilda could hear the keen disappointment behind his words.

"Yes, we must," she said. "It is not safe to stay."

"I understand."

The silence that followed seemed akin to the mood. Hilda looked at him for a moment, then stopped walking. He needed to know the truth.

Josh turned to her. "What is it?"

She took a deep breath and began slowly. "Joshua, I'm afraid that I wasn't completely honest with you at the wedding. That is, I did not tell you the whole story."

He nodded slowly. "I figured there were some things you weren't saying, especially after our meeting in France."

Hilda sighed. "I'm afraid it goes back further than that. You see, my last name is van Ostrand."

His gaze was shocked, and she saw a small hint of anger behind his eyes. "You're German?"

"In truth, I was born and raised there, but I was adopted. When I was sixteen, Jesse came to visit, and we ... became very good friends. After he left, we kept up our correspondence through letters, but when the war started, well ... we drifted apart." Hilda started walking slowly, Maria's hand clasped tightly in hers. "It was years before we saw each other again, when he first came to London as a volunteer. Back then I was ... I was different than he remembered me to be."

"Why were you in London?" Josh asked.

"Well, you remember when I said Jeffrey was a friend?" When he nodded, she continued. "Well, he was actually more than just my friend. He was my superior ... in the British Secret Intelligence Service."

Josh could not be more surprised. "British Intelligence? Hilda, are you saying that ... that you were a spy for the SIS?"

"The title was sort of thrust at me, actually. It was all accidental of course, but by the time I left Germany, most of the Nazis believed me to be a traitor. So I came to London, with Jeffrey's help, as Angelis Chevalier, a French woman seeking asylum, and the identity stuck. That is why you saw me in France, and that is why things were so awkward between Jesse and me." She stopped and turned away. "I never did get the chance to tell him the truth, so I'm telling you, hoping somehow, you will understand."

Josh just stared at her. Hilda was not sure what was going through his mind. He did not know about her father, or her brother, or the fact that her real parents were Americans. What she had just told him could seem like gibberish in his head. He finally took her arm gently.

"I think," he began, "that you're trying to apologize for something that you had no control over, Hilda. I am glad that you told me, but you shouldn't drown yourself in guilt over what you did or did not do. War is a crazy, uncertain, terrible thing, and it changes us, for better or worse. We can never go back to how things used to be, and moving forward can be extremely difficult, but we manage." He put his hands on her shoulders and looked her squarely in the face. "Jesse is gone, and there is nothing we can do to bring him back, but he knows, Hilda. He knows, and I am sure that he forgives you."

Hilda felt tears come to her eyes at Josh's words. She leaned forward and hugged him tightly. "Thank you," she murmured.

He smiled at her broadly. "I'm glad I chose to come over here and volunteer in this crazy war, because otherwise, I probably would not have met you, Hilda van Ostrand."

"I'm glad you did too," she said. Something changed in his eyes, but as quickly as she noticed, it was gone. "To be honest, I was beginning to doubt that we would win this war until you came."

He gave a little laugh, though he remained serious. "Well, I will try not to misuse your faith in us."

"I'm sure you won't."

They shared a smile and continued to walk. When they got to the hotel, she paused for a moment.

"So, I guess I'll be seeing you," she said quietly.

He nodded and watched her. "I don't know if I'll see you again before you leave. We go up tomorrow, so ..."

She shook her head. "Please don't, Josh. Don't be like that. I've already lost Jesse. I'm not about to lose you too."

He smiled at her determined voice. Hilda stuck out her hand. "Good-bye, Joshua. Maybe I'll see you again sooner than we think."

He pulled her into a hug and kissed her cheek. "Good-bye, Hilda. Be safe."

Southampton was full of people. Jeffrey slowly pulled the car up next to the port terminal and hopped out to get the bags from the trunk. As Hilda stepped out of the car, she saw dozens of sailors loading cargo onto the enormous ship that would carry them across the ocean. Hundreds of wounded soldiers crowded the dock, and nurses rushed to and fro between the medical trucks and the injured, preparing them to board. Turning, Hilda opened the other door and took Maria's hand.

"Here we go, darling," she said as she put the girl's coat on. "Stay close to me."

Maria nodded and clutched her hand. Jeffrey handed Hilda her coat and gave the bags to a sailor with the cabin number. He reached into the car and retrieved a file, which he opened.

"Here's your cabin number. I tried to get you in as comfortable a room as possible. I'm afraid you are one of the few civilian passengers, and most of them are American." He gave a little chuckle. "I'm sure you'll be able to fit right in. Here is your passport and identification card. Maria's are in the file as well. You should not have any trouble at customs." With a small breath, he handed her the file. "Good luck."

Hilda took it from him, and her eyes met his. "Thank you, Jeffrey."

"Ah, don't think of it. I was glad to help."

"Really, though. You've done so much for me already. I don't know where I would be if it weren't for you." She sighed and felt her eyes warm with tears. "I don't think I've ever properly thanked you ... for everything."

He stared at her, and his eyes softened. He gently touched her cheek. "You know I would do anything for you, Hilda."

She nodded as tears trickled down her cheeks. "I know. And Jeffrey ...

you were right, not to tell me about my father until you did. I just couldn't see past the pain to the logic behind it."

Jeffrey simply nodded. A long moment passed between them. They had endured so much together, and now she was on her own. God only knew what the future held.

"I hope I'll see you again," Hilda said.

"With your luck so far, I'm sure we will, someday," he answered. He took her coat from her hand and held it out for her to put on. "You should go. You want to be settled before you depart."

Hilda nodded slowly and slipped into the coat. She turned to him and threw her arms around him. "Good-bye," she whispered. She kissed him lightly on the cheek before pulling away. She turned from him and took Maria into her arms as she walked toward the gangway. She never looked back.

An officer at the entrance took their tickets. Hilda showed him the necessary paperwork, and after a moment, he returned them with a smile.

"Welcome aboard, miss," he stated.

"Thank you."

A steward directed them to their cabin, where Hilda found all of their bags had been brought. A half hour later, as she was putting Maria's clothes away in the dresser, she felt the engines begin to rumble beneath her, and she knew they were almost underway.

"Maria!" she called.

The girl appeared from where she had been in the bedroom.

"We're about to leave. Would you like to go up and watch?"

Maria nodded eagerly. Hilda took her hand, and in a few minutes, they emerged on the top deck. Not many people were there; most of the injured could not come up top. There were some who had arms in a sling, or a bandage around their head. She noticed several people in plain clothes snapping pictures. Reporters from the states. She was not surprised.

Going to the rail, Hilda looked for Jeffrey among the crowd of people waving farewell. There he stood, watching the ship depart from beside the car. She knew she was too far away to be recognized, but she waved anyway. She was going to miss him. He had been her rock, the one person she could turn to when there was no one else. Now, she was setting out on her own. It would not be easy, but she knew it was time.

Time to find a new life and begin a different journey.

Time to say good-bye.

"To love and admire anything outside yourself is to take one step away from utter spiritual ruin; though we shall not be well so long as we love and admire anything more than we love and admire God."

C.S. Lewis

25

Mari turned off the watering hose and brushed a hand across her brow. The glorious sunshine warmed the ground and she smiled and waved at a couple of teenage girls biking to the beach. Even in the late afternoon, it seemed too beautiful of a day to be inside. She knew, however, that she had to go in soon to prepare dinner. Danny would be home soon, and Christina was due to be there any minute.

As Mari collected the mail and sat down on the porch, she let her mind wander over the memories that had taken her months to recover from. She could still remember the day that Danny walked into the kitchen, pale and shaking. In his hands, he held a short letter and a pair of dog tags. The realization that had hit her in that moment had been so terrifying, so dreadful, that she had fainted right there on the kitchen floor. It had taken her weeks to stop crying at night, and months to finally start managing life without her son. It had come a bit easier with Christina's marriage to Nathan. He was a doctor, and the two of them had been stationed at Pearl Harbor when the Japanese attacked. When Christina had suffered a tragic injury to her leg, Nathan had been the one to stay by her side. They had been inseparable ever since.

The entire family had truly bonded together during all of the hardships they had faced. Mari sighed, content and happy. She had been at peace for a while now, but it was important to her to look back on the painful memories every now and then.

She was about to sort through the mail when she heard a car pull up to the curb. Glancing up, she smiled and stood as Nathan and Christina hurried up the path. The young woman was glowing. Mari kissed her son-in-law and gave Christina a hug.

"How was the doctor's appointment?" she asked with a twinkle in her eye.

Nathan laughed. "She looks wonderful. A good six months along, and very impatient to be a mother."

Christina joined her husband's laughter. "Hello, Mom. I'm sorry we're a little late. Did we keep you waiting long?"

"Not at all, dear. I was just on my way inside to start the soup. Now don't stand out here and catch a chill. Come on inside."

Mari hustled them into the living room and set them up with some sweet refreshment. As Nathan went to clean up, Mari called from the kitchen, "How does chicken with carrots, celery, and onions sound?"

Christina wrinkled her nose. "No carrots, please. Where's Dad?"

"He should be home soon."

Christina took a sip of the lemonade in front of her and sighed contentedly. It tasted heavenly. A knock at the door made her look up in surprise. Was Mom expecting someone? Slowly, she stood and went to the door. The descending sun shone against the backs of the visitors. Christina leaned against the doorframe and shaded her eyes.

"May I help you?"

Hilda had never felt so nervous in her life as she did standing there in front of the door on the porch of the beautiful pale yellow house. She fidgeted with the lapels of her coat, which covered a dark chocolate brown dress. She was not wearing a heavy coat, but she still felt like she was suffocating from the heat.

Next to her, glancing at the porch swing with a curious eye stood Maria, looking adorable in a sea green travel outfit. Hilda took a deep breath and knelt, adjusting the string of Maria's hat beneath her chin.

"Now, remember what I told you," she said. "Be sure to greet everyone with a smile and look them in the eye."

Maria nodded slowly.

"Good girl."

Hilda rose and smoothed her dress when she heard footsteps coming from inside. She felt the panic begin to rise in her throat, but fought it down. She could do this. If they sent her away, she would just find another way. They had come for safety. Somehow, they would get it.

The door opened to reveal a pretty young woman standing in the doorway. Studying her features, Hilda realized that this must be Christina, Jesse's younger sister. She had a kind face as she gazed at them. She looked to be about five or six months pregnant.

"May I help you?" she asked with a smile as she shaded her eyes.

Hilda faltered for a moment. "I'm sorry to bother you ... are you Christina?"

"I am. Do I know you?"

"Um, not really." Hilda paused, not quite sure where to go from there. "Is ... is Mr. or Mrs. Riker at home?"

"My mother is here, yes. Won't you come in?"

"Oh. Thank you." Hilda hustled Maria inside, and they stood awkwardly in the hallway.

"Come in and sit down. Mom put out some fresh lemonade."

They followed Christina into the living room. Hilda noticed as they walked that the young woman had a slight limp. She wondered what had happened, but only for a moment. When they entered the living room, a man stood there. He gazed at them, not unkindly, but with a hint of curiosity.

"Oh, this is my husband, Nathan. Darling, this is ..." Christina faltered with a slight chuckle. "I'm sorry. I didn't catch your name."

Hilda felt her heart begin to pound. If she said her name, would they know who she was? She did not know if Jesse had mentioned her to anyone. Glancing at the young man, she knew she could not lie. She had to give a good impression to this family.

"My name is—"

A gasp from the doorway made them all turn. Hilda had not noticed the other woman appear out of the corner of her eye. A loud crash ensued as the woman dropped the plate of crackers and cheese she had been carrying. Her eyes were wide with terror. With wonder.

"Merciful heavens ..."

In the short silence, Nathan awkwardly moved to start cleaning up the food. Hilda hesitated only a moment before stepping forward. The older woman did not move; her eyes were glued to her face.

"Are ... are you Mrs. Riker?" Hilda asked.

The woman nodded slowly.

"I wonder if I might speak to you."

Christina stepped forward, concern written on her face. "Mom, what's going on?"

The front door opened, and Hilda watched as another man entered the living room. He took in the scene—Mari, pale and shaken, the broken plate at her feet, his daughter and son-in-law with looks of confusion on their faces, and a young woman he had never seen before standing in the middle of the room, a little girl at her side.

Hilda looked at the man, and her mind burst open with memories from long past. He looked so much like Jesse. He had to be Danny Riker.

"Hello," the man said quietly, studying her face.

"Hello," she answered. "Sir, I don't know if your son told you about me ..."

"I know who you are," he said.

"Danny," his wife murmured.

"Why don't we all sit down," he said as he led Mari to one of the couches. Christina sat down in one of the chairs, Nathan behind her, and Hilda took the couch opposite the Rikers. Maria climbed into her lap and sat silently.

"I suppose you're wondering what I'm doing here," Hilda said.

"Who ...?" Mari's eyes were wide and staring.

Hilda began slowly.

"My name is Hilda van Ostrand. I met your son when he was visiting my home in Heidelberg. We became ... good friends." She looked at their unchanging faces and sighed. "I'm sorry. Maybe I should not have come here."

"Please," Danny interrupted, lifting a hand. "We want you to stay. I know this has seemed to be quite a shock, but we thought that we would never meet you. And now ..."

"Danny ..." Mari whispered.

"Not now, Mari." He stood and came over to her. "We would love for you to stay for dinner, Miss van Ostrand."

Hilda smiled slightly, encouraged by his kind manner. "Thank you."

"Mari, how long before the soup will be finished?" Danny asked as he turned to his wife.

She seemed to start out of a daze. "What? Oh, um, just a few minutes. Let me ... let me go check on it." She got up and hurried from the room.

When Danny turned back to her, Hilda asked, "Is there a place where we might wash, Mr. Riker? The journey was rather long."

"Of course. Up the stairs and to the right. The last door."

"Thank you." Hilda rose and led Maria out of the living room.

Once they were out of sight, Christina glanced at her father, a bewildered look on her face.

"Dad ..."

"Please, Christina. Not right now."

Danny left the living room and went to the kitchen. Mari was staring at the boiling pot, her eyes glazed. The moment she noticed him, she came to life.

"Danny! Heavens above, did you see? I thought I was seeing a ghost! I didn't believe ... how could we not have known?"

Danny took her arm. "Keep your voice down, Mari."

"But Danny!"

"Allie is dead, Mari. So is Luke. And so is their daughter. We must face that fact."

His abrupt statement shocked her into silence and seemed to snap her out of her hysteria. She slowly nodded. "I know. She just ... looks so much like her."

Danny nodded and put his arm around her. "I know, I know. But we can't let our dreams blind us to reality, sweetheart."

Mari wiped her eyes. "I seem to be dealing with that a lot lately."

Danny hugged her to him and kissed her forehead. Mari had been through so much pain and heartache, and the memories constantly seemed to plague her mind. The conversation following dinner would either ease her pain, or add more aching memories to her archives of hurt.

Hilda slowly wandered down the hall, glancing into doorways as she and Maria walked. There were pictures everywhere. Jesse and his sister as children, growing up, and a handsome one of Jesse in his uniform. It was the same photo he had given her after he left so long ago. It was how she would always remember him, and she smiled softly and touched his face through the glass.

"She's like you."

Hilda was surprised at Maria's statement. The girl had been silent for most of the trip, but now she looked up innocently and pointed with her little finger to a picture near the end of the gallery. Hilda studied it closely. Two couples sat at a café on the street corner, smiling and laughing over their drinks. The first was obviously Danny and Mari Riker; Danny looked exactly like Jesse at that age. The other couple caught her attention and she leaned forward. The woman was beautiful, probably a few years older than herself in the photo, with curly blonde locks and twinkling eyes. The man was tall and handsome, his arm around the woman. Hilda's focus changed, and she caught her reflection in the glass with a start. She and the woman could have been twins. There were subtle differences, but there was no denying the resemblance. She took the picture of the wall and turned it over. A small note written in an elegant woman's hand had only a few names and a date. *Danny Riker, Mari Riker, Allison Winter, Luke Pendair. 1917.*

Hilda slowly, as though in a trance, pulled from her bag the short note from so long ago, the words imprinted on her mind, those neat strokes unforgettable:

Please love her as your own and raise her in Christ's love, which binds us all. M.R.

Hilda stared in disbelief at the two notes side by side. There was no question. They were one and the same hand.

"Oh ... my ..."

Hilda slowly descended the steps, Maria following close behind her with a confused look on her face. Danny and Mari came out of the kitchen, and Christina and Nathan stood from the couch. They all stared at the look on her face and wondered what on earth was going on. Hilda stopped in front of Mari, her eyes never leaving her face.

"It was you," she murmured as tears came to her eyes. "It was you."

Danny stepped up and put an arm around Mari, looking between the two of them.

"Miss van Ostrand, I don't ..." Mari started to say.

Hilda lifted the note so that they both could see. "You wrote this ... didn't you?"

Mari slowly took it from her and stared at it, unable to believe what she was seeing. She lifted her eyes back to Hilda's face.

"How did ... it can't be ..." She stumbled as she tried to form a sentence. "Where did you get this?"

Hilda slowly entered the living room and sank down onto the couch. The Rikers followed her slowly.

"I don't know if Jesse ever told you, but I was adopted," Hilda began quietly, a watchful eye on her hosts. "I was found on the steps of a convent when I was just an infant. I was told a nurse had died trying to save my life. My father and mother adopted me a few months later. I didn't learn the truth until nearly five years ago. That I was not German by blood."

Their faces showed their surprise, and Hilda saw that Mari was entranced at her story. She continued. "My father chose not to tell me because of the coming war. After he was killed, I was given this note, along with all the evidence he had found revealing my true ancestry." She gave a wobbly smile. "And then I saw your picture on the wall ... you saved my life."

Mari slowly walked forward and sat down next to her, her face filled with an uncertain joy, as though she was afraid it was all some sort of terrible joke. "Then ... you really are ... you really are her." She touched Hilda's face slowly. The contact seemed to make it real for her, and she gave a cry and clung to Hilda's hands. "I remember wishing and praying that you were alive, and somewhere safe. I did not want to let you out of my sight, but there was an explosion ... We never heard any news, and finally ... we simply gave up hope of ever knowing what really happened." Mari's tears began to flow and she embraced Hilda with a sob. The younger clung to her, amazed at the seemingly impossible connection they had made.

Danny cleared his throat. Sniffling, Mari pulled away from Hilda and gave a small chuckle. "Oh, Danny, didn't I tell you? I knew she was alive! And when she came in ... I just knew!"

Danny stared at Hilda. His eyes tried to take in what his mind could not comprehend. Slowly, he stood and held out his hand. Hilda rose and took it. She saw his expression change from bewilderment to wonder.

"You really are ... Luke's daughter," he murmured.

She nodded as tears fell down her cheeks. "I was hoping you could tell me about my parents."

He gave her a smile and pulled her into his embrace. She closed her eyes, letting Danny fill the fatherly absence in her heart. Mari wrapped her arms around them, and the three of them stood there in the middle of the living room. Hilda sighed, a smile on her lips. They had found a safe haven at last. And they had found friends.

Hilda sat out in the Holden's backyard and watched Maria run around, squealing with delight as Nathan chased her through the flower beds. The child had made a complete turnaround in only a few short days. Christina, with her new motherly instincts, had taken her under her wing, and Maria had opened up to her and Nathan more than anyone else. Hilda laughed as the child fell in a bed of daisies, and Nathan threw her into the air. They were like the parents that Maria lacked, and the thought of Paul and Hannah threw a dark cloud into Hilda's thoughts.

Mari came out from the house and sat down next to her, a book in her hands. She smiled. "I have something for you." She handed the book to Hilda, who opened it and saw that it was a journal. The number at the top of the page dated April 14, 1916. "It belonged to your mother, Allison. She could often be found outside the hospital writing away. I think this will help you get to know her better. And your father. She wrote about Luke all the time." Mari grew thoughtful. "There was a tree she used to sit under when it got really hot. Right before they were married, Allie and Luke carved their initials into it."

Hilda watched Mari talk about her friends, and wished she had had the chance to know her parents like she had. She closed the journal softly and held it close to her heart.

"Mari, thank you, so much."

The older woman smiled. "It was helpful in reminding me of her spirit after she died. Journals, letters ... initials carved in trees," she said with a laugh. "Such things keep us close to those we love, I think."

Hilda nodded and looked down at the journal. They sat in silence for a moment, watching the antics of the others in the yard. Maria's smile and laughter were infectious, but Hilda still felt a heavy weight on her heart.

"Mari ..."

The woman turned to her with a questioning smile. "What is it, Hilda?"

Hilda sighed, feeling the tears prick the back of her eyes. "I'm sorry about Jesse."

Mari stopped and turned to her as realization flooded her being. "Oh, honey ..."

"I feel like somehow it's my fault," Hilda said. "My brother dragged him halfway across the world, and then I made him feel obligated to come back after leaving me there."

"Hilda, he didn't—"

"And then when he does come back, I ignore him and put on a ridiculous charade that I don't care anymore!" she cried, ignoring Mari's attempt to speak. "How could this have happened? How could I have turned into this terrible person who deserts her family and breaks people's hearts?"

"Hilda."

Mari's soft voice pierced into the barrage of turmoil that was radiating through Hilda's mind. She sniffed softly and looked into the woman's kind, gentle face through the waterfall of her tears.

"Hilda, Jesse's death was not your fault. It was God's will that he leave us, and nothing will change that."

"But why?" Hilda was angry now. "He was the one man who understood me, who saw what I had done and still loved me, despite everything."

"That's who he was, Hilda. For so long, I wondered how he could go through life so selflessly. It was because he always tried to be like Christ in everything he did."

"And look what He gave him in return!"

Hilda stood abruptly, clutching her mother's journal, and hurried back into the house. How could Mari just sit by and accept Jesse's death like that? There was no possible explanation. Out of the corner of her eye, she saw Danny look up from where he was working at his desk. He sent an inquiring look outside the screen door, but Mari was silent. Hilda went out to the front porch and sat down in one of the chairs. She opened her mother's journal to the first entry.

> *Well, I've made my decision. Mother and Father are none too pleased with it, but I can't be coddled my entire life. I want to do something useful, not just be a pretty face in New York society. Nothing can stop this calling. I've made my choice. Who knows what awaits me over in Europe? All I know is my entire life is about to change, for the better, I don't know, but the Lord has opened this door to me, and who am I to not trust Him in this?*

Hilda read the last words again. Who am I to not trust Him? Who am I? Suddenly, Hilda had never felt so small and insignificant in her life. The world was so much bigger than her, so much bigger than anything she had experienced.

Danny sat down in the chair next to her. Hilda had not even heard him open the door. He did not say anything, but allowed her to continue in her thoughts as she watched the tall roses sway in the afternoon breeze.

"I used to believe in God, you know," she said.

Danny turned his eyes slowly to her. "What happened?"

"I don't know. I became so caught up in what I was doing; I guess I just ... forgot."

He smiled softly. "I find that hard to believe."

Hilda looked at him for a moment before turning back to the roses. "Well, it's true. After my father died, I stopped believing that He had a plan and made my own."

"And how did that work out for you?"

Hilda couldn't help giving a short laugh, and rolled her eyes in agreement with his thoughts.

"I remember the first time I felt truly lost and alone. After Jesse died," she said as she looked back at Danny. "And I called out to Him."

"In fear," he said.

Surprised, Hilda nodded. "I suppose. I felt as though I would go insane if I didn't talk to someone ... anyone. Jesse was gone, I had no family ... I thought I could walk down the street and no one would even know I was alive."

Danny put his hand on her arm gently and Hilda closed her eyes against the tears threatening to break forth. "I just ... don't understand why he had to die."

Danny stood and knelt in front of her, forcing her to meet his eyes. He took her hands tightly.

"Perhaps he had to die so that you might live."

Hilda's eyes turned confused. "What do you mean?"

"You're lost, Hilda, and that's not a bad thing. You see your weakness, your need for someone, and you turned to the Lord. You still feel Him; you still need Him. Jesse was just in the way of you realizing that."

With that, Danny stood and went back into the house. Hilda thought on his words carefully. The impact they had was like a hard knocking on her heart. Had Jesse become her idol, the only thing worth living for? As she looked back, she realized that in her love for him, she had pushed everything and everyone away from her in the process. Dederick had been right. She had not fully lived since Jesse had waved farewell on that train so long ago. Hilda could blame her actions on the truth of her past, on the war, on Jeffrey Rolf, even on Jesse. But in the end, she was the one who blindly fell away from what truly mattered. And that truth hurt.

26

Hilda walked along the sandy beach two blocks from the Riker house and laughed at Maria's concerned face. They were in the middle of an intense discussion, and no answer seemed to please the little girl. Her brown curls bounced as she shook her head and crossed her arms with a frown.

"But where is the snow?" she asked again.

Hilda squatted in front of her, unable to contain her amused smile. "Darling, California is different from back home. It's much warmer here than in Germany, and since snow only comes when it's cold, the Rikers have sunny Christmases instead of snowy ones."

"But Christmas isn't the same without snow," Maria complained.

"I know, dear, I feel the same way. This is my first Christmas without snow too." She scooped up a pile of sand and let it sift through her fingers. "We could make a sand man instead."

Maria's face brightened, and she ran down toward the water. Hilda helped her make a small mountain, the lower body, and then sent Maria in search of eyes, nose, mouth and arms for their creation. Hilda scooped as much sand together as she could, and in the end, she was quite impressed to see that she had made a sand man, three crumbly sand balls high, that stood about three feet off the ground. Maria came bounding back, her arms full.

"Here!" she exclaimed. "Ooh, he looks so big!"

Hilda laughed. "Show me what you found."

Maria opened her hands. Two identical blue shells had to be for the eyes, a smaller one was the nose, and several rocks would be his mouth.

"And what's that around your neck?" Hilda asked.

Maria put her findings at her feet and lifted the slimy rope from her neck. "I don't know, but it's for his arms."

Hilda watched, amused, as she tried to make them straight, but they simply drooped to the ground when Maria let go.

"That's all right, Maria, he's just tired. Let's put his face together."

When they stepped back from their work, Hilda put her hand to her chin in mock thinking as she studied their sand man. Finally, she nodded affirmatively. "Yes, he looks just like you." Hilda tickled Maria and sent her into a burst of laughter. "I didn't know you had a brother!"

Maria stopped suddenly and stared at the man. Her face was serious, much too serious for a three and a half year old. She touched the sand man gently, leaving her fingerprints on the side of his cheek. She turned to Hilda.

"Auntie ... where are my parents?"

Hilda was not expecting her question and felt the painful blow to her heart fully. Maria had never asked about her parents in all the time they had been together; Hilda assumed she was simply too young to remember or even understand the truth. But now Maria looked up at her, sad as though knowing the answer would not be what she hoped for. Hilda knelt down next to her in the sand.

"Well, darling ..." She faltered, and she wasn't sure she could tell Maria the truth. She looked into her niece's eyes and took her hands. "They had to go away quite suddenly. They wanted to say good-bye, but there was not enough time."

Maria's face dropped, and Hilda quickly continued. "But you know what Elsa told me? She said they left you your mother's ring so that you would know how much they love you. They are going to do everything they can to come back to you as soon as possible. I promise."

Maria's eyes filled with tears, and she hugged her aunt tightly.

"I believe you," she whispered.

Hilda's heart broke. They turned and walked back up the beach, and all the while Hilda was pleading silently. *Come back, Paul. You and Hannah come back, no matter what it takes.*

~*~

July 8, 1918

I felt the baby move this morning. It was simply incredible. Luke is so proud. He is constantly smiling and laughing, which is good. He has been so serious. News of the war makes everyone very solemn. Mari has noticed the same about Danny. I think we are all ready for this war to be over. We are ready to go home. This past Fourth of July stood out starkly to all of us. Our time has been well spent here, but the time will soon come for us to leave our friends here and return to those in America. I constantly wonder what my parents will say when I come home. I wrote to them about my marriage as well as the baby, but I have not heard from them. No matter what, I will follow Luke wherever he goes. He is my husband, my love, my friend, and I will go where he goes.

Mari is ready to see Jesse again. How big he must be now! She and I like to fantasize that if the baby is a girl, they will get married. We always laugh about it. It would be quite fun, though.

This war should be over soon, they say. I pray with all my heart that they are right. We have made it this far; we can make it through, and then we are going home.

Hilda closed the journal silently that evening. How could they have known? They were so close, and yet God had chosen to take them. Hilda found herself once again finding it hard to accept, but she tried to push down her thoughts.

Mari joined her on the couch with two cups of tea. Hilda took one gratefully. "Is Maria asleep?" she asked.

"Yes, went down without a peep. Poor dear, she's been so exhausted lately." Mari smiled. "I think all this Christmas excitement is getting to her."

Hilda smiled. "Just this morning she was wondering how there could be Christmas without snow. Quite the debate, I must say."

They sipped their tea quietly for a moment. Mari noticed the journal in her hand. "Are you enjoying that?"

"More than you know. I wish my grandparents had been more accepting to her. It's not easy, what she did." Hilda looked at Mari. "I tried to find them in New York, you know, but ..."

Mari nodded in understanding. "Yes, we heard of their deaths several years ago. I don't think they ever spoke of Allison after her death. Such a sad family. I never could understand their unwillingness to contact her. They would have loved your father."

Hilda smiled at the mention of Luke Pendair. From all her mother's descriptions, her father was the most handsome pilot to take to the skies, and everything a woman dreamed of in a man. Gentle, yet strong; protective, yet understanding. Allison had loved him so much.

"You have his eyes, you know," Mari murmured. "Luke had the most beautiful green eyes that could pierce your soul. Allison said that every time he looked at her, she melted like butter in a pan." She swallowed as tears formed in her eyes. "The night that … they died, Luke held you in his arms and just stared at you, marveling. I don't think he'd ever felt more proud than in that moment."

"I'm glad to know a part of him is in me," Hilda said with a small smile. "He sounds like such a wonderful man."

Mari laughed and put down her tea. "Oh, how Jesse idolized that man! From all the stories we told of the war, he looked up to Luke, even though he'd never met him. He and Danny were Jesse's inspiration to become a pilot."

Hilda watched Mari talk about her son, and grew content as she told stories of Jesse growing up with his sights set on the skies. He had more passion in him than the entire Air Corps combined, Mari liked to say. Hilda smiled softly as the older woman spoke of better days. Mari suddenly grew soft and serious.

"I thought I would never recover the day we heard of his death," she murmured. "The New Year had just passed, and we had such great expectations … and then came that awful telegram, and I felt my heart shatter into a thousand pieces." Mari wiped a tear from her eye and looked down at her tea on the table in front of them. "It took months and months for me to move past his death. When Christina got married, I knew that slowly, I was beginning to heal. But it still hurts every time I think of him."

Hilda took Mari's hand gently. "I know." She paused and took a sip from her cup. "He wrote to me, you know. Right before he died."

Mari looked at her, surprised. "What did he say?"

Hilda smiled gently. "He said to live."

⁓

Christmas day dawned brightly in Los Angeles. The sun shone down on the city as Hilda and Maria stirred from their sleep and hurried down to join the Rikers at the Christmas tree. Maria received more gifts on that day than she had in her entire little life, with her favorite present being a doll with brown hair and brown eyes, wearing a beautiful floral dress, and over her heart was stitched a name. *Hannah.* A gift from her aunt.

Hilda received several presents as well, but she could not think of any better than being with her new family after having spent so many Christmases without her own. As Maria played with her new doll with Christina and Nathan and their new addition, little baby Anneliese, Hilda found herself at peace. It was only appropriate in this holiday of peace on earth and goodwill toward men. How strange to think of peace, though, in the middle of a war. It was odd, being so at ease, when far away, Europe still raged in the fight against Nazi Germany. She had no news from her friends, for none knew where she had gone, though Jeffrey knew she was somewhere in the states.

But something was changing. She read of British air raids on Berlin becoming more frequent and more deadly, and she imagined Joshua up in the skies fighting along with them. She sent up a silent prayer for him. Though Hitler still shouted victory for Germany, Hilda knew that slowly, piece by piece, his regime was crumbling. Could it be possible? That her home could return to the way it once was? She could hardly remember a moment in her life where the Nazis had not been present. Could there possibly be a future in which there was no Hitler, no terror from the Gestapo? The thought made her ache for Heidelberg, for her home and her own room. She thought of her last encounter with Dederick. She still found it hard to forgive him; a piece of her could not let go of his betrayal of their mother, and yet ... somehow she saw them coming together again. Her mother, Paul, Dederick, Hannah ... they could be a family again.

The war was changing. Hilda watched the film reels and read the newspapers. Maybe, just maybe, in a few short months, she and Maria could go home.

27

London, April 1944

P assing through the train car on the way to London, one couldn't help but notice the poised stature of the woman sitting next to the window. Not a hair was out of place beneath her white and blue hat, cocked stylishly to one side. Her royal blue overcoat stood out in stark contrast to the light sky blue color of her dress. The small girl sitting next to her wore a spotless lavender traveling suit and looked through the pictures of a book laid open on her lap.

Hilda smiled at Maria as the two glanced at each other. Their time in America had been well spent, and Hilda felt more confident and at peace than she ever had. Her parting with the Rikers had been hard, and there had been many tears, but somehow she knew they would see each other again.

"Now remember," Mari had said, her tone like that of a mother, "the Holdens are expecting you. We wrote them of your return, and they will pick you up at the station."

Hilda nodded and smiled. After several more tearful good-byes, she and Maria had boarded the train for New York with a final wave from the window.

In the few months since she had first considered returning to London, the Allies had launched several offenses on both the Ukrainian front and the Belorussian front. The British continued to lead raids on Germany,

265

including their most recent massive bombing of Hamburg. The tide was indeed turning in the Allies favor.

"Aunt Hilda, are we there yet?"

Hilda turned to Maria, newly turned four, who was staring at her questioningly. "Yes, darling, we're almost there."

"Who are we staying with in London?"

"Friends of the Rikers. Dr. and Mrs. Holden. They're picking us up at the station. Remember to be polite."

Maria nodded and reached for her small white gloves sitting next to her on the seat. Hilda assisted her in pulling them on, and then put on her own. True to her words, the train pulled into Victoria Station ten minutes later. Hilda called to a porter, and they followed him off the train as he carried their bags out of the car. She looked around and after a moment, she saw a woman come forward, a purse clutched in her white hands. Hilda slowly moved toward her, and Maria clung to her hand.

"Mrs. Holden?"

The woman nodded slowly, a wobbly smile coming to her lips. "Please, forgive me," she murmured. "I just ... never imagined ... all this time, we thought you didn't survive, and yet ... here you are."

Hilda gave a small smile in return. "I never did get to properly thank you for saving my life. I'm sorry."

Mrs. Holden gave a wave of her hand. "Don't thank me. Thank my husband. And Jesse. They both did a wonderful job."

Hilda nodded, and Mrs. Holden turned to the little girl watching the conversation silently.

"And you must be Maria," she said with a smile.

Maria nodded, her innocent eyes on the woman.

"Maria," Hilda encouraged softly.

"Very pleased to meet you," the girl piped up.

Mrs. Holden's smile widened. "The car is outside. My husband should be home early tonight, and my daughter Grace and her husband asked to come over and meet you. I hope you don't mind."

"Not at all," Hilda said. It would be good to see Jeffrey again. Strange, but good.

John Holden had not been able to take his eyes off of the woman across from him for the past hour. The resemblance to Allison Pendair was uncanny, except for the green eyes. When Hilda van Ostrand smiled, he saw Luke's eyes lighting up with laughter. He would never have guessed that Luke and Allison's daughter possessed so much of their personalities. She was like a vision, a piece of the past. But she was so real.

"You may have gotten this a lot from Mari and Danny," he said, "but you look and act so much like your parents."

Hilda smiled, and once again, John was struck by the similarities.

"Yes, they did say that, all the time," she said, "but I loved hearing it." Leaning forward, she asked, "Can you tell me about them?"

"What is there to say?" Mary said with a small laugh. "Just picture yourself, and that's what they were like."

"Please," Hilda murmured. "I'd like to know."

John smiled wistfully. "I can still remember the day I first met your mother. She stepped off the train as scared as a newborn kitten. Mari was with her, but she wasn't as nervous as Allie, who was clinging to her arm. It wasn't until a week later that I found out of her parents' anger when she volunteered."

"Did she ever see them again?"

John shook his head. "The day she left was the last day she saw them. She wrote to them while she was here, but they were so angry over her decision that they refused to even acknowledge her. I don't know that they ever mentioned her name again, all because she chose a pilot."

Hilda sighed. "He was handsome, wasn't he? My father?"

Mary smiled. "Oh, yes. Arguably the most handsome man in the whole squadron. Many a young girl vied for his attention, but he had his heart set on one. He told me later it was love at first sight."

Hilda smiled gently. It sounded like a storybook. They had triumphed over adversity to be together at last, but their union was cut short. Mari had told her how the story ended, and after many tears, Hilda finally understood what happened. It had been hard to hear, but knowing more of their love story made it easier to bear. They had not had to be parted long from one another.

"They were so in love," Hilda said quietly.

"Yes, they were," John murmured.

"I just wish I could have known them. I tried to find my grandparents, but they were dead."

"Yes, we heard of their deaths about seven years ago," he said. Watching her, he added quietly, "I'm sure if they had known you were alive, they would have wanted to see you."

Tears entered Hilda's eyes, and she felt Maria's little hand on her arm in a comforting attempt. She gave the girl an encouraging smile and put an arm around her.

The front door opened quietly. "Mum? Dad?"

"In here, Grace," Mary called.

A moment later, Grace appeared in the doorway, Jeffrey next to her. He glanced at Hilda in faint surprise. Hilda smiled slightly. He had noticed the change in her. Maria swung herself down from the couch, a beaming smile on her face, and ran into Jeffrey's open arms. Grace looked at him in surprise.

"You know them?" she asked.

Jeffrey nodded. "We've known each other for a while, Hilda and I. She came to our wedding. I met Maria only recently."

Hilda stood and stuck out her hand. "I don't know if you remember me, Mrs. Rolf. Your father tended me."

Grace studied her for a moment, then her eyes widened in surprise. "Of course! I'm sorry, I didn't recognize you."

"Do you remember when we would talk about our friends, the Pendairs?" John asked his daughter.

"The Americans? Yes, I remember."

"Dr. Holden, please," Hilda said quietly, but he continued enthusiastically.

"This is their daughter, Hilda van Ostrand," he stated with a brilliant smile.

A shocked silence fell over the room. Jeffrey stared at her, disbelief in his eyes. Hilda sighed and lowered her head. She could not bear to see his hurt look.

"Hilda, my daughter Grace, and you already know my son-in-law, Jeffrey," Mary said with a smile.

"Pleased to know you," Hilda murmured.

The awkward moment remained for a few more seconds, and Hilda thought she might scream at the silence. Luckily, the cook came in and announced that supper was ready. With a sigh of relief, Hilda stepped forward and took Maria from Jeffrey's arms. At least during supper, she would not have to sit idly and feel awkward. She glanced at Jeffrey as she left for the dining room. His face was still showing shock, and she could read the hurt behind his eyes. She had much to explain.

Hilda stepped outside the door, two cups of hot coffee in her hands. As it clicked shut, she turned to find Jeffrey staring out into the night. Inside, the faint murmurings of the Holdens and Maria's laughter in the parlor were heard. With a small smile, she stepped forward and held out the coffee. He took it silently. For a moment, they simply stood there.

"It's a beautiful night," she murmured.

Jeffrey looked down at the cup in his hand. Hilda felt her warm approach begin to freeze over like a cold hand clenching her heart. She sighed.

"Jeffrey, I'm sorry."

Slowly, he turned to her, and confused pain returned to his face. She held his eyes, hoping to make him understand her reasoning.

"How long have you known?" he asked quietly.

She lowered her eyes. "When you gave me the package from Father the night we met."

With an exasperated sigh, he ran his hand through his hair. "Why, Hilda? Did you not trust me?"

"Oh, Jeffrey, it wasn't that. I just felt as though my whole life had been ripped from me, and I finally found something that defined me, and I wasn't going to let anyone take it from me," she said as she tried to stop the tears.

"I wanted you to trust me, Hilda," he said, anguish in his voice.

"I do trust you!" she cried. "This has nothing to do with trust. It was it was something sacred that I felt could not be blurted all over London. Please, Jeffrey, try to understand."

He gave a short laugh. "You know, Hilda, I can't count how many times I've thought I had you figured out. Next thing I know, you pull out another surprise." He sighed. "I suppose I'll never fully understand you."

"I don't think I even fully knew myself," she murmured. "Not until recently."

He looked at her. "What do you mean?"

Hilda drew a deep breath. "When I first came to work for you, I thought I was in control. I could be anyone I wanted to be and no one would ever know the woman behind the charade." She caught his gaze and held it. "I was stripped of my mask this past year, Jeffrey. I'm not in control anymore. And you know? I'm more at peace, more free than I ever was when I wanted to control my fate."

Jeffrey was watching her with new eyes.

"I'm happy, Jeffrey," she said. "I don't want to continue holding down these secrets. If I do, I'll go down with them." She sighed. "So it is true, my parents were Americans. They died at the end of the Great War, and I was adopted by the van Ostrands. The rest is history. I'm here now, and I hope you understand the reason for my silence."

He held her eyes for a moment, and then slowly nodded. "You're quite a woman, Hilda van Ostrand. I have yet to meet another person who has gone through what you have experienced. It's an honor to have known you." With a slight nod of his head, Jeffrey turned to walk back in the house.

Hilda watched him stop in front of the door, and slowly turn back. His gentle eyes searched hers. "The man who wins your heart will be a lucky one, indeed."

She felt the small ache slowly inch back into her heart. Hilda stubbornly pushed it down and took a sip of her coffee. There would be another time, another life for that. Breathing in the cold night air, she slowly shook her head. But not right now.

As Jeffrey disappeared into the house, she suddenly straightened in determination. She would survive. She knew that now. She would survive, and then she and Maria would go home.

"Death leaves a heartache no one can heal,
love leaves a memory no one can steal."

From a headstone in Ireland

28

Sevastopol, May 1944

Tanya had never felt so anxious and jittery in her entire life. They had been living outside of Sevastopol for three weeks now, and she still had not seen Dederick. She had learned that many troops had been sent to try and liberate the city. Had she worked so hard for nearly two years only to have him slip from her again?

She could still hardly fathom her luck. Everything had fallen right into place. Father had been given orders to go to the camps outside the city before they started the siege. Tanya had begged to go with him and after some long hesitation, he had finally agreed. After he had left her flat, she thought she probably would have gone anyway. She would not remain in Moscow for another three months while Dederick waited in Sevastopol.

Anxiously, she paced around the flat. She and her father had relocated to a small town about fifteen miles east of Sevastopol. Nicholas would be back from the front soon, and then she would play her hardest card.

She would ask to go with him.

Tanya knew he was already suspicious of why she wanted to accompany him to a war zone. His two agents had watched her like hawks while she was in Moscow. Though they were not with her now, she knew someone was constantly watching her. She had to move carefully.

The door behind her opened, and she turned to see her father and a soviet officer enter the apartment. Smiling, she came forward.

"How was your meeting?" she asked.

Nicholas muttered something to the officer, who nodded and left. The moment the door shut, his eyes narrowed in ferocious anger, and he struck her so hard and so fast that she was more shocked than hurt.

"How dare you?" he yelled as she fell backward into a chair. "How could you even think that I would not find out?"

"What ... w-what ..."

"Don't tell me you don't know what I'm talking about!" he roared. "I knew you had a motive in coming here! But this? My own daughter, stooping so low! Traitor!"

At this, Tanya stood with a new fiery anger. "You have no idea what you're talking about!"

"Oh, don't I?" he said with a sarcastic laugh. "You would give up a life in peace and wealth ... for something you don't even understand? For a boy?" He spat the word.

"For the man I love!" she said defiantly. "You really think I would submit to hanging onto the coattails of a father who never bothered to see his daughter more than once every five years? He loves me, which is more than you could ever do!"

Nicholas slapped her again and she fell over the chair to the ground. She knew if he had the chance, he would beat her to within an inch of her life. She was dazed, and felt her eyelids begin to droop. Tanya watched him become a fuzzy black figure against the starkness of the room. Terrified that he would come at her again, she tried to crawl away toward the chair, but the motion made her head pound, and she blacked out.

When she came to, night had fallen. Tanya slowly sat up. Her father was gone, but she knew he had left his guard at the door. Her betrayal would be severely punished and if she did not leave quickly, there would not be another chance for escape. She did not know how she would get there, but she knew she had to find Dederick tonight.

Softly, Tanya walked up to the side of the door and grabbed a shovel from the fireplace with a firm grip. She knocked. The door swung open, and the officer entered. In one swift motion, she sent him to the floor, unconscious.

Tanya's heart raced as she threw some necessities into a bag. She knew she was walking into the middle of a hectic battle, but it could be even more dangerous for her to stay. The street was bustling when she hurried out of the building. Women shopped for groceries and men talked in serious tones about the war. A soviet officer could be seen here and there.

Clutching the case to her, Tanya tried to appear calm as she hailed a taxi and pulled a safely hidden address from inside her bag. She had to reach him. She had to.

⌒*⌒

Dederick could barely keep his eyes open. He could no longer remember how long the siege had been going on. The days had flowed together, and the barrage of bullets had become a steady monotony.

"Lieutenant, you're being relieved."

The voice came from a young soldier behind him. His face was grim and dirty. Dederick nodded to him wearily. A cold bed awaited him, but at least there was a mattress. He stumbled into the barracks and collapsed onto the cot. He succumbed to the darkness, but not before her face came to his mind. He missed Tanya so much. So much it hurt. *Sleep,* his mind said. *Sleep.*

A very light tap on his arm pulled him back.

"Sir. Sir."

Dederick groaned and opened his eyes to search for the person who had whispered. His eyes found those of a young soldier who looked no older than fifteen. Pain clenched his heart as he thought of the boy who had saved his life.

"What is it?" he asked, irritated.

"There's someone to see you, Lieutenant," the boy said.

"Now?"

"She says it's urgent."

"What could be so urgent that you have to wake me in the middle of the night ... she?"

With a quick look at the boy, Dederick ran out of the barracks and glanced around. The street was empty, and the occasional sound of machine gun fire could be heard. He turned quickly when a shadow detached itself from the wall. His eyes saw the shining blond hair in the moonlight and the piercing eyes that searched his.

"Dederick," Tanya murmured as she stepped toward him.

"What are you doing here?" he asked in wonder.

"I want to be with you." Her voice broke. "I'm so sorry, Dederick."

He didn't let her say another word. He crushed her in his arms, and she let him capture her lips as her tears mingled with his kiss. He murmured words of love to her between kisses, and she clung to him. After several moments, they reluctantly pulled away.

"How did you ... I don't understand ..."

"It doesn't matter," Tanya said with a shake of her head. "There is nowhere in the world I would rather be than with you."

He could not believe she was actually here. He lightly framed her face and kissed her lips. "When this war is over, I am going to marry you, Tanya Berezovsky."

Her smile lit up her entire face and she laughed. "I'll hold you to that."

He became serious and gazed into her brilliant eyes. "I love you," he said firmly. He wanted her to know the depth of his feelings. "More than anything on this earth, I love you."

"I love you too," she whispered. She brought his head down, and they shared a passionate kiss.

"I don't want to go," she murmured.

He nodded and led her down the street to an abandoned house. They walked into the first bedroom, and he drew her down onto the mattress with him.

"Stay with me," Tanya whispered. "Stay with me always."

Dederick nodded and stroked her hair as he leaned back on the pillow. For the first time in a long while, he fell into a dreamless, calm sleep. The woman he loved was in his arms, and even though a siege raged on around them, peace filled the house and the couple.

Tanya woke to the sound of rapid gunfire and shouting. With a start, she sat up. Next to her, Dederick stirred at the sound. The next moment, he was awake and alert, and his eyes glanced around quickly.

"Come on," he said, and took her hand. He led her through the house and out the back door. All around them, soldiers were running to posts, shouting orders as guns were loaded. Dederick looked around grimly.

"The Soviets must have gained the upper hand," he said. He put his hands on her shoulders and stared at her intensely. "This is getting bad. You need to go."

Tanya shook her head furiously. "I won't leave you."

"I don't want you here, Tanya. It's too dangerous. You could get hurt."

"I don't care about that, Dederick. I'll die if I'm parted from you again."

Her eyes were so full of pain and want that he could not help himself. He crushed her to him and kissed her with all of his pent-up passion.

"I'll never leave you again," she whispered when he pulled away.

An explosion sounded near them, and Tanya let out a small cry. Dederick pushed her against the wall of the house and shielded her with his body. When all of the debris had fallen, he looked at her with avid concern.

"Are you all right?" he asked. He looked her over for injuries.

Tanya took a deep breath. "I'm fine, really."

He sighed and ran his fingers through his hair. "I still can't believe this. I don't understand it, but I can't tell you how happy I was when I saw you come out of the shadows."

She smiled brilliantly. Another explosion sounded, and she glanced around nervously. "Where do I go?"

He held her gaze and came in close to her. "You have to trust me, Tanya."

"I do," she whispered.

"You need to get out of the city by the south. I will meet you at the harbor. There is a boat there called the *Neptune's Revenge*. Wait for me there. I *will* come for you."

With tears in her eyes, Tanya nodded. She drew him against her and kissed him one last time. Their eyes held for a second, and then he was gone.

"I love you," she whispered as he disappeared around the corner.

Shells exploded everywhere as Tanya ran toward the southern end of the city. At one point, she was blown off her feet and landed on something soft. She looked in horror at the mangled body of a dead German soldier. With a cry, she got up and ran as fast as she could. Within minutes, the harbor appeared, shining before her. Boats bobbed here and there with the coming of the tide, and only a few yards away swayed the *Neptune's Revenge*. With a quick glance toward the roofs and down the street, she dashed aboard and quickly secured herself inside the hold. It was dark and musty, but there was a comfortable bed she could rest on, as well as some crackers, a canteen of water, and a bottle of vodka. Trembling slightly, she lay down on the bed and closed her eyes.

"Hurry, Dederick. Please, hurry."

The sun was setting when Tanya awoke. She got up, slightly confused as to where she was. It all came back to her in a moment. She was aboard a fishing boat, waiting for Dederick. Cautiously, she opened the hatch and peered out. Not a soul was in sight. Occasionally, there was a sound of gunfire, but the battle appeared to be over.

"Come on, Dederick. Where are you?" she murmured.

Darkness slowly enclosed the harbor. All that could be heard was the lapping of the waves against the dock. The quiet was unnerving, and Tanya felt a chill begin to take over her heart. Had something gone wrong?

A sudden small movement caught her attention. A shadow could barely be seen against the blue hue that covered the buildings. Tanya watched cautiously, and then her heart leaped with joy. It was Dederick. He had made it!

Careful to stay hidden, she watched him dodge the light and steadily make his way toward the dock. The city must have fallen, for he ran as though he did not want to be seen. It didn't matter. Once he got to the boat, they would leave forever and not have to worry about the war anymore.

Dederick paused in the shadows across the street from the dock.

"Come on, Dederick," she whispered. "You're almost there."

He hesitated for a few seconds, weighing the odds.

Now, Dederick!

He dashed across the street and began to run down the dock toward the boat. Tanya began to open the hatch to welcome him, but his firm shout came rolling over the wind.

"No!"

To her horror, she heard the pop of gunshots, and watched as he ducked his head. Soldiers appeared in the street behind him, and shouts in Russian could be heard.

"There he is!"

It barely registered that the voice sounded familiar to her, for as she watched, Dederick stumbled and fell to his knees. The soldiers were almost on top of him now.

"No!" she screamed, trying to block out what she was seeing.

Dederick unsteadily rose to his feet and stumbled down the dock. He was a mere twenty feet from her, and she could see the pain etched in his face. As he stepped onto the boat, she lifted the hatch and hurried toward him. He gave a sudden cry as a bullet pierced his back and he fell forward.

"Dederick!" She ran to catch him, and they both tumbled to the deck. "No, no!" Tanya cried, tears running down her cheeks.

"Cease fire!" came the call from across the street.

Absentmindedly, she glanced up. Her father appeared from the shadows, a shocked look on his face. A gun went off somewhere, and Tanya fell to the deck, covering Dederick.

"I said, cease fire!" came Nicholas' harsh voice. "The boy is as good as dead. Back to your posts!"

There was a scurrying of feet, and then silence. When Tanya glanced up again, she met her father's gaze for only an instant before he disappeared down the street. As the darkness closed around him, she knew she would never see him again.

A soft moan came to her ears, and she turned her eyes back to the man she loved.

"Tanya ..." he whispered painfully.

"Shh, don't talk," she said, a tremble in her voice. "We have to stop the bleeding and get you to a comfortable bed."

"It's ... too late for that ..."

She hugged him to her gently so as not to hurt him, while her tears flowed freely.

"Don't you dare talk like that, Dederick van Ostrand," she said firmly. "Do you hear me? You've got to fight. You must fight!"

Her voice broke, and her head fell lightly against his chest as she sobbed. *This can't be happening. This is a nightmare.*

"Tanya, please ..." came Dederick's soft voice, and she felt his hand on her hair. She raised her head and sniffed as she wiped the tears from her eyes uselessly.

"Oh, darling, I'm so sorry! This is all my fault. If only I had come to the station that day, none of this would have happened."

"Shh," he whispered. "Don't ... don't blame yourself ..."

His eyes closed, and he took a sharp breath. Tanya's heart stopped as she watched him. "Dederick?"

He let out a slow breath and opened his eyes, a small smile on his face. "I ... I thank God every day that you came into my life," he murmured. "I ... I love you ..."

"Dederick, Dederick ..." she moaned. She leaned down and kissed him, wishing she were not as helpless as she felt. As she watched through watering eyes, the light faded from his face, and he relaxed against her chest. A sigh escaped his mouth, and he was gone.

29

T here had been whispers around the camp for the past two months, but Paul had still not had any success in contacting Hannah. The guards had tightened security, and with good reason.

The war had taken a dramatic turn.

It had all begun on June 6, during the early morning hours as the choppy waves crashed against the beaches of Normandy. The Allies' surprise attack had done more damage than they thought possible. After a long, hard fought battle, they had taken the coast from the Germans, stirring hope for the first time in months.

Whispers had ensued around camp not long after that, and the battle, which was coming to be known as D-Day, had made every inmate's hopes soar more than they had in a very long time.

If only he could get to Hannah! Paul wondered if she knew about the victorious invasion, and if she, too, felt the coming change in the wind. It was there, just out of reach, but coming closer and closer.

Freedom was near.

But with this realization, he worried. The Nazis were already trying to cover up their tracks. Rumors had been going around about concentration camps being liquidated and all traces of the camp removed. He had to get to Hannah. Somehow, he had to.

The darkness closed in around him as he followed the line of men toward the barracks. Guards stood at every corner, watching them. Paul would not be meeting Hannah tonight.

⌒n⌒

Hannah had seen Paul again. The days had been endless torture, but her eyes had brightened when she spotted her husband in a long line of men. He had seemed very preoccupied with his thoughts, and she grew worried at the endless stress he must be experiencing. His eyes had suddenly found hers, and they stared at her with a sudden intensity. She realized that he wanted to meet with her again, and she discreetly nodded her head to let him know she understood.

As she lay on her bunk quietly staring into the darkness, she listened to the murmur of the women sleeping. Her stomach gnawed at itself and groaned for food she did not have. She began to feel light-headed, and she wondered not for the first time if she would make it through to the end. She prayed that Paul had news. She had survived for this long, but how much longer?

Amid the murmurs of the sleeping women, Hannah heard the faintest sound of something tapping the wall next to her ear. She sat up and glanced through a crack in the wall. Relief rushed through her as she saw Paul's flushed face. He had obviously dodged several guards. Hurriedly, she slipped out of the bunk and discreetly stepped out of the barracks. Within seconds, she was in Paul's arms. She clung to him as though he alone could save her. They shared several passionate kisses and whispered words of love before they finally lifted their heads.

"I didn't think I would last much longer without seeing you," she whispered.

He pulled her head against his chest and smoothed her hair. "It's been so long."

"What's been happening, Paul?" she asked, her eyes wide to take in all of him.

"The war has taken a turn."

"For the better?"

"Oh yes. The Allies took control of the French coast months ago, and in the east, Sevastopol has been retaken."

"What does it all mean?" she whispered excitedly.

"It's means it's almost over. Freedom is on the horizon."

"Have you heard anything more?"

280

Paul shook his head, but Hannah had a feeling he was hiding something from her.

"I'm trying to find out more, darling. Don't despair. It's nearly over. Just hold on a little bit longer."

She nodded and sighed against him. A sudden thought came to her. "Paul, have you ever thought about what will happen when we die?"

"Hannah, don't think like that!" Paul said.

"No, no, not if we die here," she said, shaking her head. "I mean, when we die, which we will someday, what will happen to us?"

Paul stared at her, confused for a long moment.

"Judith was telling me something," she said.

"Judith? You saw Judith?"

"Yes."

"Where is she?"

"She's dead."

The reply came out bluntly, and Paul nodded in silence. They had both come to understand the value of life in Auschwitz.

"What did she say, Hannah?"

"She said she had become a ... Christian, and that Jesus Christ was the Messiah." Hannah looked up at him. "Do you believe this?"

"I did," Paul said solemnly, "but since then, my faith has been sorely tested."

She sighed. "At first I thought she was simply going insane, what with all of the hard labor, but ever since then, her words have stayed with me." Hannah pulled the now precious pages of Isaiah from inside her shirt and showed them to her husband. "She gave me these shortly before she was killed. I didn't think I could ever believe in something like this, but now ... in this horrible place, I just need something to hold onto."

Paul held her close. "You know, my father used to say to me that faith is not faith until it is the only thing you are holding onto. I never truly felt what that meant until now. When I said my faith had been shaken, I did not mean this." He gestured around them. "When Hilda left, I did not know why He was tearing my family apart. When Dederick went away to Poland, I saw the affect it had on my mother, and wondered how God could do this after we had served Him so faithfully. But to everything there is a season, and a time for every purpose under heaven." He sighed. "This has only served to make me realize how lost I am without my Savior."

Hannah stared at him in wonder. She could feel the pain in his voice, the turmoil he had gone through, and yet he had survived because of the very Man her ancestors had rejected, scorned, brutalized, and killed. Could it possibly be true? Her own suffering had given her a small glimpse of what the man called Jesus endured. Closing her eyes, she tried to speak to him. She did not know what to say, so she simply called.

"Messiah?"

The sound of running feet broke into her thoughts, and Paul pushed her back into the shadows. Six or seven soldiers ran past, and their footsteps faded into the night toward the other end of the camp.

"I've been gone too long," Paul whispered. He gave her a lingering kiss. "It won't be long, my love. I promise. This will all be over soon."

He disappeared behind the barracks, but not before she whispered, "I love you, Paul."

He blew a kiss in her direction and ran into the dark shadows. Hannah watched him go, tears in her eyes. After a moment, she snuck back into the barracks and crawled into her bunk. Tears wet the pillow as they slid down her cheeks, and she closed her eyes.

"Father?"

⁓

Paul hurriedly slipped back into his bunk and closed his eyes as he tried to slow his breathing. A whisper next to him made him turn.

"Paul?"

"What is it, Simon?"

"Where did you run off to? We heard guards run past and thought you were done for."

Paul gave a small laugh. "Not me. They haven't licked me yet."

Simon rolled over to face him fully and rested his elbow against the hard wooden board beneath them.

"You know what we heard the guards saying?"

"What?" Paul whispered.

"There's word going around that the gas chambers will be destroyed soon."

Paul sat up abruptly and stared at Simon. "What do you mean?"

"Just what I said. You know what that means ..." Simon nodded slowly as understanding spread over Paul's face. "They're getting nervous. You know the Soviets are closing in."

"Yes, but is it any better for us to be rescued by them?"

"After this hell hole, I'll take anything," Simon muttered.

Paul watched him roll back over and go to sleep. So, they were starting to destroy the camp. Did that mean that they were going to be destroyed as well? So much could happen in so little time. They all walked a very fine line between life and death. How much longer would they all last? He fell asleep with that question in his mind.

That night, for the first time in a long while, he dreamed of Maria.

She walked through a meadow of tall, sweeping grass. A smile was on her face and she was calling for someone, but he could not understand what she was saying. Suddenly, Hilda appeared and ran to Maria, sweeping her up into her arms. From where he stood, he got his first full view of his daughter. She looked older, perhaps six. She wore a ring about her neck, and he recognized it as Hannah's. How had she gotten it?

Another woman came into view, running up to the laughing pair. She looked so familiar, but Paul could not place her. Maria turned to the woman and threw herself from Hilda's arms into hers. The woman caressed her cheek and kissed her forehead.

"Papa! Papa!" Maria called, running to him.

He scooped her into his arms and kissed her cheeks. His eyes came back to the woman as she held out her arms to him.

"Paul, my love," she murmured ...

Hannah woke to harsh voices in the barracks. All around her, women were being smacked awake and forced to stand in single file lines. Confused, she stood and joined the ranks. They had not done roll call like this before. Perhaps they were being moved to a different work area.

At a loud command, the women began to march out of the barracks. The sun was just beginning to rise, covered by the smoke that rose from the camp. Hannah stared at it longingly. Somewhere not far away, a free soul was watching the same sunrise. As she observed its glorious ascent, Hannah suddenly began to pray.

Lord, You've given me a new day. When you could have struck me down, you chose to give me life. How unworthy am I? How could I have gazed upon this amazing occurrence every day and never known the joy You feel when I smile at its warmth? How could I not have seen Your love for all creatures when I looked around? Judith saw. Her face glowed when she spoke of You. I want that. I want to experience that same joy forever. Take me, please. Your Son suffered so much more than I have, and he did it for me. Despite what I have done to curse You for my plight, You have loved me through it all. You are truly amazing.

A jostle behind her made her start out of her praise. A woman was screaming, and tried to run. As they all watched, a guard took up his gun and in three shots, she was dead on the ground. Other women screamed in horror and clung to one another. Hannah glanced around in confusion as they were led on. What was going on?

They passed dozens of men breaking up rocks, and with ease, Hannah spotted Paul. She watched him, love in her eyes, as they moved along. He paused to wipe his brow and glancing up, he caught her eye. He gave her a small smile, but in an instant, it turned into a confused frown. She wondered what he was thinking, but with a soft smile, she put her fingers to her lips to blow him a kiss.

In one swift movement, Paul dropped his pick and began to race toward her. She had never seen such a look of fear in his eyes.

"Hannah!" he yelled as he struggled over the rocks to reach her.

One of the inmates grabbed him and tried to hold him back. Paul fought against him, and Hannah saw with alarm that tears were streaming down his cheeks. Her eyes grew concerned, and she tried to give him an encouraging look.

It's all right.

He grew smaller as they continued on. With a cry, he fell to his knees and began to sob.

"Hannah! Hannah!"

She felt her own eyes begin to tear. She had never heard such pain in his voice, such helplessness. She turned for one last glimpse. His friend was trying to drag him back to work as menacing guards approached

With fingers to his lips, Paul cried out in a shaky but loud voice, "I love you, Hannah van Ostrand!"

She raised her hand to him and in her heart sent him a promise. *We'll be together again soon.*

The women were herded into a cold, stone building, slightly set apart from the rest. A sinking feeling of cold dread came over Hannah. She knew where they were.

It was the gas chambers.

At first, she didn't know what to think. Feelings of fear, panic, sorrow, and horror rushed through her. With trembling fingers, she undressed with the rest of the women. Many were weeping; others clung to each other and tried to whisper words of comfort. Next to her, a young teenager was trembling, tears running down her cheeks. Hannah put her arm around the girl.

"Don't be afraid," she whispered. "The Lord is with us."

The girl cried softly into her shoulder as the crowd was led into the room that had haunted their dreams at night. The cold stone walls enclosed them, and even as Hannah realized they would be the last things she ever saw, she wanted desperately to fight it.

This can't be it, God. It can't. I want to live. I want to go home with my husband, and watch my daughter grow up. This can't be the end.

But she knew it was.

Hannah realized that Paul had known as well. He had fought so hard to save her, and yet she would die within sight of freedom. When he had shouted his love to her, he had done so for the last time.

The door clanged shut. Silence reigned, with the exception of a few sobs and whispers. The women had become hardened; to die would be a freedom greater than to live. As Hannah stood among the women, her arm still around the girl, she began to murmur, "The Lord is my shepherd, I shall not want. He makes me lie down in green pastures, he leads me beside quiet waters, he restores my soul ..."

An odd smell came to her nose.

"He guides me in paths of righteousness for his name's sake ..."

The women became hysterical and began pounding on the door, screaming.

"Even though I walk through the valley of the shadow of death, I will fear no evil, for you are with me, your rod and your staff, they comfort me ..."

She felt herself falling to her knees, the girl still in her embrace. A series of coughs wracked her body. It was hard to breathe.

You prepare a table before me in the presence of my enemies. You anoint my head with oil; my cup overflows ...

Hannah fell across the body of a gasping woman, her head feeling light. She pressed her hands against her chest, where the pages of Isaiah had once laid against her heart. Spots danced before her eyes.

Surely goodness and love will follow me all the days of my life.

Silence began to reign over the chamber that had become a tomb. Hannah sucked in one last short breath, an image of Paul and Maria going before her, as though leading her, toward the Throne.

And I will dwell in the house of the Lord forever.

30

London, December 1944

J effrey paced back and forth, unable to sit down as the screams from the other room filled the hallway of the hospital. He pulled at his hair, collar, and buttons every five seconds, and he felt as though he had aged twenty years in seven hours. How long could this possibly go on? Something had to be wrong. Another scream pierced the air and he jumped a foot.

Sitting quietly on the bench against the wall, Hilda calmly looked up at him. She set aside her magazine and folded her hands in her lap.

"Jeffrey would you please relax? You're going to make me go bald just watching you pull out your hair."

"How can I relax, Hilda? How can I relax?" His voice reached an insane level, and Hilda raised her eyebrows at him.

"Honestly, women have been having babies since before the flood. Grace will be fine." She watched him carefully. "Are you sure you don't want to go down to the nurse's lounge? Dr. Holden said we were welcome to wait there."

"I don't want to go down to the nurse's lounge, I don't want to!" He was reaching that pitch again and Hilda finally got up, took his arm, and dragged him down the hall.

Jeffrey craned his neck every time the door opened, and Hilda snapped her fingers in front of his face. "Jeffrey, stop it. Your neck will permanently be in that position if you do that one more time."

He turned again as the door to the lounge opened, and Hilda sighed.

"You asked me to come and help you through this, but you're certainly making it difficult!" He stared at her in astonishment and she smiled. "There. Got your attention."

Jeffrey gave a deep sigh and rocked his head forward into his hands. "You'd think with my line of work that I would be able to handle this kind of pressure. I'm not fit to be a dad. The child will fire me the moment he sees me, and so will Grace."

Hilda leaned across the table and took his hand. "First of all, you can't be fired from being a father, especially by an infant. And secondly, no man goes into this knowing what he's supposed to do. It's a learning process, and you just have to let the chips fall where they may."

The door opened again, and Jeffrey turned quickly. Mary walked in, a wide smile on her face. Jeffrey leapt up and ran to her.

"Is it ... w-w-wha ... yes?" he finally managed to get out.

Mary's face grew amused at his struggle, but her smile was filled with joy. "Jeffrey, you have a son."

He looked back and forth between Mary and Hilda, who both smiled at him in congratulations. He sputtered for a few moments, then a yell spilled from his lips and he sprinted down the hallway, yelling the whole way, "I have a son! I have a son!"

Hilda and Mary shared a glance, and Mary joined her at the table. "Thank you for being there for him. I doubt anyone else could have calmed him down."

"Well, it took all my wit, let me tell you," Hilda said with a smile.

"You've been a wonderful friend to him, Hilda. I don't think he would be the man he is today without you," Mary said quietly as she stared at her.

Hilda blushed and lowered her head. "Grace is the one who changed him, Mrs. Holden. She deserves your credit."

"Yes," she mused.

A quiet moment passed before Hilda stood and hastened for the door. "Well, I must be going. Maria is having a play date, and I must go fetch her home." She stopped at the door. "What are they going to name him?"

Mary smiled. "Adam. Adam John Rolf."

Hilda hurried out of the lounge, wondering why Mary had been insistent on her part in Jeffrey's life. It was in the past now; she had Maria to care for, and as soon as the war was over, a home to rebuild.

Maria skipped along beside Hilda, kicking up snow as they walked along the street toward their flat in Leicester Square. Her bright red coat was festive even though the Christmas season had passed. It had been a present from Hilda, and Maria wore it every day.

"You know, Maria," Hilda said as they walked along. "Miss Grace had her baby today. A beautiful baby boy named Adam."

"What does he look like?" the little girl asked.

"Well, he looks like any other baby right now, but soon he'll be a very cute little boy whom you can play with."

Maria paused and stared at her. "Where did he come from?"

Hilda opened her mouth to answer but wasn't sure how to put it in words for her niece. Maria was three months shy of five, nowhere near an age appropriate to share such details. She walked slowly, holding Maria's hand as she pondered the question.

"Well," she mused, "when ... when two people ... when they want to ... when they have love for each other, something happens, and it creates a baby," she finished strongly, proud of her answer.

"What happens?"

Hilda groaned inwardly. Curiosity always got the better of Maria.

"Well, something ... incredible happens to make the baby. When two people love each other, Maria, children are sure to follow. You understand?"

Maria nodded slowly and gazed up at her aunt. "Do you love someone, Auntie?"

Hilda paused as that small ache returned to her gut. "I did, yes."

"So where is your baby?"

Hilda burst out laughing, and lifted Maria into the air, hugging her. "Oh darling, I'm afraid it's something you won't fully understand until you're a bit older, all right? Let's just leave it at that."

They walked together for a time before Maria had another question. Hilda braced herself.

"Who was it you loved, Auntie?"

Hilda slowly put Maria back on the ground and held her hand. "His name was Jesse. He flew planes, just like the ones we see over London from time to time. He had brown hair and beautiful dark brown eyes, the color of cinnamon." She smiled softly. "His voice could melt my heart."

"If you loved him so much, why didn't you get married, like Miss Grace and Mr. Jeffrey?" Maria asked innocently.

Hilda looked down at her sadly. "Many things happened that kept us apart, darling. In the end, what separated us could not be bridged."

Maria was confused. "What does that mean?"

Hilda walked briskly on. "It means he died."

〰

Hilda sat in her living room and sipped a cup of tea thoughtfully. Maria had long since gone to bed, and the night was pitch dark outside, but far off, Hilda could see the lights of the Square. London never slept, even in war. A lamp glowed dimly on the table next to her, and the radio crackled with slow jazz. In front of her on the table lay her journal, open to the final entry. A blank page laid waiting, but Hilda did not pick up her pen. Her thoughts were on the version of history that she had just read, the thoughts of a young German child growing up during the rise of the Nazi power. An innocent girl whose life was drastically changed forever as she left to stand on the frontlines of battle, caught between her loyalty to family and country, and love for a young American.

As Hilda put these thoughts together, she suddenly sat up. She took a sip of her tea and lit a cigarette quickly. Going to the dresser against the wall, she pulled out her typewriter and a large stack of paper. She set up the typewriter on the coffee table, sat down on the couch, and stared at the blank page that she had inserted. She took a slow drag on her cigarette and blew it out thoughtfully, staring out the window. Then she began to type.

〰

The night of December 31 was cold and cloudless. A beautiful white moon shone down as Hilda walked to the New Year's Eve Party that the Holdens were hosting in the multi-purpose room of the hospital. Her slimming black dress shimmered beneath her long white fur, and peeking out from beneath her hem were her bright red boots to keep her feet warm and dry until she could change into more festive shoes. Grace and her friend Abigail had kindly offered to watch after the children while the adults went to the party. Hilda had wished Maria a Happy New Year before blowing her a kiss and slipping away.

The hospital came into view before her, and dozens of strings of lights had been hung across the porch to welcome guests to the party. Once inside, she checked her coat and changed into a pair of silver heels. Soldiers mingled everywhere, some injured, some not, but all were gaily laughing and drinking champagne as couples danced around the floor to the live band playing from the corner. Tables were everywhere, festively decorated in gold and silver. A sideboard of food lined one wall, and Hilda made her way toward it. She was halfway there when she spotted Jeffrey in the crowd. She waved vigorously and he hurried over and hugged her with a smile.

"It's so good to see you!" he said above the music.

"And you! How are the new mother and father doing?" she asked, smiling.

"I think we were sent an angel. Adam goes to sleep when we put him down, wakes up to be fed and goes right back to sleep. He's an absolute delight." He glanced around. "In fact, I'm only staying for a little while before heading back home to them. How have you been since I last saw you? Busy?"

Hilda nodded slowly. "I have actually. I've taken up my pen again."

Jeffrey put his hand on her shoulder. "That's good, Hilda, very good. I'm glad." He spotted someone in the crowd and moved away. "I'll see you later. Save me a dance!"

She nodded and turned back to the line. The food was delicious, some prepared in Mrs. Holden's own kitchen. Hilda missed her cooking. It was so nice having her own flat with Maria, but she had never really had the time to become domestic over the past several years. She and Maria had lived on soup most of the time, because Hilda tended to burn everything else. Mary's cooking topped the evening for her.

The night sped by as Hilda danced with countless soldiers wanting her arm, and she obliged, happy to give them a moment's rest from the grim war outside the walls. She laughed and danced and ate and drank the night away. As if in a haze, she noticed Jeffrey sidle up to her and give her a kiss good night. It was nearing eleven o'clock, he said, but she just nodded and smiled, tapping her foot to the music.

"Maybe I should call you a cab," he said, pulling her toward the door.

"No, Jeffrey, I'm quite all right," she said as she moved back toward the dance floor. "I need a night out, you know. And what better night than New Year's Eve?"

"I'll look out for her," came a third voice, and Jeffrey's eyes narrowed slightly when he looked behind her.

Hilda, however, turned in surprised and beamed. "Josh! Oh, it's lovely to see you again!" And she threw her arms around him. She turned back to Jeffrey. "You go on home to Grace and Adam. I'll be fine."

Jeffrey nodded slowly and left the room. Hilda watched him go for a moment before turning back to Joshua with a huge smile. "Well, I'm so glad to see you still in one piece! The Nazis didn't get you, did they?"

"Nothing but a few bumps and bruises," he said with a laugh. "Dance with me?"

"Absolutely!"

Joshua led her out onto the dance floor just as the music slowed down. He stared at Hilda for a moment, then took her in his arms, and they slowly swayed back and forth to the music.

"I wondered about you, Josh," she murmured against his chest. "Every time I read about the air raids, I hoped you were safe."

"It's nice to know you were thinking of me," he said. "I hoped you did."

She looked up at him. "Of course I did, Joshua. You're my friend, aren't you?"

He stared long and hard at her, and for the second time, Hilda saw that intense look in his eyes, only this time it didn't go away. She couldn't look away as he spoke softly.

"Am I? I hope I can be more than that, Hilda."

Hilda licked her suddenly dry lips, the wooziness leaving her confused at what he was saying. She could not put words past her tongue, and luckily, Dr. Holden came to her rescue as he took the stage.

"Ladies and gentlemen, it is almost midnight! Find that partner and get ready to sing!"

Hilda came out of her daze and slowly moved toward the door, but Josh stopped her. His voice was so passionate, but she could not understand why that bothered her. Hadn't she decided to live? Jesse had been dead for five years. If she did not try now, when would she ever get another chance? But the confusion in her brain would not go away.

"Hilda, please, listen to me. I want us to try this," Josh murmured.

"Try what?"

"I think we can be more than friends, don't you? I see the way you look at me, and when we were dancing ... please Hilda," He pulled her to him.

"Josh, I don't know ..."

"Ten! Nine! Eight! Seven!" The countdown began.

"Hilda, I know you lost someone already, but I promise, I won't leave you. Ever. I'm a fighter, and I will come back to you," Josh insisted.

I will come back to you, Hilda. Wait for me.

"Three! Two! One! Happy New Year!"

The band broke into a chorus of 'Auld Lang Syne' as couples across the room shared a toast and a kiss to the New Year. Hilda stared at Josh's chest before slowly raising her eyes to meet his. He still held that passionate look, and before she could utter a protest, he embraced her, whispering, "Happy New Year." And he kissed her.

His lips were warm from the alcohol and the heat of the dance floor, but Hilda knew his mind was sound as he cupped the back of her head and met her lips again. She sagged against him, dizzy and overcome by the power of his embrace. She couldn't help but respond; Josh was a handsome man, with strong loyalties and gentle attributes, everything she admired in a man. When he finally broke away, Hilda slowly raised her eyes to him. As another chorus of 'Auld Lang Syne' began, she whispered back, "Happy New Year, Josh."

31

E verything was a blur. Days turned into weeks, weeks turned into months, and still nothing changed the cold, hard reality of what had happened.

Hannah was dead.

Paul had never felt so powerless in his life. At night, he lay in his bunk and stared into space as one lost to the world. With every beat of his heart, the devastating truth pounded him like a drum. She was dead, and she was never coming back. This horrible nightmare he had thought to escape had suddenly become a gruesome reality, and he felt his heart clench until he thought is would burst with the pain.

She would not be coming home with him. She would never hold her daughter in her arms again. They would not grow old together, or sleep in each other's arms, or watch Maria grow up.

Hannah was gone.

Simon came up to Paul one day as he mechanically broke up rocks. His eyes were concerned, and he took up his own pick next to him.

"Paul, what's wrong with you?" he asked as they worked.

"Don't," Paul said.

"Don't what? Don't say the truth? You're killing yourself, Paul. You don't need to be in a death camp to let that happen. After all you did to encourage her, to keep persevering, you're just going to give up and die?"

"I couldn't save her."

"No, you couldn't. And you're not alone. Every single person in this camp has lost someone they love. My wife was killed the moment she stepped off that train. My daughter was sent to a German camp to be used in whatever way the soldiers saw fit. Do you think they would want us to stop living because of them? The only way they can be remembered is through us. We must keep going for them. We must survive for them."

Paul glanced over at Simon, who stared at him intensely. "She was my life," he murmured. "And now she's gone."

"You have your daughter, Paul," Simon said. "She is waiting for you to come home. She has already lost her mother. Don't leave her an orphan when this war is over."

Paul's mind drew up an image of his daughter. Her smiling mouth, laughing blue eyes, curly brown hair framing her oval face. He remembered the dream he had the night before Hannah was killed. She had looked so grown up, full of life and love. He did not want to miss that. He wanted to be with her, to watch her grow up, to love her as he had not been able to for four years.

"Paul," Simon muttered.

Paul glanced up, and they looked around. Guards were everywhere, shouting orders as they herded people toward the barracks. The two men joined the mass of people moving in that direction. As they walked, they looked at each other, bewildered. Something was different.

The doors to the barracks were slammed closed, and the running footsteps and shouting voices faded away. No one dared to move; heavy breathing was heard, but no one spoke. Simon and Paul glanced at each other.

"What's happening?" Simon whispered.

Paul shrugged, and he slowly moved to a crack in the wall. His feet dragged, and his eyes grew blurry. He fell to his knees and peeked through the slit in the wall. Nothing stirred; the camp seemed silent, deserted. Here and there, picks and shovels lay on the ground where people had discarded them in their haste to reach the barracks. Far away toward the entrance of the camp, the distant rumble of engines could be heard. The sound grew softer and softer until it dissolved into silence.

"What is it, Paul?" Simon asked as he and the other men waited for the verdict.

"It's nothing ... nothing," he murmured. His head felt light, and he rested it against the wall. His body slid to the floor as blessed darkness consumed his exhausted hungry state. The last thing he heard was Simon urgently calling his name.

⟡

A bright flash of light made Paul squint in his sleep. His head felt heavy and he had an awful taste in his mouth. He was in desperate need of water. The murmur of voices surrounded him. Slowly, he opened his eyes, and they adjusted to the dusk that had settled. He saw all of the men crowded around the door, straining to see through the cracks.

"Simon," Paul croaked out. His throat felt as though it were full of dust.

The man turned from where he was trying to see. His eyes turned surprised, and then a smile split his face and he hurried over to the bunk.

"Hey, welcome back," he said. "Are you comfortable enough? We tried to put as many blankets on it so that it would be soft."

Paul slowly raised himself up and rested against the beam behind him. He closed his eyes and sighed before turning to his friend.

"What's going on?" he asked.

"Someone's coming."

"Who?"

"We aren't sure, but I don't think it's the Nazis."

"What do you mean? They didn't come back?"

"No. After you lost consciousness, we waited and waited, expecting them to return. But they didn't." Simon's eyes grew excited. "I think they fled."

Paul held his breath. "From who?"

"The Soviets."

The words hit Paul like a tidal wave. The immense relief that he felt at their deliverance was joined with the unease of what the Russians would do with them. The Soviets cared for no one but themselves. The single reason they had allied themselves with England, France, and America was because Germany had betrayed them. Once the war was over, they would return to their hostile and horrific ways.

The sound of marching feet and rumbling tanks grew louder. It came closer and closer, and all in the barracks waited with baited breath. What came toward them would determine their future. Would they be liberated only to be sent into persecution once again? Paul's body was weak, but his determination to return to his daughter was greater than any physical malady he had.

"Simon," he whispered.

Simon glanced at him from where he sat on the bench.

"Promise me that no matter what happens, no matter who comes, you will help me get back to Heidelberg. Back to my daughter."

Simon slowly nodded his head, his eyes meeting Paul's.

"I promise."

⌇

Paul couldn't remember falling asleep, but when he awoke, he saw something he had not seen in four years.

Snow covered trees.

Slowly, as though in awe, he sat up and looked around. Gone were the meager wooden walls of the cold barracks. A crisp breeze blew through an opening in a clump of trees. He was in some kind of forest, wrapped in several blankets and sitting on a dry piece of ground at the base of a tree. At the center of the opening, Simon was coaxing a fire into life. Paul looked at him in slight confusion. "What happened?"

Simon started at the sound of his voice. "Well, hello again," he said with a smile. "You lost consciousness again. You're pretty weak, Paul." He came over and sat down next to him. "It was the Soviets. They liberated us, Paul. You should have seen the people's faces when they walked through the gates. I had never felt so free in my entire life."

Paul looked around. "Well, then, where are they now?"

"We branched off from them late last night. I remembered what you said that night a few months ago. By the looks on those soldiers' faces, they could care less whether we lived or died."

"How did we get away?"

Simon smiled. "I'm not without skill, Paul. Don't forget I used to work for the government before that awful man came to power."

Simon's face was bitter as he stood and went back to his fire. Paul watched his stiff posture as he knelt down and fed the fire.

"How long did you mourn them?" he murmured.

Simon's shoulders slumped, and he hung his head. "Years," he whispered.

The wind whistled through the trees as an awkward silence reigned between them. Paul rose unsteadily, clutching the blankets to him, and walked to the fire.

"Do you know if she's alive?" he asked.

"My daughter? No, I never saw her again after we got off the train. The only reason I knew what happened to her was because one of the inmates saw her being shipped off." Simon ran a hand through his hair. "I wanted to die. I told myself I had nothing left to live for. But then, one day, I saw a young woman struggling to dig a grave. She had tears running down her face. And that's when I realized that I had to be strong for her. For everyone else who was alone and afraid."

"I don't think I could have done that," Paul murmured, staring into the flames.

Simon put his hand on his shoulder. "Yes, you could have," he said. "If not for them, then for your daughter."

Paul stared at his friend for a long moment, a grateful look in his eyes. "You live up to your name well, Simon."

"What do you mean?"

"Any time I've been angry or depressed, you were the one I could come to and talk with. You always listen to me, no matter what."

Simon gave a short laugh. "I wasn't always like that."

"Maybe not, but when I needed a friend, you were there."

The two looked at each other, and Simon grew serious. "I will do my best to get you back to your daughter, Paul. I'm sure she is waiting for you to return."

"You don't think she has forgotten all about me, do you?"

"I'm sure that whoever is taking care of her is making sure that she remembers you. It would be hard not to."

Paul wistfully thought of Maria. She would be five in March. She had not even had her first birthday when he and Hannah had been arrested. Despite Simon's encouraging words, he was uneasy. Would she really know him? Did she have a picture of him?

Paul rubbed his eyes as all of the possibilities ran through his head. He was beginning to feel tired again, and he lay down by the fire and closed his eyes.

"It's good that you get rest," he heard Simon say. "We have many days of travel ahead."

Though he was next to the warm fire, he heard the whistle of the brisk wind, and felt the chill of the snow around him. Paul shifted onto his side, but opened his eyes in surprise when he encountered something small and hard. He stared at a brick that lay inches from his face. It was crumbling, and looked as though it had been torn from a wall. One side was stained with blood. He saw all of the horrors he had experienced in that small thing. All of the sorrow and pain was right there in front of him, in the substance of the object that had been made by the hands of a prisoner. A prisoner, who had been beaten, cursed, spit on, humiliated, and scorned. It represented everything he had lost.

"Paul, are you okay?" Simon asked. He was staring at him from across the fire.

"Where did you get this?"

"You don't remember?" Simon shrugged. "That's understandable. You came to as we were leaving and asked me to cut out a brick for you. You wanted to remember everything you had suffered." He looked at Paul strangely. "Why would you want to do that?"

Paul kept staring at the brick as if in a daze. "I suppose I wanted something to remember her by. I need to remember her, Simon. Without her, I'm lost."

"She would want you to keep on living, Paul. It is good that we hold onto those memories, but to be consumed by them makes us dead to the world. We have to keep living."

Keep on living. After what they had been through, death would have been merciful. Had they even been living these past few years? The life that had once been so prominent now seemed so distant, so unreal. How could they go back? Their lives had been forever changed. No matter what happened from now on, everything was different.

They traveled for several days, sleeping by day and walking by night. Every village they went to, they heard more and more news. Soviet troops were surging ahead, crushing German forces in the east while the Allies pushed from the west. There were rumors of the Big Three meeting at Yalta. Though President Roosevelt, Winston Churchill, and Joseph Stalin did not have much in common, they were all ready for the war to be over. For Paul, it was over. His beloved wife was dead, and he wanted to go home. He knew not what waited there, but anything had to be better than what was behind him.

Simon tried to keep his spirits up by telling jokes and stories from his childhood. Paul was grateful for his company, but the pain within him remained very prevalent. Every so often, he would pull out the brick he had taken and stare at it. He felt his stomach clench at the thought of Hannah lying in the dirt of that horrible place. There was no way he could know where her body had been laid to rest. Somewhere, around those cold, dark buildings, beneath the bloodstained earth, Hannah's body would remain.

Paul closed his eyes to shut out the harsh memories. He had to look to the future. Somewhere ahead of him, little Maria waited. The thought of his precious daughter brought his mind back to the dream he had had the night before Hannah's death. He had spent endless hours of the day trying to understand what it meant.

"Simon," he asked as they rested against a cold, prickly stack of hay bales in a field. "I had a dream the night before … a while before we were liberated, but I haven't been able to figure out what it means."

Simon looked at him curiously. "Would you like to tell me?"

Paul nodded slowly. "I see Maria walking through a field, and she is wearing Hannah's ring around her neck. Then my sister and another woman I don't know appear. They're all laughing and talking like they've known each other their entire lives. It's strange because Hilda has never met Maria, and the other woman looks so familiar." Paul sighed and looked over at Simon. He was listening intently. "This woman talks to me as though she has known me in a way only a wife can."

Simon leaned forward slightly. "And then?"

"And then everything fades," Paul finished. "It's been tormenting me ever since."

"Maybe you will meet this woman soon," Simon said.

"I may, but why now? What does it mean?"

Simon stared at him for a long moment, his face serious. "Maybe there will be another woman in your life, Paul."

Paul's eyes narrowed, and he stood in anger. "No! I will never love anyone as much as I loved Hannah, as much as I still love her. She was the only one who could ever hold my heart. And she is gone."

He stalked a few yards away and sat down on the cold hard ground. He was furious. How could his friend dare to suggest such a thing? Did he think his loyalties would shift that easily? There would never be another woman he could love with such capacity as he had Hannah. He and Maria would be fine on their own.

Wouldn't they?

Paul felt a lone tear fall down his cheek. Could he let his daughter grow up without the loving hand of a mother? She needed a woman to help her grow. To teach her grace and poise and gentleness.

Could he consciously deprive her of that love?

Could he deprive himself?

32

The cold was just beginning to diminish and in the city, the snow was quickly disappearing. As Elsa walked back from the grocer, a meager bag of food in her hands, she felt the wind whip up the street and steal in between her coat. The chill hit her to the bone, but she did not notice as she hurried down the street, for the undeniable, the incredible, the inevitable was happening.

The Nazis were losing.

Slowly, little by little, they had been pushed back, defeated, broken. It would only be a matter of months before they would give up. Surrender was on the horizon. The war in the Pacific still raged, but the European front of this Second World War was nearing its end. Elsa guarded herself. There could be obstacles along the way, no matter who currently held the upper hand, but deep inside Elsa firmly believed it. They were all ready for this war to be over. It was only a matter of time.

As Elsa lifted her head, a long figure caught her eye. There was nothing spectacular about the person, but the fact that she was standing in front of the old van Ostrand house made her pause. She crossed the street and approached the woman.

"Excuse me ..." she began, but as the woman turned, Elsa dropped her groceries in shock, and tears came to her eyes. She let out a sob and threw her arms around her dear friend. "Oh Benny! Benny, I thought you were gone for good!"

Benedikta hugged Elsa as tightly as she could; her arms were fairly weak. Tears ran down her cheeks as she leaned back and took in her best friend.

"Oh Elsa, I so hoped to find a friend when I was released," she murmured. "Oh, I'm so sorry, you've dropped your groceries."

Elsa laughed and waved her hand in the air. "Dash the groceries! Oh my dear, I thought you were dead. When Paul returned unsuccessfully from Berlin, we gave up any hope of seeing you again."

"Paul went to Berlin?" Benedikta asked. "To try and release me?"

"Yes, Benny. Oh, he fought so long to try and free you, but in the end ..." She stopped suddenly, and Benedikta noticed Elsa's gaze falter.

"What is it, Elsa? What happened?" But she had a feeling she knew deep down the answer to her question. "They took them, didn't they?"

Elsa nodded sadly. "Not long after your arrest. It happened so suddenly, and after the deportations in 1940, they thought they were safe."

Benedikta's face turned to one of terror. "Oh god, Maria!"

Elsa calmed her down as Benedikta began to cry again. "Now, now darling, don't fret. Maria is safe. She wasn't there when they took her. She was with me."

Benedikta looked up, hopeful. "You have her?"

"No dear, but she is safe. Here, come with me, and I'll tell you all about it ..."

⁕

Paul and Simon trudged up the road, and Paul stared up at the buildings he remembered so well. Surprisingly, nothing had been bombed by the Allies. The city looked relatively normal, as though not a part of the war at all. It remained untouched.

"I say, does Heidelberg know there's a war going on?" Simon joked as they walked on.

Paul nodded his head slowly. "It is strange isn't it, that they haven't touched the city. But trust me, the Wehrmacht know there's a war coming their way."

Simon kicked a bag that blew up the street and squinted against the bright sun. The cold had decreased, but a wind still blew the spring away for the moment. "So where are we going, Paul?"

Paul stopped and glanced around. "Honestly, I don't know. Nowhere seems to be home anymore. I guess ..." He faltered, not sure what he thought. Everything was different now, with Hannah gone. All he knew was that he had to find Maria and start over, somehow.

"Where should we start looking for your daughter?" Simon asked.

Paul began walking again. "The last time I saw her, Elsa had her. She was a friend who took in Jews in need. We need to find her first, but I don't know where she would be now. She may not even be in the city anymore."

Simon glanced down at the ground. "Your call."

Paul looked ahead and recognized the street crossings. Only a few blocks ahead was the bridge leading out of the city, and not far from there was his old home. It seemed like a good place to start.

"Follow me," he said.

Benedikta stared out the window and sipped her cup of tea. No one was in the streets today. The army headed for them had pushed all the citizens of Heidelberg into their homes. The city was silent.

She and Elsa had returned to the old van Ostrand home, and for the past few weeks had been reviving the rooms and gardens. It was the only home Benedikta had ever really known, and she wanted to start over with the family she had left. Dederick was gone. She could not bring him back. The pain was still too near for her to tell Elsa the story. Benedikta prayed that her other children would find their way home. Paul, Hannah, and Hilda. And dear Maria. Wherever she was, she was in the best hands.

As she watched the wind whip up the street, two men came into view. Benedikta studied them intently. From where they stood she could not make out any features, but one looked older than the other. But what shocked her most was when they began to walk up the path that she and Elsa had weeded just yesterday. She put down her cup and hid behind one of the drapes, fear riding up her spine. As they drew closer, she began to notice their appearance. One man had graying hair and looked to be in his late forties. His eyes were tired, but he appeared to be very relieved about something. The man next to him was younger, with a torn blue and white striped uniform underneath a worn brown coat. His shaggy blonde hair fell over his face, but Benedikta could not miss the piercing blue eyes that looked up at the door in hope. She gasped in astonishment and ran into the hall. She threw open the door and simply stared.

The men were startled at the thin, pale woman in front of them, but a shock of recognition spread across the young man's face, and he took a staggering step toward her.

"Oh, Paul, my dear boy ... you're here ... you're really here ..." Benedikta sobbed as her son fell into her arms.

"Mother ..."

The two embraced tightly, fearing to let go should they be separated again. Benedikta heard Elsa come down the stairs and gasp in delight at the sight of Paul home at last. After a long moment, Paul stepped back.

"This is my friend, Simon. If it weren't for him, I wouldn't be here," Paul said, bringing him forward.

"Well, that's not exactly—"

He was cut off as Benedikta hugged him tightly. Any friend of Paul's was hers as well. So many were starting over. They needed to come together. As she looked at her son, she noticed something more emanating from him than just relief at being home. His joy was evident, but hidden beneath it was something that had nothing to do with his homecoming. As Paul hugged Elsa tightly, Benedikta realized what was amiss.

"Paul ... where's Hannah?"

His face came up, and the pain she read there was enough. Her heart broke as her son slowly shook his head, and his shoulders hunched as wrenching sobs came from his lips. Benedikta took him in her arms and led him into the parlor. Simon and Elsa followed close behind.

"Oh, Paul," she murmured as they sat down on the couch. "I'm so sorry."

"There was nothing I could do," he said quietly, staring down at his hands. "I just watched as they led her away. I've never felt so helpless in my life."

Paul looked up at his mother, despair in his eyes. She looked at him and saw the boy he used to be, who came to her when he was afraid. "I don't know what to do, Mother. I feel so lost."

Benedikta took his hands and squeezed them tightly. "We'll start over. Both of us."

He looked at her, trying to reign in his sorrow. Finally he spoke, this time searching her face. "How did you come to be released?"

Benedikta stopped. Now it came to it. She could hold back from Elsa, but she could not hold back from her son. It would not be fair, and would only prolong the pain. She stood slowly and went to the window.

"I was sitting in my cell," she said, and she felt her hands tremble. She had to be strong. "A guard came in and escorted me to a hearing, where ... they told me I was free to go."

When she turned, the room was looking at her in confusion.

"Did they say why?" Paul asked.

"I thought just as you do, Paul. Since when had this cold country allowed supposed traitors to go free?" Benedikta sighed, her breath shaky. "They told me that it had been the dying wish of one of their most loyal soldiers. I wondered who would possibly want to help me. They said the letter had been found with his things, and after further consideration, they agreed to the request."

The three seemed to lean forward in anticipation.

"Who was it?" Elsa asked.

Tears escaped Benedikta's eyes as she gazed at her son. She struggled with her words, returning to his side and taking his hands. "Oh Paul."

Paul stared at his mother and slowly shook his head in horrified shock.

"No ..." He stumbled to the window to hide his anguish. Not Dederick. Not his brother. Please, God, not his wife and his brother. Had he not suffered enough? He hung his head, and his tears dripped to the window sill. How many more would be taken? Would they ever have peace?

"He is in a better place, Paul," Elsa said softly from her chair as her own tears fell. Simon sat silently in the corner, his face serious, and looking at his friend reminded Paul of why they had come here. After the dismal news, he dreaded asking his next question.

"Elsa ... where's Maria?"

The whole room grew still, turning to the woman. Benedikta seemed to brighten at the mention of the little girl's name, and to Paul's utmost relief, a smile slowly crossed Elsa's face. She stood and walked over to him, taking his hands.

"She is safe, Paul," she assured him.

He almost sagged to the floor in relief, and he gripped Elsa's hand tightly. "Where? Where is she? Take me to her."

Elsa led him to the couch and sat down across from him. Paul did not understand. He wanted to see his daughter now.

"Paul," Elsa said slowly, "Maria is with your sister."

Paul started. It was the last thing he expected to hear. "With Hilda? Why is she with Hilda? When did she return?"

"I happened upon her here a few years ago, and I told her everything that had happened. I told her that Maria needed a safe place, and I knew the rumors had been going around that Hilda was in London, so I asked her to take her back to England with her."

"You did what?" Paul stood, angry at first. What right did Elsa have to send his daughter away?

"Paul, you must understand," Benedikta reasoned. "It was too dangerous here in the city. Elsa only had Maria's well-being at heart when she sent her away. Don't worry. She is in excellent hands with your sister."

Paul paced back and forth, trying to organize his thoughts. "Where are they now?"

The two women grew silent and stared at one another. Elsa spoke slowly. "After they left, I didn't hear from them again. I ... I don't know where they are, Paul."

Paul stared between his mother and her friend. His wife. His brother. And now his daughter was missing? He could not take much more. If anything had happened to Maria, there would be no more reason to live.

Simon slowly stood and put a hand on Paul's arm. The younger man seemed to come back to the present at his friend's touch.

"Paul, you're exhausted. We both are. Don't think too hard on this right now." Simon squeezed his shoulder encouragingly. "I remember you talking about your sister. You always described her as strong, able to withstand anything. She was a survivor, were your words. I'm sure Maria is perfectly safe, and they are waiting for the war to end before they return."

Paul nodded slowly as reason returned to his head. "I did say that about her, didn't I? You're right, Simon. Silly of me to worry. She's fine, I'm sure ..."

Elsa stood and she and Benedikta led the men upstairs to their beds where they could rest. Much had to be done in the wake of this news, but for now, everyone needed rest.

A small, sad group gathered around the grave that afternoon. The March air was warming considerably, but a cold silence held court over the van Ostrand family and their friends. Benedikta put a handkerchief to her eyes beneath her veil as Paul placed a wreath under the name on the smooth stone. *Dederick Adrian van Ostrand. 1919 – 1944.*

He was laid to rest next to his father below a towering oak in the cemetery. It was a constant reminder of life's changing seasons, and

Benedikta had never felt it more keenly than when her son was buried next to her husband that day.

Dederick had been her happy child. The son she would always see as a boy and never fully as a man, in a way only a mother could understand. Her heart clenched, and fresh tears poured from her eyes. That son was no more.

Paul clung tightly to his mother's arm, steadying her as they slowly moved away from the gravesite. He recalled his last meeting with his brother, when he told him about Maria. How could that have been their last meeting? He longed so much now to take it back, to try and express his love for his brother, but it was too late. All he could do now was pray for forgiveness from Dederick and move on.

As they got to the car, Paul turned back and was surprised to find a young woman standing before his brother's grave, solemn in a black suit. He had not noticed her among their friends, but she looked familiar.

"Simon, help Mother into the car, would you?" he asked. Simon took Benedikta's hand and helped her onto the seat as Paul began to weave his way back through the cemetery. The woman turned to him when she heard him approach, but he still could not place her.

"Excuse me, Fraulein ..."

"I'm sorry, I did not wish to disturb your memorial. I only wished to pay my respects," she murmured.

"Did you know my brother?" Paul asked.

The woman smiled sadly. "I did." She looked at him. "Do you not remember me? We met briefly in Berlin."

Paul stared at her, and the face of the woman with his brother came rushing back to him. "It's you! Of course, you were with him that day. I'm sorry he never introduced us."

She held out her hand. "My name is Tanya Berezovsky."

"Paul van Ostrand."

She smiled. "I knew you had to be brothers. You could have been twins."

Paul nodded slowly and looked down at the grave. He and Dederick had been told that often as children. But no more.

"I'm so sorry for your loss," she said softly. "I was ... there when he was killed."

Paul looked up at her, surprised. "You were in Sevastopol?"

"Yes. I went to find him. We were ... supposed to be married after the war."

Paul looked at Tanya with new eyes. Slowly he brought his hand to her arm, and she glanced up at him, tears glistening in her eyes.

"When was the last time you ate?" he asked quietly.

"Oh, I have a room in town," she said, but he held up his hand.

"No. You must stay with us. My mother would not have it any other way," he said, and he led her down the hill toward the car.

"Thank you for your kindness," she murmured. "I have no family left to return to."

Paul looked at her gently. "We are your family now, then." He suddenly grew strangely silent, studying her. Her face was more than familiar from Berlin. He remembered it from a dream, not so long ago.

As they returned to the car and Tanya was introduced to the rest of the family, Paul watched her. He could not understand the feelings running through him, but he remembered Simon's words when he'd told him of his dream. Maybe there will be another woman in your life.

It couldn't already be happening. So much was changing, and much too fast. It was the war, and Hannah's death, and Maria's absence that made him feel this way, nothing more. He did not want anything to change yet. He just wanted a time to mourn.

But change was coming, despite Paul's efforts to stop it. That night, a loud explosion woke him from his bed, and he jumped up and looked out the window to find the bridge within view from his room engulfed in flames. Another explosion sounded further off, and then all was silent again, but flames glowed softly in the night light.

The Wehrmacht, Germany's armed forces, were abandoning Heidelberg, blowing up two of the city's bridges in their wake. Paul would wake the next morning to a changed city, as the United States Army entered Heidelberg following a peaceful surrender from the civilian population.

"I know not what the future holds, but
I know who holds the future."

Unknown

33

Heidelberg, August 1945

The war was over.

After six long, bloody years, it was finally over. In April, the Allies liberated Buchenwald, Belsen, and Dachau, horrified at the sight of the starving, persecuted people emerging from the concentration camps. The Soviets finally reached Berlin, and not long after that, Mussolini was captured and hanged by the Italian partisans, allowing the Allies to take Venice. Two days later, Hitler committed suicide.

Five days after German troops surrendered in Italy, on May 7, 1945, German forces surrendered unconditionally to the Allies, and Victory in Europe ensued. The Reich government was rounded up and imprisoned, and the Allies divided Germany and took control of the government.

A few months later, on August 6, the United States dropped the first atomic bomb on Hiroshima, Japan. The defiant Japanese refused to surrender, even though one of their cities had been flattened by the most powerful bomb ever made. Three days later, a second bomb was dropped on the city of Nagasaki, and after its horrific demise, the Japanese Empire agreed to an unconditional surrender.

The war was over.

Hilda stepped down from the train, helped by a handsome American soldier who stood on the platform. They were everywhere. Jeffrey had told her that the Americans had set up their headquarters in Heidelberg months ago, but it had taken her longer than she anticipated to pack up her and Maria's life in London and return. Jeffrey had insisted on her staying until the war in the Pacific ended, just to be safe. For Hilda, the summer had passed too slowly after the war in Europe ended. She had heard no news of her family, though lists were beginning to pop up everywhere of the victims of the holocaust. She couldn't look. Jeffrey had seen the lists, and Paul's name did not appear. Of that, Hilda was grateful. It meant there was still some hope.

Now as she finally looked around her home again, a smile split her face and she turned to help Maria down the steps. The little five year old could not remember much of her birthplace, but she knew it was home, and she stared in awe at all of the soldiers who mingled amongst the citizens of Heidelberg.

Hilda took their small bags in one hand and Maria in the other as they made their way out of the train station to the street. The bright August sun shone down, and she glanced around in awe. Not a single building showed any sign of the war; every Nazi swastika had been destroyed, and besides the bridges being rebuilt near her old home, everything stood exactly as it had when she had last been there. The Allies had not bombed the city, and Hilda felt tears come to her eyes. Her beloved Heidelberg still stood as beautifully as it once had.

Maria tugged her along, and Hilda began looking for a taxi. A soldier came up to them with a smile on his face.

"Can I help you, miss?"

She nodded as Maria hid behind her skirt. "Yes, we are trying to find a taxi."

"I'm afraid most of the taxis aren't in commission at the moment, miss, but we'd be happy to take you in one of the trucks to wherever you are headed." He gestured behind him at a military car that stood on the street.

"That's very kind of you," Hilda said with a smile. She handed him the address, and he escorted her to the car.

"What brings you to Heidelberg, miss?" he asked as they drove. "Got a fellow in the army, have you?"

Hilda slowly shook her head. "No, actually ... I was born here."

The soldier looked at her cautiously. Her accent was so flawless that he had not even guessed. "I ... didn't even realize. You don't sound German at all, if you don't mind my saying," he said, slightly uncomfortable.

Hilda did not blame him; while the Americans had treated the citizens well, there was still prejudice to be had within the city.

"I left Germany before the war started, in '38," she explained. "I tried to help with the war effort as best I could in London."

"Interesting," he said, though he still seemed hesitant. "And now you've returned home ... to rebuild?"

"To start over, hopefully," she said. "My niece's parents were victims of the holocaust and I hope to find them." Hilda did not add the possibility that they might be dead.

The soldier softened at this, and he turned to her helpfully. "There are lists posted in headquarters to help relatives locate each other. I could take you there if you like."

"No, no thank you," Hilda replied firmly. "Just up here is fine."

The soldier pulled up to the curb and hurried around to let them out. Hilda was relieved to see that Maria had been engrossed in the sights of the city rather than their conversation.

"Thank you," she said, and he smiled as he pulled away and drove down the street.

Hilda looked up, and across the street, she saw the house of her childhood, but it was different. It had been covered in dust and the garden overgrown the last time she had been home. Now, tall roses bloomed in front of the house, and the pathway had been freshly weeded. A new coat of paint was on the wall, and a welcoming set of chairs sat on the front porch. Someone was home.

Hilda swallowed, suddenly very afraid of what she would find. Had she gotten her hopes up for so long, only to return to find a stranger living in her house? She turned her back quickly, and her breathing came in short gasps. Perhaps there had been no word from her family for that very reason. There was no one left. The thought made her hand come to her mouth as she tried to push down the dreadful feeling in her stomach. A gentle touch made her look down. Maria was pulling on her hand, and she pointed across the street toward the house. Hilda turned.

A woman had come out onto the porch, her hand shading her eyes as she stared across the street. She had pulled back her wispy gray hair into a neat bun at the nape of her neck, and she wore an apron over a bright floral dress. Hilda slowly crossed the street, Maria close behind her, and stood on the other curb, staring at her. She gasped as the woman's hand came down from her forehead, her own blue eyes filled with shock. It had been seven long years, but Hilda knew exactly who it was standing on the porch.

"Mother ..." The word escaped her lips in a hushed whisper.

Benedikta van Ostrand let out a small cry at the sound of her daughter's voice. With tears streaming down her cheeks, she opened her arms wide. Hilda raced into them and their tears mingled as they clung to one another.

Her mother was here. At last, she had found some of the family she thought had disappeared from her life. Hilda drew a shuddering breath and held her mother tighter. So much had been lost. So much had been taken. And yet the Lord had brought them home again.

"Oh, Hilda," her mother whispered. "How I've missed you! And look how much you've grown! Oh, my darling, I love you."

"I love you, too, Mum," came Hilda's muffled reply.

A small cough drew them apart. Hilda watched as her mother's eyes took in the child before them.

"Is this ...?" Benedikta's voice drifted off, and she simply gazed at Maria in silent disbelief.

Hilda went to the little girl and brought her forward. "Mother, this is Paul and Hannah's daughter, Maria. Maria, this is your grandmother."

The child put out her hand. "Hello."

In awe, Benedikta took it and murmured, "Well now, my dear. The last time I saw you, you were just a babe. What a lovely young lady you've become."

Maria smiled shyly. "Thank you."

Benedikta clasped Maria's hand as she pulled her daughter into her embrace once more. The small family stood on the porch for a moment.

"Oh, darling, how I've missed you," she said again. "I wondered every day where you were."

"There is much to tell," Hilda said as she pulled away and wiped her eyes.

Her mother looked at her solemnly. "Yes, there is."

The door behind them opened and they all turned. A thin man stepped out, his eyes wide with shock. Hilda couldn't speak, so great was her joy at the sight of her brother. He was pale and gaunt, but he was alive. That was all that mattered. No one said a word as Hilda and Paul stared at each other, but it was a small voice from behind Benedikta that broke the silence, and sent Hilda into tears.

"Papa," Maria cried, and she pushed between her grandmother and aunt and threw herself against Paul's legs, hugging him.

Hilda watched through her blurry eyes as Paul slowly knelt down and cupped his daughter's face in wonder. He touched her eyes, nose, lips, and hair, as though afraid it was all an illusion. The resemblance to Hannah was undeniable. A moment later he pulled Maria into his arms and buried his head in her shoulder, muffling his sobs.

"Maria, my dear little Maria, you're here, you're safe," he said. "Oh, honey, I love you so much!" He shuddered as relief flooded through him, and it was several moments before he stood, lifting Maria into his arms, and found Hilda's eyes once more.

"Hilda," he murmured, and took a staggering step forward. "My god, look at you ..."

Tears rolled down her cheeks, and a cry of joy left her lips as she stumbled forward and hugged her dear oldest brother. Maria put an arm around her aunt, her smile contagious as they all laughed at their tears.

"Oh Paul, I've missed you! I can't believe it. This is more than I could ever have imagined coming home to!" She shook her head and touched his cheek. "I've wondered for so long about you ..."

"I didn't know if I would ever see you again. I have always hoped ..." he said softly.

Hilda nodded, and suddenly caught a glimpse of Elsa standing in the doorway, a hand over her heart as she watched the small family reunited. Hilda smiled and embraced the older woman, who patted her cheek with a grin.

"I always knew you would make it," Elsa said. "I never gave up hope that you would return."

"Thank you," Hilda said quietly. She glanced back at her family: Paul with Maria in his arms and Benedikta next to him, his hand in hers. She could not believe the blessings she had received in this one day. Her heart was nearly full with the joy of their reunion, and at that thought, she looked past Elsa inside the house.

"Is anyone else here? Hannah?"

Elsa had taken Maria up to bed, and Simon was settled in the library with a book when Hilda, Paul and Benedikta gathered in the parlor. A single light burned on the table next to the couch where Hilda and Paul sat. Tears were in the eyes of every person as Paul told the story of the last few agonizing months he spent in imprisonment. Hilda had wondered if such a thing would happen, but she had never truly thought she would have to face the death of her best friend. She placed her hand softly on Paul's arm, as if needing to know that he was real and not some ghost. So many had been taken from her. Loss had come to be a common word in the face of the Nazi regime. She prayed this was the last she had to come to terms with.

"Oh, Paul," she murmured when he had finished. "I'm so sorry."

"There was nothing I could do," he said. "I should have been able to save her."

"You can't let guilt rule your life, Paul. Think of Maria. You have years ahead of you with her," Hilda encouraged.

He smiled at her. "Yes, thanks to you. You've done so much for her. I don't know how I could ever thank you enough."

"I would do all that and more for that little girl. She's far more precious than anything on this earth," she said softly.

"Yes, she is."

Benedikta leaned forward from where she sat. "We'll help you, Paul. You're not alone."

The front door closed suddenly, and footsteps sounded in the hall. A moment later, a woman's voice rang out. "Hello? Paul?"

"In here, Tanya," he called.

Hilda watched as a beautiful young woman entered the parlor. She smiled at the party, her gaze stopping on Hilda. She came forward and held out her hand.

"Hello. I'm Tanya Berezovsky," she said warmly.

"I'm Hilda van Ostrand."

Tanya's eyes grew surprised, and she looked at Paul with understanding. "The sister you were telling me about! Oh, it's so wonderful to meet you at last. Benny and Paul talk about you all the time."

"Is that so," Hilda said, confusion in her face. "I'm sorry. I'm not sure how you all are acquainted."

Tanya looked as though she was about to speak, but Paul stood and put a hand on her arm. She looked back at him and remained silent.

"What's going on?" Hilda asked.

Her mother stood slowly. "There is ... more news, Hilda dear."

She looked between the three of them. "Well? What is it you've heard?"

They all looked at each other, and Hilda grew irritated with their silence. A sense of dread was growing in her. "Mother?"

Benedikta stared down at her daughter with sadness. "It's ... Dederick."

Hilda shook her head slowly in disbelief. "No ..."

"He was killed in Russia some time ago," Benedikta said quietly.

Hilda stood slowly, and a hand came to her mouth as she choked down a sob and turned away. "No, no, no ... not my little brother." She bent over and shut her eyes tightly against the pain. This could not be happening. Her brother, whom she had just begun to understand and love once more ... he couldn't be dead. "I never got to ... he so wanted the chance ..." The agony stole her words away.

A touch came on her arm and when she turned, she was surprised to find the woman Tanya Berezovsky next to her, tears in her eyes. "I'm so sorry," she murmured. "I knew Dederick in Berlin. We were ... going to be married."

Hilda gave a cry and suddenly embraced the young woman. He had found love. After all the hatred and coldness, Dederick would have been married. How cruel this war had been, to her, to Tanya, to her family. Her heart broke as Tanya cried softly into her shoulder. She must have loved him so much.

How long would the suffering continue before healing could begin?

It was a solemn group that gathered in the cemetery that stood on the hill just outside the city. Hilda stood in solemn black, a scarf tied over her brown hair. Next to her, Maria clung to her black-gloved hand. Benedikta and Paul stood together silently. Though his face was still pale and thin, Paul stood straight and tall in his black suit. He clasped his mother's hand tightly as she wiped her eyes.

Before them stood a fresh grave. At long last, they were able to lay to rest the woman who had changed Paul's life, who lay in a mass grave far away, but whose spirit was with them now. Maria stepped forward, a simple white rose in her hand. She laid it at the base of the stone marked *Hannah Katharina van Ostrand.*

"I love you, Mama," she whispered.

It had been hard, telling Maria that her mother was gone. At first she had not understood, but the realization had dawned on her soon after that, and she had cried well into the night. Hilda stayed with her, comforting her. Maria had held onto her hopes that her mother would return, but like so many other things, the war dashed those hopes to pieces. As the days went by, Maria had gotten closer and closer to her father, and they had learned to love each other again through their shared sorrow.

When Maria stepped back from the grave, she was whimpering softly. Paul took her into his arms and cradled her, whispering words of comfort. Benedikta stepped forward and simply stared at the graves before her. So many she loved had been lost, and the tears poured freshly down her cheeks. Paul took her hand and led her down the hill to where the car waited.

Hilda knelt down in front of the new grave next to her father. Her fingers reached out and traced the name. *Dederick Adrian van Ostrand.* The vivacious little boy, who became the zealous teen, who became the wiser man. She would never forget his melodious laughter, his heartwarming smile, his unwavering passion.

She looked down at the red rose she held in her hand. With care, she placed it at the foot of the gravestone.

"I'm so sorry, Dederick," she whispered. "I forgive you."

34

Hilda hurried up the path and pushed open the door to the house with her free hand, the other laden with groceries. Everywhere was humming with activity. Elsa was in the kitchen singing as she put together a small cake as a treat for lunch. On the landing above her, Maria screamed with delight as she charged up the stairs and into her room, Simon close on her heels impersonating a bear. Tanya hung the washing in the backyard, where the sun shone down brilliantly on the flowers. Her mother and Paul were somewhere in the house, she knew, and she laughed softly as she entered the kitchen and placed the groceries on the counter.

"How was town?" Elsa inquired as she placed the cake in the oven.

"Busy. Everyone is out and about now that the initial fear of the Americans is gone." Hilda left quickly to put away her hat in the closet before returning and putting on her apron. "I was able to find some fresh vegetables at the market. We can put them in the soup."

"Oh, wonderful! They'll give it a nice flavor." Elsa went over to where she was boiling chicken broth.

"Do you need any help, Elsa?"

"Oh, no, dear, you've been out all morning. I believe your mother is in the library reading. Go and join her. I'll be fine in here."

Hilda smiled her gratitude and left the kitchen. The library door was closed. Hilda hesitated outside for a moment before she gave a soft knock and opened it.

Benedikta sat on the deep green leather couch, a glass of water in front of her on the coffee table. A book lay open on her lap, but she was not reading it. Her eyes were on the window in front of her, her gaze caught in the sunshine. She did not appear to be in a daze; her look was wistful, and a soft smile graced her lips.

Hilda slowly came in and stood beside the couch. "Mother, how are you today?"

Benedikta turned to her daughter with a smile. "I'm fine, dear. Come, sit with me." She patted the seat next to her, and Hilda slipped out of her shoes and tucked her feet beneath her as she sat down on the soft couch.

"What are you reading?" she asked.

Her mother closed the book and showed her the cover. "*Pride and Prejudice.* It's made me feel young again, back when I was searching for my Mr. Darcy. I've read this book so many times. I used to dream about it when I was younger. Of course, I was Elizabeth, and Mr. Darcy walked into my parlor to propose to me. Instead, your father came in and asked me if he could find his ball that had come into the backyard. Not exactly what I had imagined, and he was an absolute pest for the next several years. But I knew from the moment I saw him that there was something different about him." Benedikta put her arm around Hilda. "And there was."

"I wish I could have what you had," Hilda murmured. She leaned her head into her mother's shoulder and sighed.

"What about Jesse? Have you talked to him?"

Hilda did not say anything for a moment. She couldn't. Her voice quavered when she finally spoke.

"I couldn't tell you," Hilda whispered brokenly. "I didn't want anything to dampen the joy I felt at being with you all again."

Benedikta looked at her in confusion. "What's wrong, Hilda?"

Hilda sniffed softly and murmured, "Jesse was killed ... fighting in the Eagle Squadron."

"Oh, honey!" her mother cried, taking her in her arms. "I'm so sorry. I'm so sorry."

"I violated his trust to the end, Mother. It hasn't been easy moving past it."

"What do you mean?"

Hilda glanced at her mother before sitting up slowly. So, her most precious secret would now be revealed. She would never allow her mother to go on without knowing the truth.

"Mother, the real reason why I left ... there is more to it than you realize."

Benedikta sat up and listened intently.

"I discovered something ... the night of Kristallnacht," Hilda said. "I met someone who told me that I wasn't who I thought I was."

"I don't understand."

"Mother, my whole life I assumed I was German."

Benedikta stared at her for a long moment. "You're ... not?"

Hilda shook her head.

"How do you know?"

"This person I met, he gave me something ... something from Father. It was his old journal and several old papers. I knew after reading them that I had to leave Heidelberg."

Her mother leaned forward. "Darling, what did they say?"

Hilda took a deep breath. "They say that ... I'm an American. I was born at the end of the Great War to a pilot and a nurse."

Benedikta stared at her in shock. A minute ticked by.

"American?" she whispered.

"Yes, and you'll never believe it, Mother, but Jesse's parents and mine were best friends."

"The Lord works in mysterious ways," Benedikta murmured. She looked at her daughter in understanding. "I now see why you had to flee. I only wish I could have helped in some way."

"It's in the past."

Benedikta studied Hilda curiously. "Why did you feel you had violated Jesse's trust, darling?"

"I worked for the Secret Intelligence Service in London, specifically the military intelligence section. I was given a whole new identity, and no one outside of my superiors could know who I really was. I had to pretend to be someone I wasn't whenever I saw Jesse. It nearly did me in."

Benedikta was speechless as Hilda stood and went to the window.

"I have learned to accept my mistakes and move past them. That is the only way I can keep going," she said, adding softly to herself, "The only way I can keep living without him."

A moment of silence passed, and Hilda heard her mother stand and move toward her. Benedikta smoothed the hair away from her daughter's face. "My brave girl," she said. "So much have you been through ... have all of us been through. We need to start over." She stepped away and clasped her hands. "But first, I must confess something to you."

Hilda turned to her, surprised. "What?"

Her mother looked at her, contrite and sad. "Oh darling, I was so afraid, you must understand, and after the Gestapo gained so much power, I didn't want them to take you away."

"What do you mean?"

Benedikta swallowed. "The reason ... I was put in prison ..."

But Hilda took her hands to stop her words. "Mum," she whispered, brushing her cheek, "I know. I know."

Her shock was clear on her face. "How ... how could you know?"

"When I came back and found Maria ... I also saw Dederick," she said.

"You saw him?" Benedikta asked, wistful jealousy in her voice. "How did he look?"

"Oh, Mother, he was so changed from what I once knew him to be. I think we have Tanya to thank for that." She moved back to the couch and sat down. "He confessed everything to me about turning you in." She looked at her mother. "He told me you hid the letters to protect me."

Benedikta hurried to the couch and sat next to Hilda. "Oh darling, I was so afraid that your contact with Jesse would be seen as suspicious to them. I couldn't have you taken away from me."

"It's all right, Mother. We were both changed regardless of our correspondence. There's nothing to be done about it now."

They sat there quietly for a moment before Hilda stood. "I meant to help Tanya with the laundry. Excuse me."

She left Benedikta with her thoughts, and hoped things would change for the better soon.

~

Tanya heard a laundry basket drop beside her and looked up at Hilda, who smiled. "I thought I'd help you with this."

"Thank you, Hilda. It's a lovely day to be outside anyway."

"Yes, it is." Hilda pulled some pins from the line and began hanging up a bed sheet. After a moment, she turned. "I'll be honest. I had another motive in helping. We haven't really had a chance to get to know each other."

Tanya lifted a pillowcase to the line and smiled. "I confess, I've been slightly worried at that. Your family talks about you so much that it sounds hard to live up to."

Hilda was surprised. "There is nothing to live up to. I simply want to know more about you and Dederick. You said the two of you met in Berlin?"

Tanya smiled, remembering. "He came to my rescue in Poland, actually. It's a bit of a long story. My father works in the Russian government, for the NKVD. Let's just say he tried to drag me to Moscow, and Dederick was there. My knight in shining armor."

Hilda slowly lowered the shirt she was holding. "He loved you despite that? Then he grew even more than I thought."

"Our relationship wasn't easy, but I would not be the person I am now without him," Tanya murmured.

Hilda thought of Jesse. "I know what you mean."

"You lost someone?"

"Yes."

"Does it still hurt sometimes?"

"Every time I think of him," Hilda whispered, hanging the shirt slowly. "He was my life for so long."

"He still is mine," Tanya said, tears in her eyes.

Hilda took her hand and looked at her squarely. "Tanya, don't be afraid to let go of him. He will always be in your memories. If we hold on to those in the past, we will never seek to have a future. I know. I thought I would never be able to live again after Jesse died. But I learned to move on with my life." She picked up her empty laundry basket. "I haven't forgotten him, and I never will, but it doesn't tear my heart out to think of him. Don't be afraid to live."

With that, she went back inside and left Tanya pondering her words. As she crossed the hallway, she noticed Paul at the window, staring out into the garden where Tanya worked. She slowly came up behind him and saw his gaze.

"She really loved him," Hilda murmured.

Paul nodded slowly, still staring at Tanya through the glass.

"Perhaps she was meant to find you," she continued.

"What do you mean?" he asked as he turned toward her.

"You've both lost someone very dear to you. You can comfort her."

Hilda stared at him. Paul suddenly realized her meaning, and anger filled his face. "Don't ask me to forget Hannah."

"I'm not. But she wouldn't want you mourning forever." Hilda walked away and up the stairs, leaving Paul still for a moment. He watched Tanya a moment longer before pushing the door open determinedly.

Tanya stood out in the backyard with her hands on her hips and stared at the clothing hanging from the line. She could not get her mind off what Hilda had said. *Don't be afraid to live.* But she was. Every time she looked at Paul, she was.

At the sound of the door opening, Tanya turned. Paul came outside and glanced around. She could tell he was looking for her. For some reason, she ducked behind the laundry and waited for him to go back inside.

"Tanya?" he called.

She closed her eyes and remained where she was. A slight breeze blew through the yard and rustled the grass.

"Tanya?"

Startled, she opened her eyes to find him standing inches from her. She took a step back and ran into the laundry basket. She would have toppled over had Paul not grabbed her arms to stop her fall.

"Are you all right?" he asked as he held her. "What are you doing?"

"Nothing," she said hastily as she put some space between them. "I was just ... thinking."

He studied her carefully. "About what?"

"Nothing important," she murmured, turning to the laundry so that she did not have to look at him.

After a moment, Tanya felt Paul's hands on her shoulders, and he lifted her so that she had to meet his eyes. He looked so sincere, so gentle, and she felt tears begin to build behind her eyes.

"What's the matter?" he asked softly.

She stared up into his eyes and tried not to give in to her tears. "This war has torn everything from me that I loved. I don't think I'll heal from it very easily, and I don't know where to begin."

Paul nodded in understanding. "When my wife died, I just wanted to give up. I didn't care about the pain or the horror anymore, I just wanted to die ... to be with her. And then Simon told me a story about his daughter being wrenched from his arms. He wasn't sure he could live with it until he saw a scared young woman in the camp one day. He had to go on for her, he said. He had to find that light when everything else was covered in darkness. It's the only way you can see where you're going."

Tanya listened as he spoke. She could not imagine the pain he must have felt watching his wife being dragged away to die. "How did you survive the camps?"

He looked at her steadily. "I found my light. It was my daughter, Maria. And my wife."

They both shared a look. So much was said in their eyes, and Tanya could not find the strength to break away. Her feelings were laid bare before him, and she could see that he noticed. Paul cleared his throat and turned.

"Paul."

He turned slowly back to her. She shook her head and closed her eyes, and a few tears escaped them.

"I can't compete with her," Tanya whispered.

She waited, and did not hear a reply. A light touch to her forehead made her eyes fly open, and she saw him raising his head from where he had kissed the still tingling spot.

"You don't have to," he murmured.

Hilda brushed some hair out of her eyes and kneaded the dough firmly against the board. Elsa was busy chopping vegetables to steam, and Benedikta had fallen asleep in the library, so it was Maria who answered the knock that no one else heard. A moment later, she bounded into the kitchen.

"Aunt Hilda, that man from England is here to see you," she said innocently.

Hilda's eyes widened and she turned Maria over to Elsa. "Thank you darling, but next time, please get me before you answer the door."

She hurried out, brushing flour from her face and hoping there were no spots on her dress.

"Hilda!"

Startled, she looked up at the voice calling her name. A smile of shocked surprise came over her face. "Josh!"

She ran into his arms and gave him a hug. She had not heard anything from him since they had parted ways in London before the war ended. She did not even realize how happy she was to see him until she pulled away and looked up into his smiling eyes.

"What on earth are you doing here?"

He laughed. "Looking for you, beautiful."

She let the endearment slide as he looped her arm through his and they walked into the parlor. He was here, he was in one piece, and he was alive.

"How have you been?" she asked.

"Busy. You might not think it with the war over, but it's been crazy. I was home for a few weeks before I came back."

"Why did you come back?"

Josh shrugged. "I guess I just feel like this place has become more of a home than where I grew up."

Hilda looked at him, confused. "This place?"

"Europe. While I was home, I couldn't stop thinking about this place. What I've done here, who I've met." His eyes met hers.

Hilda gave a little laugh in an attempt to lighten the heavy mood. "And you always boasted that you had left your heart in Texas."

He stopped in front of the fireplace and turned toward her, taking her hand. She looked at him awkwardly, not sure where he would take the conversation.

"I think my heart is somewhere else now," he murmured.

Taking a deep breath, Hilda took a small step away from him. "Josh ..."

He held up his hands to show he did not want to push her. "Look, I know that things have been rather odd between the two of us, but I really want us to try. I have ... strong feelings for you, Hilda. You must know that."

She nodded and looked up at him. Their kiss over New Year's Eve had left her with many questions, some of which she did not like the answers to, but the war was over now. Everything was behind her. She studied Josh, and he cocked his head at her look.

"Am I under scrutiny? Because I'm rather unprepared," he joked, straightening his jacket.

Hilda laughed and put her hand to her cheek. "No, no, I'm sorry. I was just thinking." She smiled at him. "I am very happy to see you, Josh."

His gaze changed, and Hilda searched for another topic. "However did you find this place?"

"Your pal Jeffrey. He gave me the address when I returned to London."

"How is Jeffrey?"

"Doing fine, just fine. He and the wife and boy seem quite happy. They miss you," he added.

Hilda nodded. "I miss them too." She took his arm. "You must stay for dinner, Josh. You can meet my family."

Josh put his hand over hers. "Darling, I wouldn't miss it for the world."

35

Paul walked into the house, whistling. He looked around for Tanya or Maria as he came in, but saw only his mother sorting through the post. She looked up and smiled at him.

"Hello, darling," she said as he kissed her cheek.

"Mother, where is everyone?" he asked as he put his coat in the nearby closet.

"Tanya and Maria are in the yard. Mr. Sauders found some baby kittens, and the girls have become quite attached. Oh, this one is for you." Benedikta looked at the postmark. "It's from the states, dear."

Curious, Paul took it and opened the envelope. A short note lay inside, but its contents caused Paul to blanch.

"Who is it from, Paul?" Benedikta asked, concerned.

Paul just shook his head back and forth slowly. "Oh god ... oh Mother, how can I ..." He suddenly reached into the closet again for his coat and ran for the door. "I'm sorry, Mother, I must go! Don't worry about waiting for me for dinner, I just ... I'll be back!"

Benedikta watched him go, wondering what on earth had just happened. After a moment, Elsa came into the hall.

"Was that Paul I heard?" she asked.

"Yes," Benedikta mused. "He just ran off in the most astonishing manner."

"Whatever for?"

"I've no idea. He received a letter, and then bolted for the door as if the devil himself were on his heels."

Elsa frowned. "Well, I hope it's nothing too serious."

Benedikta kept her eyes on the door. "Yes, so do I. So do I."

Hilda glanced into the parlor where her mother sat reading. The sun would soon set, and a warm, dull glow filtered through the window onto the couch where she sat.

"Mother," Hilda said from doorway, "I hope you don't mind, but I need to step out for a few minutes, take a walk."

Benedikta looked up and studied her daughter's face. She looked calm and composed, but she knew that behind those deep green eyes, a silent storm raged. The pain was still there.

"Of course, darling. Don't worry about dinner. Tanya and I will take care of it," she said.

Hilda nodded her thanks, seeming a bit far away, and closed the door behind her.

She walked around the edge of the city aimlessly for less than an hour. Parties and dancing were everywhere. It was a night on the town. Couples strolled down the street with glasses of champagne in their hands. The sun had barely gone down, and already, the nightlife was in full swing. Finally unable to find the peace and quiet that she sought, Hilda made her way outside the city to the only place she knew would give her silence.

The headstones in the cemetery looked black against the sunset, and Hilda made her way slowly to her family's plot. The only sound was the wind moving through the grass between the graves. She knelt down and simply closed her eyes, listening to the whisper it made.

Oh, Lord, please. Let the pain go away. I don't want to feel this for the rest of my life. I want to be whole again, in You. It's like he's holding me back from being a new person. I want to be released from my sorrow. Please, release me ... release me ...

No answer came for her plea, and Hilda hung her head in defeat. Her loose hair blew softly around her face and covered her tears. She had to be missing something. God would not put her through such heartache if there weren't a reason. Hilda thought suddenly of Josh. He had been such a dear friend to her in hard times, and now that he had returned, maybe this was her chance to find love again.

As she stood, she glanced back down at the graves of her family. She could not wallow in sorrow forever. They would not want her to. She could find happiness again, and maybe, just maybe with this new found love, her pain over Jesse would ebb away.

The following morning was so hot that Hilda and Josh reclined on chairs in the garden, watching Maria and soaking up the final summer rays. Hilda raised her head and lifted her curls from the back of her neck before leaning back and closing her eyes. Josh lounged next to her and attempted to read the paper for news from the Pacific. He glanced up as Maria started counting her jump ropes again.

"Did Paul ever come home last night?" he asked.

"No," Hilda mumbled, slightly asleep from the warmth of the sun. "Mother said not to worry, he will be back. And he's been working quite hard lately, you know. I'm sure he'll return soon."

"Odd, how he left so suddenly though," he mused.

"Mm."

Josh looked at the paper again and pointed to a long convoluted phrase. "What does that say?"

Hilda leaned over and read it quickly. "Last ships of soldiers will return in the next few weeks. Our boys are coming home."

He nodded and went back to his reading attempts. Hilda studied him from behind her sunglasses. The past couple of weeks, they had grown closer in their friendship, united by the common pain of a lost friend and love. She would be lying if she said she didn't find him handsome, and his Texan drawl only added to his appeal. She could see herself going down that path someday soon. Josh lifted his head and caught her gaze.

"What?" he asked.

"Nothing."

"Come on, beautiful. What's up?"

She sat up and studied the flowers that had been skillfully planted and mothered by Benedikta and Tanya. They still held to summer's glow, but would soon be buried in the autumn chill. So hopeful, and yet when they became their most beautiful, they were forced to wither to the ground.

"I still miss him, Josh. I can't help it."

"I know."

She turned to him, removing her sunglasses and letting the shade from her hat fall over her face. "But soon ..."

He put his paper aside and took her hands. His were strong, and she felt encouraged by their strength.

"You deserve to be happy, Hilda. Maybe that means me, maybe it doesn't, but I'm glad you are reaching for it." He laughed a little. "I hope it includes me, though, I'll admit."

Hilda smiled. She liked Josh. Maybe not the way he liked her, but she could get to that point. They stared at each other for a moment. He leaned in suddenly, and her heart jolted for a moment. Too fast. But it was only for a moment, and she found herself angling her face toward him. It felt right, and yet ... she couldn't find anything to counter her emotion.

"Hilda."

Her brother's voice found the interruption she couldn't, and she pulled back abruptly. Josh didn't let go of her hands, but she stood and freed herself when she saw Paul standing there, still and serious, a look on his face that went beyond discomfort in what he had come across. In fact, he didn't seem to know what to do with himself. His eyes darted between the two of them, then down to his hands, and he shifted on his feet from time to time. Hilda hurried over to him and touched his arm.

"Paul! We wondered where you'd gone," she said with a smile, but it dropped at his expression. "Whatever is the matter?"

Paul looked past her. "Maria, be a dear and run inside to your grandmother. Josh, if you wouldn't mind giving my sister and me a moment in private?"

Josh nodded and followed after Maria, who skipped into the house shouting for Benedikta. Hilda stared at her brother, afraid at what she saw in his face.

"Paul? What's wrong?"

He took her arm and led her to the bench in the corner of the garden. "Hilda, something unexpected has come up."

"What is it?" she asked, concerned.

"Well ..." he began, looking away toward the house. He struggled to find words.

"Paul, what happened? Is it Tanya?"

"No, no, she's fine," he mumbled.

"Well then, what's wrong?" she asked, crossing her arms. "You look like you've seen a ghost!"

He laughed, almost insanely. "You might put it that way."

Out of the corner of her eye, Hilda saw her mother come out onto the porch, Elsa behind her. They both wore expressions of mixed concern, disbelief, and wonder. Josh stood just behind them, a similar expression on his face, but he also looked sad.

"Paul, would you please just tell me what's going on? You're beginning to scare me!" she said.

Paul turned to look at her. Hilda tried to read his face but found it difficult to understand the emotions there. He slowly drew a letter from his pocket and held it out to her.

"I received this letter yesterday. That is why I left so suddenly."

Hilda stared at him, but did not take the letter. Nervously, she glanced down at the address she could see. It was familiar to her.

"It's from the Rikers," she said quietly. "I didn't know you corresponded with them."

"I don't," he replied. He paused in his thoughts and stood, moving a few feet away from her. "Hilda, do you know what I wish more than anything else?"

Hilda was confused. "What? Paul, what does this have to do with the letter?"

"I wish I could have one more moment with Hannah," he murmured, not listening to her. "A minute would be enough. They are so precious, so few. It's painful to waste them."

"This is about Hannah?" Hilda asked.

"No. Oh, I'm not doing this right. How does one say such things?" he asked himself.

Hilda stood slowly and put her hand in his. "Paul, I've heard terrible things in my lifetime, I'm sure I can handle it. It can't be that bad," she insisted.

"It's not!" he said, as though not believing his own ears. "In fact ... it's wonderful. Shocking, but wonderful."

Hilda sighed and led him back to the bench. "Then just tell me."

He struggled again for a moment, and then took a deep breath and dove in. "Hilda ... someone precious ... has come back to us."

She was confused again. "Who? Did Danny and Mari write to tell you this? Who could they possibly know that ..."

Sudden realization spread through her whole being, and Paul nodded slowly. She felt her heart rip wide open as another figure caught her eye on the porch. She glanced over Paul's shoulder and stood slowly.

It was him. He stood tall and straight in his dress blues, just as she remembered him from the first time she had laid eyes on him ten years ago. Those beautiful brown eyes soaking up her image just as she did his. He slowly took the steps down to the garden, and Hilda felt like her feet were cemented in the ground. It wasn't possible. It couldn't be possible.

"Hilda."

When he spoke her name she gasped, and her thoughts crashed back to earth. She took a couple steps backward and held up her hands. He stopped.

"You can't be real," she whispered painfully. "You died."

Paul's voice seemed to come from far away. "He was a prisoner of war. The plane crash caused him to lose his memory. No one found his body, just his tags. Nobody could have known."

Hilda tried to sort through the jumble of emotions that were racing all over her at once. She knew she must look ridiculous, standing there with her eyes wide open, jaw dropped in shock, and tears running down her face, but she could not help it. When she finally got control of her functions again, she did the first thing that her mind told her to do.

She ran.

Jesse laid a hand on Paul's arm as he started to follow Hilda into the house.

"Please ... let me go," he said quietly, and walked determinedly after her, past the silent threesome on the porch. The parlor door slammed, and Jesse followed Hilda into the room, shutting the door quietly behind him. He turned to her slowly, but her back was to him, her gaze locked on something through the window.

"I know you must have some questions," he said.

"*Some* questions?" came her broken reply, and her hand raised to her mouth. "Oh, Jesse ... you have no idea."

He slowly walked toward her, but stayed a few feet away. "Please let me explain."

"Yes, why don't you?" Still, Hilda did not turn to him.

Jesse clasped his hands behind his back to keep them from reaching for her and began slowly. "There was a crash, like Paul said. I must have hit my head. When I woke up, I was in an isolated room with one high window. My tags were gone, and I knew absolutely nothing. Not my name, not the date ... nothing. It took me a few days to realize that I was in some sort of prison. I didn't recognize anyone, and none of them knew me. I felt like I was on a different planet."

Jesse paused for a moment, and he noticed that Hilda had become silent. Her hands leaned against the window, the tips of her fingers white as she pressed against the window panes, trying to understand his story. He continued on.

"I didn't really have a sense of time. I remember when there was a scare running through the camp because some POWs had been executed. Everything else was a blur. When we were released, we were transported back to London, where Dr. Holden found me in the hospital. Ever since, he's been trying to help me remember."

Hilda turned for the first time, and he saw that her guard was up against him, as though afraid that this was all some sort of awful joke.

"Help you ... remember," she said slowly.

"Yes, I'm afraid my memory is still a little rusty. I don't remember much before the crash. I even had trouble with my own parents, but Dr. Holden says it will come back in time."

Hilda did not say anything, and Jesse stepped forward hesitantly. "Oh Hilda, you can't imagine how hard it was. I wanted to know so badly, but every time I reached for a thought, it slipped away." He ran his fingers through his hair and began to pace. "All that time in the POW camp, I wanted to die. I was going mad just sitting there staring at the wall. I don't want to be like that for the rest of my life." He caught her gaze firmly. "I need you to be with me, help me remember."

As Jesse watched her digest his words, he thought back to his Channel crossing only a few short days ago. All he had had to go on were her beautiful green eyes, the ones that stared at him so confused now. He remembered thinking that she was on the other side, a link to what he had lost. No matter what he remembered when he saw her, he knew that he had loved her. It had been years, but at the thought of Hilda, something jumped inside him. Maybe, just maybe, that something would be released, and he would discover what he had lost, and what he so desperately wanted back.

"You want me to help you remember," came her soft voice.

"Yes," Jesse pleaded, taking her hands for the first time.

Hilda studied him for a long moment, and in a second Jesse saw the despair, the anger, the pain in her eyes, and his heart fell.

"Oh, Jesse, in another life, I loved you," she sobbed. "But I've spent the last five years coming to terms with your death. I've moved on. I can't do it any more, it's too painful."

Hilda turned and stumbled toward the door. Jesse turned slowly and watched the woman he knew deep inside he loved disappear into the hall. He could not fully remember the time they had spent together in the past, but all he could feel now was the shattering of his heart into a thousand pieces as she exited his life once more.

36

Paul slowly entered the parlor, where he found Jesse still watching the door that Hilda had just fled from. He put his hands into his pockets and went up to his friend.

"It's been hard on her, Jesse, I know it has. She just needs some time to come around, that's all," he said.

Jesse smiled, but shook his head. "No, she doesn't Paul. It's been five years. We were so young when we were together." He looked up as Josh came and stood in the doorway. "A lot has changed since then."

Paul turned and noticed the two glancing between each other. He shifted on his feet and moved toward the door. "I think I'll go check on her."

"No, let her be," Jesse said quietly.

Paul nodded slowly and hurried from the room. Jesse and Josh stared at one another for a moment. Josh seemed to be wondering whether or not Jesse was going to come at him with his fist.

"Wow," he began, moving into the room. "I ... this is ... really unexpected."

Jesse followed him with his eyes. "Tell me about it."

Josh glanced up at him and shook his head. "Jesse, you have to understand ... we thought you were dead. Otherwise—"

"You don't have to explain anything, Josh. I understand."

Josh was about to say more when Tanya burst into the room, her eyes wide. She found Jesse, and with a cry she ran over and gave him a hug.

Jesse was confused, but returned her embrace. When she pulled back, her smile was filled with joy.

"I can't believe it!" she exclaimed. "When Hilda said the man she lost was Jesse, I didn't even think there could be a connection, but ... oh, I'm so happy to see you again!" And she hugged him again.

"I'm sorry, I ..." Jesse stammered, and Tanya pulled back suddenly.

"Oh, yes, I'm so sorry. I just got back from town and Paul explained everything that happened. When he mentioned your name I couldn't believe it." She took his hand in hers. "I'm Tanya. Berezovsky. We met on the crossing to England. I thought you were a steward."

Jesse's eyes widened as his thoughts worked to come together in his head. "I remember," he said slowly. "Your father was Russian and your mother was German."

"Yes," she said with a smile.

"You were having trouble deciding which side to take in the war," he continued.

"You remember correctly. I ended up in Berlin, so I guess that answers your question."

"I'm so glad to see you again, Tanya. It's nice to have another familiar face in my memory," Jesse said, but his eyes were still full of sadness.

"Hilda must be overjoyed to see you alive," she murmured, touching his arm.

He laughed softly, painfully. "I don't know about that. More like her entire world turned upside down again." He looked at her and shook his head. "It's been so long, but I guess ... a part of me hoped she still might ..."

Tanya wanted to encourage him, but she was afraid that if she said anymore, she would only be pushing the knife deeper into his back. Paul came back into the room and stood next to her with a hand on her back. They shared a resigned look.

"Paul, thank you for coming to get me at the station," Jesse said as kindly as he could. "Would you mind taking me back to my hotel now?"

Paul nodded, shared one last look with Tanya, and went to get the car. Jesse held out his hand to Josh, who shook it slowly.

"It was good to see you again, Josh," he said with a forced smile. "Tanya, so glad we could meet again."

Jesse leaned forward and quickly kissed her cheek, and she nodded with a smile. "Stay in touch, Jesse," she murmured.

He moved slowly back toward the hallway. Paul appeared next to him, the keys in his hand. "The car's all ready, Jesse," he said quietly.

A silence hung over the room. No one dared speak for fear the flood of emotion hanging above them would come crashing down. Slowly, Jesse turned back into the room.

"You take good care of her, Josh," he said firmly before placing his hat on his head and striding out, Paul on his heels. The front door shut soundly a moment later, and the house was quiet.

Tanya brought her hand to her mouth and slowly shook her head. "This is wrong."

Josh looked at her absentmindedly, his thoughts still on what had just occurred. "What do you mean?"

"She still loves him," she said. "I know she still loves him. I know it."

"How do you know?"

Tanya turned to him, her eyes earnest as she spoke. "I loved her brother, Josh. And when he died, I thought I'd never be whole again." She looked up to where they knew Hilda was, somewhere, trying to get past the shock of what just happened. "I saw it in her eyes, clear as day, when she talked about him. I've never seen a love as strong as hers for Jesse."

Josh slowly walked to the window and watched as Paul drove off with Jesse down the street toward the center of town.

"No," he said quietly. "I suppose not."

Benedikta looked into her daughter's room and found Hilda standing beside her bed, her gaze lost in something beyond the window pane. On her desk, her letters from Jesse lay scattered about, and her chair was overturned as though she had risen suddenly, upset at what she read. Benedikta stepped quietly inside the room.

"Paul just phoned," she murmured as she closed the door behind her.

Hilda nodded slowly, but her eyes continued to stare blankly out the window.

"He said that Jesse's decided to leave on the afternoon train," her mother continued.

Hilda looked at her and nodded in an attempt to keep her composure. "It's probably for the best."

"Darling—"

"Mother, please don't make this harder than it already is," Hilda said.

Benedikta sat down on the edge of the bed. "That's it, then? You're willing to give up the most wonderful thing that ever happened to you; after all you've been through—"

"But we haven't, Mother!" Hilda cried. "That's just it. We've been worlds apart for so long, and he doesn't know the first thing about what I've done."

"He doesn't know many things, Hilda," her mother said firmly. She pulled Hilda down next to her on the bed. "That is why you must tell him."

"I can't, Mother, I can't! Things are too different now ... I've moved past it. Josh has been a wonderful friend to me, Mother," she said earnestly. "I think that—"

"Josh?" Benedikta sighed. "Oh my darling. Josh is a nice man. And I can tell he cares for you deeply." She took Hilda's face into her hands. "But Jesse *loves* you. He truly loves you. I saw it in his eyes the moment he saw you."

Hilda shook her head and stood. "No Mother. He doesn't, because he doesn't remember."

"That's why he needs you, Hilda," came her mother's voice, "just as much as you need him."

Hilda tried to shut her ears to what she heard. There was a part of her mother's words that nagged at her, but she could not go back. The possibility of losing him a second time was too great.

"I'm sorry, Mother," she said. "But anything that used to be between us is gone."

Benedikta rose slowly from the bed and stood in front of her daughter. "Then you owe him a descent farewell," she said firmly. "Do not let him leave with the thought that you don't care. Because I know you do."

With that she turned and strode out of the room, and Hilda closed her eyes against the light, her family, and the world. A tear escaped from her eye and slowly created a river down her cheek.

⌒⋇⌒

Hilda walked down the street, unsure of why she was even going to the hotel. It seemed to make no sense in her mind, and yet deep within her, something was telling her to keep walking. As she drew near, she questioned herself again.

Why go through all of the intense pain again? She had already spent weeks trying to mend over her lost brother and friend, and it had taken years for her to move past Jesse's death. Now, God seemed to be mocking her efforts by returning him to her life. Was this a test? If it was, she failed miserably. Jesse's return was like a lifeline in a raging storm, but she was afraid that if she reached for him, he would slip from her fingers once again, and this time, he would never come back.

When had she become so guarded? Was it when she realized that home had no longer been safe? Or her first mission as Angelis Chevalier? Too many possibilities ran through her mind, and by the time she reached his door, she had run out of excuses. She squared her shoulders, determined to say her good-byes and be gone.

Jesse opened the door, surprised to find her there. He smiled widely until she stepped formally into the room, and he realized that nothing had changed.

"I've come to wish you safe journey," she said slowly, glancing at his partially packed bag on the bed.

He nodded, and she could tell her words pained him deeply, but there was nothing more to be done.

"You are leaving on the afternoon train?" she asked formally.

"Uh, yes. Paul was kind enough to have me put in first class. But then the military will set up their injured heroes nicely however they can."

"I'm sure you're lodgings will be very comfortable," she said.

Jesse lifted his hand, and an irritated look came into his face. "Hilda, please just stop. If you've only come to see me off, than I'd rather you just left. If you have more than that to say, then please say it now." He caught her gaze steadily. "My feelings have not changed. Not from this morning. Not from ten years ago," he said. "That much I know."

Hilda studied him for a long moment. His eyes were pleading, hoping to be filled. His heart begged her to show him the truth, but deep down within her, she knew she could do nothing. Anything she told him would fall on deaf ears. He was here, but a huge part of him was missing. He would hear, but he would not understand. He was lost to her and she could not find him.

Jesse seemed to notice her thoughts, and he turned and pulled a photo from his bag. "My mother gave this to me when I got home. Before that, I couldn't remember anything. Then Mom told me about your visit … and about your real parents."

Hilda slowly took the picture from him. It was from the Christmas she had spent with the Rikers. She, Maria, Danny and Mari stood smiling in front of the Christmas tree. Hilda closed her eyes. So then he knew about the Pendairs. That saved her a long explanation, at least. She felt him come nearer, and she looked up at him.

"I was lost," he whispered, "until I saw your face."

Hilda sighed and shook her head as she moved away. "You honestly expect me to believe that for five years, you had amnesia?"

"Please, Hilda, I know it sounds crazy," Jesse tried to explain. "You can ask Dr. Holden. He said I was off my rocker when I first got back to London. I was going crazy not knowing a thing about myself." He tried to catch her gaze again. "Please, Hilda."

Slowly she turned away, too pained to see his expression. "I've moved on, Jesse," she murmured. "I've moved on, and that's that."

He nodded, a grieved, resigned look in his face, but he kept his eyes on her. "I understand."

She moved to the door.

"Hilda." His voice gave her pause. She heard him come and stand close behind her. "I'm still me," he said gently. "Deep down, I'm still me, and I still love you."

Wiping her eyes, Hilda slowly walked away from the man she loved. She felt her heart shattering, but she knew that there was no other way. If she tried to cling to him, she would end up broken in body and soul. It could never be. What they had shared was in the past, and there it would have to stay. She had to move on, for Jesse and for herself.

Jesse moved back to his bag, and Hilda turned the knob. Tears escaped her eyes, and her feet seemed planted to the floor. *Move.* She forced one foot in front of the other, and the door shut silently behind her.

Josh took a seat silently next to Hilda. She sat on the porch, lost in her thoughts as Maria played in the yard. For a moment he just watched her face, and what he saw made him finally understand. She still loved him. Whether she believed it or not, she did.

"Hey," he said.

She started a little bit, but when she saw him, she smiled and went back to watching Maria. "Hey."

"How are you doing?"

She laughed shortly and stared down at her hands. "I've been better, but I'll be all right." She looked at him after a moment with a pained smile. "That was definitely the most astonishing thing that's ever happened to me."

Josh didn't say anything, and Hilda began to lay out her thoughts to her friend. "I just ... I thought I was done with this wild roller coaster of a romance. I just want to bury it once and for all," she murmured.

"Do you honestly think it will stay buried?" he asked.

Hilda stared at him. "I will make it stay there."

Josh sighed and took her hand. "Hilda, I know."

"Know what?"

"I know why you won't take Jesse back," he said. "You're afraid."

"Afraid? That's ridiculous," she began to protest, but Josh put his other hand over her mouth, stopping her in surprise.

"You're afraid you're going to lose him again, just like you lost your father, and your brother, and your sister-in-law," he said gently. "You're afraid that if you try to love him, he'll be taken away again. But Hilda, it's different this time. There is no shadow of war, no one is chasing you. There is nothing to fear but what you have created in your head."

Hilda slowly turned back to watch Maria, but her thoughts were not on the child. Josh continued slowly. "You came home to start over. So start over. With Jesse."

Hilda wiped the silent tears that fell from her cheeks and clasped Josh's hand tightly. "I don't know if I can," she whispered brokenly.

Josh rose and bent down, kissing her forehead gently. He tilted her chin up so she was forced to meet his eyes. He smiled encouragingly.

"The ball's in your court, Hilda. It's up to you to decide what to do with it."

The clock chimed the four o'clock hour as Jesse and Paul drove up to the station. A silent moment passed before Jesse slowly got out of the car and pulled his bag out. Paul watched him from behind the wheel, his face betraying the sadness he felt inside. Jesse gave a small smile and reached inside to shake his hand. "Thank you, Paul."

"Jesse, I'm so sorry that things ... didn't work out," Paul stated, his eyes cast in shadow. "I know that we all wished it would be so."

Jesse nodded resignedly and turned toward the station. "I suppose I couldn't have expected much else. It had been so long; she wouldn't have waited for me." He gave a short wave. "Hopefully I'll see you around, Paul. Good luck with Tanya. She's quite a lady."

Paul waved back and watched as Jesse moved toward the entrance to the station before slowly pulling away from the curb.

Jesse put one foot in front of the other, each feeling as though it weighed fifty pounds. He should not have gotten his hopes up and he knew it. His friends in London had tried to warn him, but something in him had so strongly declared, *She waited for you. Go to her.* Now it all seemed silly. Nothing more to do now than to go home and begin again with his family.

Steam rose steadily up from the tracks as he searched for his platform. Soldiers everywhere seemed to be traveling home that day as well, but Jesse felt no kinship to them at the moment. Right now, he just wanted to find his seat and be alone with his thoughts. It was all he could manage at the moment. He cleared his throat and smoothed his coat as he made his way toward the designated platform along with the sea of other uniforms.

"Jesse!"

At first, he didn't hear it, but the call came again and again. Jesse stopped and looked around. It did not take him long to find the one young woman among the mass of soldiers who pushed and shoved her way through the crowd toward him. He dropped his bag and waited as Hilda stopped about ten feet from him. Now what?

Hilda looked upset, and Jesse felt his heart descend even lower. If she was going to give him another excuse for them not to be together, he might throttle her. Hadn't she hurt him enough? A man could only take so much before he snapped.

Her eyes were determined, and yet she seemed uncertain as she looked around the station. Jesse folded his arms and cocked his head.

"What do you want, Hilda?"

She looked back at him, despair in her eyes and in her voice.

"Jesse ... I've lost ... so much in this war," she said, trying to keep her composure. Around them, the crowd of soldiers thinned as they herded onto the train. Hilda wiped a single tear from her eye. "I know ... that if one more happiness disappears, my heart will never mend."

Jesse listened intently, and his arms slowly fell to his sides. What exactly was she saying? She suddenly pointed her finger at him, her words now strong and deliberate. "You can't ... *ever* ... leave me again, do you hear? So help me God, you can't ever leave me again!"

The last words were barely out of her mouth before Jesse swiftly closed the distance between them, took her in his arms, and kissed her as though he would never let her go. The feeling of her lips on his rushed over him in a wave of glorious passion. To think he had forgotten what it was like to kiss this woman. How could he have ever resigned himself to living without her? Jesse tightened his grip around her waist and deepened the kiss, oblivious to the cat calls and whistles coming from the train. He pulled away slowly after a time, and Hilda clung to him tightly, unwilling to let go.

"Wow," he whispered. "I remember this. We were here, weren't we?"

Hilda glanced around with a smile and sniffed. "You were leaving to go back to America, and you jumped off the train, pulled me into your arms and kissed me. You said you were falling in love with me, and to wait for you."

Jesse brushed the hair away from her face and kissed her again. "Yes, and you said you would. How could I have forgotten?"

Hilda brought his hands to her chest and kissed them. Jesse leaned his forehead against hers.

"It was long ago, and so much has happened since then," she murmured. "There is much to share."

"And all the time in the world to do it. I promise you, I will never leave you again," Jesse said, and he kissed her deeply. "My precious Hilda. Tell me about your life."

As the two slowly walked out of the station arm in arm, the light of the afternoon began to fade. The darkness of war had fallen upon them, and they were older now, wiser in the ways of the world. Countries had fallen, lives had been lost. Trials had been fought, and the battle had been won. Now, the light of dawn would bring a bright future, and a promise of faithfulness and love awaited them.

"Hope is the word which God has written
on the brow of every man."

Victor Hugo

Epilogue

Hilda woke to find the other side of the bed cold and empty. She glanced around with sleepy eyes and found Jesse standing at the big window in their bedroom, staring out at the sunrise that came up over the rooftops behind their house. She sat up slowly and watched him. The muscles in his back rippled as he placed his hands against the windowsill and hung his head.

"Oh, God," she heard him whisper. "There has to be an easier way."

With compassion in her eyes, Hilda walked over to her husband and slipped her arms around his waist. She held him that way for a moment, simply letting the feel of his warm, smooth skin wash over her.

"Another dream?" she murmured.

Jesse nodded slowly. "I can't get the faces out of my head. Faces, but no names." He turned and took her into his arms. His face displayed a quiet, confident look, but she knew that beneath it, turmoil stirred relentlessly in his mind. Jesse's memory had not fully returned. The years leading up to the crash were easily forgotten. He did not fully recall his time with Dr. Holden in London, or when he went home to his parents.

In spite of it all, Jesse had been the blessing in her life for over ten years, when she first saw him step off the train that day so long ago. He was her constant support, and she loved him.

"I keep having these constant headaches. It's as though I'm trying to

343

take in all of this information, and my mind can't handle it," he said with a deep sigh.

"Then don't distress yourself," she said, framing his face with her hands. "It will come back to you in time."

Jesse walked back to the bed and sat down on the edge, shaking his head. Hilda went over and stood before him.

"It scares me, Hilda," he murmured, looking down at his hands. "It scares me when I look at my friends and forget their names. It scares me to look at little Allison and forget she's my daughter. What if, one day, I suddenly wake up and don't know her at all?"

She knelt down in front of him. "That is not going to happen," she said firmly. "You love her, Jesse. Above everything else, for as long as she lives, she will know that."

Jesse gazed at her for a long moment. "And when I look at you," he murmured. "How can I look at you at times and not remember your beautiful face?" He touched her cheek gingerly.

Hilda's heart broke slightly at his words, but she rose and retrieved a pile of torn letters. They had clearly been perused several times. " Here," she said. "These will help."

Jesse took them and rubbed his fingers over Hilda's fine script. "Yes, I remember. Our love letters."

Hilda knelt in front of him once again and took his face in her hands. "I will never let you forget me, or Allison, or our friends. Never."

Jesse nodded and kissed her gently, and Hilda reminded him once more of the passion they shared. It was several minutes before they let go, and Hilda pulled him toward the door. "Come, I want to show you something," she said.

They quietly made their way down the hall and into Hilda's study. Jesse flipped on the light and watched as she slowly removed a fat stack of papers from her desk drawer. She brought them over and sat down on the couch, tapping the seat next to her. Jesse sat down and stared in awe at the tall stack.

"I was going to wait until morning to show you, but now seems as good a time as any." She patted the papers in her lap.

Jesse turned his head and read slowly. *Two Lives Entwined: The Memoirs of Angelis Chevalier. By Hilda B. Riker.* He stared at her, a wondrous smile on his face.

"I finished it last night," she murmured. "They're all in there. Every last one."

Jesse put his arm around her shoulder and kissed her forehead. "Sweetheart, this is incredible. You finally finished it."

"Look at the dedication," she said, and Jesse flipped open a few pages to the short note at the front.

"'To my loving husband,'" he read slowly, "'so that he may treasure our love story forever.'"

Jesse sighed and kissed Hilda deeply. "I love you," he whispered.

"I love you, too," she said, and she clung to him for a long moment.

Jesse suddenly pulled away and gazed at her for a long time. She watched him quizzically.

"Do you know what I love about your eyes?"

Hilda looked surprised. "What?"

"I love waking up every morning and wondering what color they will be. Sometimes they are a deep, rich green, like the color of evergreens. Other times, they're so bright I have to blink when I look at you. But my favorite is when they're the color of the ocean, with the sun sparkling off of its liquid depths."

She smiled. "Poetic. Why is that your favorite?"

Jesse looked at her, gentleness on his face. "Those are the times when you tell me you love me. When I can see straight through those green liquid depths to your heart. And I wonder how I could ever have forgotten you."

Hilda sighed deeply and closed her eyes. "C'est doux."

Jesse smiled. "Merci."

"How could I have ever lived apart from you?" she asked quietly.

"Luckily you never had to answer that question," he said, leaning toward her mouth.

"Luckily," she murmured before his lips took hers in a passionate kiss. How she loved this man. She would always love him.

Hilda's memoirs were published three years after the end of the war and became an international success. She and Jesse lived out the remainder of their life in the English countryside, making frequent visits to California to see Danny and Mari. Frederick van Ostrand's wish was fulfilled as Hilda and Jesse watched their children grow up and marry. They remained lifelong friends with Paul, Tanya, Jeffrey, and Grace.

Jesse never fully recovered his memory, though he continued to improve. He never truly forgot his love and devotion to his wife and children.

Hilda found peace at last and embraced both her German and American heritage. She found the home she longed for with her husband and children, and was blessed with sixty five years of love and joy with her family. At the memorial service held in honor of her life, over two thousand people attended, including ambassadors from the United Kingdom, Germany, and the United States of America. She was laid to rest next to her husband in the cemetery above Heidelberg, where her father, mother, and brothers were also buried. At her memorial service, her niece Maria read a simple, unforgettable excerpt from the last page of Hilda's memoirs.

I have seen many things, many dark things in the course of my young life, and I have come to realize that even in the darkest of nights, when all the lamps have gone out, there is always hope for those who have the courage to seek the Light.

THE END

Chronology of World War II

1918

November 11 – World War I ends with German defeat

1919

April 28 – The League of Nations is founded
June 28 – Signing of the peace treaty of Versailles

1921

July 29 – Adolf Hitler becomes the leader of the National Socialist 'Nazi' Party

1926

September 8 – Germany is admitted into the League of Nations

1930

September 14 – Germans elect the Nazis, making them the second largest political party in Germany

1933

January 30 – Adolf Hitler becomes Chancellor of Germany
July 14 – The Nazi party is declared the only party in Germany
October 14 – Germany quits the League of Nations

1934

August 19 – Adolf Hitler becomes Führer of Germany

1935

March 16 – Hitler violates the Treaty of Versailles by introducing military conscription
September 15 – German Jews are stripped of their rights by Nuremberg Race Laws

1936

February 10 – The German Gestapo is placed above the law
March 7 – German troops occupy the Rhineland

1937

November 5 – Hitler reveals his war plans during the Hossbach Conference

1938

October 15 – German troops occupy the Sudetenland; the Czech government resigns
November 9/10 – Kristallnacht – The Night of Broken Glass

1939

March 15/16 – The Nazis take Czechoslovakia
May 22 – The Nazis sign the 'Pact of Steel' with Italy
August 23 – The Nazis and Soviets sign the Pact
August 25 – Britain and Poland sign a Mutual Assistance Treaty
September 1 – The Nazis invade Poland
September 3 – Britain, France, Australia, and New Zealand declare war on Germany
September 5 – The United States proclaims neutrality
September 17 – The Soviets invade Poland
September 29 – The Nazis and the Soviets divide up Poland

1940

January 8 – Rationing begins in Britain

May 10 – The Nazis invade France, Belgium, Luxembourg and the Netherlands; Winston Churchill becomes British Prime Minister

May 15 – Holland surrenders to the Nazis

May 28 – Belgium surrenders to the Nazis

June 10 – Norway surrenders to the Nazis; Italy declares war on Britain and France

June 14 – The Germans enter Paris

June 22 – France signs an armistice with the Nazis

July 10 – The Battle of Britain begins

August 13 – German bombing offensives against airfields and factories in England

August 15 – Air battles and daylight raids over Britain

August 23/24 – First German air raids on central London

August 25/26 – First British air raid on Berlin

September 3 – Hitler plans Operation Sealion, the invasion of Britain

September 15 – Massive German air raids on London, Southampton, Bristol, Cardiff, Liverpool and Manchester

September 27 – The Axis Pact is signed by Germany, Italy, and Japan

October 12 – Germans postpone Operation Sealion until spring of 1941

October 22 – First deportation of local Jews, including 281 from Heidelberg

December 29/30 – Massive German air raid on London

1941

May 10/11 – Heavy Germany bombing of London; the British bomb Hamburg

July 12 – Mutual Assistance agreement between the British and the Soviets

September 1 – the Nazis order Jews to wear yellow stars

September 3 – First experimental use of the gas chambers at Auschwitz

October 2 – Operation Typhoon begins, the Germans advance on Moscow

October 30 – The Germans reach Sevastopol

December 5 – The German attack on Moscow is abandoned

December 7 – The Japanese bomb Pearl Harbor

December 8 – The United States and Britain declare war on Japan

December 11 – Germany declares war on the United States

1942

January 26 – The first American forces arrive in Great Britain
May 8 – The German summer offensive begins in the Crimea
May 27 – SS Leader Heydrich is attacked in Prague
May 30 – The first thousand bomber British air raid, against Cologne
June 4 – Heydrich dies of his wounds
June 5 – Germans besiege Sevastopol
June 10 – Lidice is liquidated in reprisal for Heydrich's assassination
July 3 – The Germans take Sevastopol
August 12 – Stalin and Churchill meet in Moscow
August 17 – The first all-American attack in Europe
October 18 – Hitler orders the execution of all captured British commandos
November 11 – The Germans and Italians invade unoccupied Vichy France
December 17 – The British Foreign Secretary tells the House of Commons of mass executions of Jews by the Nazis

1943

January 10 – The Soviets begin an offensive against the Germans in Stalingrad
January 27 – First bombing raid by Americans on Germany at Wilhelmshaven
February 2 – The Germans surrender at Stalingrad in the first big defeat of Hitler's armies
February 18 – The Nazis arrest White Rose resistance leaders in Munich
May 13 – German and Italian troops surrender in North Africa
September 8 – The surrender of Italy is announced
November 18 – Large British air raid on Berlin

1944

January 6 – Soviet troops advance into Poland
March 4 – Soviet troops begin an offensive on the Belorussian front; the first major daylight bombing raid on Berlin by the Allies
March 18 – The British drop three thousand tons of bombs during an air raid on Hamburg, Germany

April 8 – Soviet troops begin an offensive to liberate Crimea

May 9 – Soviet troops recapture Sevastopol

May 12 – Germans surrender in the Crimea

June 6 – D-Day landings at Normandy

August 19 – Resistance uprising in Paris

August 25 – Paris is liberated

October 21 – Massive German surrender at Aachen

October 30 – Last use of the gas chambers at Auschwitz

November 25 – The crematories at Auschwitz are destroyed

December 17 – The Waffen SS murder 81 U.S. POWs at Malmedy

1945

January 26 – Soviet troops liberate Auschwitz

February 4 – Roosevelt, Churchill, and Stalin meet at Yalta

March 29 – The Wehrmacht abandon Heidelberg after destroying two of its bridges

March 30 – The civilian population surrenders Heidelberg to the American troops without resistance

April 12 – Allies liberate Buchenwald and Belsen concentration camps

April 21 – The Soviets reach Berlin

April 28 – Mussolini is captured and hanged by Italian partisans

April 29 – American troops liberate Dachau

April 30 – Adolf Hitler commits suicide

May 2 – German troops in Italy surrender

May 7 – Unconditional surrender of all German forces to Allies

May 8 – V-E (Victory in Europe) Day

May 23 – SS Reichsfuhrer Himmler commits suicide

June 5 – Allies divide up Germany and Berlin and take over the government

July 1 – U.S., British, and French troops move into Berlin

August 6 – First atomic bomb dropped on Hiroshima, Japan

August 9 – Second atomic bomb dropped on Nagasaki, Japan

August 14 – Japanese agree to unconditional surrender

September 2 – Japanese sign the surrender agreement; V-J (Victory over Japan) Day

CPSIA information can be obtained at www.ICGtesting.com
Printed in the USA
BVOW011111040413

317309BV00007B/145/P